FROM
THE
SHADOWS

Billy Boyle
The First Wave
Blood Alone
Evil for Evil
Rag and Bone
A Mortal Terror
Death's Door
A Blind Goddess
The Rest Is Silence
The White Ghost
Blue Madonna
The Devouring
Solemn Graves
When Hell Struck Twelve
The Red Horse
Road of Bones

On Desperate Ground
Souvenir
Shard

FROM THE
SHADOWS

A Billy Boyle World War II Mystery

James R. Benn

Published by Soho Press, Inc.
227 W 17th Street
New York, NY 10011

Library of Congress Cataloging-in-Publication Data

Names: Benn, James R., author.
Title: From the shadows : a Billy Boyle World War II mystery / James R. Benn.
Description: New York, NY : Soho Crime, [2022]
Series: The Billy Boyle WW II mysteries ; 17
Identifiers: LCCN 2022012206

ISBN 978-1-64129-298-6
eISBN 978-1-64129-299-3

Subjects: LCGFT: Novels.
Classification: LCC PS3602.E6644 F76 2022 | DDC 813/.6—dc23
LC record available at https://lccn.loc.gov/2022012206

Printed in the United States of America

10 9 8 7 6 5 4 3 2 1

Dedicated to my wife, Deborah Mandel

He is the half part of a blessed man,
Left to be finished by such as she . . .
—William Shakespeare, *King John*, Act II, scene ii

THE PARTISAN

When they poured across the border
I was cautioned to surrender
This I could not do
I took my gun and vanished.

I have changed my name so often
I've lost my wife and children
But I have many friends
And some of them are with me.

An old woman gave us shelter
Kept us hidden in the garret
Then the soldiers came
She died without a whisper.

There were three of us this morning
I'm the only one this evening
But I must go on
The frontiers are my prison.

Oh, the wind, the wind is blowing
Through the graves the wind is blowing
Freedom soon will come
Then we'll come from the shadows.

Lyrics: Hy Zaret, adapted from the original
French by Maurice Druon and Joseph Kessel.
Music: Anna Marly, 1943

FROM
THE
SHADOWS

CHAPTER ONE

THE SEA WANTED to swallow me whole. I wouldn't have minded if it had been quick.

Wave after wave crashed over the side of the fishing boat, water sluicing across the deck and soaking me as I clung to a knotted rope strung along the gunwale. Crewmen of the small caïque shouted to each other, and the captain hung on to the tiller, trying to keep the thirty-foot craft on course.

I'd ceased to care where we were headed, as long as it wasn't underwater. I was flat on my rear, snug against the hull, hoping and praying that the next wave wouldn't wash me overboard. This was supposed to be the sunny Mediterranean, but it felt more like a nor'easter off Gloucester when the November winds blew hard and cold.

Two days ago, I was in Cairo, relaxing at the bar in Shepheard's Hotel, enjoying a bit of rest, hardly suspecting what was coming around the corner. Now I was listening to my chattering teeth and the British skipper ordering his five-man crew—two Greeks, two Englishmen, and one silent, swarthy fellow of uncertain nationality—to hold on tight.

He didn't need to tell me twice.

I saw the skipper bracing himself, the tiller hard to starboard as he maneuvered the wooden fishing boat to avoid being sideswiped by a giant roller. The problem was, that left us with only one alternative.

Head straight into the wave.

Time seemed to slow down. The wave kept coming, growing larger, the crest towering over our mast with its furled sails. The long, sharp bow bit into the trough as the frothing breaker spat foamy white and encompassed the small boat.

I felt weightless, floating in air, tethered only by a length of rough hemp rope twisted around my wrist. I was standing upright in the wave itself, pieces of ship's gear floating around me, the world either silent or so filled with this deafening downpour that every other sound was flattened into oblivion.

I hit the deck hard, sliding toward the bowsprit as the caïque came through the wave and dropped to the churning surface. The rope held, stopping me before I crashed into the bow, nearly breaking my wrist in the process.

But I was alive, on the right side of rough water, and the next wave wasn't higher than our mast. Lucky me.

A crewman, one of the Greeks, came forward to check the rigging.

"Hey English, you still here?" he said, pulling at the forestay line.

"American," I said, pulling myself up. "Where is here, anyway? Are we getting close?"

"Close, yes," he said. "To windward shore. Wind not so bad, waves not so bad. Relax, English, we have you there soon. After dark."

"American," I said again. Not that he could tell from my uniform. I wore sun-bleached khakis that could have been standard issue from any army in the Med, along with a dark civilian jacket. Aside from my captain's bars and dog tags, there was nothing to identify me as US Army. The idea was to escape notice by the Germans but still have enough of a uniform to not be shot as a spy.

"Sure, sure. American, English, all the same to me. I am Erasmos Papadakis," he said, extending his hand.

"Billy Boyle," I said as we shook.

"Bill-lee Boyle. Strange name, but okay. I am your guide tonight. I take you ashore," Erasmos said. Before I could ask any questions, he moved on with his steady seaman's gait, leaving me to lurch about as the boat crested another wave and its bow slammed down, over and over.

I managed to stay upright, grasping the rigging as I gazed at the horizon. A thin line appeared and soon developed into hills fronted by jagged cliffs.

Crete. Home to thousands of German occupation troops, a few hundred thousand Greeks, or *Kritikoi*, as the natives of this island were known. And a handful of British Special Operations Executive teams who were busy arming the resistance fighters and keeping the Germans busy burying their dead.

So why add one American to the mix? For some damn reason, one of the Brits couldn't be located, and the brass wanted him brought out for some SOE business in the south of France. That's all I was told because that's all I needed to know. Need to know is a big thing in this war, a concept I never much liked. As I gazed out over the unwelcoming shore while we rolled on the dying swells, I would have preferred to know why I was risking my neck. Or maybe not. Finding him might be nothing more than the whim of some senior officer heading off for cocktails right about now.

The warm air began to dry my clothes as I stood in the bow, thankful that the mountains of Crete had finally blocked the hard winds coming out of the northwest. It was the first bit of luck since I'd been plucked from the hotel bar in Cairo and given this job by my boss, Colonel Samuel Harding. He said the orders had come from on high, which must've been damned high since Harding worked for General Eisenhower at Supreme Headquarters, Allied Expeditionary Force.

But SOE had plenty of strings to pull, and Cairo was a long way from London. All Harding could tell me was that a British colonel from SOE headquarters in Algiers was behind the mission. So here I was, ready to be taken ashore to locate Captain Richard Thorne, who had unaccountably stopped responding to radio messages. Which meant I was dependent on Erasmos to help me find him. And get him out. Well, I'd survived the trip here from Tobruk, despite the storm that had brewed up a few hours after we'd left Libya, so I figured the return trip couldn't be worse.

I'd take what luck I found, I told myself as I strolled back to the skipper, Lieutenant Marchant, still at the stern. It was nice to be able to take a step without the deck rising or falling four feet.

"If I'd known about that blow, I wouldn't have set sail," he said. "But we're through it, so all's well. They brew up out of the north sometimes with no warning."

"You sound used to it," I said, looking at his hands in the fading light, white-knuckled on the wooden tiller.

"All in a day's work for the Levant Schooner Flotilla," Marchant said. "Glad to help."

The Levant Schooner Flotilla was one of those small, semisecret organizations the Brits operated with flair, using volunteers who scrounged, stole, or requisitioned caïques and other small vessels to smuggle agents and commandos on missions in the eastern Mediterranean. They refitted fishing boats with engines pulled from British tanks and radios from American fighter planes. Marchant had been a yachtsman before the war and looked like he was enjoying himself despite the heavy weather.

"How do we get ashore?" I asked. The sea was calmer, but I didn't want to take a swim in it.

"We'll be in the Gulf of Loutro soon," he said. "Nice anchorage. Erasmos will paddle you ashore in a dinghy, along with some supplies. Food for the villagers, mostly."

"It is good to bring gifts," Erasmos said as he joined us. "Food and bullets."

"The villagers will help us locate Thorne?" I asked.

"Maybe," Erasmos said. "But these people are Sfakian."

"What does that mean?" I said.

"It means you'd better hope they take a liking to you," Marchant said. "Otherwise—"

He took one hand off the tiller long enough to draw it across his throat.

CHAPTER TWO

THE LIGHT OF a half-moon still makes for a dark night, especially when you're going over the side of a boat into an inflatable raft. We were within the calm waters of the Gulf of Loutro, the sea an inky black splashed with shimmering moonlight, the stars above putting on a splendid show.

I climbed down the rope ladder as Erasmos steadied the raft. Crew members handed over containers of food and ammunition. Plenty of .303 cartridges for the Lee-Enfield rifles the British were dropping to the SOE groups, along with a decent supply of 7.9 mm Mauser rounds to be used with captured German rifles. Not to mention the tins of bully beef and biscuits. Once all that was aboard, our tiny craft was awfully low in the water.

"See you tomorrow night," the skipper said in a hushed voice from the caïque. "Good luck."

"We'll need luck to reach the shore before going under," I said, pushing off and digging in with my oar. I could hear Marchant laugh like a pirate watching some poor slob walking the plank.

"Just row, Bill-lee," Erasmos said. "It will be good to have gifts for the Sfakians. Best to keep them happy."

Erasmos and the skipper had filled me in on the people of this mountainous region. They lived a harsh and rugged life amidst the gorges and mountains of the interior or in small villages along the coast, none of which were connected by roads. The Sfakians were renowned as rebels, fighting the Venetians and the Turks long before they turned against the German invaders.

"Paddle harder, English," Erasmos said. "To starboard. See the lights?"

"Okay," I said, noticing that we'd drifted off course. Tiny, soft lights came into focus. Not electrical lighting, but oil lamps or candles illuminating the cluster of whitewashed houses glowing in the faint moonlight. The buildings hugged the terrain, blending into the folds of the ground, tight against the cliffs rising behind them.

"No roads?" I said, gasping between strokes. I couldn't help wondering if the Germans ever sent out patrols to enforce a blackout.

"No roads," Erasmos said, his breathing a lot steadier than mine. "Paths through the gorges. Trails for goats and sheep. Germans only come, never leave."

"Killed by the Sfakians?"

"After some time, yes," Erasmos said. I didn't press for details or ask exactly what he meant.

The surf demanded our attention as we came close to shore. Rocks jutted out amidst the churning water and we zigzagged around them until a rolling wave lifted the dinghy and deposited us on the pebbly beach, pretty as you please.

We dragged the cargo-laden craft up the beach, past the tide line, and I readied the Thompson submachine gun I'd slung behind my back. I didn't think anyone could have heard us with the pounding of the surf and the tumbling beach stones, but I didn't want any surprises.

"No, English," Erasmos said, patting me on the shoulder as he sat on the prow of the dinghy. "We will be honored guests of the Sfakians, God willing. No need for that."

A pebble rolled downhill and bounced off my foot. Then another. I looked up and made out a half-dozen forms silhouetted against the gauzy yellow light of the closest windows. Men with rifles.

Aimed at us.

I slung my tommy gun and stood, arms outstretched, figuring I'd let Erasmos do the talking. He did plenty, unleashing a torrent of Greek that I hoped contained many friendly greetings and news of the gifts we'd brought.

The villagers descended a rocky path, sure-footed even in the dark. None of them spoke in answer to Erasmos's cascade of words.

"I think they heard you," I said to Erasmos. I could see he was nervous, maybe more nervous than he should have been. Had he recognized one of the villagers? He slowed down, the last few words sputtering out into the dark, disregarded by the men who gathered around. Their rifles were no longer pointed directly at us, but they held them at the ready. Several men looked up and down the beach, satisfying themselves we were the only visitors.

Erasmos began jabbering at them again, probably telling them over and over what they'd already figured out.

"It's okay, Erasmos," I said, watching the men watch us. They wore black boots. Sashes tied around their waists were topped with knives and cartridge belts. They seemed very much at ease, as if they normally lazed around the house fully armed, waiting for intruders by land or sea. Thick beards were the order of the day, a few of the men sporting twirled mustaches.

I could understand Erasmos being jumpy. I wasn't exactly calm, but I did a better job of hiding my nerves than he did.

"Erasmos Papadakis, I am surprised to see you again," said one of the men, pointing with his rifle. "We do not need another SOE agent. We need guns." His English was clipped and precise, as if he thought carefully about every word. I hoped he gave as much consideration to the pressure his finger was exerting on the trigger.

"He is not SOE," Erasmos said. "American. He comes to take an SOE man out."

"I'm Captain Billy Boyle, United States Army," I said, trying to make sense of what was going on. I waited for someone to take notice or introduce themselves, but all eyes were on Erasmos.

"Which Englishman?" asked the *Kritikos*.

"Thorne. Do you know where he is?" Erasmos said. "Can you take us?"

"What is in the raft?"

"Food and ammunition," Erasmos said. "For the villagers. For you."

"Who is this guy?" I said, looking at Erasmos as I stepped closer to the fellow doing the talking. "You know him?"

"We know each other all too well, my American friend. I am Solon. Follow me." He snapped his fingers, and men grabbed the supplies before herding Erasmos and me up to the village. I wanted to quiz Erasmos on whatever beef he and Solon had going, but they kept us apart on the narrow path.

We passed several small houses of whitewashed stone where flickering lights were doused as we drew near. Best not to show much curiosity about armed men in the middle of the night, even if they were from your own village. We arrived at a courtyard, the gate opened by another bearded fighter, rifle at the ready.

"In here," Solon beckoned, opening a stout wooden door. One of his men entered with us as the others carted away the supplies. "Sit."

We arranged ourselves around a rough wooden table. The room was lit by an oil lamp on the wall and a squat candle on the table. A fireplace took up one corner, charred wood spilling out onto the stone floor. Solon leaned his rifle against the wall behind him, and I did the same with my Thompson. Erasmos, armed with only a pistol, made a big deal of keeping his hands on the table. The fourth guy busied himself at a cupboard, his rifle slung over his shoulder. The room smelled of gun oil and wet ash.

"Solon. Isn't that the name of some old Greek?" I asked. I wasn't getting any answers with direct questions, so I figured I'd try out what I remembered from my ancient history class. Unfortunately, that didn't go much beyond the name ringing a faint bell.

"Besides myself?" Solon said, smiling as his pal set down plates of bread, cheese, and olives. Solon had a scattering of gray around his temples, and while he was older than I was, he wasn't *old*.

"A lawmaker and sage of ancient Athens," Erasmos said. "Solon is well regarded by all Greeks." I wasn't sure if he was giving me a history lesson or buttering up the current Solon.

"I practiced law before the Germans came," Solon said. "But that is all in the past. It seemed as good a choice as any for a *nom de guerre*. Now, eat, you must be hungry. A sea voyage makes for an appetite once it is over, does it not?"

"Thanks," I said, taking a plateful of food and a glass of whatever Solon's silent partner was pouring.

"To many dead Germans," Erasmos said, raising his glass for a toast.

"*Ya mas!*" Solon said as I joined in, clinking glasses. They downed the clear liquid with enthusiasm, so I followed suit. It was firewater.

"Good stuff," I said, setting down my glass with a thud and stifling a cough.

"Raki," Solon said. "Like the Italian grappa."

"Yes. A little sweeter," I said.

"In this village they flavor it with honey," Solon said, pouring us another.

"You're not from here?" I asked, beginning to steer the conversation back to what I needed to know.

"No. My men and I have come to pay our respects. One of our fighters was of this village. He was killed two weeks ago," Solon explained. "We visited his family and recruited two young men. We leave in the morning."

"You just happened to be here when we landed?" I asked.

"Indeed. A lucky coincidence for you, Captain Boyle. The local fighters would not know where Captain Thorne is."

"You do?"

"Of course. I know everything that happens in this part of Crete," Solon said, his hooded eyes turning on Erasmos. "Everything."

"If you know everything, tell me what you've got against my friend Erasmos," I said, taking a drink.

"Erasmos is not your friend," Solon said. "He works for the British. And maybe the Germans."

"No!" Erasmos said, slapping his hand on the table. "You know this is a lie."

"I don't believe it," I said to Solon. "If he was a traitor, he'd be dead, not sitting here drinking raki with us."

"Perhaps. He makes things difficult for me by returning. I told him to stay away," Solon said, looking straight at Erasmos. "Didn't I?"

"Yes," Erasmos said. "I am sorry, but I could not refuse. If I say no, the British will not allow me to fight with them. It is the only way left."

"Wait, what's going on between you two?" I asked.

"Erasmos would be dead, if only on suspicion," Solon said, "if he were not my cousin. He enjoys my protection. But I do not enjoy granting it."

Both men went silent, the tension between them unrelenting. I'd walked into a family feud that threatened my mission, if not my health. There was only one way to clear this up.

I poured more raki.

After a few glasses, the story came out. Erasmos had been part of Solon's resistance group. He had been a trusted messenger, taking verbal instructions from one group to another and rendezvousing with SOE teams at their hideouts. As a result, he had known about drop zones for arms and supplies as well as the identities of guerilla leaders. Solon had trusted his cousin.

Everyone trusted Solon, since he had a ferocious reputation in combat and took on the Germans whenever they ventured into his mountainous territory. On this, Erasmos readily agreed.

Three months ago, an arms drop was scheduled. Erasmos delivered the messages. Solon and a small group would receive the weapons. Men from several groups would gather at a small village the next day where the weapons would be distributed. The village was chosen because it was isolated and neither the Germans nor the *Kritikos* guerillas had been in action anywhere close by.

A safe place.

But Solon was a careful man, which is why he was still alive. At the last possible moment, he dispatched Erasmos with a change of plan. The meeting place was switched to another village ten kilometers away. Erasmos traversed the gorges and plateaus for more than twenty-four hours, delivering the news.

As Solon spoke, Erasmos nodded in agreement. So far, so good.

The arms drop went off perfectly. Solon and his men loaded the gear onto donkeys and began the trek to the village in the dark. In this part of Crete, the only roads were tracks, barely wide enough for a man and a donkey, but each knew the way.

Solon heard the firing as dawn broke across the horizon.

He saw the smoke as the sun rose.

They found the bodies an hour later.

The Germans had been waiting. They surrounded the small village and massacred the resistance fighters and all the villagers. Men, women, and children.

Every resistance leader whom Erasmos had told of the change in plan lay dead in the gritty dust, while Erasmos, exhausted, slept soundly far away.

There was only one conclusion; Erasmos had betrayed them. How else to explain the presence of the Germans? As Solon put forward that question, Erasmos buried his head in his hands and stated with great weariness that it was not him. It must have been someone else. Who, he could not imagine.

"Because he is my cousin, I gave him the benefit of my doubt. Also, I was trained as a lawyer," Solon said. "The evidence against him is heavy, but circumstantial."

"Your men were not so understanding," I said.

"No," Erasmos said. "This is Sfakia. A blood debt is not forgiven. Brothers, fathers, cousins, all killed."

"Honor demands blood," Solon said. "I told Erasmos to leave Crete."

"This I did," Erasmos said, as if that settled it. "Now I am back. I will find who did this. Crete is home."

"You have no home," Solon said. "You will stay here, under guard, until we return. I will take Captain Boyle to Thorne in the morning. Now, sleep."

Solon extended his hand to Erasmos, palm up. Not for a friendly handshake. Erasmos withdrew his revolver slowly and handed it over. Solon glanced at his man standing guard and motioned for him to take Erasmos away. I trailed them into the street, lit by the faint light of glittering stars.

"I'm sorry," I said, although I wasn't sure for what. Maybe Erasmos had sold out to the Germans. But if he had, why return to Crete? Was clearing his good name more important than his life? And if someone slit his throat, he'd have neither. I couldn't figure him.

"Me too," Erasmos said. "Very sorry." With that, he followed his guard into the shadows, looking like a man who knew his grave had already been dug.

Solon showed me to a small room at the rear of the building, empty except for a pile of wool blankets. I asked him what he thought of Erasmos, but all he did was sigh and tell me to sleep.

"Erasmos will be alive tomorrow," he said. "Pray to God we will be as well."

CHAPTER THREE

A SHARP RAP on the door woke me in time to see a rosy light cresting the hills behind the house. I got up off the floor and stretched my aching muscles, hoping Erasmos was doing the same.

I washed at a pump behind the house, filling a wooden bucket and dumping it over my head. The air was cold and the water even colder, but I knew the day would be a warm one. No clouds in the sky, and we'd be hiking uphill all day. A recipe for heatstroke in the Mediterranean.

I carried my gear into the kitchen. Solon was heating water at the hearth.

"You will leave the submachine gun here," he said, wasting no breath on a morning's greeting. "It marks you as an American. *Kritikoi* carry rifles. A man needs to fight and hunt. A German might spot us at a distance. A few fighters would be nothing new for them. But an American in their midst will bring them running."

"If you say so. It's a handy weapon."

"Yes. If I came upon a house filled with drunken Germans, I would put it to good use. But I prefer a rifle. Any fool can pull a trigger and let a dozen bullets fly. It takes the skill of a hunter to kill a German with one bullet, and live to do it again," Solon said.

"Rifle it is," I said, sensing that there was something in the code of the Sfakians that frowned on the unwise expenditure of ammunition.

"Coffee," Solon said. He poured hot water into cups and tossed me packets of soluble coffee from the supplies we'd brought in. "Not very good, but in wartime we make sacrifices. The food we gave to the old people of the village. But the coffee and bullets we keep."

It was hot, and with the bread and cheese left from last night, we made a breakfast of it.

I sipped the hot joe. "Were you in the Greek army?" I asked.

"No. But when the Germans descended on us, I fought. We all did. My grandfather killed a German paratrooper with a stone in his olive grove. My grandmother slit the throat of another before he could untangle himself from his harness. The people of Crete have been fighting invaders for centuries. The only thing new is how these came. From the sky."

"It must have been a shock," I said, remembering the news stories back in '41, before America was in the war. The airborne invasion was massive, and bloody.

"The British fought well, as did our Greek troops," Solon said. "But there were too many Germans. They were everywhere. We battled to allow the English time to escape, many of them through Sfakia itself."

"You didn't leave?"

"No. I stay to avenge my family. Many of them were killed in reprisals," Solon said. "The Germans will pay."

"That would be Erasmos's family as well," I said. "Are you sure he betrayed you?"

"At the start of this war, I would have said no, it is impossible. A man of Sfakia would never go over to the murderers of his kin," Solon said. "But after three years of war, I have seen too much of human weakness. Now I say it is possible. Still, he is of my blood, and I will allow no one to harm him. Unless I find proof of his treachery, then I will choke the life out of him myself."

Solon ripped a hunk of bread apart and tore at it with his teeth. The conversation seemed to be over. I drank the last of the coffee as Solon's ever-present bodyguard wrapped what was left of the food and stuffed it into a sack.

Solon rose and left the table, taking his rifle with him. His face was dark, and his jaw clenched, as if he was in pain from telling me so much about his losses. Outside, I was given an ammunition belt.

Wearing it and toting my rifle—a captured German Karabiner 98k—I probably could blend in at a distance as a *Kritikos* resistance fighter. One who couldn't manage a dark bushy beard, that is.

I followed Solon and his men out of the village, up a steep path that twisted through a landscape of boulders and scrub brush. Within minutes, we'd lost sight of the village as it vanished behind gray rock and stunted trees sculpted by the wind. The ground was stony, each step a grueling challenge as the incline increased and Solon led the way like a rabbit bounding across open fields.

As we crested a ridge, Solon called a halt. Just in time. I leaned back against a boulder, and shielding my eyes against the sun, looked out over the blue waters of the Mediterranean to the south. It was a beautiful sight, but I was more interested in great gulps of air.

"We couldn't have taken an easier route?" I asked as soon as I got my breathing under control.

"This is the best route, since it is the only route," Solon said, his voice soft and low. "Do not speak, you make enough noise with your feet. No reason to add your mouth to the clatter. Germans have ears, you know."

I thought I had been light on my feet, but maybe not by mountain goat standards. A canteen was passed around, and I took a small drink, following the example of the others. No need to be thirsty greedy as well as foot noisy.

We moved on, down into a gorge and up the other side, then across a plateau where olive trees stood in neat rows. My aching thighs were glad of the break.

Solon halted, a hand raised in the air. He cocked his head in one direction, then the other.

I heard it too. An airplane. Not the growl of a fighter or the heavy, high engines of a bomber, but rather the purr of a light aircraft. A German spotter plane.

Solon rasped out an order that didn't need translation. We ran under the branches of an olive tree and grasped the trunk, eyes down. If a low, slow-moving aircraft is looking for you, the last thing you want to do is look up. Faces are bright shiny objects when everything around you is shades of gray and brown.

Were they looking for us? Who knew we'd be coming this way? I wasn't sure how the Germans could even spot the desolate track we'd taken, but no sense taking chances. Besides, there was some comfort in not looking. If I can't see them, they can't see me. Right?

The engine revved and the plane climbed and circled around as the pilot took a good look at the olive grove. Then the noise faded until there was nothing but a faint and distant buzz, like an annoying insect that had finally given up.

"We go," Solon said, looking worried. Or maybe that was the way he always looked on patrol. We went single file, staying under the shade of the leafy branches.

"Do you think we were spotted?" I whispered, trotting to catch up with Solon's long strides.

"We were not," he said. "I don't think he was looking for us. His route took him too far out over the valley."

"Someone else then," I said, "hiding from the Germans."

"Everybody hides while in the mountains. There are thieves and brigands. Deserters. If you meet a man on this path and do not know him or his people, he may kill you," Solon said.

"I hope you know a lot of people," I said.

"I do. Now, save your breath."

It was good advice. Up and down two more gorges, then clambering over rocks until we came to a grassy slope dotted with shrubs and a few bent trees. Below was the valley Solon had mentioned. On one side, a jumble of fallen rocks and boulders hemmed us in, and on the other, one of the many gorges that decorated the landscape dropped off sharply.

We sat under a tree, which gave shade and cover. The canteen was passed around along with bread and cheese. But Solon didn't join in. He stood, leaning on his rifle, and stared at the rockfall, turned, and looked back the way we came. He stood like that for a long time. I glanced at the men around me and shrugged a question their way, nodding my head toward Solon.

One of them cupped a hand around his ear and swiveled his head.

He was listening. For men he might not know? For whomever the Germans were searching for?

I didn't have a chance to ask. Solon moved out, and we followed as he led us into the valley, keeping close to the shadows cast by the boulders. I tried to listen, but all I heard were my own footsteps and the wind sweeping uphill, brushing back tall grass.

CHAPTER FOUR

AT THE BASE of the hill, we halted again. Solon climbed up a boulder and scanned the ground ahead. His men knelt, silent, as if praying. Solon swiveled his head, listening intently to the silence. I swear he even sniffed the air, trying to catch a stray scent.

The Germans had their own smell. On a hot day you could catch a distinctive odor of sweaty leather and ersatz tobacco whenever they got close. But there was nothing on the dry wind here except dust and grit, not even the slightest aroma of Fritz.

Solon slid down from the rock and took a drink from the canteen. He passed it around, and we each had a swallow before it was empty. Solon spoke with his men, and one went on ahead, taking point.

"We are close," he said as we walked. "In a kilometer we come to a road. Then a village. Thorne will be near."

"In the village?" I said, enjoying the notion of an actual road.

"When we get there, you will know," Solon said. No need to burden me with a location. I might still be captured, after all.

"Are we being followed? Who were you watching for?"

"I watch. I listen. I do these things because I wish to live," he said. "A man must be careful."

"You didn't answer my question," I said.

"That is because I am still listening, but not to you," he said, putting a finger to his lips. He must have been listening, because he sure as hell wasn't talking much.

We came to the road, which wasn't more than a dirt track the width of one vehicle. But that was a major motorway around here. It curved around a hill, bringing us to the base of a small village, about ten stone houses clustered together, the pink stonework set into the hillside like stepping-stones. Two men armed with rifles stood on the roof of one building. They must have been listening for us.

Solon waved and shouted a greeting. More people came out to watch us take the flat stone steps into the village. We were brought onto a shaded terrace where food and drink suddenly appeared. Everyone ignored me, my disguise fooling nobody. I didn't mind, being too busy falling into a chair and accepting a glass of cool water.

"I told them you were English," Solon said from across the table. "Fewer questions that way. English come through here all the time. An American will just get them excited. Many Greeks want to go to America after the war."

"Is Thorne here?" I asked, not caring much about the villagers' travel plans.

"Close," Solon said. "We eat, then we go to Thorne. Tomorrow, we go back."

"How close?" I asked.

"Not far. But higher," Solon said. "Eat."

I took one slug of raki just to be sociable but stuck to water after that. After an hour of gabbing with the locals, Solon and I set out alone, taking a path out of the village that led straight up. Or so it seemed.

"Thorne is at his *mitatos*. A shepherd's stone hut in the mountains," Solon said as we climbed. "Very secure. It cannot be spotted from the air. Even the roof is stone."

"Are you certain he's there?" I asked, between heaving breaths as we trudged upward.

"Yes. The villagers say he is planning something. Runners have been sent out to other fighters," Solon said.

"He'll have to put that on hold," I said. "His orders are to come back with me immediately."

"You have not met Captain Thorne, have you?"

"I can't wait," I said, feeling the ache in my thighs as the rifle strap dug into my shoulder.

After an hour, the setting sun was at our backs, and I could feel the temperature drop. The incline lessened as the path emptied into a rocky field where the wind whistled over outcrops of stone.

"Halt," Solon said as we stepped into the field. "There, ahead."

"That pile of rocks?" I said. It was the perfect camouflage. Nestled against the hillside, the stones taken from this very field, was a round structure with one door. The domed roof was made of the same material and would be near impossible to spot from the air. We were thirty yards away and I hadn't seen it.

"Thorne!" Solon shouted.

"Right here. Steady on, boys," a voice said from behind. Standing on a rock mound ten feet above us and armed with a casually aimed Sten gun was a figure who looked half British and half wild *Kritikos*. His trousers were stuffed into leather boots like Solon's, and he wore a black scarf wound around his head as many men did. The battledress jacket marked him as British, but the thick beard looked right at home on this mountain.

"Captain Thorne, is that the way to greet a friend who has travelled far to see you?" Solon said, stretching out his arms in mock surprise.

"Solon! Didn't expect to see you here. Didn't expect anyone until tomorrow," Thorne said, jumping down off the rock in two leaps. "Who's this chap? Please say he's my new radio operator."

"Afraid not, Captain Thorne," I said, offering my hand. "Captain Billy Boyle. I have orders to escort you out."

"Out of where, and since when do Yank captains give orders to the SOE?" Thorne snapped. "Oh, never mind, let's get inside where you can explain yourself properly. Solon, where'd you get this fellow?"

"He washed ashore at my village," Solon said. "With Erasmos in tow."

"Sorry to hear it," Thorne said as he stooped to enter the *mitatos*. I wondered if he meant sorry about me or Erasmos. "Welcome to my abode, Captain what-was-it?"

"Billy Boyle," I said, following him into the darkness. "Call me Billy."

"You Yanks and your given names," Thorne said as he struck a match and lit two candles. "Call me Thorne and tell me what the hell you're all about. Have a seat while you do it."

The room had a wide stone bench around it which, by the look of the wool blankets scattered over the flat gray stones, also seemed to serve as a sleeping platform. It wasn't as uncomfortable as it looked, or maybe I was too dead tired to care.

"I've got your orders here, Captain Thorne," I said, taking out a sealskin pouch and ignoring his crack about first names. Some Brits didn't take well to easy familiarity.

"Set it down," Thorne said, glancing at a spot next to him. "First, a toast."

I tossed the pouch down next to him and waited as he poured a round of raki into battered tin cups.

"To absent friends," Thorne said, raising his cup. We clinked cups and drank. Absent friends, a toast for the dead.

"*Ya mas*," Solon said. "To our health." We clinked again, finishing off the liquor. Thorne refilled the cups, and looked to me, waiting for whatever toast I'd offer.

"*Fad saol agat*," I said, raising my cup. "Long life to you." Thorne laughed as we clinked.

"God help me, I'm surrounded by optimists, and one of them an Irishman to boot. Health and long life on the run in Crete, that's rich," Thorne said, taking another slug. "Do you know why we touch glasses when we toast, Boyle? Solon told me the story."

"Can't say I do."

"Turns out it's a custom from ancient Greece. When they clinked full glasses together, the liquid would slosh into the other chap's glass. Therefore, if he were trying to poison you, he'd get a taste of his own medicine. Keeps everyone friendly, that's the idea," Thorne said, eyeing me over the rim of his cup. "Now tell me, Boyle, what poison have you brought me in that pouch?"

"Your superiors at SOE are wondering why you haven't maintained radio communications. Is your radio dead?" I asked.

"No, but my wireless operator is. I'm a fair hand myself, but only fair. Too slow. It gives the Germans an advantage with their radio detection vehicles," Thorne said. "There's a signals platoon about an hour from here. They've been nosing around and nearly nabbed another SOE team. A bloody nuisance. But what the hell does SOE want with me? What's so urgent?"

"Another assignment," I said. "It's all in there. You and I are supposed to provide security for some SOE commander on a trip through southern France. He requested you specifically."

"Southern France?" Thorne said, opening his orders. "That's mostly liberated ground, isn't it?"

"Yes. This guy's job is to gather information from Resistance groups about Vichy officials and other traitors who either escaped with the Germans or got phony papers and are hiding in the cities or countryside. There's a lot of them, and they won't like being hunted," I said. "But the accommodations will be an improvement. Nice is our first stop."

"Bloody hell," Thorne said, reading through the orders by flickering candlelight. "It's Stewart."

"Royal Navy Commander Gordon Stewart," I said, recalling the name from Harding's briefing. "You know him?"

"Well enough to know he'd be happy to see me dead," Thorne said. "Maybe that's what he has in mind, although tomorrow may increase his chances."

"Who is this man?" Solon asked. "An enemy of yours?"

"It's a long story," Thorne said. "He's done well for himself, even though he does think I ruined his life. He's head of Section F in Algiers."

"What is Section F?" Solon asked.

"Section F is responsible for SOE operations in France," Thorne said. "Southern France, in this case. It makes sense Stewart would want to review who betrayed whom and bring the culprits to justice, if he can find them before they disappear. But why he wants me along for the ride, I can't imagine."

"We need to leave in the morning," I said. "A boat is standing off-shore."

"Oh, no, Boyle," Thorne said. "I am otherwise engaged tomorrow morning. We are inviting the German signals platoon to a party. Should be fun. You can stay here or come along, old chap. More raki?"

Thorne grinned as he topped off my cup. I could see he was having fun, and there wasn't much I could do to dissuade him, so I had some more to drink and decided it was a swell idea to go along and keep an eye on him tomorrow.

"What is your plan?" Solon asked Thorne.

"I have the radio hidden in a cave not far from here," he said. "It's on the northern slope, close to the main road. In the morning, I report in. I'm slow enough at the Morse key that Jerry will have plenty of time to get their radio detection vehicles moving."

"You're going to ambush them," I said.

"Exactly," Thorne said. "I have three groups, all local fighters, ready to take up positions along the road Jerry will travel."

"You are certain they will come?" Solon asked.

"Absolutely. They've been active in this area, and I've been quiet, as you noted, Captain Boyle. They will jump at the bait, I'm sure. Probably take it as a sign of a new SOE team. Our objective is to destroy the vehicle with the radio detection equipment. It will make life easier for everyone."

"Okay. Now tell me why Commander Stewart wants you dead, Captain," I said.

"Oh, do call me Dickie, will you? I can see you're a decent fellow," he said. Solon laughed, and I could see how much Dickie Thorne liked to put on a show.

"Will do, Dickie. Now spill."

"Well, it was back in 1941. They'd sent me to a demolitions course in Haifa. Palestine, you know. Gordon Stewart was running the show and there were about thirty of us there," Dickie said, rubbing his chin as he conjured up the memories. "It was a large army base, and the SOE contingent occupied a very small section of it. Anyway, back then Stewart was itching to leave SOE and get a command for himself. A motor torpedo boat squadron, I think he fancied. A good man with explosives, but he preferred the regular navy to behind-the-lines stuff."

"I do not like him already," Solon said.

"You'd like him even less if you met him," Dickie said. "Very officious. He volunteered some of us for other duties at the base, to ingratiate himself with the brass, I always thought. My job was to assess base security."

"Since SOE missions might involve infiltrating an enemy base," I said.

"Just so. My job was to review all procedures and passwords. I worked with soldiers from the Jewish Brigade, Palestinian Jews, mostly. The army wasn't sure what to do with them, so they kept them busy as guards and laborers," Thorne explained, then drained his cup. "One day a truck pulled up to the gate as I was making my rounds. I watched as the guard examined their paperwork and waved the truck through. Looked quite proper, except that the truck went straight to the armory where they filled it with rifles and ammunition. The blighters drove out the same gate, picking up the Jewish Brigade guards as they left. It was a Haganah operation."

"Haganah?" Solon asked.

"Jewish militia in Palestine," Dickie said. "They're stockpiling arms for when the war ends. They used their lads in the Jewish Brigade to pull off this theft. Very well done, I must say."

"Didn't you get in trouble?" I asked.

"Oh, I stood at attention for a while as an assortment of majors and colonels told me what they thought of my skills and the SOE. But the real casualty was Stewart. He was the one who'd put an idiot like me in charge of security. Didn't do his reputation much good. He wasn't cashiered, but he was told straightaway there'd be no sea command for him. They sent him to Cairo for a desk job, then I heard he'd made it back into SOE's good graces somehow. Probably the only lot that'd have him."

"Why the hell does he want you along on this southern France junket?" I asked.

"Excellent question, Billy," Thorne said, flashing a smile. "*Ya mas.*"

CHAPTER FIVE

WE HIKED DOWN into the valley early the next morning. At a prearranged rendezvous, we met up with two groups of fighters Thorne had summoned for the ambush. Solon's men were with them, having learned of the action when the others came through the village.

"The two groups have assigned positions along the road," Thorne said, drawing a curved line in the dirt. "Here, where the road bends, one group will open fire on the lead vehicle. Then, from behind, the others join in, trapping the bastards."

"How many Germans do you expect?" I asked.

"They usually send out two trucks to escort the radio detection vehicle. Perhaps a staff car for the officers," Thorne said.

"Usually? What do they do for the unusual times?" I asked.

"They also have two armored cars, but we haven't seen them in a while," Thorne said, shrugging as if it was nothing to be concerned about.

"Armored vehicles with machine guns, and all we have are rifles?" I said. "Listen, rifle rounds can wreck radio equipment easy enough, but all they'll do is annoy a Kraut machine gunner. He'll spit out more lead in a minute than everything these men are carrying."

"We target the radio detection vehicle and then get out," Thorne said. "Everyone knows the plan. No heroics. If all goes well, five minutes after we open fire we'll be scattered into the hills."

"Where will you be?" Solon asked, staring at the line drawn on the ground while I thought about how long five minutes can be.

"Just around the bend," Thorne said. "There's a cave where the radio is. Jerry will be headed for it, and straight into our guns. As soon as they get close, I scramble up to the top of the ridge and start tossing grenades."

"I'll stay with you," I said, wondering if I'd gone around the bend myself.

"As will I," Solon said, scuffing the dirt with his boot. "We have two new men, boys really, and the experienced men will watch them. I go with you."

"Glad to have the company," Thorne said, reaching into his pack and handing us each a grenade. "Party favors."

Thorne trotted away, keeping off the road and moving over tufts of grass. The road was well-packed dirt, but even the slightest impression of a boot heel might give the game away. A little thing, but little things kept you alive out here.

We circled around the ridgeline, Thorne pointing out the cave, nothing more than a narrow cleft in the gray, crumbling rock. He clambered up and I followed. Solon melted into the terrain, easing himself behind a boulder while watching the road in either direction.

"Help me with this," Thorne said, pulling camouflaged parachute silk away from two cases. I grabbed one by the webbing and he got the other, along with a smaller bundle wrapped in canvas. "Automobile battery. It'll give us enough juice to get the job done."

Thorne opened the cases and began setting up the radio at the mouth of the cave, staying in the shade and keeping one eye on the road. He handed me a spool of antenna wire, and I climbed up the rocks, stringing yards and yards of the stuff. By the time I returned, Thorne had connected the battery to the power supply and was soon tapping out Morse, slowly and deliberately, on the keypad.

"How long before they pick it up?" I asked.

"They listen all day," Thorne said, pausing between the dots and dashes. "They'll pick it up within the hour at most, then send out their direction-finding vehicle. We know they have two, so there's a chance they'll send both to triangulate our position."

"But not on the same road," I said.

"Right," he said, his eyes flicking back and forth between the key and a crumpled paper with a series of letters. His pre-coded message.

"They'll get a bearing on the signal. This road is the best around, so one vehicle is certain to come this way, using its signal-strength detector to find us, or at least get close. It will cripple the bastards to lose it, plus the signals personnel."

"What do you know about Erasmos, Dickie?" I asked, glancing in the direction of Solon, just out of earshot. Thorne shook his head as he slowly finished a sequence of code.

"Don't know. I'd have shot him myself, but it could have been someone else," he answered. "Doubtful though. Unless he bragged to the wrong person. There's a lot of status being associated with Solon and the other leaders in this area. Might be hard to resist puffing yourself up."

"You think he informed. You would have shot him," I said. Dickie took a deep breath and stopped sending.

"I think it likely. Likely enough to have earned Erasmos a bullet, if only as a warning to any others considering the same. It's not a pretty war out here, Billy," he said. "It can be vile."

He went back to tapping out the stream of Morse code, neat and tidy in three-letter groups. Probably no hint of executions or other ugliness, but who knew? This was SOE, and they weren't exactly on speaking terms with the Marquess of Queensberry.

"Done," Dickie finally said. "If they haven't noticed that they must be napping. I'll send out another message in five minutes to be sure they stay on the scent. Ask Solon to climb to the top of the ridge and keep a lookout like a good lad, will you?"

I am a good lad, so I gave Solon the message and watched him climb to the high ground. He waved from the top, and I looked up and down the road. Nothing.

Or did I hear something off in the distance?

A stone landed at my feet. I looked up to find Solon waving his arm. He pointed down the road and cupped a hand to his ear. He'd heard it clearly from up there. Germans headed our way. I scrambled up to the cave and told Dickie, who tapped out another string of code.

"Quick off the mark, those Teutons," he said. "Bring in the wire, will you?"

I rolled up the wire while Dickie packed the radio. We stashed it back in the cave and clambered up the ridgeline. Solon was shading his eyes and pointing to a haze of dust.

"There," he said. "Not far."

"All right," Dickie said, checking our field of fire. On either side of us a mound of dirt and rock reached out to the road like two grasping claws, blocking our view in either direction. But straight on, we had a direct line of fire. "Perfect."

He stood and waved his Sten gun above his head. Across from us came a signal from one ambush group. At the bend in the road, another fighter waved, then ducked. Everyone was ready.

"They must stop the lead vehicle," Solon said, gesturing toward the group at the bend. "If not, they will get in behind us."

"They know," Dickie said. "They concentrate on the first vehicle while the rest of us target the radio truck. They have grenades, don't worry."

I didn't say anything. Grenades weren't a lot of use against armored cars unless you rolled one under or popped one through a hatch. Otherwise, it just made the gunner mad. But all they had to do was slow them down so we could fill the radio vehicle with lead. Then we'd skedaddle. My kind of plan.

The growl of the advancing vehicles came nearer. The sound grew insistent as it clarified itself, the grinding gears, rumbling tires, and revving engines signaling imminent danger. It was the moment—I've had them before—when you realize that the plan you've agreed to is no more than a plan, and that the men with weapons headed your way might not be in complete agreement with it. They'd much prefer to kill you and get back in time for dinner.

The column churned up dust, a cloud of it moving across the stony horizon. I kept my head down, my cheek pressed against cool rock, my hands gripping the rifle. I could sense Dickie rising, peering over the edge, watching for the right moment.

"Now!" Dickie shouted, unleashing bursts of fire from his Sten gun. I jumped up, zeroing in on the radio truck, a big boxy vehicle with a telltale circular antenna on top. I fired, working the bolt, and targeting the rear compartment with its equipment and radio operators.

Explosions burst at the front of the column, the ambush group at the bend showering the lead armored car with grenades. It skewed to a halt across the road, and for a second, I thought it had been disabled.

"Grenades," Dickie shouted. Solon and I pulled out our grenades and tossed them downhill toward the radio vehicle. Dickie reloaded his Sten and kept up a stream of fire even as the grenades exploded, bracketing the truck.

I reloaded and kept shooting, watching my bullets strike home. The truck began to smoke, but the driver was still alive and pulling it off the narrow road. Dickie dropped his Sten and tossed two grenades, his face twisted in anger as both the armored car and the radio truck kept moving.

The armored car's machine gun fired, targeting the men trying to stop it. The grenades had had no effect.

Across from us, I could see heavy fire directed at the other ambush group. Rapid machine gun fire from down the column, probably a second armored car. The Germans had recovered from the surprise attack, and now soldiers were moving forward, trying to flush out their attackers.

"Look," I shouted to Dickie, the noise from the battle too loud to be heard over. I pointed to the lead armored car. It was ignoring the rifle fire and grenades and moving forward, the radio truck following, slowly, belching smoke.

Fire broke out beneath the truck, the driver diving out of his cab only to be cut down.

The truck exploded, its gas tank igniting and sending a plume of fire and black smoke skyward. German soldiers scattered, falling back against the onslaught of heat and flame.

"Yes!" Dickie shouted, pumping his arm up and down as he signaled to the other groups. "Fall back!"

"The armored car," I said, pointing to the bend in the road. The vehicle was moving, trailing white smoke from its engine. A half dozen Germans on foot crept behind it, fading from sight as it turned the bend. "It's getting behind us."

"Hurry, boys," Dickie said. "We have to beat them, or they'll have us."

He didn't have to tell me to hurry. I could hear firing pick up as the

Germans behind the burning truck worked their way to our position. If we could get across the road behind us and into the rocks, we'd get clean away. If not, we'd be caught between two groups out for blood. We'd killed too many of them in a sudden ambush to expect anything but a bullet.

We rushed down, past the cave and almost to the road as the armored car rumbled into view. Bursts of machine gun fire zinged into the stones, forcing us to take cover. Above us, grenades went off, the Germans from the other side assaulting our position.

"We have to make a run for it," Dickie said. "They'll be on us in minutes."

I aimed and fired at the Krauts coming out from behind the armored car. They knelt and fired, but not before I noticed flames coming from the rear compartment. The truck explosion must have damaged the engine. The machine gunner kept us pinned as crewmen bailed out of the burning vehicle and took cover, then he jumped out, smoke swirling around him.

"We must go now," Solon said, even as small arms fire filled the air and ricocheted off stone. "There is no other way."

"He's right," Dickie said, looking me in the eye. "The others had orders to pull back as soon as I gave the signal. There's no one to help us." He leaned out and let go with his Sten, making the Germans keep their heads down. For now. We couldn't go up and we couldn't cross the road.

"The smoke might give us cover," I said, watching the armored car as gray smoke poured out of it.

"We don't have time," Dickie said, eyeing the ridgeline.

I heard a familiar sound. One that didn't belong here.

The rapid-fire bursts from a Thompson submachine gun.

"What the bloody hell?" Dickie said. I could see Germans turning away, seeking out this new threat. More bursts, and two Krauts fell dead. "Let's get out of here."

Before we could move, three Germans bolted from cover and headed toward us. Behind them, through the smoky haze, I could see the muzzle flashes from my Thompson. It had to be mine.

One of the Germans fell. Solon and I dropped the two others while

Dickie aimed his Sten at the ridge above us, watching for more of them to come over the top.

For a moment, the road was quiet, except for the sound of snapping flames. A figure came out of the smoke, short and stocky.

Erasmos.

"I could not let you go alone, cousin," Erasmos said to Solon, his face drawn and anxious. "Nor you, English."

Solon spoke to Erasmos in Greek, words that came from a place between heartache and anger. Before he could finish, a rifle shot cracked, and Erasmos dropped. Dickie sprayed the heights, and I got off a couple of rounds, enough to buy us a few seconds.

"Get him out of the road," I said, training my rifle on the ridge.

"He is dead," Solon said. He handed me the Thompson as if we had all the time in the world, then hefted Erasmos across his shoulders and set off down the road, leaving smoke, fire, and death in our wake.

CHAPTER SIX

WE LEFT THE road quickly, following a goat path that led down-hill and out of sight. Solon grunted as we stepped over rocks and downed limbs, struggling to keep his balance under the weight of his burden. His cousin, his blood.

The path evened out, going through a growth of scrub pine, and emptying into a gently sloping field of green grass dotted with field-stone. Below us the valley floor spread out in a latticework of farms and fields, faint wisps of smoke marking the comforts of home and hearth.

"Here," Solon said, laying Erasmos out on the grass and taking in a deep breath. "Here."

"We can't bury him," Dickie said, looking back at the way we'd come. "No shovels, no time."

"Stones," Solon said, checking Erasmos's pockets. If the Germans found his body, they'd search it for any trace of his identity, then go after his relatives and his village. Solon came up empty, then arranged Erasmos's arms across his chest, laying them on top of the terrible wound over his heart.

"I'm sorry," I said, and began to carry pieces of fieldstone to Solon, who took off his jacket and covered Erasmos's face with it.

"As am I," Solon said as he began stacking stones around his cousin. Dickie went back up the trail to listen for any sounds of pursuit as I continued to carry burial stones. By the time he came back to say all was quiet, we had the body nearly covered. With Dickie's help, we were done quickly, a large flat rock serving as a headstone.

"Do you want to say anything?" I asked Solon, who hadn't said much at all.

"Erasmos is in Crete. His bones will always be here. He died fighting the invaders and saving his own blood relative. Whatever else he did, he ended well," Solon said. "Not every man does."

He walked away.

I made the sign of the cross and followed, wondering about that comment, *whatever else he did*. Solon hadn't absolved Erasmos, but he buried him with heavy stones and honorable words, on a hill looking out over his homeland.

Maybe Solon believed Erasmos. Or maybe part of him was glad he wouldn't have to defend Erasmos against those who wanted their blood revenge. Was that what Erasmos was seeking? When Solon stopped to listen all those times, did he sense his cousin shadowing us, waiting for the moment to prove himself?

These weren't questions I'd dare ask Solon. He tromped on, his face a grimace of silence, and his back rigid. I followed, too tired to talk, as my boots carried me numbly through the miles. We stopped at a village for food and drink. Solon sat in the shade of an olive tree, gulping water. Dickie was chatting with the locals like a politician, shaking hands, telling the story of the ambush, and saying his good-byes.

Without a word, Solon stood and departed. That was our signal to follow.

It was dark when we finally came to the village where we'd left Erasmos not that long ago. One of Solon's men had a bandage around his head and a story about Erasmos getting the drop on him, from what Dickie translated for me.

Solon grunted and said nothing. He sat down heavily at a table in the courtyard. His man with the bandage brought a bottle of raki and three glasses, spoke with Solon, and left. Dickie and I joined Solon as he lit a candle.

"Erasmos," he said, raising his glass. We clinked hard, the liquor sloshing and running down our fingers, marking us all as victims. We drank and kept our peace as the quiet of the night settled in around us.

"The boat came last night," Solon finally said. "It will come again tonight. Last time."

"I hate to leave this island," Dickie said in a low voice, gazing up at the stars. "It's terrible and wonderful at the same time. The rest of the world is simply terrible, unless things have changed greatly since I was last there."

"They haven't," I said, reaching for the Thompson that I'd leaned against the wall. "Here, Solon, you should have this."

I handed the tommy gun to him. It wasn't much of a remembrance, but Erasmos had been clever and courageous as he carried it.

"Thank you," Solon said, and set the weapon on his lap. In one hand he held his drink, and with the other he caressed the wooden stock.

He was still at the table as we stood to walk to the beach and watch for the boat. Candlelight flickered in the shadows, casting flashes of light and darkness across his face. We shook hands, but Solon was somewhere else, some place between drunkenness and grief, his eyes focused on the darkness beyond us. Before today, Erasmos had been a problem, unsolvable if Solon were to stay true to his blood relative and his cause. Now, Erasmos had solved the problem, not to mention saved our lives, and that had broken Solon in a way that I could barely understand.

Solon's men brought the raft to the beach, and we watched the water for the signal light.

"Was it the Levant Schooner Flotilla chaps who brought you over?" Dickie asked.

"Yeah. Marchant was at the helm," I said, my eyes on the inky black sea. "Helped by the biggest wave I ever saw. There!" I pointed to a pencil-thin point of light that flashed three times. One of Solon's men returned the recognition signal and we shoved off, paddling hard to leave the rocky shore behind.

THE FIRST THING Marchant asked me about after we were hauled aboard was Erasmos.

"He's staying on Crete," I said, without going into how permanent the arrangement was.

"Good show," Marchant said. "Make yourselves comfortable, and the boys will get you some grub. Smooth sailing home, Billy. Good to see you in one piece, Dickie!"

Marchant returned to the helm as his crewmen brought us blankets and bully beef sandwiches.

"Southern France will have its advantages," Dickie said, staring at the food. "Still can't imagine what old Stewart wants me there for, unless the whole thing's going to fall apart, and he needs someone to blame."

"Hard to see how it could go south," I said, taking a bite. The British corned beef was a step up from Spam, but it was still meat from a can. "It's talking to Resistance people in liberated areas."

"Did you learn nothing from your brief island sojourn, Billy? Resistance fighters can be out for each other's blood, and not just on Crete."

"You have a point," I said, leaning against the rails and watching the thankfully calm water flow under the bow. I thought about the Resistance groups I'd run into in Normandy, all united in their hatred for the Boche and divided by their vision for France after the war. Some were Marxists, some Catholic, and others favored de Gaulle, or even a restored monarchy. Whatever unity they'd enjoyed during the Occupation may not withstand the Liberation and peace. "If Stewart is looking for collaborationists, each faction is capable of offering their political enemies to meet whatever quota he has."

"You're a smart one, Billy, for a Yank," Dickie said, drawing a blanket across his shoulders. "No offense, but your lot can be a bit naive. How'd you come to be in this line of work? With the OSS?"

"No, not that crew," I said. The Office of Strategic Services was America's version of the SOE, and OSS teams had been dispatched throughout occupied Europe. "Although we'll likely run into them on our grand tour."

"Say, Marchant, you must have some rum on this tub, old boy?" Dickie shouted in the direction of the helm. Marchant laughed and sent one of his men to fetch a bottle. "So, what's your outfit then?"

"SHAEF," I told him. "Supreme Headquarters, Allied Expeditionary Force. My boss is Colonel Sam Harding, who runs the Office of Special Investigations. He reports to General Eisenhower."

"Rarified circles, indeed," Dickie said, nodding his thanks to the crewman who handed him a bottle. "But what are you investigating besides this year's harvest of Chenin Blanc grapes?"

"What Colonel Harding told me was that this venture had to be a joint American and British effort since we'd be working with both OSS and SOE personnel. We'll have a French officer in charge, of course." I stopped to take a swig as Dickie passed the rum.

"Right. Old Charles de Gaulle wouldn't have it any other way," he said. "He has to convince the French he's won the war all by himself. Is that the real reason SHAEF is involved?"

"I think that has a good deal to do with it," I said. "Part of the reason is that I was on hand in Cairo when they needed somebody. But to tell the truth, it's also because I have a personal connection to General Eisenhower."

"Do tell," Dickie said, as I took another swig and handed over the bottle.

It was a good night for a story. Warm breezes, calm seas, and a bottle of hooch. So I laid it all out for him.

Back when the Japanese sucker-punched us at Pearl Harbor, I was a newly minted detective on the Boston Police Department. It was sort of a family business, my dad and uncle both being detectives. I'd been a patrolman for a few years, but when you have relatives on the Promotions Board and the questions for the upcoming detective's exam mysteriously appear in your locker one morning, it's not all that hard to get ahead.

Some people may say that's not right. Me, I think it works. No one else is gonna look out for us Boston Irish, so we look out for ourselves. If you're Irish, you understand. My grandfather never forgot all the NO IRISH NEED APPLY signs he saw when he looked for a job, and he made sure we remembered as well.

"I didn't know General Eisenhower was Irish," Dickie said, interrupting the flow.

"Hang on," I said. "I'm getting to Uncle Ike."

There I was, ready to start my career as a plainclothes detective, when suddenly, I find out there's not enough deferments to go around. Last hired, first drafted. In my family, we believe in a united Ireland,

and we're not exactly fans of the British Empire. Although I admit to Dickie that I've met some decent Englishmen since coming over here in '42.

My father's older brother had been killed in the World War, back in 1918, and he'd decided that was the last Boyle who ought to die to pull England's fat out of the fire. As so often happened in my house, it was my mother who first came up with a plan. Her notion was to keep me alive and out of the shooting war. She was related to Mamie Doud, who'd married Dwight David Eisenhower before I was born. Mom put the touch on Mamie, who suggested to her husband, then an unknown colonel in Washington, DC, that he should take me on as an aide. The idea was that I'd sit out the war doing my bit by shuffling papers and not getting shot.

All well and good, but what we didn't know was that Uncle Ike had been named to head US Army forces in Europe, and he fancied the notion of a detective on his staff to investigate low crimes in high places. He needed someone he could trust to keep his mouth zipped and not spill military secrets, so me being a relative was a bonus.

That landed me in London more than two years ago, wondering if I was up to the job, and how angry Uncle Ike would be if he found out the story of my promotion to detective.

"Stewart will love this," Dickie said. "Rubbing elbows with the influential is his idea of heaven."

"Dickie, if I had any influence, I would have found somebody else to drag you off that damned island," I said. "Don't make trouble for me, okay? Let's have a nice time in France. Good food, wine, and soft beds. You be decent to Stewart, and we'll get along fine."

"I can't wait for you to make the acquaintance of Commander Gordon Stewart, Billy. You'll see how far decency gets you. Cheers," Dickie said, handing me the bottle. "Ought to be fun."

I'd trust Dickie in a fight any day. But could I trust him to keep his head when it was words being tossed instead of grenades?

CHAPTER SEVEN

WE SAILED IN to Tobruk harbor under the midday sun, where a British army sergeant met us at the dock. Tobruk was still pretty much a pile of rubble, having been thoroughly destroyed a few times over as the Germans and Commonwealth troops fought for it during the early desert war. Now it was a busy rear area filled with stockpiles of supplies and streets almost cleared of debris.

We shook hands with Marchant and wished him well, following our escort to a waiting staff car. He drove us to a nearby barracks, where we were issued new uniforms and gear. The soldier handing out razors and soap took one look at Dickie's beard and dug out a pair of scissors.

After the hot water sluiced away layers of dust and salt, I began to feel human once again. I dressed in clean khakis, stretched out on a cot, and waited for Dickie to appear.

"Come on, Billy, let's get some grub," said a British officer who peeked his head inside the room. He looked vaguely familiar.

"Is that you, Dickie?" I asked, rolling off the cot. "Didn't know you had a baby face under that foliage." He looked about ten years younger without the beard.

"I miss it already," he said, rubbing his bare chin.

We made for the mess hall and attacked the food in silence. It was the first square meal I'd had in days. Maybe longer for Dickie. When we were done, our sergeant told us to grab our gear. Our flight for Algiers was in one hour.

"That's fifteen hundred miles," Dickie said with a sigh as we packed our stuff in haversacks. "I'd rather be back in my stone hut than sit on a hard metal seat for half the day."

"Just think about southern France," I said. "Too bad they're not taking us straight there."

"Oh, I don't mind Algiers," Dickie said as we walked outside. "Decent food if you know where to look. And the chaps at SPOC will want to brief us fully, I expect."

"I don't know that one," I said, as I looked around for our ride.

"Special Project Operations Center," Dickie rattled off. "SOE and your OSS decided to join forces, along with a few Frenchmen from DGER."

"Okay, I know what the Office of Strategic Services is, but what's DGER?" I asked, pronouncing it the way Dickie had, *dee-ger*.

"Free French intelligence," Dickie said. "*Direction générale des études et recherches*. In plain English, the General Directorate for Study and Research. Sounds so academic and innocent, doesn't it? Well, here's our car."

I expected a ride out of town to an airbase, but instead the driver returned to the harbor. There, moored one hundred yards offshore, was a beautiful sight. A Short Sunderland flying boat, a four-engine aircraft roomy enough for bunks and a galley kitchen.

"Well, I'll say this much for Stewart, he knows how to arrange first-class transport," Dickie said as we got into the launch. "Those things are flying hotels."

We took full advantage, catching up on sleep on a real mattress with clean sheets. Fifteen hundred miles slipped underneath our wings quickly, and we were roused by a crewman serving coffee and sandwiches. Commander Gordon Stewart went up a notch in my estimation.

The aircraft landed with a few thumps in the calm waters of the Bay of Algiers. A launch motored out to take us off. As we headed for the dock, whitewashed stone buildings and the many minarets of the city sparkled in the sun, and ships of every size dotted the anchorage. The last time I was here, the Luftwaffe was still dropping by and leaving five-hundred-pound calling cards.

"I assume someone from SOE is meeting us?" Dickie said, holding onto his cap as a warm breeze blew against our faces.

"No, one of my crew," I said. I shaded my eyes and scanned the crowd of khaki on shore, trying to pick out Kaz. Lieutenant Piotr Augustus Kazimierz, that is. A lowly lieutenant in the Polish Armed Forces in the West, Kaz was also a baron of the Augustus clan. And my best friend. We'd met when I first came to Great Britain in 1942, and he was working as a translator on General Eisenhower's staff. Fluent in most European languages and having a nodding acquaintance with several others, he'd been quite in demand because of those talents. Back then, no one had any idea of his other skills, such as being a deadly shot with his Webley revolver and saving my skin on a regular basis. Before too long, he'd been brought in by Sam Harding to the Office of Special Investigations, and two years later, we'd logged a lot of miles tracking down murderers and traitors.

I spotted a figure on the wharf waving a peaked service cap, his immaculately tailored tropical uniform evident even at this distance. While everyone else wilted in the heat, Kaz looked like he'd just had his khaki drills cleaned and pressed, which could well be the case. Kaz liked a nice crease in his trousers.

"Our ride's here," I said to Dickie as the launch halted at the wharf. I waved and called out to Kaz, who stepped forward.

"Wait," Dickie said, skidding to a stop as soon as we stepped out onto the wharf. "Is that you Piotr? It can't be."

"Dickie," Kaz asked, "Dickie Thorne?"

"One and the same, old boy. But you're hardly the same, are you? My god, that scar! And you've got meat on your bones, haven't you?"

Kaz and Dickie shook hands and clasped each other's shoulder, in what was an enthusiastic display of emotion for an Englishman.

"We haven't seen each other since Oxford," Kaz said, sparing me a glance.

"Balliol College," Dickie added.

I knew Kaz before he got that scar, but by now it was as much a part of him as his sandy hair and high cheekbones. It went from the corner of his eye down to his jaw, a jagged reminder of the explosion that had killed the woman he loved and nearly destroyed him.

"Bit of an accident," Kaz said, fingering his scar. "Makes shaving a bother."

"Rough luck," Dickie said. "But you were a skinny old thing when we last parted. Now you look a proper soldier. And you're associated with this Yank?"

"Indeed," Kaz said. "We have worked together since the spring of forty-two. I had no idea you were the SOE chap Billy was sent to find. What a shock to see you, Dickie."

Kaz and Dickie rambled on for a bit, each asking the other about old school chums. Some were dead, others cast to the four corners, a few still hitting the books.

Besides lacking a scar, Kaz had been a skinny kid when I first bumped into him, more suited to translating documents and reading top secret reports. But along the way, he'd built himself up, working out with dumbbells and doing remarkably fast walks through Hyde Park. He'd dedicated himself to the war effort, seeking revenge for his family in Poland, all of whom were executed by the Nazis.

Or so he'd thought, until he'd received word that his youngest sister, Angelika, had somehow survived. She'd become a courier with the Polish underground and had been captured in a roundup. Luckily, Angelika had been part of a prisoner exchange several weeks ago, and against all odds, she'd been reunited with Kaz. Right now, she was recovering at the country home of Sir Richard Seaton, father of Daphne Seaton, who had died in the explosion that had scarred Kaz. She was being tended by Diana Seaton, Daphne's sister.

Diana and I are an item. I wish I were with her just as much as Kaz wishes he were with Angelika. We're an odd bunch, Yanks and Poles and Brits, working stiffs and aristocrats, people who never would have crossed paths but for this war. Now, we are bound together by the ties of shared experience and unthinkable terror, and I can't imagine life without them.

"Ah, excuse me," Kaz was saying. "So sorry, Colonel, I was taken with the excitement of seeing an old friend." Kaz stood aside as he presented us to a smartly outfitted French officer wearing a flat-top kepi service cap and a thin mustache that looked like a copy of the one General Charles de Gaulle sported.

"Captain William Boyle of the United States Army and Captain Richard Thorne of the British Army," Kaz said, standing ramrod straight. "Allow me to introduce Lieutenant Colonel Maxime Laurent of the French First Army."

Colonel Laurent looked like he expected a salute, which was his due, of course, so I snapped one off, as did Dickie, doing that flat-handed English version.

"Gentlemen," Laurent said, returning the salute. "Welcome to *Algérie française*. I am attached to the Special Project Operations Center and will be working closely with you. Shall we go?"

"Are you with DGER? *Direction générale des études et recherches*," I said, trying my best at a French accent. All the French I knew came from dealing with French Canadian criminals in Boston, plus what I'd picked up in Normandy.

"I am glad your French is so atrocious that no one nearby can understand you, Captain," Laurent said. "Otherwise, I would be forced to report a security breach to Commander Stewart."

"You know the commander, Colonel Laurent?" Dickie asked, rolling his eyes behind Laurent's back.

"Yes, an excellent officer, in my opinion," Laurent said, waiting for a driver to open the staff car door for him. Kaz smiled as he got in the front seat, the kind of smile that spoke of long-suffering forbearance.

"So Captain Thorne was telling me," I said as we settled into the spacious staff car. "Right, Dickie?"

"If Commander Stewart is involved, we can all count on a fair bit of excitement," Dickie said, staring out the window as the automobile drove through the narrow, crowded streets.

"A well-planned venture need not be exciting," Colonel Laurent said.

"Of course, you're right, Colonel," Dickie said. "I would just like to know exactly what Commander Stewart has planned. For all of us."

CHAPTER EIGHT

THE SPECIAL PROJECT Operations Center was headquartered at Villa Magnol, a grand house on a cliff overlooking the Mediterranean. Palm trees swayed in the breeze, and a grove of small pines, bent against the winds off the water, lent to the feel of a luxury resort.

For some. Colonel Laurent was billeted at the villa, which was richly decorated with archways and scrollwork in a Moorish design, like a film set for *Road to Morocco*. I half expected to see Bing Crosby and Bob Hope scampering up the steps, but all I saw was the hindquarters of Laurent as he left us to find our quarters. He'd told us to appear in the briefing room in one hour.

"This way," Kaz said, leading us toward rows of Quonset huts, tents, and a few wooden structures of recent vintage. No filigreed scrollwork in sight. "The villa was originally the headquarters for the OSS. When SPOC was formed, SOE and the French moved in."

"The brass gets to live the high life, huh?" I said, following along as we made our way around tent pegs and taut ropes.

"The red carpet is out for Colonel Laurent," Kaz said. "Politics. But not to worry, this is the cool season. It could have been worse. Ah, here is our tent."

"Delightful," Dickie said, dropping his kit bag onto a cot. "I'm not sleeping on rocks and no one's shooting at me. You won't hear me complain."

"You can draw supplies from the quartermaster, Dickie. It is one of the wooden buildings we passed," Kaz said. "Billy, there is your duffle."

"Is this a command performance we're going to?" I asked as I unpacked my clothes and gear. "Fancy dress?"

"No idea," Kaz said, sitting on a wooden folding chair that was the mainstay of our furnishings. A warm breeze came in from under the loose tent flaps. This place would be an oven in summer. "Colonel Laurent shares little with me, since I am, after all, only a lieutenant."

"You're a baron, Piotr," Dickie said. "He'd probably go for that."

"I share that when it amuses me to," Kaz said. "The colonel fails to engender frivolity."

"What about Stewart?" I asked, glancing at Dickie, who gave me a look but said nothing about his prior relationship with the commander. I busied myself shaking the wrinkles out of my cotton khaki shirt as Kaz gave a slight shrug.

"An able administrator, as far as I have been able to determine, or care to," he said. "He spoke at dinner last night of going into politics after the war. As I understand it, he lobbied quite hard for this assignment. It will be his first venture to France."

"Which is a nice way of saying he's a desk jockey who pulled strings to get a safe assignment which he will later sell to the voters as a dangerous mission in occupied France," I said.

"Billy, you have become such a pessimist," Kaz said with a laugh. "This may not be such a simple mission, you know. There is much talk of hunting down French fascists. Stewart seems genuinely committed to that."

"I'm going to the quartermaster to get some fresh clothes," Dickie said. "You can fill Piotr in on my past dealings with Stewart. Maybe you two sleuths can come up with a clue as to why he wants me along."

I told Kaz about the Haifa heist. The first thing he did was laugh about Dickie unwittingly letting in the Haganah infiltrators.

"Oh, I shall have to tell that story at Oxford if ever Dickie and I return there," he said. "But it does raise questions, does it not?"

"What questions?"

"The first is why Commander Stewart recommended Dickie for a promotion, if there is still bad blood between them," Kaz said. "Stewart told me he had arranged it but never brought up the name, except to say it was a step up to major. I did not mention it yet to Dickie since I wanted it to be a surprise."

"Interesting," I said. "What's the other question?"

"Either this is Stewart making amends for Haifa, or he is going to take his revenge on Dickie," Kaz said.

"By making him a major? What a dastardly plot," I said. "You're overthinking it, Kaz."

"Well, you were the one spinning a theory about Stewart going to France in order to bolster his military record," Kaz said. "I would say everything is more innocent than our disturbed minds will allow us to consider. Stewart has fought the war from behind a desk, and like many others he wants to get close to the front before it's over. Hardly uncommon. Whatever happened years ago in Palestine, he at least knows Dickie, and obviously trusts him. Enough to recommend him for promotion. Deviousness is not always the order of the day, Billy."

"Maybe," I said, grabbing a towel and my shaving gear. "You think I have a disturbed mind?"

"We have seen the world at its worst for the past few years, haven't we?"

"So no, not really disturbed?"

"Not at all, Billy. Enjoy your shave. Be careful with the razor."

"When did you get to be such a wise guy?" I said, heading out to wash up.

"How long have I known you?" Kaz said to my back. Fair point.

CLEAN-SHAVEN AND SPORTING fresh khakis complete with field scarf, known as a tie to normal people, I headed to the villa with Kaz and Dickie. As we climbed the steps, I took in the expanse of this camp. Besides the tents and buildings, there was a dusty field where small groups of men jogged and did calisthenics. Farther away, close to the pine forest, a shooting range was set up, the faint *pop-pop-pop* of small arms fire punctuated by the occasional explosion.

"Demolition training," Dickie said. "Stewart loves blowing things up, his own career included."

"Dickie Thorne, there you are!" a voice boomed from the doorway.

Wearing Royal Navy khakis with the rank of commander on his shoulder boards, it had to be Gordon Stewart. Dark-haired with a wide face, he wore a mustache and gave off a hearty exuberance. He stood in the doorway, the stone sill giving him an inch or two on us as we approached. Yeah, I could see him as a politician. He looked like he was straining to keep a speech from spilling out of his mouth.

"Commander Stewart, sir!" Dickie responded, snapping off a salute. Kaz and I followed suit.

"Good to have you on board, Dickie," Stewart said, returning the salute and shaking Dickie's hand. "Ah, Captain Boyle, yes? The baron has told me much about you."

"Kaz has an active imagination, Commander," I said, looking up at Stewart. He was tall enough not to need the height advantage, but I could see he enjoyed it.

"Well, come in, will you," Stewart said, as if he hadn't been blocking the entrance and we were somehow at fault for still being out on the terrace.

Stewart moved aside and a series of explosions sounded from the direction of the firing range. I instinctively turned to look and heard a sharp sound, followed by a sting at the back of my neck.

"Inside!" Dickie yelled, grabbing Kaz by the arm and pushing me through the door.

"Good god, you're bleeding," Stewart said, looking at my neck. I put up my hand and it came away sticky red as Stewart shouted for a medical kit.

"I saw the round hit the building," Dickie said. "A stone chip hit Billy when he turned."

"I believe I will need a new hat," Kaz said, holding his peaked cap by the brim. The bullet had scored the cloth right at the top, missing Kaz's head by inches.

"I believe I'll sit down," I said, moving to one of the chairs that lined the hallway. "Who the hell's shooting at us?"

"Must have been an errant round," Stewart said as a soldier arrived with a medical kit. Dickie fetched a glass of water and cleaned up the blood with a handkerchief. He said it hardly needed a bandage but slapped one on anyway.

"It almost killed Kaz," I said. "It could have hit any of us. Who's running things down at the firing range?"

"Let's go look," Dickie said.

"Wait, we've got something laid on," Stewart said. I knew he was going to spring the promotion on Dickie, but I also wondered if he was worried about another scandal. He'd apparently put Haifa behind him, but a near miss involving officers from SHAEF, that might be troublesome. I saw him glance down the hall to one of the rooms where Colonel Laurent stood by the door, waiting for the surprise party to kick off.

"Please excuse us, Commander," Kaz said, nodding to me. Dickie and I followed outside.

"What are we doing, Kaz?" I asked.

"Testing a theory," he said, stepping out into the sunlight and putting on his hat. "I was standing just here." He planted his feet and stood still.

"Your theory is that gunman needs another chance?" I asked.

"No. If it was accidental, it will not happen again. If not, the sniper has made his escape," Kaz said, with his usual impeccable and precise logic. "Use my cap."

Dickie was quicker off the mark than I was. Taller than Kaz, he stood in front of him and squinted along the furrow that the bullet had left. He turned to check the mark on the stonework where the bullet had hit, then went back to sighting along the peaked cap.

"Not the firing range," he said, stepping back. "Those woods, the hill off to the left of the range." The pine woods ran atop the ridge facing the sea. A small hill jutted out from the ridgeline, capped by scrawny trees.

"I make that five hundred yards, maybe more," I said.

"Decent range for a Lee-Enfield with a scope," Dickie said. "Same for one of your Springfield sniper rifles."

"What's all this talk about snipers?" Stewart demanded. He hadn't been there a minute ago. Waiting to see if one of us was picked off?

"Simply a theory, Commander," I said. "I'd suggest alerting your beach patrols if you have any out. We'll be right back."

The three of us piled into a jeep parked along the drive and sped down the dirt track leading to the open ground. Dickie drove like a maniac, spitting gravel and sending up a cloud of dust.

"He is a worse driver than you, Billy," Kaz shouted, hanging onto the back seat.

"We only have sidearms," Dickie responded. "We have to make him think we mean business."

"Right, because we'd have to be idiots to drive straight at a sniper armed only with pistols," I said. It almost made sense.

Dickie at least swerved a few times, sending up even larger swirls of dust. I saw a column of men running in formation break and scurry for cover as we approached. Others came from the direction of the firing range and demolitions area to see what all the ruckus was.

Dickie drove straight for the base of the hill, slammed on the brakes, and slid to a stop. We jumped from the jeep and fanned out, pistols drawn, making our way up the hill. I doubted anyone was still there, but there was no sense offering an inviting target. Slouched and moving from tree to tree, I tried to keep Kaz and Dickie in view.

A shot cracked. Close. We all ducked.

Another, then another. A ragged volley, each shot spaced apart by a few seconds.

I looked at Kaz and shrugged. It didn't seem like anyone was firing at us. I saw Dickie look upward, then shake his head. No clipped branches, no *zing* of bullets.

"This is ridiculous," Kaz said. "They must be shooting out to sea." He stood, his Webley still at hand, held down at his side. We joined him, making our way through the pines as the shots kept on. It was an odd feeling, knowing that we'd been nearly hit by one round a few minutes ago, and here we were, walking toward even more rifles. But there was something methodical about the firing, hardly the frantic pace of shots fired in anger.

We were about to the crest when I heard voices, a combination of French and English. I could hear the bolts being worked. Dickie made it to the top first.

"Bloody hell," he said, holstering his pistol.

Not ten yards down the slope, a dozen men knelt in a shallow trench overlooking the beach, aiming their Lee-Enfield rifles with telescopic sights out to sea. Standing behind them was an American corporal, counting off in French. On each count, a man fired at a buoy outfitted with a large target. The corporal checked each shot with his binoculars, giving each man a *bien*, *mal*, or *terrible*.

They were so intent on shooting, and the corporal so focused on the target, that they didn't notice us. Which gave me time to study the area. The soft, sandy soil was freshly dug, evidenced by the shovels and picks scattered about. A small boat was beached on the shore below, probably used to bring the target out to the buoy. The Yank was a Negro, a bit surprising since Uncle Sam liked to keep the races apart in this man's army. But Villa Magnol wasn't exactly the regular army, and things were different here. In my experience, it was the enemy who usually tried to kill me, not my own people.

"Corporal!" I shouted, timing it between gunshots. He jumped, then turned to face us.

"Captain," he said, coming to attention and offering a salute. "So, you've come for me at last."

CHAPTER NINE

THE RIFLEMEN IN the trench turned in our direction, suspicious eyes narrowing as we faced the corporal who'd obviously been expecting somebody.

"Hold on, Corporal," I said as we drew closer. "We're not looking for you, unless you're the guy who took a potshot at us."

"We're shooting into the sea, Captain," he said. "Don't get many ricochets out that way. Sir."

"What's your name, soldier?"

"Corporal Elwood Drake, Captain." Drake's eyes moved between us, alert for a threat. Moments ago, he'd looked resigned, but now appeared confused. Why should he be any different than the rest of us? "Just to be clear, sir, you haven't come for me?"

"Let's talk about your guys with sniper rifles first," I said. "Then we'll get to you. Who are they?" Kaz and Dickie moved closer to each end of the trench, keeping an eye on the Frenchmen who'd been whispering among themselves. Their weapons weren't pointed out to sea anymore. Not at us either, but at the ready. Seemed like Drake wasn't the only guy who was suspicious of three officers showing up at his back.

"We are with the Maquis du Vercors," one of the men said, stepping out of the trench. "Some of the few who still live. I am Jean-Paul. *Caporal-chef* Drake is helping us prepare for our return to France." Jean-Paul was of average height, lean and muscular. He had wavy dark hair and good looks that were enhanced, rather than spoiled, by a scar along one cheekbone. He sported thin lips and an off-kilter nose that might have been broken once or twice.

"Captain Billy Boyle," I said, then introduced Kaz and Dickie. I knew better than to expect a full name. Most French Resistance fighters used a *nom de guerre* to protect their families, and the Germans still held a good chunk of real estate in their nation.

"Does anyone else speak English?" I asked. The men muttered among themselves, giving elegant Gallic shrugs. I'd have to ask Kaz later if he picked anything up.

"No, no, I translate for them," Jean-Paul said. "The *Caporal-chef* knows a little of our language, but if you have any questions, I will help." He said all that in a tone that told me he'd be no help at all.

"Corporal Drake, I assume you are the firearms instructor for this group?" Dickie asked, looking back at the ridge behind us, a short walk to a decent view of the villa.

"Yes sir." Drake looked to Jean-Paul and the others. "They've done well." The men grinned and nodded at Drake.

"Well enough to hit a target at five hundred yards?" I asked.

"Depends on how big the target is," Drake said with a straight face. Jean-Paul translated the exchange for the men, and it got a laugh.

"Let me put it this way," I said, feeling the bandage pull at my neck and tiring of the evasion, no matter how funny the line. "Could you hit a man at five hundred yards? And don't say it depends on the man."

"Yes, I could, Captain Boyle. Right here," Drake said, thumping his chest.

"I applaud your enthusiasm," Kaz said. "What about these men? I assume you are training them to do the same?"

"Sorry, sir, I am not at liberty to say," Corporal Drake proclaimed. "I'm sorry if a stray bullet went in your direction, but it wasn't from this group. They know which way the target is."

"Depends on the target, Corporal," I said. "May I use your binoculars?" It wasn't really a request, but I figured it best to act nice, given the suspicion of these Frenchmen, their seeming loyalty to Drake, and the firepower they packed.

Drake handed them over, and I focused on the buoy. Fixed to it was a large plywood sheet with what looked like a life-size outline of a man on it. The edges were peppered with plenty of holes, but there were a good number in the torso. Even a few in the head.

"You trained them well," I said, handing back the binoculars. "But why use the buoy? Isn't the firing range set up for five-hundred-yard shots?"

"The motion of the water forces you to account for movement," Drake said. "More realistic than a stationary target."

"Useful for hitting a man walking, for instance," Kaz said.

"*Certainment*," Jean-Paul said. "The Boche, they do not stand still for us."

"Corporal, were you with these men the entire time? I assume you walked here from the firing range?" Dickie asked.

"Yes, I took the motorboat to the buoy to set up the target. Jean-Paul brought the men here to dig the trench."

"You were in the boat alone while these men were here?" I asked, trying to understand the sequence, and who might have had a chance to sneak away.

"I left the firing range at the same time they did," Drake said. "Took me a while to pick up the boat at the dock and then to strap the target to the buoy. By the time I got here the trench was ready."

"Who's in charge?" I asked. "When you're not around, I mean."

Jean-Paul grumbled in French, and a young man cursed, eyeing me as he spat into the sand.

"That's enough, Danton. *Cesse.* Captain, what exactly are you accusing us of?" Drake said, keeping his eye on Danton, who looked ready to blow his top, if not someone else's.

"This," Kaz said, holding out his service cap, the line of the bullet clearly visible. "I prefer to keep my brains on the inside, don't you?"

"Where were you?" Drake asked, fingering the groove in the wool cap.

"On the rear terrace, about to enter the villa," I said.

"Jean-Paul, did everyone stay together?" Drake asked, a leaven of anger in his voice.

"*Oui, oui*," Jean-Paul said. "All of us, we dug the trench."

"You are quite sure?" Dickie said, a hand resting on his holstered pistol.

"*Oui!*" Jean-Paul said, his jaw clenched in anger. He rattled off a few lines in French that got his boys all riled up.

"We shoot Boche," Danton said. "*Américains,* no." The kid was twenty or so, tall and skinny, with dark curly hair and a face flushed with anger. A couple of guys shook their fists at us to show their indignation. We weren't making any friends here.

"Jean-Paul, take the men back to the firing range and have them clean their weapons," Drake said. "I'll be along in a while. Nothing to worry about, okay?"

"*Oui,*" Jean-Paul said, throwing a casual salute in our direction. The men gathered their tools and rifles and began to walk down to the beach. They all wore nondescript khakis without rank or insignia, and I was curious as to what they were all about. Drake, too, for that matter. But those questions could wait.

"Let's take a look, sir," Drake said, pointing to the ridge above.

"You don't believe your men?" I asked as we retraced our steps.

"They're not exactly my men," Drake said. "I'm training them. They listen to me, but I don't have any actual authority. Okay, stop." He held up a hand. "Sorry, stop, sir."

"Don't worry about it," I said. "What are we stopping for?"

"So we don't disturb the shooting position," Dickie chimed in.

"Exactly, sir," Drake said. "If one of them snuck up here to take a shot, they'd find a good spot. The ground slopes down, so they couldn't go prone, they'd have to sit or kneel. Let's spread out and go slow. Look for indentations in the ground."

"You don't believe Jean-Paul?" I asked as we moved apart and worked our way through the branches.

"I don't know why I shouldn't," Drake said. "But I'd be more comfortable if we didn't find anything. I respect these guys. They've all fought with the Resistance."

"Here," Kaz said, about ten feet off to my left. He knelt to study the ground and as we gathered around, I saw what drew his eye.

"Scuff marks in the sand," Kaz said. "Perhaps a heel dug in."

"Perhaps," Dickie said, not sounding convinced.

Drake sat, bracing himself with his heel on the slope, and looked to the villa. "That's a fair distance. Probably five hundred yards, same as the buoy. Where'd the shot hit?"

"See that door off the terrace, the one nearest the driveway?" Dickie said. It looked damn far away from here. Drake looked through the binoculars and whistled.

"You're lucky he shot high, Lieutenant," Drake said.

"We were bunched together," Kaz said. "Billy took a stone fragment in his neck, and it almost hit Dickie."

"Came close to Stewart too," Dickie said. I could tell he held back any comment about the shooter doing us all a favor.

"Commander Stewart?" Drake asked.

"Of the Royal Navy," Dickie answered. "You have much to do with him?"

"I'm about to," Drake said. "He's taking me with him on a mission to France. Glad he wasn't hit. With all due respect to you gentlemen."

"Looks like we're going to get to know each other, Corporal," I said. "We're headed to the Riviera with Stewart ourselves. But first, we need to figure out which of your Frenchmen wanted to kill one of us."

"I can't figure it, Captain," Drake said. "It sure as hell looks like it wasn't an accident. But why? And right before they're due to ship out."

"Could it have been a warning of some sort? Or a deliberate miss?" Kaz asked.

"No. I trained them too well for that to have been a deliberate miss," Drake said. "Any of those guys could've placed a round two or three feet over your heads. This was meant to be a kill shot."

CHAPTER TEN

"YOU WENT UP that hill yourself, all three of you!" Stewart snapped. "Any one of you could have left that sandy ground disturbed, right?"

"That wasn't the route we took, Commander," I said. We'd found Stewart on the terrace, waiting for a report. He hadn't liked it much.

"No shell casing? None of the Frenchmen saw anyone leave?"

"No casing was found, Commander," Dickie said, speaking calmly, or at least trying to. "But since it was only one shot, the shell might not have been ejected there. They could have easily waited until they were back in the firing slit, where it'd be mixed in with dozens of others."

"Are you seriously suggesting that it is likely an entire unit covered up an attempt to murder one of you? Preposterous," Stewart said. "Some idiot discharged his weapon in the wrong direction, that's all. And don't try to convince me with that cap again either. My god, if you were turned two inches in the other direction, it would point at the firing range. Obvious to a child, I would think."

"The shot could have been aimed at you, Commander," I said, hoping a sense of self-preservation might calm Stewart down.

"Listen to me, all three of you," Stewart said, his arms akimbo and his face flushed. "I need level heads about me on this mission. No galivanting off at the drop of a hat, understand?"

I saw Kaz trace the groove the bullet had made in his hat, and I gave him the slightest nod *no*. I'm all for making senior officers look the fool, but there was nothing to be gained here by commenting on his choice of words. Stewart was a pressure cooker about to burst, and I didn't want Kaz getting burned by the steam.

"Understood, Commander. We were mainly concerned with your safety. It won't happen again," I said, choosing my words to amuse Kaz.

"See that it doesn't," Stewart said, oblivious. "Captain Thorne, come with me."

"Perhaps he's having second thoughts about taking me along," Dickie whispered as we trailed after him. "One can only dream."

"Don't get your hopes up, Dickie," Kaz said. "It's far worse."

Stewart led us into a room where we found Colonel Laurent deep in conversation with several French officers and civilians. They hushed up as we entered, and there was that uncomfortable silence you feel when people stop talking about you but can't figure how to start a new conversation. A couple of British SOE officers entered with two Americans. One of them I knew well. Colonel Sam Harding, my boss.

"What's going on?" Dickie asked, practically tugging at Kaz's sleeve. Kaz told him to mind his manners and introduced him to Harding.

"Glad to see Captain Boyle got you out in one piece," Sam said, giving me a wink. "Good to see you too, Billy. Everything go well?"

"Easy enough, Colonel," I said. I had no idea what Sam's relationship with Stewart was, and it didn't make any sense to set off alarm bells about snipers until I did. Besides, we wouldn't be hanging around here much longer. Once I could get Harding away from all this brass, I'd fill him in. Kaz gave me a discreet nod. He understood.

"Colonel Edwin runs this place," Sam said, nodding in the direction of a balding fellow who was glad-handing with the French. "It takes a special talent to get the English and the Americans to work together. Throw in the French, and it requires a master touch."

Sam shook his head as if in relief that he hadn't drawn such duty. Ramrod straight, a veteran of the last war, and with gray flecks at his temples, Sam Harding was the kind of officer who'd rather face a dug-in enemy than a gathering of brass and bureaucrats.

"Colonel, if you have any influence here, perhaps you could get these two to tell me what's going on," Dickie said. "Everyone seems to know but me."

"Dickie and I studied at Oxford together," Kaz said, launching into a story about two girls in a boat. Before he could finish, Stewart cleared his throat and motioned Dickie forward. I spotted Laurent slipping out. Perhaps he'd been warned about the possibility of a speech. Smart guy.

"In light of our previous work together, I am pleased to be the one to announce the promotion of Captain Richard Thorne to the rank of major, effective immediately," Stewart said, his voice booming as if he were addressing an outdoor crowd. "Time to lose the pips, old boy, and don the crown."

Stewart went to work unfastening the three pips on each shoulder tab, designating the rank of captain, and replacing them with a single crown. Dickie looked dumbstruck.

"Well done," Kaz said, shaking Dickie's hand as the gathered brass politely applauded.

"You deserve it, my lad," Stewart said in his loudest and most condescending voice. "But for what, we're not allowed to say, eh?"

"Thank you, Commander," Dickie managed, although he was unable to hide his surprise. "Although I'm not sure what I've done to deserve it."

"Modesty becomes any officer," Stewart said, clapping Dickie on the shoulder. "One day your story will be known, I'm sure. Difficult decisions during difficult times, indeed."

"Excuse me, sir," a voice broke through from the door. It was Drake, his face swathed in sweat as he gasped for breath. "Colonel Edwin, it's the Maquis du Vercors. They're gone."

"Explain yourself, Corporal Drake," Edwin said, breaking away from the French civilians he'd been talking to. The colonel was short on hair and had the kind of scowl you'd expect from anyone riding herd on this bunch. "You took them to the range today, didn't you?"

"Yes, sir. Everything went smoothly at first, but there seems to have been an incident," Drake said, his eyes wide as he took in the brass in the room. When you're the only enlisted man around, and you're bringing bad news to senior officers, things have a way of going downhill fast. For the enlisted man, that is. Make it a Negro enlisted man and that slope just got a lot steeper. "I told them to return to the range, but when I came back from mooring the boat, they weren't there."

"We've only just given Commander Stewart an initial report," I said to Edwin. I didn't want to embarrass Stewart in front of everyone, as tempting as that was. He'd look to dump the blame on the likeliest subject, which for once wasn't me. "A slug hit the villa from the general direction of the firing range."

"These your two, Sam?" Edwin said to Harding. Harding admitted to it and introduced us.

"We were standing near the door, speaking with the commander," Kaz said, taking his cap and showing Edwin the bullet's mark. "The round missed us all only by inches."

"Someone gunning for you, Stewart?" Edwin asked, his voice betraying suspicion and incredulity battling for top billing. I got the fleeting impression he wasn't at all surprised to hear Stewart might have found himself in the crosshairs but couldn't come up with a reason why.

"Not at all, Colonel," Stewart said. "Most likely an unsupervised trainee. This French group was fairly undisciplined when they first came here, as you recall."

"Well, where the hell are they now, Commander?" Edwin barked, turning away from Stewart and addressing Dickie. "Major Thorne, time for you to earn your keep as a major. Begin a search. Take Corporal Drake and Sam's boys with you. Find them. No one takes potshots at my villa and then walks away. Go."

As we left, I saw Stewart move to a window, standing a couple of careful feet back. His cheeks burned bright red, and he quickly covered it up by rubbing his face. Was he hiding his embarrassment, worried about another Haifa haunting his career? Or was he angry, looking to spot a rogue Frenchman with a high-powered rifle?

"I'll drive, sir," Drake said as the four of us got to the jeep. "It's my job."

"Take us to their quarters," Dickie said, nodding his agreement. "I thought you were a firearms instructor?"

"It's a long story," Drake said, backing up and gunning the engine. "Right now, we need to get to the main gate. Then their quarters. Okay, Major? Hey, weren't you a captain a few minutes ago?"

"You missed an episode," I said from the back seat. This was beginning to feel like a Flash Gordon one-reeler, complete with sudden escapes from unknown villains. Kaz gave me a quizzical look, but the explanation got knocked out of me as Drake put the jeep through its paces, spitting gravel as it barreled over open ground toward the main road. Drake hadn't waited for approval from Dickie over the change in destination, and Dickie was too engrossed in not falling out of the jeep to say much about it.

"He's a better driver than you, Billy," Kaz shouted, grabbing for his cap and missing as it flew off his head. "Oh well, I need a new one anyway."

The main gate appeared ahead, shaded guard towers on each side. Drake hit the brakes at the last second and wrapped a flurry of dust around the guards.

"Sergeant," Drake yelled at the guard. "A truckload of Frenchies come through here just now?"

"Sure did," the noncom said, saluting smartly as he took in Dickie's brand-new crowns. "Ten minutes ago."

"They have a pass?" I asked.

"No sir. They wasn't on leave or anything. Training exercise, they said. Happens all the time around here."

"Open up, Sarge," Drake said. Dickie nodded, following his lead, and the guards swung the gates open.

"You have any idea where they're headed?" Dickie asked Drake, sounding hopeful.

"The docks, maybe. Or the airfield. DGER has any number of ways to get them back," Drake said, driving a bit slower now as we shared the road with lumbering trucks and donkeys pulling carts.

"Shouldn't we have Colonel Edwin contact the airfield?" I asked.

"Doesn't work that way, Captain," Drake said. "DGER does what it wants. They use us for training because it's convenient. But this is

France, remember, and the French are damn touchy about it. They need us, but once they get what they want, that's it."

"So the Maquis du Vercors could be boarding a Free French vessel or aircraft and there's no way to stop them?" Kaz asked.

"That's the way General de Gaulle likes it," Drake said.

"I haven't heard much about a Free French air force," I said. "Do they have aircraft?"

"Some. A few transport planes to help get their people around," Drake said. "They also put together a squadron of older aircraft from all their colonies. Not much to look at, but it's what they would have used to send in their paratroopers to the Vercors."

"What paratroopers?" I asked.

"The 1st French Parachute Regiment," Drake said. "They were slated to drop during the invasion, but de Gaulle pulled them out because he wanted them used farther inland in support of a Resistance uprising. He didn't have the airlift to do it alone, so he cobbled together a makeshift air force. Word was the regiment would be dropped into the Vercors, but they just ended up cooling their heels in Algiers. Still there, far as I know."

"Why? You'd think de Gaulle would jump at the chance. So to speak."

"Scuttlebutt was his senior officers were against it. Too risky to chance an elite unit in a lost cause, that sort of thing," Drake said, taking a corner at high speed. "One guy, Brigadier General Michel Robine, showed up for some meetings with Colonel Laurent. He seemed to be the one who put the kibosh on the plan. Laurent was all for it, but his side lost out."

"That's fascinating, but remind me why we are in hot pursuit of these fellows?" Dickie asked. Seemed like he was still trying to get the hang of this majoring thing. "They're not exactly escaped convicts."

"Two reasons, sir," Drake said. "First is we might catch up with them before they get too far. Second is I want my truck back."

"What's so important about the truck?" I asked. "The army has plenty of them."

"This is a very special truck. If it's gone, I'm gone," Drake said as he downshifted and took us around a corner at thirty miles an hour.

CHAPTER ELEVEN

"YES!" DRAKE SHOUTED, banging the steering wheel with one hand. Up ahead, a US Army truck was pulled over to the side of the road, its canvas flaps hanging loose. He pulled in behind it and jumped out of the jeep, pulling the rear flaps aside.

"Empty," Drake said.

"Hold on," I said, drawing my pistol and moving to the front of the truck. The back was empty, but that didn't mean the cab was. I heard someone scrambling around up front and dashed up to the driver's side door, pulling it open and thrusting my .45 automatic right into the face of an Arab kid, wide-eyed and all of maybe ten years old.

"Skedaddle," I said, stepping aside and motioning with my free hand. It didn't require any translation. He dove past me, hit the ground running, and vanished between two run-down buildings.

"Still warm," Drake said, laying his hand on the hood. "If we'd been here any later that kid's pals would have stripped her for parts."

"This is your truck, the one that's more important than finding our sniper?" Dickie asked.

"Major, we almost got them," Drake said, somewhat sensibly. "They were probably met by a couple of cars. Less noticeable that way. If we'd caught them making the switch, we could have grabbed them."

"Did they take their Lee-Enfields?" I asked.

"They weren't at the firing range, so I'd say yeah, they did."

"Perhaps it is best then," Kaz said, holstering his Webley. "We would have been outgunned. Given what you said about French jurisdiction,

I doubt we could have compelled a dozen armed men to turn around. Not with pistols, certainly."

"Good point, Lieutenant," Drake said. "But I'm sure the major will want to report that we came close to capturing them, without going into detail about how it wouldn't have been possible."

"You're wise in the ways of officers, Corporal," I said.

"Man in my position, Captain, he gotta be. Should we head back now, Major? Check out their quarters?" Drake climbed in the cab of his truck and started it up. "Sir?"

"Let's go," Dickie said. Corporal Drake turned the big truck around and we followed in the jeep. Seemed like we were in his wake a fair bit. We rolled back into camp and parked at the end of a row of Quonset huts. Drake led us to the third hut, which had a tricolor French flag flying from a small pole.

Inside the curved metal structure, it was warm and stuffy and smelled like a room where twelve men, reeking of sweat and dirty clothes, lived together. Newspapers and magazines lay scattered about, along with a few books. Haversacks were shoved under each cot, packed with clothing. Holstered pistols on leather belts were left on a table at the back, curled around bottles of cognac. A Sten gun was propped against one cot.

"They left in a rush," Dickie said. "Looks like they didn't even bother stopping here."

"On whose orders, I wonder?" I said, dumping the contents of a haversack and pawing through them.

"They could have gotten nervous, grabbed the truck, and headed out," Drake said. "Hey, what are we looking for, anyway?"

"Evidence. Clues. A clean shirt. Toss the place," I said. "If that sounds okay to you, Major."

"Oh, do shut up," Dickie said, emptying a bag. He grimaced as the aroma of old socks blossomed in the fetid air.

"Here," Kaz said, fingering what looked to be a much cleaner piece of cloth. "The flag of the Free Republic of Vercors." He shook it out, a tricolor flag of blue, white, and red. In the center panel was the cross of Lorraine, the Free French symbol, surmounted by the letter *V*.

"What free republic?" Dickie asked.

"It's where these fellows were from," Drake said. "The Vercors plateau, up near the Swiss border. You heard about it, right? They proclaimed a republic and tried to organize an army to hold off the Germans until we invaded the south of France, back in July."

"I've literally been living in a cave these past months, my good fellow," Dickie said. "Not to mention on a German-held island, so tell me more."

"You have heard of D-Day?" Kaz asked. "Normandy. Lots of Germans?"

"Yes, *Lieutenant*," Dickie said, rolling his eyes. "That was big news. SOE radioed us to spread the word among the guerilla fighters. Morale booster."

"The *maquis* forces were strong in the Vercors," Kaz said. "The Germans didn't have any troops stationed on the plateau. For the most part, the *maquis* were unarmed men evading the work details that would have sent them to Germany for slave labor."

"But then D-Day got them all riled up," Drake said, finding another piece of cloth with the same design, this one an armband. "They started hitting the Germans whenever they could. Arms started to be flown in, along with OSS and SOE teams. The *maquis* figured southern France would be invaded right away."

"There was confusion. General Eisenhower had asked for an uprising by the Resistance to impede German forces advancing to the Normandy invasion," Kaz said, kicking a pile of clothing under a cot. "General de Gaulle followed suit, but he called on FFI forces everywhere in France to fight."

"Then Maquis du Vercors jumped the gun," I said. "At the invitation of Charles de Gaulle."

"Yes," Kaz said, nodding. "They proclaimed the republic and raised the flag in the village square of Vassieux-en-Vercors. That was early July. By the end of the month the republic, and the village, were no more."

"They expected reinforcements and heavy weapons," Drake said. "They got neither and were slaughtered."

"Sad business," Dickie said. "The Nazis love their reprisals, don't they?"

There was no need to answer. I'd seen reprisals in France. I prayed that the killers would find their own terrible ends on the battlefield soon or be brought to justice when the war finally ended. Rough justice it may be, but nothing compared to what they inflicted upon the combatant and innocent alike. If only the Maquis du Vercors had waited. In August, the Allies hit the beaches of southern France in large numbers. By September, French troops had marched through the Vercors with little opposition.

"I remember when these guys came in from France," Drake said. "They didn't have much except the tattered clothes on their backs. But they had their flag and those armbands. That tricolor hanging out front, it's got the same design."

"Now they've got our sniper rifles and new clothes," Dickie said, throwing down a shirt in disgust. "Their pals in DGER will outfit them with whatever else they need. Do you know what their assignment was?"

"No. I doubt they'll all stay together, but I don't really know," Corporal Drake said. "They're intelligence agents, not a combat unit."

"Let's ask Colonel Laurent, then," I said. "If he doesn't know then maybe he could put us in touch with someone who does."

"I doubt it, Billy," Kaz said, running the flag between his fingers. "Have you noticed the material is silk? Parachute silk, if I am not mistaken. The blue and red sections are sewn on, see?" He displayed the careful stitching. It was the same on the flag and the armbands.

"White parachute silk?" Dickie said. "You don't use that stuff for arms drops. Stands out for miles. They must have had these done here."

"No," Kaz said. "The corporal told us they came with these things. They would not have had the opportunity."

"It could have come from a downed flier," I said. "I'm pretty sure they use white chutes."

"Maybe," Kaz said, nodding the way he does when he's being too polite to say I'm wrong. "But it tells us one thing. These men left in a great rush. Wherever the silk came from, these are important objects. The flag of their republic. The armbands that served to proclaim who they were."

"Someone wanted them far away, and fast," I said, remembering how Laurent had darted out of the speechifying. "Anything else in here?"

"Look at this," Dickie said, taking a pistol out of a haversack. "A Welrod."

"An assassin's pistol," Drake said, watching as Dickie checked the magazine and declared it unloaded before he gave it to him.

The Welrod was made for stealth and nothing else. It looked more like a foot-long lead pipe with a handle than an actual pistol. It wasn't just that it was silenced. It *was* a silencer, with the sound suppression built in. The SOE claimed that it was accurate up to thirty yards, but always followed that up with the suggestion that it be placed in direct contact with the target to be sure of a kill.

"This model takes .32 caliber ammo," Drake said, carefully examining the Welrod. "None of those pistols on the table do. They could have just asked me. I'd have given them plenty and tried it out on the range. Clean and oiled, it's well taken care of."

"It is not an unusual weapon for the *maquis* to have," Kaz said. "But it is odd that they did not mention it to you."

"None of this makes sense, and I find it hard to believe all of them are in cahoots to nail one of us," I said. "Corporal, take charge of that pistol. Then let's find Laurent and see if he clams up. That oughta tell us something."

"Let's take this silk," Dickie said. "I'll give an armband to Laurent as a gift and see how he reacts."

"Excellent idea, Major Thorne," Kaz said, folding the flag.

"Lieutenant, you may take this as a standing order," Dickie said. "Do shut up. Now let's go."

"Do you still need me, Major?" Drake asked.

"Oh yes, you stay with us Corporal. You have a story, and I want to hear it," Dickie said, heading out of the stuffy metal hut. "It may be the best part of this bloody day."

CHAPTER TWELVE

"YOU GUYS GO on and talk to Laurent," I said. "I'm going to check something out. Let's meet on the terrace, then we'll report to Colonel Edwin."

"Do you want me to go with you?" Kaz asked.

"No, I'm just going to check out a hunch. Give me the flag, I'll stash it back at our tent."

Kaz gave me the flag and a raised eyebrow. I shook my head, a quick message that I didn't want to talk openly. He picked up on it and went off with the corporal and Dickie, chatting away as if this had been a terribly amusing jaunt.

But I was betting he had the same suspicion I had. Was one or more of these Frenchmen flying a false flag? Could a double agent have infiltrated their group? If so, he—or they—would be able to do a lot of damage once they took to the field. A few weeks at a top secret SOE and OSS training camp would reveal a lot of high-level information.

I had a few secrets myself, mainly the orders that I'd been carrying. They were still wrapped in oilskin in my duffle, and they contained names and specific information about our mission. It wasn't win-the-war level stuff, but it could tip off a few suspected collaborators. If there was a bad apple or two among the *maquis*, maybe they'd decided to search our stuff.

I was suspicious, but I really couldn't see how any of us posed a danger to them, if there even was a double agent. I'd been halfway to buying the notion of an accidental discharge to explain the round that zinged Kaz's cap. But the Welrod bothered me.

Specifically, the empty magazine.

Why keep an empty weapon? Why keep it hidden and not ask for ammo to be issued?

I didn't like where those questions were leading me, and I hoped I was dead wrong. Make that just plain wrong.

I reached our tent and walked around it, dodging stakes and guy-lines, looking for any sign of entry. Anybody could be spotted going in the front, but on each side there was plenty of space to crouch down and sneak in under the flaps. The tents were set on wooden platforms, with the sides tied down tight. In hotter weather, they'd be rolled up. But today was chilly by north African standards, and the canvas was well secured.

Which made it easy to spot the two small holes on one side. I backed up into the walkway that ran between the rows of structures, gauging where the shooter would have stood. I looked around. Plenty of activity, but no one was paying much attention to me. I walked closer, raised my arm as if I had a weapon. Easy.

Inside the tent, I found the other holes. Most likely the exit holes since they lined up with a pair of holes through the neighboring tent. How did they miss us? The trajectory traversed the tent. If Kaz were sitting in the chair when they were fired, it would have been a near miss, high and to the side.

I checked the orders. Everything was still in place, exactly as I'd left it. I tossed the silk onto my cot and tried to think this one through.

What sense did it make to fire blind into a tent?

And who pulled the trigger? The Maquis du Vercors were with Corporal Drake, heading out from the firing range when we were in the tent. Or was this a parting shot? No, since they didn't come back to their tent. A warning, perhaps? But from who?

Who fired the last two rounds, then cleaned the weapon and placed it in the haversack? It didn't have to be one of Drake's *maquis* boys. It could have been anyone who knew where the Welrod was kept.

Next, I checked the tent beside ours. It was stacked with supplies. There were two neat holes at the rear corner, and it looked like the slugs were embedded in a wooden crate of K rations. There were too many damn boxes to move, but I didn't much care. At least the bullets hadn't hit anyone. The Welrod was a low-velocity weapon, and they wouldn't have gone far, but they could have done some damage at close range.

I stopped to look around. The area was filled with men on the move—carrying gear, stopping to light up a smoke, laughing and talking. The accents of America and the British Empire mingled in with French and even the faint strains of Italian. No one paid me any mind. If I had a silenced weapon under a coat thrown over my arm, no one would have noticed a thing.

Wait.

Shell casings. There would have been two, and stopping to pick them up might have attracted attention. I retraced my steps, looking for the giveaway glint of brass.

I found one. The other could have been kicked aside or covered by loose soil. It hardly did any good, but it was at least a connection to the shooter. Unfortunately, it was a .32 caliber casing, which didn't narrow things down much. Remingtons, Berettas, Walthers, and other guns made in Europe all used that caliber. Any of them could have found their way here, with SOE and the OSS often arming their agents with weapons found locally.

It was hopeless. I stuffed the shell into my pocket and headed for the villa. I found Kaz and Dickie on the terrace, seated on a low stone wall.

"Enjoying the weather?" I said. "Looks sunny with a chance of hot lead."

"There is little else we can do," Kaz said. "Do you like my new hat?"

"What's going on? I thought you guys were going to question Laurent?"

"He's vanished," Dickie said. "Took the time to pack his gear. Odds are he's on his way to France with the rest of them."

"Colonel Edwin was not pleased," Kaz said. "He issued an order that no one could leave or enter the base without his permission."

"So you decided to go to the quartermaster for a new hat? I could've thought of a few more useful things to do," I said.

"I merely said this was my new hat, Billy. They're hanging about inside, so I had my choice. I shall leave it to someone else with more time to visit the quartermaster."

"I should have had him arrested, of course," Dickie said. "But instead, we searched Laurent's office. You'll never guess what we found."

"More of these?" I asked, tossing him the shell casing.

"How did you know? And where did you get this?" Dickie said, surprise clear on his face.

"On the walkway outside our tent," I said, and told them about the two bullet holes.

"We found a full box of .32 caliber rounds in the back of a desk drawer," Kaz said. "There were various files and reports from DGER agents in France, all from before the invasion. He may have taken the recent files with him."

"Meaning the Maquis du Vercors," I said.

"The name does not appear anywhere in his files," Kaz said. "I looked for the two names we know of, Danton and Jean-Paul, but there is no mention of them."

"Edwin was hopping mad, let me tell you," Dickie said. "He took charge of the bullets, but I saved you a souvenir."

As he handed me the round, I compared it with my shell casing, then realized what I'd overlooked. The headstamp. Most bullets had a maker's mark on the bottom of the casing. I compared the two.

"Identical," I said, showing Kaz and Dickie. Stamped on the metal of each was RG 32 43.

"RG is probably one of the Royal Ordnance factories," Dickie said. "The numbers indicate .32 caliber, produced in 1943."

"While it doesn't prove anything, it does raise certain questions," Kaz said.

"Yeah, like why Laurent is trying to kill us," I said.

"No," Kaz said, fingering the casing as if it held some secret. "Rather, why he failed to do so."

I was about to ask Kaz to explain that one, but Drake pulled up in his jeep and joined us. He explained that Colonel Edwin had him lock down the armory and confirm what weapons were gone. Only the sniper rifles were missing. I filled him in on what I'd found at our tent and the matching bullets, then asked if he knew what Laurent carried for a sidearm.

"Sure. It's an automatic. A Webley & Scott," he said, stopping as his eyes went wide with realization. "That's a .32 caliber model. The SOE supplied them to the Resistance for a while. Equipped with silencers."

CHAPTER THIRTEEN

COLONEL HARDING CAME out of the villa waving a piece of paper and pointing at Drake.

"Corporal, take me into Algiers," he said. "Orders from Colonel Edwin."

"Where are you going, Colonel?" Dickie asked.

"DGER headquarters. They're at the Hôtel St. Georges, and I'm going to demand some answers about Laurent and this disappearing act," he said.

"I'm ready, sir," Corporal Drake said. "But you should hear about these bullets first."

Dickie launched into a summary of our tent being ventilated and the shell casing matching the rounds left in Laurent's desk.

"I've seen Colonel Laurent's sidearm, sir," Drake said. "It's a Webley & Scott, a .32 automatic. It takes a silencer."

"Are you saying Colonel Laurent of DGER shot up your tent?" Harding said, shoving his service cap back on his head as if it might help him think.

"Colonel, it is not impossible that the round that hit my cap was fired from a short distance away," Kaz said. "We assumed it was from the direction of the rifle range because of the firing going on there. But perhaps that was a coincidence."

"Or a convenient cover," I said, stepping over to where Kaz had been standing. There was a clear line to the firing range area and the ridge, but there were also trucks parked nearby, along with two jeeps and a staff car. "Any of these vehicles could have been used for cover. We can't be totally certain of the angle."

"I'll have to ask about Laurent's time in France," Harding said. "He could have gotten that pistol in an arms drop. I know SOE stopped sending them at least a year ago. The silencer was large and heavy, too big for a small automatic."

"It is a nice pistol," Drake said. "Small enough for an officer's sidearm. I can see why he kept it, silencer or not."

"Okay, if you haven't yet, search Laurent's room," Harding continued. "Top floor, end of the hall. And here's another surprise. Our departure has been moved up. We fly out tomorrow morning."

"Why?" I asked, wary of any last-minute changes.

"Colonel Edwin wants us out of here," Harding said. "Can't say I blame him. We'll probably be safer in France anyway. Stewart is holding a final briefing along with dinner for our group at 1800 hours. We'll be back before then."

"With me at the wheel, Colonel, no problem," Drake said as they got into the jeep.

"Shall we?" Kaz said, arching an eyebrow in the direction of the villa entrance.

"Listen, you two seem to know more about searching rooms," Dickie said. "Why don't I track down Stewart while you ransack Laurent's quarters? I want to see what he thinks of all this. He did seem worried, even with all that bluster and puffery."

"Good idea," I said. "Don't let on about the parachute silk or the bullets. No sense in letting word get around."

"Listen, Gordon Stewart is a bit of a twit, as well I know," Dickie said. "But are you saying you can't trust him in this matter?"

"No, Dickie," Kaz said. "It's just that the commander likes to talk, doesn't he? No reason to broadcast the little we do know, or suspect. Loses us the advantage, does it not?"

"All right, I see," Dickie said, half reluctantly. "I will fill him in on our pursuit of the truck. Not much more to say than that."

"We want to know if there's any information he's not sharing," I said.

"Like why suddenly we're old school chums?" Dickie said. "I'd like to know that myself. Good hunting, boys."

There wasn't a lot of hunting to be done in Laurent's room. He'd had a partial view of the Mediterranean, a soft bed, one armoire, and a small desk. A breeze brushed the curtains aside, and I wondered if Laurent was going to miss his cozy quarters. I would.

"Nothing under the bed," Kaz said, brushing the dust from his knees. He opened the armoire. "Nothing anywhere, it seems."

I checked the desk. The side drawers held a few paperclips, one broken pencil, and a well-used eraser. The center drawer was locked, which at least offered an intriguing possibility. I tried to force it open, but no dice. I could have picked it if I had a knife with me, but that was back at the tent.

"Kaz, does this desk look like an expensive antique?" I asked.

"No, certainly not," Kaz said. "Old enough to be relegated to a guest room, but not old enough to be valuable."

"Good." I turned it over, exposing the bottom of the drawer. It was a thin veneer, and it gave way under my boot with a single sharp kick. I pulled a couple of pieces off and felt around inside. I came up empty except for a small box of wooden matches.

"The Fleur de Sel. In Digne," Kaz said. "Appears to be a French restaurant."

"Flower something?" I asked.

"Flower of salt," Kaz said. "Refers to sea salt gathered from marsh basins after the water has evaporated. Very highly regarded as a finishing touch to garnish a dish. It is quite expensive. Perhaps we can visit. Digne-les-Bains is just north of Nice, our first destination."

I rattled the little box, decorated with bright images of wine bottles. It wasn't full. I opened it and out spilled seven matches.

"This one is broken," Kaz said, holding up one match snapped nearly in two. "Odd."

"Kaz, how many people are going on this mission?"

"Well, Colonel Laurent, if he ever reappears. Colonel Harding. You and I, along with Dickie and Corporal Drake. And Commander Stewart, of course."

"Seven people," I said. "Is that broken match a message of some sort?"

"A decidedly odd delivery mechanism if it is," Kaz said. "How could Laurent know we'd look in the drawer, if it was even Laurent who put it there? It could have been dropped in there a month ago. A year ago."

"Maybe," I said. It was a helluva coincidence, and I didn't like coincidences. Seven men, and one of them had already been targeted, either by a sniper's shot or a silenced pistol. It didn't make any sense at all, but it had to make sense to someone.

"There is something about this room that does disturb me," Kaz said. "The others obviously ran without stopping to gather their belongings. A sudden rout. But Colonel Laurent left with everything, leaving the room bare. No sense of rush here, is there?"

"What does that tell us?" I asked, feeling a good head scratch coming on.

"He was prepared. For what, I do not know. It will be quite interesting to see if he shows up tonight," Kaz said. "Also, if he had a silencer, packing and leaving was a clever way to smuggle it out. Meaning he may want to use it again." We had a lot of possibilities and questions, none of them helpful.

"If he pulls out a smoke, I'll offer to light it with one of these," I said, shaking the box. "That might get a rise out of him."

"You know, I haven't seen Laurent smoke at all. The room has no ashtray, no smell of stale cigarette smoke. Which tells us these matches have some meaning for him."

"I wish they meant something to me," I said. "Why lock them away? Why not leave them out on top of the desk?"

"I have no idea," Kaz said. "Perhaps we are clutching at straws. One of which is broken like a man's back."

I turned the desk upright and put it back where it had been. It felt like the most useful thing I'd done all day.

"NOTHING AT DGER," Harding said later that evening as we gathered for the briefing. "The Hôtel St. Georges was locked up tighter than a nunnery at night. The lobby was wide open, but all the stairs and elevators were guarded. All I got from the soldiers standing sentry was that their orders were to let no one in without written permission from the appropriate authority. Meaning the French government."

"You couldn't get anything else out of them?" I asked. We kept our voices low, the five of us gathered in the corner of a large conference room. Tables had been pushed together to make room for the assembly, already set for dinner.

"No, but Corporal Drake did," Harding said, nodding to him to explain.

"I stayed out front, waiting for the colonel," Drake said. "Got to chatting with the doorman. Turns out a dozen guys were brought in through the kitchen earlier today. Ten minutes later, there were guards everywhere."

"Did he say anything about Colonel Laurent?" Kaz asked, just as Stewart entered. Without a word, Stewart took his place at the head of the table and began shuffling a pile of papers.

"Just that a whole bunch of senior officers and guys in suits showed up right after that. Hotel staff was told to mind their own business. Lucky for me the doorman has a side business selling information for cigarettes and candy bars."

I told Harding we hadn't found anything in Laurent's room. The matches weren't enough of a clue to bother about. But I did keep them. Dickie had found Stewart, who appeared unruffled about the whole thing. But he had stationed a guard outside his office.

"Stewart told me to expect Laurent here tonight," Dickie said. "Said it wasn't unusual for the man to go into Algiers."

"With all his gear?" Harding asked.

"Commander Stewart suggested Laurent might stay in Algiers for the evening," Dickie said, eyebrows raised. "For amorous purposes."

"That'd be heavily armed purposes, judging by the firepower at that hotel," Drake said. I laughed but was cut short by Colonel Laurent strolling in and taking a seat next to Stewart. He looked at us and nodded a greeting as if this were oh, so normal.

"Gentlemen, do take your seats," Stewart announced, gesturing for Harding and Laurent to sit on either side of him. He stood, adjusted his jacket, and launched into his speech. I watched from across the table as Dickie's eyes rolled.

"As you may have heard, we depart tomorrow morning for Nice. Our assignment is to meet with Resistance groups and put together a list of known turncoats, those who have betrayed their comrades to the Germans," Stewart said, looking to Laurent.

"The French government desires to bring these collaborators to justice," Laurent said. "Not the rough justice of the moment, but a judicial justice, carried out by the state. This is of great importance, as I am sure you can imagine. We also wish to determine who has escaped with the Germans as they retreated, and to gather information on those Germans who perpetrated crimes of war against our people. There will be justice for those they slaughtered."

"All of this information is known to *maquis* groups throughout southern France," Stewart said. "Our job is to pull it together and identify the bastards so they can be hunted down. What we learn will be shared with various intelligence services, the US Seventh Army, and the French First Army, both currently operating in southern France and advancing to the German border. Of course, if the opportunity presents itself, we shall apprehend these collaborators ourselves and turn them over to the French authorities."

"We begin tomorrow evening in Nice," Laurent said, consulting a paper that Stewart handed him. "The Maquis Luc Robert is waiting to speak with us. Then we go on to Digne-les-Bains, Chambon-sur-Lignon, and several other villages as we get closer to the Vosges front."

"Colonel Harding will be at Seventh Army headquarters providing what support we need," Stewart said. "Corporal Drake will serve as driver for Colonel Laurent and myself. Major Thorne, you and Captain Boyle will act as security. We will likely come up against those who do not wish this mission to succeed. Some secrets are buried deep, and we aim to uncover them. Lieutenant Kazimierz, I may need you as an interpreter for when Colonel Laurent and I are not together. My French is passable, but only so."

"As we draw closer to the front lines, we will also seek men to serve with the American forces as guides. *Maquis* who know the land," Laurent said. "Scouts for the advancing troops."

"Is that what the Maquis du Vercors was training for, Colonel?" I asked.

"Not all," Laurent said. "Some, certainly."

"So, we won't be seeing them again?" I asked. "Too bad, because they left in such a hurry, they forgot their flag. Handmade from parachute silk, with their unit's symbol sewed on."

"Please bring it with you, Captain Boyle," Laurent said. "I am certain Jean-Paul would be happy to have it returned. If you ever see him again."

Now it was Colonel Harding who was rolling his eyes, in my direction, so I shut up. Stewart went on for another twenty minutes giving us five minutes' worth of information. Thankfully, he wrapped up as the food was brought in.

We dined on garlic soup and baked sea bass, with plenty of wine to wash it down. I watched Stewart as he chatted with Harding and Laurent. His table talk was directed at the higher ranks, which left us to chew on the food and everything that had just happened.

"Who thinks today was just a horrible misunderstanding?" I said to Drake, Kaz, and Dickie, keeping my voice low.

"That could be a possibility," Kaz said, watching Stewart. "The commander is certainly enjoying being the center of attention. He may turn a blind eye to this threat if it might halt the mission before it begins."

"It would be like him to sweep it under the rug," Dickie said. "And then trip over it."

CHAPTER FOURTEEN

LAURENT LEFT THE dinner early, announcing that he had matters to attend to and he'd see us at the airport tomorrow. Stewart stayed for a while making small talk, but soon took off, making it clear that he, too, had matters of high import waiting for his attention. Harding turned in his chair to face us, a sigh of relief escaping his lips.

"Sounds like a cakewalk, Colonel," I said as Harding drained his wineglass.

"Don't count on it," he said. "Our primary objective is to identify the worst of the collaborators who have managed to escape justice and alert all Allied forces and intelligence services to be on the lookout for them. Think about what a threat that poses."

"We already have a good idea, Colonel," Dickie said. "I'm wondering who can be trusted."

"Everything I've heard about Colonel Laurent is that he's all right," Harding said, lowering his voice. "He was an army officer when the Germans invaded and refused to give up when France surrendered. He made it here and joined de Gaulle, then returned to France to organize Resistance groups. He's been fighting this war longer than any of us."

"But still, let's keep our eye on him," I said.

"Agreed," Harding said. "I'll have some help on that front too. I just got word that Big Mike has been released from the hospital and will join me at Seventh Army HQ."

"Good news," Kaz said, at the same time Dickie asked who Big Mike was.

"Staff Sergeant Mike Miecznikowski," I said. "He hurt his leg jumping out of an airplane, and he's been in a Cairo hospital healing up. It was worse than they thought at first."

"Actually, it's First Sergeant," Harding said. "His promotion finally came through."

"Splendid," Kaz said. "It will be good to have him back, with even more stripes."

"He's from Detroit, just like you, Drake," Harding said. "He was on the police force."

"Perhaps you know each other?" Dickie asked.

"A Detroit cop with a name like that? He's definitely from the other side of the tracks," Drake said. "He may have chased me a time or two though."

"That reminds me," Kaz said. "I want to hear about how you ended up with the OSS. Tell us a story, Drake." Dickie encouraged him by filling his wineglass.

"It's a good yarn," Harding said. "The corporal filled me in on our drive to Algiers." With that, Harding left, and we all topped off our glasses.

"It's no big deal, sirs," Drake said, leaning back in his seat, suddenly modest.

"Hey, it's just a bunch of guys having a few drinks," I said. "Cut the *sirs* and spill."

"Do tell, Drake," Dickie said with a grin. "Your major orders it."

"Okay, okay," Drake said, one hand raised in mock surrender. "It was back in early forty-three. I was with a quartermaster truck company out near the harbor, doing repair work and ferrying supplies to the front. There were a few Colored quartermaster companies in Algiers, but mine drew the job of supplying this base. One day, an officer strolls into our shop. Captain Jerry Sage of the OSS. Says he needs to requisition one of our trucks. My commanding officer didn't like to loan out trucks since they never seemed to come back. So he told Captain Sage, sure you can have a truck, but it's gonna come with a driver so he can return it when you're done."

"Your CO is pretty smart," I said. He'd be the one to answer for any missing vehicles.

"Yeah, but so was Jerry Sage," Drake said. "At first, he tried to argue. Top secret OSS stuff and all that. But it didn't work. Finally, Sage gives in and signs the requisition which says he will return the truck, with driver, when it is no longer needed. He's not happy having me around with not much to do except take care of the truck, and truth be told, neither was I. So I asked if I could join in their training. Judo and all sorts of knife-fighting stuff. Blowing things up. Target practice with every weapon in this man's army and the Wehrmacht's to boot."

"That's how you ended up training the *maquis*?" Kaz asked.

"Yep. Captain Sage saw how I took to it and said he'd try to get me permanently assigned to the OSS, him not being too concerned with crossing the color line. Meanwhile, he put me to work training agents. Every time my CO would call and ask about me, the captain would say he still needed the truck."

"Where's Sage now?" Dickie asked, draining his glass.

"In a German POW camp," Drake said. "When the Germans rolled through Kasserine Pass and chewed our boys up, the brass rushed everyone to the front to plug the hole in the line. That meant Captain Sage and his OSS team. I asked to go along, but he wouldn't take me, not while I was still officially with the quartermaster truck company."

"That's a waste of trained OSS men," I said. "They're not meant to be line infantry."

"That's what Captain Sage thought too," Drake said. "But he knew they had to go. He was even excited about it. But they got overrun. Some dead, the rest wounded or captured. Heard from the Red Cross that he was in a POW camp in Germany a month or so later."

"But you were able to stay here?" Kaz asked.

"Seems like I proved my worth. Colonel Edwin didn't mind having another instructor on hand, so now when my CO calls, he tells him Captain Sage still requires the truck," Drake said, slapping the table as he laughed.

"Which is why you were so gung ho about getting it back," I said.

"Damn straight, sir. This mission may not be behind enemy lines, but it's important. Commander Stewart is giving me a chance to do my part. That's all I want. That's all a lot of other Colored guys want. A chance to fight."

"I know," I said. "There might not be a lot of fighting, but there are dangers. I'm glad you're along for the ride." I raised my glass, and we drank. I thought of my childhood pal, Too-Tall Tree, a Negro who'd made it into a tank destroyer battalion back in England. We'd reconnected shortly before D-Day when Tree needed help getting one of his pals out of a serious jam. The 617th Tank Destroyer Battalion was one of the few Colored outfits ready to see combat, but instead, they'd ended up stripped of their armored vehicles and sent to work in quartermaster companies. Lots of heavy lifting and no chance to prove their mettle in combat.

Funny how there are plenty of guys who'd be happy to stay out of the fight, working behind the lines in supply units or driving trucks. But tell men like the Negro soldiers I knew that they weren't good enough to fight, and they'd do anything to get up front on the sharp end of this shooting war.

"A bit of advice, Corporal," Kaz said, setting down his drink. "I have my own reasons for fighting this war. The Nazis have destroyed my nation and murdered those I love, so I often feel a certain zeal when it comes to this enemy. You have your own reasons for fighting and your own righteous zeal. But do not let it control you. Keep a level head. A dead man proves nothing."

"Good advice for us all," Dickie said. "Someone may try to take a run at us again."

"What I can't figure is how firing on us helps," I said. "If this mission puts a French collaborator in the crosshairs, wouldn't it make more sense for them to disappear? They can't kill all of us."

"Need I remind you we are all flying on the same aircraft in the morning?" Kaz said, holding out his glass for Dickie.

"It's hard to believe," Drake said.

"That someone's out to get us?" I asked, not wanting to think about our aircraft going down over the Mediterranean.

"No. That someone who's kept their head down this long would risk showing themselves in an attempt to stop us," Drake said. "I mean, I understand about collecting the dope on these guys and putting out an alert. But I'm thinking what I'd do if I were some Pierre who'd betrayed his own people."

"What then?" Dickie asked.

"Cash out," Drake said. "Take whatever I could and scram. And I'd do it quietly. Head to Spain or Switzerland. Get new identity papers. Not make a big show of shooting and missing. All that did was rile up a nest of hornets."

"There's something to that," I said, swallowing the last of my wine. I had the nagging feeling that we were looking at this all wrong, and I tried to separate out what we knew from everything we'd simply assumed or feared.

There wasn't much left over after that. I tried to think it through again, but everyone was so busy drinking and yakking it up that I couldn't hear myself think. Not that the sound of too few clues rolling around in my head was all that deafening.

CHAPTER FIFTEEN

I TRIED NOT to think about Kaz's comment from the previous night as we boarded our C-47 aircraft at the dusty airfield outside of Algiers. We were all flying together, and if there was a conspiracy to sabotage our mission, this would be the place to catch us at our most vulnerable. We didn't have to worry about the Luftwaffe this far from the front, but even a small bomb would be deadly twenty thousand feet over the Mediterranean.

I couldn't help noticing the gear being stowed aboard as we took our seats. I wondered if the stuff had been searched, and at the same time, cursed myself for getting carried away with the whole idea. The best thing would be to forget about it, I told myself. Get on with the mission and stop seeing threats everywhere.

I'd almost talked myself into it when Laurent took a seat directly across from me. He carried a bulging leather briefcase that gave off a loud *clunk* as he set it between his legs. At that moment, the hatch was slammed shut and the C-47's engines started up, making conversation impossible and sending my mind spinning nearly out of control. Was he carrying a bomb? More likely a few bottles of cognac.

I distracted myself by scanning the other passengers. In addition to our group there were six others. Two French civilians, government officials of some sort, along with two French officers, and two Yanks. It was the usual assemblage of ranking officers and dignitaries who rated access to Uncle Sam's air service. No one looked ready to take a potshot at any of us, so I leaned back and closed my eyes.

After a few hours on a hard metal seat in a steel fuselage vibrating to the tune of two thunderous Pratt & Whitney radial engines, I was almost ready for the distraction of a Kraut fighter on our tail. Thankfully, we began our descent as the coastline of southern France drew near, sunlight shimmering on the water below. I almost relaxed. The easy duty that I'd envisioned at first seemed possible once again. We were far from Algiers and the enclosed environment of the training camp, so why not? Once Big Mike caught up with us, we'd have another set of eyes to watch our six.

The airfield ran right along the coastline. We landed on the dirt runway and passed the ruins of several buildings that the Germans must have blown up when they left town in a hurry back in August. We halted at an intact hangar, and fresh, cool air filled the aircraft as the hatch was opened.

"Welcome to the Riviera," Dickie said as we made our way onto solid ground and stretched our cramped limbs.

"This isn't a vacation, Major," Stewart said. "You'll do well to remember that."

Dickie did another eye roll as Stewart swaggered off to where a staff car and two jeeps stood waiting. Harding noticed and did his diplomatic best to suppress a smile as we waited for our gear to be unloaded. Me, I was traveling light. I grabbed my haversack and my Thompson from a crewman. Drake gathered up his bag and Stewart's heavy duffle, muttering something about golf clubs, which drew a laugh.

As we got to the vehicles, Laurent stopped to open his briefcase, withdrawing two large stones. He saw the expression on my face and explained as he tossed them aside.

"There are confidential documents in this briefcase, Captain. If for any reason our aircraft went down over water, I wanted to be sure it would sink to the bottom. An over-abundance of caution, perhaps, but after years of intelligence work, one tends to see the world in terms of threats, you understand?"

"Sure, Colonel," I said, glad that I wasn't the only one concerned about a watery grave. "Better safe than sorry."

"*Exactement*," Laurent said, closing his briefcase and making for the staff car with Stewart.

"The drivers will take us to the hotel," Harding said. "Then these vehicles are ours. Let's go." Harding and Dickie went in one jeep, while Kaz, Drake, and I piled into the other and followed. Our driver wore an American uniform of familiar khaki, but with a beret and the tricolor shoulder patch of France. He didn't speak English, so Kaz asked where we were headed.

"The Excelsior, a small but elegant hotel, he says. Near the train station, which causes me to wonder at his understanding of elegance. Still, it sounds serviceable," Kaz said.

"I'm guessing it's not one of the fancy hotels on the waterfront?" I asked.

"No, he tells me those are all taken by his government and the American army. Those that the Germans did not ruin, that is. Mines are still being cleared from the beach. Fittingly, he says, by German POWs."

"Fancy or not, this is going to be a new experience for me," Drake said from the passenger seat.

"You've never stayed in a hotel?" I asked.

"Oh, I have, Captain," Drake said with a smile. "Just never with white people. Say, I noticed you eyeing that briefcase on the plane."

"Yeah," I said, as Drake glanced at the silent driver, who may well have understood English. "Pretty smart."

"Well, maybe so, Captain. But given that Italy's on our side now, and that there's damn few Jerries left anywhere in the Mediterranean, just who would've picked up a floating briefcase anyway? Makes ya think, don't it?" Drake said.

It did.

"Interesting notion," Kaz said, as we zipped through narrow cobblestone streets, the old buildings painted in subdued pastels, marred only by the occasional spray of bullet holes from fighting during the liberation.

Drake had a good point. What was in Laurent's briefcase, and why was he worried about it washing ashore in Allied-controlled territory? What secrets did it hold?

The Excelsior was a five-story joint with an ornate exterior that had seen better days. It was close enough to the railway station that I could hear train whistles echoing down the street. We left the vehicles in the courtyard and carried our gear into the lobby. This time Drake went ahead, leaving Stewart to lug his own stuff.

"We shall convene in the main conference room in one hour," Stewart said after we'd been handed our keys. He pointed across the lobby to where double doors opened into a darkened room. "Colonel Laurent and I will review the matters to be discussed with the Maquis Luc Robert before their arrival. Questions?"

"The only question I have is how well-stocked the bar is," Dickie said, in a low voice. "As far as I'm concerned, this *is* a vacation, no matter what Stewart says."

There were no questions, so we hoofed it up the staircase, the elevator being out of order. The hotel looked like it had once been grand but had descended into shabbiness, with grubbiness not far behind. Laurent, Stewart, and Harding were on the second floor, the rest of us one floor up.

"We'll find some booze and food once we're finished with the *maquis*," I said to Dickie as we made for our rooms, all in a row overlooking the street.

"I hate the thought of leaving Colonel Harding with Laurent and Stewart," Kaz said as he unlocked the door to his room.

"The price of high rank," Dickie said. "See you in an hour."

I FRESHENED UP, knotted my field scarf exactly right, and headed down to the lobby ahead of schedule. I'd spotted a display of postcards at check-in and figured it would be a good time to jot down a quick note to my folks. A card from a fancy hotel in Nice, far from the front lines, would put my mom's mind at ease. I wrote out a few lines, addressed it, and gave it to the concierge to post, along with a few francs for the stamps and his trouble.

I checked my watch and there was still time to kill. I wandered into the spacious lobby and found Colonel Laurent deep in muted conversation with Danton, one of the Maquis du Vercors.

"Ah, Captain Boyle," Laurent said, catching my eye. "Look who I found in our hotel. You have met Danton, he tells me."

"Yes, we have met," I said. He'd been in uniform then, but today it was civilian clothes. "You were holding a recently fired Lee-Enfield. Right, Danton?"

"Yes. Shooting at the empty sea," Danton answered, giving me a polite nod of recognition. "Soon it will be at the Boche."

"You left the camp rather suddenly," I said. "And Colonel Laurent offered no explanation."

"I go where my orders take me," Danton said. "And I go when they tell me to go. Not Colonel Laurent."

"I see, Captain Boyle, you think I have authority over Danton and his *maquis* group?" Laurent said. "No. I am with the intelligence branch of DGER. It is Operations that gives Danton his orders. A different department, you understand. Security."

"Okay," I said. I did know how compartmentalized these secret agencies were, which made sense. "What brings you here, Danton? On assignment?"

"Sadly, I cannot say."

"You left very quickly," I said, trying another approach to shake any information out of him. He may have been not much more than a kid, but he was firm in all his answers. "Why?"

"An airplane was available," he answered. "We had to make haste."

"Captain, first, please do sit and join us," Laurent said. I took a chair next to him so I could study Danton's expression. "Second, let me explain that although your army has provided us with many supplies and weapons, we are often in the position of requesting aid, which includes air transport. Some activities we would rather engage in ourselves. Sensitive matters, you see?"

"I think so. You're saying one of your own French aircraft became available, but it couldn't wait. So Danton and the others had to hustle out of camp."

"Hustle? Yes, they needed to make haste," Laurent said. "Nothing more than that."

"I understand your air force is pretty thin," I said. "Not enough aircraft to go around. Is that why those French paratroopers were never dropped onto the Vercors Plateau?"

"It is true our air force has not been fully rebuilt," Laurent said, avoiding the question.

"It could have been done," Danton said. "If General Robine had not been such a coward."

"We have argued this point often, Captain Boyle," Laurent said. "As you can see. There were many dangers, and it is sad we will never know if it could have succeeded. The *maquis* on the plateau were constructing a landing strip, but the Germans came in gliders first."

"And slaughtered the villagers of Vassieux," Danton said, looking away as if the vision of that massacre was passing before his eyes.

"All right. Now tell me what you're doing here," I said. "In this hotel at this time of day."

"So suspicious," Danton said. "You should work with Colonel Laurent. He also questions everything."

"We are working together," I said. "What are you doing here?"

"It is of little importance. I was first with the Maquis Luc Robert, the group led by Cathedral. Then I went north, to the Vercors, when they announced the republic. Many of us flocked to them, thinking it was the beginning of our liberation," Danton said, his face hardening. "But it was not. We were betrayed by those we thought would help us. You. The British and their SOE."

"How?" I asked.

"It does not matter now," Laurent said. "Look, here comes Cathedral."

"*Excusez-moi, s'il vous plaît*," Danton said, rising from his seat and making for a tall, thickset man in a gray suit.

"Cathedral?" I asked.

"Some people keep their code names," Laurent said. "They have become part of who they are. Many of us created ourselves anew in this war and would not recognize, or perhaps even like, our previous selves. Others, young men like Danton, came of age during the war and know little else."

"Danton doesn't seem happy about his allies," I said, watching as he and Cathedral shook hands and headed into the bar.

"The Vercors was a bad business," Laurent said, a faint, wistful sigh escaping his lips. "Ah, here is Commander Stewart. Shall we?"

"We are waiting, gentlemen," Stewart grumbled as Laurent led the way. I had the feeling the colonel was glad to leave the subject of what happened in the Vercors behind. Which meant I needed to know more about it.

We followed Stewart into the conference room, which held a large table and several rows of chairs. Kaz and Harding were already seated, with Drake hustling into the room ahead of me. Only Dickie was missing. A map of the coastline, still marked with German notations, covered most of one wall. Ours was obviously not the first military meeting in this chamber. Two chandeliers lit the room, one with flickering bulbs that provided more irritation than illumination.

"Major Thorne is five minutes late," Stewart said, glancing at his watch. "Corporal, would you kindly rouse the major?" Drake nodded and left the room in a shot.

"While we wait, Commander, could you review what we're discussing here?" Harding asked. I detected an edge of disapproval in his voice, sensing that Stewart hadn't shared much, if anything, with him.

"A chap code-named Cathedral is the head of the Maquis Luc Robert," Stewart said. "He has provided a list of names. Several have been revealed as informers, and others may be pro-Vichy fascists who adopted new identities."

"We can have those names cross-checked at DGER," Laurent said, which kicked off a discussion of how best to investigate these people. It was beginning to sound like a bureaucratic wrangle, until it was interrupted by the sound of heavy footsteps coming down the stairs outside the room.

"It's Major Thorne," Drake said, standing in the doorway. "He's dead."

CHAPTER SIXTEEN

"WHAT?" COMMANDER STEWART said, looking at Drake's stricken face. "Are you certain?"

"Let's go," I said, getting out of my seat and locking eyes with Drake, who looked like he was about to go into shock. I grabbed him by the arm and steered him toward the staircase, leaving Stewart's shouts and questions behind. I was aware of Kaz right behind us, but all I could do was try and focus my thoughts. "Tell me what happened."

"I just found him. Dead."

"Start from leaving the conference room," I said as we passed the first floor. "Did you see anyone on the stairs?"

"Yeah, one guy coming down," Drake said. "Civilian. I didn't pay him any mind, really, I was taking the stairs two at a time. I didn't want the major to get in hot water, you know?"

"I know," I said, stopping at the next landing. "Take a deep breath and think hard. Who else did you see?" Kaz was next to me now, and I could sense his impatience. Dickie was a pal, but I needed to hear from Drake before things got too confused.

"Nobody else. Just the guy in the suit. Looked to be a Frenchman, don't ask me why, it's just a sense I got," Drake said, closing his eyes. "Dark blue suit. Burgundy tie with some sort of design. Black hair. That's it. I didn't look at his face, I was too much in a hurry. No, wait, there was something. A scar over one eye. Part of his eyebrow was gone, it stood out."

"All right, that's good, Drake. Come on," I said as we headed up the last steps. "Kaz, you want to wait outside?" I was worried about

Kaz seeing his friend dead. Hell, I didn't like the notion myself. Dickie was—had been—a great guy. I didn't much want to see his corpse either.

"No. We must do this, Billy," Kaz said, his jaw clenched.

We were almost to Dickie's room when it hit me.

"Wait," I said, holding back Drake who was reaching for the door. "How'd you get in?"

"I opened the door," he said. "Knocked first. When I got no answer, I tried the latch. It opened right up."

"Odd," Kaz said from behind me. "Why would Dickie leave his door unlocked?"

"Maybe he was surprised as he was leaving," I said. "Pushed back into the room."

"Time to find out," Kaz said, opening the door.

Directly ahead of us, Dickie lay facedown on the floor, a blossom of blood on his back. One arm was jammed awkwardly against the bed frame, the other limp at his side. The room was a mirror image of mine, with the bathroom off to my right. The curtains were still pulled shut. Dickie's bag sat on the bed, and he was still wearing the clothes he'd traveled in. The room key had been tossed onto a small table by the door.

"Drake, stand outside," I said. "Don't let anyone in without my okay, got it?"

"Will do, Captain," he said.

"Wait," Kaz said as I held the door open. "Did you come all the way in, then open the door on your way out?"

"No, Lieutenant," Drake said. "I took one step in and knew he was dead. No need to go any farther. That's a killing stab wound right there. A thrust under the shoulder blade. Tricky, you got to slip past the ribs. But if you get that right and give the blade a little twist, it's lights out. Never done it myself, but I've taught it to a lot of guys."

Drake went out just as Harding, Stewart, and Laurent arrived.

"Is it true?" Stewart asked, his hand going to his mouth as he saw Dickie's body over my shoulder.

"It's true, Commander," I said. "Right now, I can't have anyone else in here. We must conduct a search. Colonel Laurent, can you contact the police? We need someone to check for fingerprints." Kaz was already at work, checking the bag and patting down Dickie's pockets. It can't have been easy for him.

"I will," Laurent said. "But then this will become a local matter. Or should you conduct the investigation? What do you think, Commander?"

"I'm not sure," Stewart said, for once at a loss for words. "Is this some random attack? A robbery? Perhaps the local police will know."

"Nothing's missing," Kaz said. "His bag is unopened, and he has a quantity of francs in his pocket. This was not a robbery. But look at what I found on the floor beside him." Kaz held up a piece of white silk. Parachute silk, which had been used to wipe the blade clean of blood.

"We need fingerprint people, and we need to lock the doors to this hotel. Now," I said. "If we want to have a chance at finding who did this."

"I'll call the MPs and get this place cordoned off," Harding said.

"I will contact the *Police Municipale* and request technical assistance," Laurent said. "We can discuss jurisdiction later."

"Yes, yes," Stewart said. "I must talk with Cathedral and fill him in. You may find me in the meeting room." He craned his neck to look back into the room, his face going pale as he spotted the telltale red. He turned around, one hand to his eyes as if to rub the image away, then started to walk down the hall.

"Are you okay?" I asked Kaz as soon as Stewart cleared off.

"I am capable," Kaz said, standing over Dickie's body, his eyes darting about the room. "To die here, after all he endured, it is beyond sad. Mournful, in the truest sense."

"We've got reinforcements coming," I said. "You could take a break."

"No," Kaz said, flicking his hand as if he were chasing off a bothersome fly. "No. I will stay. For Dickie. Now, see here. He walked in, dropped his bag on the bed, then made for the curtains."

"That's exactly what I did."

"Yes. He makes it two steps past the corner of the bed and is stabbed. Quite expertly, according to Corporal Drake," Kaz said, his gaze turned to the armoire along the wall.

"It looks like he was stabbed by someone who came in with him," I said.

"Or someone who was already here," Kaz said, snapping open the armoire and stepping back. It was empty. "And we know no one went in with him, because we all entered our rooms at the same time."

I knelt to check Dickie's pockets again. I knew Kaz had done it, but it was best to recheck. No matter what he said, this was a friend, and I couldn't have blamed Kaz for missing something. Except he hadn't. There was nothing but the crumpled franc notes they'd given us in Algiers.

"Do you think the parachute silk was a message?" I asked.

"It may be, since it's the same as the Maquis du Vercors used for their armbands."

"Was your room dark when you went in?" I asked.

"Yes. No light on and the drapes closed. It would have been difficult to see everything clearly."

"Right. Except for someone who'd been waiting in the dimness, their eyes accustomed to the minimal light."

"The bathroom," Kaz said. We walked around the bed to the bathroom. The door was wide open. The floor was white tile, chipped and cracked in places, but clean. Except for two scuff marks. Right where a guy would place his feet if he'd sat on the edge of the bathtub, waiting. Then he hears the key in the door and shoves off, a sudden rush of adrenalin and anticipation propelling him into the next room. Kaz studied the scuff marks and nodded.

"Dickie never had a chance," I said. "The killer lay in wait for him, his eyes acclimated to the gloom. If Dickie bothered to glance into the bathroom, he wouldn't have seen him."

"And if he had come in here first, the killer still would have had the element of surprise," Kaz said. "A fair bit of planning went into this murder. But why? Why Dickie?"

"There's another question we have to answer first," I said. "How did the killer know in which room to wait?"

CHAPTER SEVENTEEN

I STARED AT the lifeless form of Major Richard Thorne, trying to figure out what forces had contrived to bring Dickie here, to this room, where a killer took his life. Nothing made sense. Not the gunshots in Algiers, not the knifing in Nice.

Outside in the hallway, I could hear Kaz and Colonel Harding arguing with a French police officer about who had the responsibility to run this investigation. Harding got hot under the collar a few times, but his basic French gave out before he went too far. Kaz picked up the argument with his soothing tones of elegant French, which seemed to mollify the detective.

Inside the room, I watched the fingerprint guy dust the usual surfaces while I leaned against the wall, staying out of his way. I didn't know if the French believed possession was nine-tenths of the law, but I knew if I left the room, I'd never be let back in. So, for now, it was the fingerprint guy and me. I watched as he swung the door mostly shut and dusted the handle and doorframe, then used a transparent tape to lift whatever prints he'd discovered off the surface.

"*Le travail est terminé,*" he announced, rapping on the door to get the attention of his boss on the other side, where the conversation sounded more subdued. The door opened, revealing two uniformed cops with a stretcher.

"They are going to take Dickie to the morgue," Kaz told me. "They will do his fingerprints there and match them to those found in the room."

"Captain Boyle, this is Inspector Charles Vigot of the *Sûreté,*"

Harding said, as the two uniforms entered the room with the stretcher, and I stepped into the hallway. "It appears he will be heading the investigation."

"Colonel, you realize there are serious security issues," I said, not even wanting to mention the letters SOE and OSS.

"Please, Captain, everyone in Nice knows of the secret meeting being held in this hotel today," Inspector Vigot said in very precise English.

"Wait, I got the impression you didn't speak English," I said, looking to Kaz, who'd been translating. He was distracted by the sight of Dickie being strapped onto the stretcher.

"I have apologized to your comrades already," Vigot said. "When faced with both the American and English military, I wished to have the slight advantage of pretending not to know the words that passed between them. Which you can understand, I trust. Of course, my superiors at the *Sûreté* chose an inspector with the proper command of the language. Otherwise, how could I investigate the murder of an Englishman among his own people?"

"Sure. It gave you an edge. I guess it worked out if you're in charge now," I said. "Although I can't see how it's a civilian matter."

We all stood aside in silence as Dickie was carried out of the room, a sheet, thankfully, covering him.

"First, let me convey my sympathies on the loss of your friend, as I already have done with Lieutenant Kazimierz," Vigot said. "Then I must have a word with my colleague, who works miracles with the fingerprints."

Vigot went into the room and shut the door behind him.

"Where's Drake?" I said, looking to Kaz and Harding.

"He's in an office near the lobby," Harding said. "Awaiting his interview with the inspector. He wants to talk with the both of you too."

"Don't tell me," I said. "We're all suspects so that's why he gets to run the investigation."

"Exactly," Harding said. "It is a persuasive argument from his point of view. Remember, the French are in the process of reestablishing control over their territory. Sovereignty and jurisdiction are touchy subjects. He could make a lot of trouble for us if he wanted."

"Even though the local rumor mill seems to know of our mission here, we don't want it spread any further," Kaz said.

"There's some logic to letting him work here while we hit the road," I said, thinking it through. "We may still run into trouble ahead. The killer, or killers, might not be done with us."

"Okay, then we won't raise a fuss," Harding said. "I'm going to find Stewart and see what's going on with Cathedral and his men."

"Does Inspector Vigot know about them?" I asked as Harding walked away.

"He says everyone does," Harding answered. "But few are glad of it."

"What's your impression of Vigot?" I whispered to Kaz as we waited in the hallway like a couple of errant schoolkids.

"Clever," he said. "Pleased with himself."

"Ah, my friends," Vigot said, opening the door and holding it as his colleague donned his hat and gave us a curt nod. "I can tell you that there are only two sets of fingerprints in this room. One, judging by where they were found, is from whoever cleaned this room last. The other set, found only on the key and the small table by the door, is most likely from Major Thorne. We will know once we get him to the morgue."

"Anything else?" I asked.

"Yes. We are certain the door was opened from the inside by a person wearing gloves. Lambskin gloves, most likely."

"How can you know that?" Kaz asked.

"We are skilled not only in the fingerprint from the skin of the finger, but the glove print as well. In France, it is illegal to wear a glove in the commission of a crime. To do so earns the criminal an additional charge. So we have made a study of the types of impressions left by certain gloves. Lambskin is quite identifiable."

"Lambskin would be worn by any fashionable person, yes?" Kaz asked.

"Or a well-off man of the country," Vigot said. "It is not much help, I know."

"You saw the silk? Parachute silk?" Kaz said.

"Indeed. It may have a bearing, but you must appreciate there have been many parachutes descending around us. Supplies to the Resistance, your excellent parachute troops in the thousands. The silk does not go unused. It may have been the killer's handkerchief."

"How did the killer get in the room?" I asked, seeing that he wasn't impressed with the silken clue. "Have you checked to see if any keys from the front desk are missing?"

"All in good time, Captain," Vigot said. "Now, please come downstairs so I may take the facts of the case from each of you. This is important, you see, since your four rooms were the only ones occupied on this floor."

Kaz looked at me.

I looked at him.

Two suspects on their way to be interrogated.

"Please wait here, *messieurs*," Vigot said when we reached the lobby, gesturing to chairs next to some potted ferns. "I shall not be long with your corporal." With that, he snapped his fingers and another uniformed cop trotted over, clasped his hands behind his back, and stood watch over us.

"We need to remember that it was only months ago these police served the Vichy regime, and then the Germans," Kaz said. "Be careful what you say."

"I get the feeling Vigot would be happy nailing one of us for this murder," I said. "It'd be easier than going through all the work of figuring out who else had a key. And his bosses probably wouldn't mind a Yank or an Englishman being the fall guy."

"Thank goodness he has nothing against the Poles," Kaz said, leaning back in his chair. Funny guy. "We need to find out who made the arrangements for this hotel. Who knew we were coming?"

"Sounds like half of Nice had a good idea," I said.

"Setting aside the question of why Dickie was targeted, for which I have no answer at all," Kaz said, "how did the killer know where to ambush him?"

"We were gabbing for a while in the lobby after we checked in," I said. "Someone could have overheard. Or been tipped off."

"Right. Even a few moments' head start would have been enough. The desk staff should be the first to be questioned," Kaz said.

"Ask this guy," I said, looking toward the check-in desk and seeing the same two people on duty. Kaz and the cop exchanged a few short sentences.

"He says to ask the inspector. He is just a lowly *gardien*."

"Does he know Cathedral?"

"He says it is a short walk from here. Seventeenth century," Kaz said with a grin. "He gives very little away."

"That's perfect, since we don't know very much to begin with."

We cooled our heels for a while until Vigot escorted Drake out of the room and asked him, nicely, to wait with Kaz. He gave orders to the cop that I figured were firmer on that subject.

"Come in, Captain Boyle," Vigot said, holding the door open like a gracious host. We sat at a small table in a room that housed somebody's office, obviously taken over by the police. Saved time, I guess, since we didn't have to go down to the station.

Vigot opened a notebook and asked me to go over everything that had happened since we'd arrived at the hotel. I went over my movements in detail, knowing he was building a timeline of who'd seen what when.

"You say that the four of you all entered your rooms simultaneously?" he asked.

"Pretty much," I said.

"Yes, but that is not simultaneous, is it? You had four rooms, all in a row. It is not reasonable that you all entered at the same second, is it? Or was it a military formation?" Vigot gave a little laugh, showing how foolish he thought this was. Good technique.

"Well, we were talking, you know. I was in the process of opening my door when Dickie was. We talked about going out after the meeting."

"And the corporal and the lieutenant?"

"They were down the hall. I didn't time them, if that's what you mean."

"No, no, of course not. But you entered your room and shut the door. Did you see Major Thorne shut his?"

"No. I couldn't. I was in my room."

"Ah. So one of the others could have taken the few steps from their door to his. Before it was closed. Who was closer?"

"Drake was in the room next to Dickie. Then Kaz," I said.

"Yes, I see. Now, you came downstairs before the meeting started, yes? You spoke with Colonel Laurent?" I told him I did. "And when you entered the meeting room, were the lieutenant and the corporal already seated?"

"No," I said, not liking where this was going. "Kaz and Harding were there. Drake came in as I did."

"Which means he was the last to leave your floor, yes?"

"I don't know when he left his room. Only when I saw him," I said. "I suppose you are also speaking with the hotel staff. How many duplicate keys are there for that room?"

"Captain Boyle, I ask the questions here. Please leave the investigation to me. Tell me, how long have you known Lieutenant Kazimierz?"

"Since 1942, more than two years," I said. "We've been through a lot together."

"And Corporal Drake?"

"Two days."

"Ah."

"Okay, Inspector, I get it. You've got the idea it had to be Drake. An American, and a Negro at that. Who's to say you're wrong in this city? But you've got to question the hotel staff, at least to make your case look good."

"You do not give the orders here!" Inspector Vigot shouted, slamming his hand down on the table. He sat back in his chair, taking a deep breath, as if he regretted the show of emotion. "Forgive me, Captain, but I have seen too many years of others ordering us about. First the Vichy fascists and the Italian occupiers, and finally the Germans after the Italians gave up. Perhaps it is this hotel. Do you know its history?"

"No, Inspector. Only that it looks like it's seen better days."

"The Germans used it to house Jews they'd rounded up. When the Italians occupied us early in the war, they did little to enforce the anti-Jewish laws Vichy had passed. Therefore, many Jews came here to hide and seek forged papers. When the Nazis swept through, they rounded up all the Jews in Nice that they could find. Most spent their last night in Nice in this hotel, dozens crowded into each room. Then a march

to the train station and off in cattle cars to those camps from which
there is no return. Forgive me, Captain, if I have had enough of for-
eigners, even our liberators, when it comes to murder. There will be
an investigation, a proper one, I promise you. But Corporal Drake will
remain with us. Jailed on suspicion of murder."

CHAPTER EIGHTEEN

"I REALIZE THAT, Colonel, but I must continue this mission," Stewart said to Harding. "And I shall."

I'd walked into the briefing room and found them going head-to-head after Vigot had Drake taken into custody. Kaz was still being interviewed by the inspector, but I'd had time enough to tell Kaz to question the desk staff as soon as he could.

"You don't abandon your men, Commander," Harding said, standing close to Stewart, his hands on his hips. "Not in my army, at least."

"I'm not abandoning Corporal Drake," Stewart insisted. "His interests will be looked after by SOE, and I invite you to involve the US Army since he is also one of yours. We've lost two men now, one dead and one in prison, and I take both seriously, let me assure you."

"We can count on Inspector Vigot and Captain Boyle to obtain information from the hotel people," Harding said. "But what about Cathedral and his group? What do they have to say?"

"Cathedral left," Stewart said. "Rather abruptly. He didn't seem to like the police activity. Remember, he's been on the run from the police and the Germans for years. Old habits and all that."

"You didn't think that had anything to do with Dickie being murdered, sir?" I asked, trying hard not to let my sarcasm show.

"Oh come now, Boyle. You don't seriously suggest someone of Cathedral's stature would volunteer to help us and then suddenly decide to kill one of us?" Stewart said, his voice rising. "It's sheer lunacy."

"Okay, let's just decide what to do next," Harding said, seeing this was getting us nowhere. "But for the record, did Cathedral say anything at all regarding Dickie's death?"

"Well, naturally, he asked what all the fuss was about. He'd been in the bar with Danton, one of Laurent's chaps, and a few of his men. He came out as the *gendarmes* arrived. When I explained, he suggested we postpone our conclave so we could allow the investigation to proceed," Stewart said. "While I don't think Cathedral had any role in the murder, I do suspect some of these Resistance groups are finding it hard to give up their outlaw ways. Probably a good deal of black market business going on, enough to make them nervous around the police."

"I have to say, it doesn't seem likely he'd bring his men here and wait around while a murder was being committed if he was involved," Harding said. I had to agree.

"Well, I'm glad we're in accord about that," Stewart said. "Cathedral wants to meet tomorrow morning, but not here. In Falicon, a small village in the hills above Nice. Perhaps you and Lieutenant Kazimierz could take on that task, Captain?"

"You're not going?" I asked, surprised. This is what our trip was all about.

"I'll be in touch with SPOC in Algiers by radio," Stewart said. "Colonel Edwin needs to be informed immediately. Now, when dealing with Cathedral, be careful. Get the information he has for us and get back as quickly as you can. We don't know if all the danger has passed."

"Corporal Drake should be informed," Kaz said. "He needs to know what's being done to help him."

"Agreed," Stewart said. "I'll get to the *préfecture* and inform Drake I am seeking legal representation for him through SOE channels."

"I'll get in touch with Seventh Army HQ," Harding said. "Maybe the provost marshal's office can help."

"Just make sure the provost marshal's MPs know we want to help Drake, not get him hung," I said.

"Don't worry, Boyle, we'll get him out of this," Harding said. "Now, try to track down Laurent and see what he knows about Danton. It's strange that he showed up the same time we did."

"He was originally part of Cathedral's group, so it's not a complete surprise," I said. "But we do need to find him; he's the only link between the shooting in Algiers and the murder here." Besides all of us, including Drake, but I left that unsaid.

Stewart went off to make some calls, saying he needed to schedule access to a secure radio link to SPOC in Algiers, using the Royal Navy base at the harbor. Harding went off in his jeep, aiming to secure a radio link to Seventh Army. We agreed Kaz and I would take on the meeting with Cathedral in the morning, leaving Stewart and Harding to focus on springing Drake.

Our job was to get the list of names from Cathedral and figure out, with his help, which traitors might be quickly rounded up and which needed to go on an Allied manhunt list. Easy, right? Just drive an hour into the hills and find Café Bernard in the village square. Cathedral would be there, and maybe we'd have a nice cup of coffee. Or there'd be another dead body. Who knew?

I found Kaz in the lobby, leafing through a newspaper as a plain-clothes detective questioned one of the hotel staff at the desk. There wasn't exactly a line at check-in, the reputation of this run-down joint probably making it the last choice for anyone who knew the score. Apparently, that score was news to Stewart and whoever planned this jaunt.

"Inspector Vigot does not think me a killer," Kaz said, folding the paper neatly.

"He just doesn't know you well enough," I said, flopping down in a chair.

"It is the distance from my door to Dickie's," Kaz said. "He insists I could not have reached it in time to follow Dickie in."

"But Elwood Drake could have."

"Yes. And you as well. You were equidistant."

"But here I am, and Drake's in a cell," I said. "Separate, but equidistant."

"I take it that is a reference to your nation's antiquated racial laws," Kaz said. "But remember this is France, and the same extreme attitudes do not hold. It may be Vigot prefers a soldier of lower rank to put on the ice, so he has someone to charge if the investigation fails to find the killer. And he is smart enough to know the American army will do more for a white officer than a Negro enlisted man."

"Hey, the cop's leaving," I said, nudging Kaz. "And it's 'on ice.'" Kaz was a big fan of American jargon, especially the gangster stuff. He'd gotten pretty good at it, but still needed the occasional correction.

"Thank you. Now get out the long green," Kaz said, heading for the desk and letting me know I was going to grease the guy's palm. "And give me your room key."

I handed both over, not sure what game Kaz was playing but ready to follow his lead. He drew the clerk aside, speaking quietly, pointing to me and the two keys he'd laid on the desk, along with a few francs.

The clerk swept up the cash, seeming to agree with what Kaz asked for. He reached back, got another key, and handed it over. Then he and Kaz chatted some more, the clerk all smiles when Kaz slipped him the rest of the long green I'd given him.

"We are moving to another floor," Kaz told me. "A large room where we can watch out for each other."

"Good idea," I said. "But what else did you learn?"

"Cathedral has stayed here before, along with his cousin. During the Occupation, the hotel manager often let them stay off the books. He was eager to demonstrate his loyalty and show the hotel itself was not to blame for how the Nazis used it."

"Great. Who's the cousin?"

"Danton. He and Cathedral had the run of the hotel," Kaz said. "And it was Cathedral who recommended it to Stewart, through Danton."

"Because he knew he could get at Dickie, maybe," I said.

"The clerk, Pascal, also said that many keys were lost when the Germans requisitioned the hotel," Kaz said. "They used it for about two weeks during the roundup and left it in great disarray. A locksmith made new keys, including master keys."

"Are any missing?"

"Pascal wasn't sure," Kaz told me. "It was a time of much distress, and he thinks a proper inventory was never taken."

"So basically, anything's possible. Dozens of people, Cathedral and Danton included, could have swiped a key. Let's find Laurent and see if he can tell us any more about Danton."

"I saw him leave not ten minutes ago," Kaz said. "In great haste."

"Not a bad idea," I said.

We grabbed our gear and made the move to a more spacious room two floors up, then headed out to find a place to eat, both of us unwilling to dine in this hotel that had seen so much heartache.

We had a lot to think about. Cathedral, Stewart, the hotel, Dickie, and what this mission still held for us. But it had been a long day, and as soon as we found a restaurant, all I could think about was toasting the memory of a good man and enjoying a meal. If I didn't feel too guilty about it.

CHAPTER NINETEEN

AFTER A FITFUL night's sleep, with pistols close by and a dresser pulled in front of the door, we took off early for the village of Falicon. On the map, it didn't look far, but that was if you were a crow. The route took us through a series of switchbacks as we climbed higher, each tight turn traversing an increasingly narrow track. No wonder Stewart chose to stay at sea level in Nice.

The last turn finally became a straightaway that allowed me to shift into third gear, which brought us into a small hilltop village with the usual church spire overlooking the village square. I parked the jeep, switched off the ignition, and turned to look back.

The view was breathtaking. I'd been too focused on not running off the road to see the broad expanse of the Mediterranean, the deep blue sky, and rays of golden sunlight glinting off the water.

"It's like a painting," I gasped, the beauty of the scene below overwhelming.

"The south of France is exquisite," Kaz said. "Unless you've just spent the night in a jail cell. Let us hope Stewart has managed to get help for Drake."

"Maybe he has, maybe he hasn't," I said as I got out of the jeep and drank in the view. "But Harding won't stop until he's done everything possible, I'm sure of that."

"Over there," Kaz said, pointing to the other side of the small square. Café Bernard was tucked into a corner of the plaza, on the ground floor of a stucco building painted in an orange pastel with robin's-egg blue shutters. A few tables were set up outside, and I recognized Danton at one of them. The rest of the men were at odds with the picture-postcard setting, a half dozen rough fellows who seemed to have given up shaving but not given up the habit of packing heat.

"Danton," I said in greeting, eyeing the pistols the others wore. "Where's Cathedral?"

"*Il est ici*," a voice announced from the doorway of the café. It was Cathedral, thumping his chest with his fist and laughing. His men stood to make way and to give us room at one of the small tables. He wore a black suit, a once-white shirt, and a three-day growth of beard. Not to mention a Colt .45 in a shoulder holster.

"Are there many Germans around?" I asked as Cathedral sat next to Danton. Cathedral answered, and his men responded with cackles of laughter as Danton quickly translated.

"Yes, in their graves," Danton said. "Cathedral speaks some English, but it is better to have me translate, yes?"

"Good English," Cathedral said with a smile, pointing to Danton.

"You must be glad to have your cousin back with you," Kaz said.

"*Ferme-la*," Cathedral said in a snarl. The men standing behind him stiffened. Looked like when Cathedral wanted you to shut up, he put a lot of muscle behind it.

"No, no," Danton said. "No references to family. These are still dangerous times."

"My apologies," Kaz said. "I certainly know how dangerous Nice was for Major Thorne, but here, in this quaint village? The front lines are hundreds of miles north, are they not?"

"The Maquis Luc Robert knows no front line," Danton said, grinning at Cathedral, who seemed to understand him just fine. "They are everywhere. So, they must be careful everywhere."

"When all Boche are in the ground or to *Allemagne*, we stop," Cathedral said, summing up my thoughts perfectly. Dead or gone, that's how I liked my Nazis. A waiter came out with a tray, carrying four cups of coffee. The tension lessened as we busied ourselves with sugar, stirring away while Cathedral lit up a Lucky Strike, cupping it in his meaty hand. Another cautious habit.

Another man strolled out of the café, coffee cup in hand, and gave us a curt nod of recognition.

"*Bonjour*, Jean-Paul," I said, raising my cup in his direction. I hadn't expected to see another member of the Maquis du Vercors here.

"*Bonjour, mes amies*," Jean-Paul said, flashing a toothy grin and leaning against the wall.

"Are you and Jean-Paul here on assignment, Danton?" Kaz asked, taking in the village square with a wave of his hand.

"No, this is a visit. A family visit, as you have discovered," Danton said. "Tomorrow I go north with Jean-Paul and several other fighters. I will be scout and translator for your 36th Division."

"Dangerous work," Kaz said. "You will know the front lines, certainly."

"I grew up near the Vosges," Danton said. "My father was a woodcutter. I know those mountains. I am not worried."

"Jean-Paul, you are from the Vosges also?" Kaz asked.

"*Non*, my home is in the Vercors," Jean-Paul said, absently fingering the scar on his cheekbone. "The village of Vassieux. But I am unable to visit my family. I have other duties."

"Good luck to you both," I said, wondering if that remark was directed at Danton for this unscheduled stop, if that's what it was. Either way, Danton would need a lot of luck. The 36th Division was part of Seventh Army's push to Germany, near the Swiss border. When the Allies landed in southern France a lot of Germans took off. It wasn't a cakewalk, but it wasn't a meat grinder either. Until now. In those mountains, with Germany at their back, the Fritzes had dug in deep.

The GIs had called southern France the Champagne Campaign. I don't know what they called the Vosges, but I bet it was no joke.

"*Merci*," Danton said. "And on behalf of the Maquis Luc Robert, I offer *condoléances* on the death *tragique* of your comrade."

"Thank you," Kaz said. "He was a friend. I wish I knew who killed him."

"Any idea who might have?" I asked, looking to Danton,

Cathedral, and Jean-Paul. "Or why?" Cathedral spoke quickly in French, pounding the table with his hand and rattling the coffee cups.

"He says there are many debts to be settled," Kaz explained. "Many things that can never be forgiven. Perhaps our friend was caught up in such acts. Or was about to take revenge himself and was stopped. It happens." Cathedral watched us, shrugged his shoulders, and sat back.

It happens.

"But Major Thorne had never been in France," I said. "I don't see how he could've riled anyone up that much."

"Riled?" Jean-Paul asked.

"Angered. Stirred to action," Kaz explained.

"Ah, yes, I understand," Jean-Paul said. "But remember, your Special Operations Executive has a long reach." With that, he went back inside the café, leaving me wondering what Dickie could have done in Crete that got him killed in Nice.

"Now, to our business," Danton said. "We have names for you. A list of eighteen traitors from this area. Cathedral has prepared it, along with descriptions, crimes, and last known locations. Three of them are living under false identities, all former Vichy serving with *la Milice*."

I knew the *Milice* all too well. Fascist thugs who tortured and killed for their German masters.

"We look," Cathedral said, withdrawing two sheets of paper from his inside jacket pocket. "But *poof*, gone."

"This is excellent information, very detailed," Kaz said, scanning the papers and the densely printed descriptions. "You are certain of their guilt?"

"*Oui, coupable*," Cathedral said, then he took a small piece of paper from another pocket and handed it to me. It held one name, Marie Schenck, and an address in Digne-les-Bains.

"Who's this?" I asked, recognizing the town from the matchbox found in Laurent's room. I handed it to Kaz, who responded with a raised eyebrow.

"Marie Schenck is Alsatian," Danton said. "More German than

French. She has informed on many people. She went into hiding when the Allies came, but Cathedral has learned she will be at that address tomorrow night. She plans to reclaim her possessions and flee."

"You must take her," Cathedral said. He drained his cup, set it down, and went back into the café.

"It is the price for the list," Danton said. "It must be done tomorrow. Otherwise, the other *maquis* groups will undoubtedly hear you cannot be trusted."

"It can be done," I said, knowing that the town of Digne was next on our list. "But tell me, why don't Cathedral and his men pick her up? Or any of these others?"

"That time has passed," Danton said. "Resistance justice was harsh, but necessary. Now, we must live according to the law. Also, there will be less retribution if your army takes them. The killing cannot go on and on, *n'est-ce pas?*"

It was hard to disagree.

"We'll do it," I said, figuring a pickup was better than a noose in the night for this woman. "Now tell me, what was Jean-Paul upset about?"

"Of that, I have no idea," Danton said. "I have only known him for a month or so. We both were part of the Maquis du Vercors, but we served in different companies. He is always moody. But willing to fight."

"Kaz, was Dickie in France at any time prior to his mission in Crete?" I asked, considering Jean-Paul's remark about the long reach of the SOE. Dickie's radio operator had been killed, but other than that, I really didn't know much about his time there.

"Crete? Commander Stewart told us Thorne had been in Algiers, then sent on a mission," Danton said. "I have no idea if it was France or Crete."

"I'm certain he hadn't been to France," Kaz asked. "He did mention he'd been training in Cairo and Palestine before his work in Crete. The incident with Stewart and the rifles, remember?"

I did, but remembering that didn't help things add up, so we wished Danton well and headed for the jeep. As I got into the driver's seat, I looked back toward the café. A few of the men returned to their seats, but the rest had gone inside. Upstairs, from a third-story window, Jean-Paul looked down on us, his expression grim. He didn't wave, but he did look glad to see us go.

CHAPTER TWENTY

"STRANGE FELLOW, OUR Jean-Paul," Kaz said as I maneuvered the jeep down the steep incline and around the tight corners. "He seemed upset about something. Angry."

"Danton said he was moody. Do you think he knows something?" I asked.

"I sense that everyone knows a little more than we do about everything," Kaz said. Which was pretty much how murder investigations went, even in peacetime. In a war where many people used their *nom de guerre*, it became more confusing. Who were Jean-Paul or Danton or Cathedral, deep down?

"What we don't know is who these Resistance people really are," I said. "Their actual names, where they're from, who they love, and what they want. It makes it hard to trace a motive when all we have are false identities."

"But their old selves are gone," Kaz said, leaning in as I took another sharp turn. "Their homes might be destroyed, and their dreams and desires from before the war shattered into a million pieces. It might be more accurate to say that what they show of themselves now is their true self. Everything else has been burned away."

I knew we were talking about the *maquis*, but as Kaz's words trailed off, I was pretty sure he'd described himself as well. Before the war, he was a student of languages, part of a large family that hoped to settle in England before the shooting started. By the time I met him, he'd lost most of his family but at least had found a woman to love. Then she was taken from him. Yes, everything that Kaz loved had been burned away, leaving his soul bared.

"What does that leave us with?" I asked, eager to avoid questioning what had been burned away from my own soul. Innocence had been the first thing to go, that much I knew.

"Well, we have one thing. We know of nineteen people Cathedral wishes to be rid of. One very much," Kaz said. "Perhaps we should learn more about them."

"Do you think Inspector Vigot may know any of them? It might help us convince him to spring Drake if we give him something," I said.

"Commander Stewart did say these names were to be put on a manhunt list," Kaz said. "Why not start with the local police?"

"I like it," I said. "Especially since I can't think of anything else to do right now." At the base of the hill, I stepped on it and headed for the *Préfecture de Police* to find Inspector Vigot.

One thing I've learned since arriving in Europe is that desk sergeants in police stations are all the same. This guy had all the right qualities. Old enough to know his way around and not be swayed by self-important types—like us—and calm enough to tell us to cool our heels and keep quiet several times without seeming irritated. He was a pro, even down to pretending not to know where Inspector Vigot was, or possibly even if he existed.

After waiting half an hour, we heard Vigot's voice as he came in through the main entrance, with Stewart right at his side.

"*L'inspecteur est là,*" the sergeant said, with such deadpan grace that I had to tip my hat to him.

"And you'll hear from the Americans as well," Stewart said, fuming at Vigot who held up his hand as if warding off the words.

"It makes no difference, Commander," Vigot said with a weariness that told me it wasn't the first time he'd said it. "This is a police matter, not a military one."

"Excuse me, Inspector," I said, not sure either one had noticed us. "May we have a word?"

"Why not? Everyone else has had words for me," Vigot said, waving his hand at the sergeant and leading us down a hallway. A portrait of de Gaulle looked down on us, and I could discern faded paint on the wall around the frame. A slightly larger portrait of General Pétain, the leader of Vichy France, had probably had the place of honor until a few months ago.

"First it was the American Seventh Army," Vigot continued. "Then a British diplomat from Algiers. Then Colonel Laurent. Have they saved the most persuasive for last? We shall see." We followed Vigot to his office, Stewart calming down enough to take notice of us.

"Where have you two been?" the commander demanded, as if we were late to class.

"Obtaining the list of names from Cathedral," Kaz answered. "A task, I recall, that was the very purpose of this mission."

"Yes, yes," Stewart said as Vigot held the door open for us. "Fill me in when we're done here."

"How well do you know Jean-Paul, Commander?" I asked.

"Later. You can ask Drake if we get him out of here," Stewart said, as we arranged ourselves in front of Vigot's desk. The inspector sat, not suggesting we do the same. He looked to be enjoying himself.

"We have a crime," Vigot said. "And I have a suspect, one who was in the right place to commit the crime. What have you to say?"

"If you have a strong case against Drake, I'd say you should keep him locked up no matter the pressure put on you," Stewart said. "But it's not a strong case. You have no evidence. Is it really worth it?"

"Are you suggesting I release a suspect due to political pressure?" Vigot asked.

"I wonder if you're keeping him locked up due to political pressure," I said. "This must be a sensitive case. A British officer murdered in the same hotel used by the Vichy state to house Jews before they were sent off to their death. Bad publicity."

"I must point out, Captain Boyle, that when the Germans rounded up the Jews who had found refuge in Nice, the Vichy state no longer ruled any part of France. The German army did. Refugees were never hunted by my men," Vigot said, with enough energy that I knew he had taken offense. Good. I didn't know what pro-Vichy sentiment he might still have.

"Now look here, Inspector, surely we can come to an understanding,"

Stewart said, trying to be reasonable but sounding like a twit. "I really do need Corporal Drake for this mission. It's quite important."

"Yes, yes, the hunting of fascist informers," Vigot said. "I do agree, it is best done officially, in full cooperation with the local authorities."

"Perhaps we could be of assistance," Kaz said, pulling a chair to the side of Vigot's desk like an old friend come to visit. "You must be interested in apprehending traitors to France?"

"I am interested in arresting those who are guilty of breaking the law," Vigot said. "Always."

"I cannot claim to be an authority on French law," Kaz said, withdrawing Cathedral's list from his uniform jacket. "But I am certain some of these eighteen people engaged in activities which resulted in the deaths of many citizens."

"Is that from Cathedral?" Stewart said. "You can't bandy that about, Lieutenant."

"Commander, we've heard from both you and Colonel Harding that these names are to go on a manhunt list all across France," I said. "No reason not to start in Nice, right?"

"No," Stewart said, after giving it a moment's thought. He was the kind of officer who didn't like initiative, especially if it didn't make him look good. But he had brains enough to see Kaz was up to something that might spring Drake, so he backed off.

Kaz began to rattle off names, places, and crimes.

Pascal Devillers of Colomars. Informed on three wounded Resistance fighters being cared for in a neighbor's house. All were picked up by the Gestapo, tortured, and killed.

Nina Delaplace of Le Broc, whose husband served with *la Milice*, betrayed a family of Jews who came to her café, desperate to obtain false papers. They were picked up by the Gestapo.

Remi Dimont of Toudon, who tortured and killed with particular gusto as a member of *la Milice*, was now living in Aspremont as Marius Robiquet, working as a farm laborer.

"Enough," Vigot said, holding up his hand. "We have been looking for Dimont. He had a hand in murdering one of our officers. If we find him, I will release Corporal Drake."

"No," Kaz said quietly. "Release him now, please. Otherwise, I am certain Commander Stewart will not allow me to give you the other names. *Fifteen* other names."

"Very well," Vigot said. "You have my word. But allow me to copy out the other names, I am interested in all that Monsieur Cathedral has to offer. This is what he came to the hotel to deliver?"

"Yes," Stewart said. "He left before we could conclude our business."

"The police make him nervous, I could see," Vigot said, scribbling in his notebook. "We know he plays with the black market. But we also know he was a real fighter, not one of those who donned the tricolor armband at the last moment. I must give him a warning soon, to go back to what he did before the war."

"That can be difficult for some, Inspector," Kaz said.

"I stayed at my post during Vichy," Vigot said, finishing up with the papers. "No man can tell me what is difficult. Now, let us go to your corporal."

"Thank you," Kaz said as he stood. A piece of paper, the note that Cathedral had given him, fluttered to the floor. It must have been dislodged when Kaz took out the other sheets.

"Another name?" Vigot asked. "Schenck in Digne?"

"No, that's a separate matter," I said, not wanting to get into Cathedral's personal vendettas.

"Wait, did you say Schenck?" Stewart said, grabbing the note from Vigot. "Marie Schenck? Where did you get this?"

"From Cathedral," I said, now that the cat was out of the bag. "He wants us to pick her up tomorrow night. He's received word that she'll be back in Digne, and he wants us to grab her."

"That's absurd, man," Stewart said, then turned his attention to Vigot. "Surely you must have heard of that affair with Christine Granville and the escape from the Gestapo prison in August?"

"*Une femme formidable*," Vigot said, nodding. "Her fame is spread wide. Marie Schenck? Wait, was there not a Gestapo officer named Schenck?"

"Indeed, there was," Stewart said, smiling at whatever he knew that we didn't. "Captain Albert Schenck worked as a liaison between the French police and the Gestapo. He was from Alsace, half German and half French, but his wife Marie is from around here."

"I don't understand," I said, not for the first time. "Why does Cathedral want Marie picked up? Why not Albert?"

"Because Albert is dead," Stewart said. "As for Marie, I'd say it has something to do with the missing francs. All two million of them."

CHAPTER TWENTY-ONE

I HAD A lot of questions, maybe two million or so. But I kept it zipped up while we followed Vigot down into the cells. He signed off on Drake's release and a few minutes later we were standing outside *la préfecture*, the corporal blinking in the bright sunlight.

"It must feel good to be free, Corporal Drake. I daresay it was close there for a while, but we brought out the heavy guns. SOE, Seventh Army, and the very persuasive Lieutenant Kazimierz," Stewart said, embroidering his own role as the master planner to whom Drake owed his release.

"I never doubted you'd do all you could, Commander," Drake said, leaving open to question exactly how much he'd expected of Stewart. This corporal had the makings of a diplomat.

"Commander, can you explain what this business with Marie Schenck is all about? It's the first time we've heard anything about two million francs," I said.

"All you have to do is ask around about the marvelous Miss Granville," Stewart said. "Anyone with the slightest acquaintance with the Resistance, which these days is every living and breathing Frenchman, can tell you the entire thrilling story, including the missing francs."

"You talking about Christine Granville, sir?" Drake asked. "She's a legend."

"Exactly so," Stewart said. "But I'll have nothing more to do with this. I don't want SOE insisting on getting their money back.

I'll be damned if I'll be their debt collector. But you two are obliged in some manner to Cathedral, it seems."

"It was the price for the list," I said.

"Danton said that if we did not comply, Cathedral would spread the word we could not be trusted," Kaz said. "It seemed like a simple quid pro quo, since we will be in Digne tomorrow anyway."

"Well, you're on your own," Stewart said. "Don't do anything rash and turn the woman over to the local *gendarmes*. It wouldn't do for men under my command to be in the middle of a Resistance vendetta. Understood?"

"Perfectly, sir," I said, if only to get rid of Stewart. I didn't understand a damn thing.

"We leave at 0800 hours in the morning," Stewart said, heading for his jeep. "Don't keep me waiting, Corporal."

"What a piece of work," Kaz muttered.

"Don't ask me," Drake said. "I never speak ill of an officer. To other officers. How about a lift?"

"You can tell us everything you know about this business on the way there," I said. "You hungry?"

"Fresh air and freedom do wonders for the appetite, Captain," Drake said. "Want me to drive?"

"Sure," I said. As we got to the jeep, Kaz jumped into the passenger's seat, leaving me in the back.

"Take the corners as sharply as you can," Kaz said to Drake while giving me a wink. "Dinner is on me." Drake checked the traffic and gunned the jeep, neatly inserting himself into the flow of civilian and military vehicles. I was about to press him on what he knew about the two million francs, but as he took the first corner, I realized Drake was going to earn himself a fine meal.

We arrived back at the hotel, my stomach trailing by a block and my hat, by some miracle, still on my head. Kaz was laughing and Drake managed to suppress a smirk as he parked in front. I had to admit he was a good driver. The turns were hard enough to be worrying but not drastic enough to send me flying into the gutter.

"Reminds me of a ride at the carnival," I said. "Except back then I was strapped in."

"You okay, Captain?" Drake asked as I unwound my legs from the back seat.

"I could use a drink," I said.

"I owe you one after that ride," Kaz said, still enjoying his revenge. "Shall we meet in the restaurant in one hour? Corporal Drake may want to freshen up."

"That'd be great," Drake said, sniffing his shirt. "I smell like *eau de donjon*."

"Then you owe us the story of the two million francs," I said. In the lobby, we got another room for Drake. Luckily, Pascal from yesterday was on duty, so we didn't need to explain things. Kaz slipped him a few francs, reminding him to keep our locations secret. After Drake was settled in, we returned to the lobby. The clerk was all too glad to see the heavy tipper again.

"Kaz, ask Pascal about Jean-Paul," I said. "Was he here with Cathedral yesterday? Remember to mention his scar."

"And his good looks," Kaz said. "The man could grace a film poster."

Kaz began to describe Cathedral and Jean-Paul, his hands showing their height and width. Once he swept back his hair as if combing it, and I knew that had to be Jean-Paul.

"No," Kaz said, after stripping off a few more francs from his diminishing bankroll. The telephone began to ring but the desk clerk waited until he'd received the cash to answer it. "He doesn't recall Jean-Paul. But he remembered Cathedral going into the restaurant yesterday. There is a separate entrance on the street, so anyone could have entered that way."

Pascal finished his telephone call, hung up the receiver, and looked to us on the off chance we wanted to fork over any more dough.

"A telephone call," I muttered to myself. A call to Dickie's room could have interrupted him as he entered. It had looked like he'd just walked in and set down his bags, but what if he'd answered the call? He might have left the door open for his killer.

"Ask if Dickie received any calls after we checked in," I said to Kaz.

"Pascal says he would not know," Kaz said after they finished. "Any calls, including those from the guest telephone in the lobby, would go through the switchboard. And before you ask, yes, they are noted."

"Let's see it, then," I said.

"Unfortunately, Inspector Vigot has the ledger with the call listings," Kaz said. "Odd that he thought it important enough to take, but not important enough to mention."

As we crossed the lobby to the dining area, I explained my theory of a call made to Dickie. "I wish we knew what else Vigot uncovered when he had the staff questioned," I said.

"Or if he even pursued the questioning diligently," Kaz said. "Yesterday he was quite satisfied to have Drake as his prime suspect. But what about the scuff marks we found in the bathroom? Doesn't that argue in favor of a killer lying in wait?"

"That could be a haphazard cleaning job. This isn't exactly the Dorchester. Our problem is we have too many possibilities," I said, stepping into the restaurant and letting my eyes adjust to the muted lighting in the bar area. "Including a police inspector who might have made his mind up too quickly. Or maybe he has a superior who's putting pressure on him to wrap this up. I've seen the type. Drake could've been his insurance policy. Doesn't mean he wasn't looking elsewhere."

"You are the expert when it comes to the gradations of police corruption, Billy," Kaz said. "So, I give the inspector the benefit of your doubt. Now, let me speak to the maître d'."

Kaz sauntered over to the head waiter's station while I looked around. There was an on-street entrance off the bar, so it would have been easy for anyone to bypass the front desk. I approached the barman while Kaz was still chatting up the maître d' and asked if he spoke English.

"A little," he said. "*Un peu.*"

"*Un peu* me too," I said, taking a seat and ordering a brandy. That much French I knew.

I introduced myself as he set the drink down and I fanned out several franc notes, telling him to keep the change. Not a Kaz-level tip, but a solid one. His name was Baptiste and the first thing he made clear was that he'd started working here only a month ago. He wanted me to know he wasn't connected to the history of this joint during the Occupation. I couldn't blame him for wanting to make that clear.

"The maître d' wasn't working that early yesterday," Kaz said, settling onto the barstool next to me.

"Ask Baptiste," I said. The attentive barman was standing by, cleaning glasses, and waiting for customers. It was early yet, and we were ahead of the dinner crowd. Kaz went through his description again, right down to the dark wavy locks.

"Yes," Kaz said, ordering a Lillet, an *apéritif* he preferred. Baptiste set it down and Kaz took a drink, nodding his approval. "Jean-Paul, or someone like him, was in yesterday, along with Cathedral, whom he recognized. Baptiste had the morning shift, and he said it was easy to remember since there are few customers in at that hour. Some come for *café*, others for liquor."

"Did he hear any of their conversation?" I asked.

"Nothing. Except that they were most convivial. They seemed to be celebrating," Kaz said.

"Just the two of them?"

"Yes, Danton came in after Jean-Paul departed," Kaz said after a quick consult. Baptiste topped off our drinks, waving his hand when I reached for my cash. We were all pals now, booze and bills cementing friendships in no time. "But he didn't recognize Danton, except from my description. Nor does he recall if any of them was wearing a burgundy tie, as was the man Drake saw on the stairs."

"Okay, so we know Jean-Paul was here," I said.

"And he never thought to mention it," Kaz said. "Why?"

"Because he killed Dickie? Because he didn't want to be associated with Cathedral?"

"But he already was," Kaz said. "He must have known we'd be at the Café Bernard this morning. He wasn't worried about showing himself there."

"A connection to the hotel, then. It could be Dickie, or it could be something else. Remember Cathedral lit out of here pretty damn quick himself," I said.

"All this is speculation," Kaz said. "We have no understanding of *why* Dickie was killed. Knowing that would help make sense of things. All we have now are the comings and goings of people associated with our mission, which amount to little more than Vigot's reasoning for taking Corporal Drake into custody."

"Somebody mention my name?" Drake said, taking the stool next to Kaz.

"Did you know Jean-Paul was here the morning Dickie was killed?" I asked. "And Danton as well?"

"*Un cognac, s'il vous plaît,*" Drake said to the barman, then turned his attention first to Kaz. "You're paying, right, Lieutenant? Dinner and drinks?"

"Indeed, and it is my pleasure," Kaz said. "I've had to ride in the rear seat while Billy drove like a maniac so many times, I thought I should return the favor. Well done. Not a bad accent, by the way."

"I picked up as much as I could in Algiers," Drake said. "A lot of it from Jean-Paul. And no, Billy, I had no idea he was here. Why?"

"Baptiste said Jean-Paul had a conversation with Cathedral in here," I said, pointing to the barman. "We saw him this morning in Falicon, along with Danton."

"Danton was here too? Strange that neither of them came to find me. We were on good terms. I helped them with their English, and they coached me on French," Drake said as Baptiste set down his drink. "*Merci.*"

"Danton said he and Cathedral are cousins," Kaz said.

"That's true," Drake said, smacking his lips in satisfaction after the first sip. "Or at least he said he had a cousin who was a Resistance leader. No names, though."

"What do you know about Jean-Paul's background?" I asked.

"Not much. He fought in the Vercors uprising as they all did," Drake said. "Had family there. Worked as a mining engineer before the war, I think he said. Lots of coal in those mountains."

"But no reason why he might be hanging around with Cathedral?" I asked.

"Other than the obvious? He and Danton are buddies," Drake said. "Maybe he had time to kill before his assignment."

"Any idea what the assignment is?" I asked.

"No sir. My job was to train them on firearms and explosives, and to be sure they were proficient with the long-range scopes. No reason for me to know more," Drake said. "Jean-Paul was a big help with the explosives, that much I can tell you. He was used to setting charges for mining operations. My guess would be they'd use him for demolitions work."

"We need to ask Colonel Laurent about this," Kaz said, "as well as Danton."

"Right. We haven't seen Laurent since he lit out of here yesterday," I said.

"I find the best place to let the world come to you is a hotel bar," Kaz said. He suggested we move to the lounge area with a low table and a good view of the entrance. Once we got comfortable, I told Drake it was time to tell the story of the two million francs.

"There's probably a lot I don't know," Drake began. "But if half of what I do know is true, Christine Granville pulled off the con to end all cons. She was the courier for an SOE network run by Francis Cammaerts. Together, they organized arms drops and kept in radio contact with Algiers."

"Where does the money come in?" I asked. "Two million francs is a lot of dough, right?"

"Around forty large," Kaz said, once again showing off his tough-guy slang.

"That's right," Drake said with a smile. "Forty thousand bucks. But hang on, you asked for a story, so there's no sense starting at the end. I guess it began with the Vercors uprising. You know how that went south in a hurry, right?"

"Yeah. The Resistance jumped the gun and called for a general uprising against the Germans," I said. "Right after D-Day in Normandy."

"Yeah. They expected reinforcements and arms drops of heavy weapons from the SOE, and for the invasion to hit the beaches of southern France right away," Drake said. "For whatever reason, that didn't happen. The Germans launched a major attack on the

Vercors, and it was a massacre. Granville and Cammaerts barely escaped with their lives."

Drake finished his brandy and Kaz signaled Baptiste for another round. Storytelling was thirsty work, and it was best to keep Drake's voice lubricated. He nodded his thanks and went on with the rest of the tale.

Cammaerts had to meet two newly dropped agents close to Digne. Christine had another assignment in the opposite direction, near the Italian border. Her mission was to encourage troops of Polish nationality who'd been pressed into service by the German army to surrender. She'd been picked for this assignment because she was Polish. Her real name was Krystyna Skarbek, and she was the daughter of a Polish count and a Jewish mother. Making secret contact with the Poles, she told them to turn on their German officers and surrender when the first Allied troops reached them. They got to it right away, and over sixty of the Poles eagerly joined the French Resistance.

Meanwhile, Cammaerts was making his rendezvous with two new SOE agents. They'd been sent with cash to help finance operations in support of the upcoming invasion. Cammaerts found a driver and picked up the two agents. Once on the road, they decided on a story. They were hitchhikers, picked up independently. The SOE men had brought a large quantity of cash, so much so that Cammaerts decided it was better that they divide it among them, so if searched no one would be carrying such a large sum.

They were stopped at a Gestapo roadblock and searched, but nothing was found. The Gestapo officer was about to let them drive on when he decided to check the francs they carried more closely.

SOE had made a crucial error. The serial numbers on the banknotes were sequential. The men could not be random hitchhikers. The driver, pleading ignorance, was let go, but Cammaerts and the two agents were taken to the Gestapo cells in Digne.

As soon as Christine heard, she dashed to Digne. Circling the prison on her bicycle, she whistled the tune to "Frankie and Johnnie," a favorite of hers and Cammaerts's. Once she heard him whistle back, she knew he was alive.

Drake paused in his storytelling to drain his glass. It was only then that I noticed Laurent standing near us.

"Do not allow me to interrupt," he said. "You tell the tale well. Continue."

Christine, realizing that torture and execution were not far off, took an immense gamble. She marched into the office of Captain Albert Schenck, an Alsatian serving as a liaison between the French police and the Gestapo, and announced that she was a British agent.

"Schenck?" Kaz asked. "He has a wife, Marie, right?"

"I don't know about the man's wife, I just know the story as it was told to me," Drake said. Kaz raised his eyebrows at me and took a drink as Drake continued.

She embroidered on the truth a fair bit. She said she was Cammaerts's wife, which was untrue, although they were lovers. She also stated she was the niece of British general Bernard Montgomery, and that the invasion was imminent. She was not related to Montgomery and while she guessed the invasion was at hand, she was uncertain of the date.

She threatened Schenck with horrible retributions if any harm came to the prisoners. Then she sweetened the pot with a bribe. Two million francs if the prisoners were released immediately.

She could have been shot on the spot. Or tortured. Instead, Schenck received word that the invasion forces had landed. That sealed the deal. He put Christine in touch with an SS officer who would get the prisoners out in return for his safe conduct out of France. Christine radioed SOE in Algiers and the funds were dropped in the next day. Schenck got his money, and the SS officer, a Belgian, freed the prisoners and brought them to Christine. She kept her word and got the man out of the area before the advancing troops or the Resistance could get their hands on him.

"She told Schenck to hightail it out of there," Drake said, wrapping up. "He didn't listen. He was killed a short time later, probably by the Resistance. Nobody knows where the money got to. Maybe that wife of his?"

"Maybe," I said. "You never know."

"Perhaps you can ask her tomorrow," Laurent said. "In Digne. I understand Christine Granville, or rather Krystyna Skarbek, will be there. Baron, she is a fellow Pole. A countess, or at least her mother was."

"I shall be pleased to make her acquaintance," Kaz said.

"You know her, Colonel?" I asked.

"No one really knows Mademoiselle Granville," he said. "A woman most *extraordinaire*."

CHAPTER TWENTY-TWO

"HAVEN'T SEEN YOU since yesterday," I said to Laurent as story time broke up. Kaz had invited the colonel to dine with us, but he'd demurred, and Kaz had gone to check on our table. "Have you discovered anything useful?"

"Only that you appeared to be more persuasive with Inspector Vigot than I," Laurent said. "How did you accomplish that?"

"We gave him a look at the names Cathedral gave us. Turns out he wanted one of them himself and considered it a fair trade," I said. "Which also told me he never thought Drake was the guilty party."

"I agree," Laurent said. "It was most likely a salve to his superiors. I wonder what he will do now?"

"He hasn't asked you about Jean-Paul?" I said.

"What about him?"

"He was here when Dickie was killed," I said. "Baptiste at the bar confirmed Jean-Paul was in the bar talking with Cathedral."

"I wasn't aware he knew him," Laurent said, looking genuinely surprised. "Danton must have brought him along."

"No, it doesn't look like it," I said. "They weren't seen together, but whether that was by design or not, I don't know. Baptiste said Cathedral and Jean-Paul looked pleased with themselves."

"Why they would, I cannot say," Laurent said, his voice tinged with curiosity.

"What can you say about Danton's reason for being at the hotel yesterday morning?"

"As you know, he was part of Cathedral's *maquis,* before going off to the Vercors. And they are related, I believe. Quite natural he would wish to see him," Laurent said.

"The two of them were still with Cathedral and his men at Falicon this morning," I said. "Aren't they supposed to be on a mission?"

"Yes, I would have thought they would be on their way by now," Laurent said, rubbing his jaw. It looked like something wasn't adding up, but he stayed silent on the subject. "But I do recall Danton mentioning something about recruiting for more scouts."

"He wasn't recruiting anyone up in Falicon," I said. "What exactly have you been up to since Dickie was killed, Colonel?"

"Captain, I am distraught over the death of Major Thorne," Laurent said, doing a good job of not looking upset at all. "But I have many duties to attend to. I spent much of the time at the French Second Corps headquarters using their radio facilities. Where I now must return. Enjoy your dinner, Captain."

Well, that didn't tell me much, but it did give me an idea. Time to make a call of our own. I found Kaz and Drake perusing the menu and discussing the selections in French, with Kaz speaking slowly and tossing out the occasional correction.

"You sound like a native, Corporal," I said as I joined them.

"He possesses a decent accent," Kaz said. "The words will follow."

"I'm thinking of staying," Drake said, setting the menu down. "After the war."

"How come?" I asked.

"Because Jim Crow never made it over here," Drake said. "I can walk into a nice hotel, get a room, a drink, and a meal. All without using the side door or being turned away like I'm a piece of trash. It's not like I've never heard a remark about the color of my skin, but the French don't go all crazy over it. They don't pass laws keeping the Negro down, you see what I'm sayin'?"

"Yeah, I do," I said. I'd learned a lot from my pal Tree, back in Boston when we were kids and not long ago again in England. Life wasn't easy for a Negro in the States, and the army wasn't any better. Worse in some ways. "You have family back in Detroit?"

"My daddy's dead a few years now. My momma lives with my sister and her husband. They'll take good care of her. But back home—that doesn't have the same ring for me. I want to be a free man, not wondering if some white guy is gonna come up against me and get away with it."

"I wish you luck," Kaz said. "If I am unable to return to Poland, I think France would make a fine new home."

"Well, I'm going home to Boston," I said. "You fellas are invited to drop by anytime."

"Now that we've settled on our postwar plans, we should order dinner," Kaz said.

"First, could you make a phone call?" I asked. "See if you can get Inspector Vigot to meet us early tomorrow morning. I'd like to get a look at that call register."

Kaz looked disappointed as he waved the hovering waiter away and left to make the call from the lobby. Drake reviewed the menu offerings for me, and all I could do was believe him and pray this wasn't another joke at my expense.

"That was excellent timing," Kaz said as he returned to the table. "I caught the inspector just as he was leaving. He is done with the telephone register and agreed to drop it off himself."

"He's going to let us take a look?" I asked.

"Oh, yes. When I told Vigot we were dining at the hotel, he said he'd heard good things about the chef. Apparently, the Hôtel St. Georges is attempting to regain its reputation, starting with their kitchens."

"The inspector will be dining with us, then?" Drake asked.

"Of course," Kaz said.

"See? That's another difference between France and the States," Drake said. "Back home, I doubt I'd be having my supper with the cop who arrested me the day before."

Vigot arrived fifteen minutes later, the thick volume tucked under his arm. He greeted Drake as if they were pals, apologizing for the necessity of his overnight stay in the cells. Drake rattled off something in French. Kaz and the inspector responded with laughter, and we moved on to the most important business.

Ordering. There was a lot of consultation with the waiter, who appeared to think each selection better than the last. I asked Kaz to order for me, trusting he was done with practical jokes for the day. Finally, after Vigot had a glass of wine before him, he set the ledger on the table and opened it.

"Gentlemen, there were very few calls made to or from the rooms your group occupied that day," Vigot began. "The hotel staff log all calls, whether from other rooms, the lobby, or an outside line. There were two calls."

He turned the ledger around so we could see, his finger underlining the entries.

"See here? A call was put through from the lobby to Colonel Laurent, forty minutes before your meeting was to begin," Vigot said. "Unfortunately, the staff does not record the name of the caller."

"That has to be Danton," Kaz said. "Billy found the two of them in the lobby shortly before the meeting."

"I'm not sure about that," I said. "Laurent made a point to say he'd run into Danton unexpectedly."

"Either the colonel was misleading you, or someone else called him," Drake said. "What was the other call, Inspector?"

"Again, from the lobby, but this one was to the room occupied by Major Thorne. It was placed minutes after you checked in," Vigot said. "I have spoken to the switchboard operator, and she cannot recall anything about the voice. A man, but nothing else."

"You were right, Billy," Kaz said. "Dickie must have let his killer in."

"No. I mean, I was wrong to think it was one or the other," I said. "A call would be just the thing to distract him. The phone rings, and he stops. Turns toward the telephone, which puts his back to the bathroom hall."

"A knife thrust by a pro, and it's done," Drake said. "Hang up the phone, and it's all over."

"Yes, I thought the call may have been a ruse," Vigot said. "The timing works perfectly. But this is of little help. It tells us nothing."

"It tells us that Colonel Laurent has something to hide," I said. "I bet it was Danton who called him, and that he had something important to say. That was no chance meeting in the lobby."

"Reporting on his successful killing of Dickie?" Kaz asked.

"Maybe," I said, trying to think through the lies and deception. "But what was the motive?"

"You said Danton spoke angrily about the SOE and betrayal," Kaz said. "Perhaps Danton was in league with Laurent to take revenge on members of the SOE?"

"And started with Dickie, who's been in Crete for the past few months? It doesn't add up," I said.

"Just because Danton was angry with the SOE doesn't mean he murdered Major Thorne," Drake said. "A lot of those guys were bitter. They felt they were left to face the Germans alone in the Vercors."

"This is true," Vigot said, sipping his wine. "Everyone expected an invasion soon after Normandy. Local Resistance groups were called upon to make acts of sabotage. Naturally, this was in support of the invasion on D-Day. But many thought it heralded landings here. Every day, people looked to the sea."

"I heard things in Algiers," Drake said. "There were arguments about what to do when the Vercors uprising was announced. The Resistance kept asking for heavy weapons, anti-tank stuff, and Allied parachute troops. But the Allied high command never planned for such a huge operation. And no one in Algiers expected the Maquis du Vercors would announce a free republic."

"Yes, it was a deliberate provocation," Vigot said, nodding sadly. "I think the Resistance thought it would force the Allies to rush to their aid. Instead, it brought the Boche."

"There were a lot of arms drops," Drake said, sounding like he needed to defend the SOE and OSS. "The Army air force even sent in over seventy B-17s at low level in daylight to drop canisters of bazookas and other arms to the Resistance on the Vercors plateau. I know, since I got pulled in to haul the weapons to the airfield."

"Oh, yes, it was a grand show, they tell me," Vigot said. "All those huge bombers dropping hundreds of bright white parachutes. It drew the attention of the Germans, most definitely. They followed with their own aircraft, dropping bombs and strafing wherever they saw those white markers on the ground."

"Which is why the Maquis du Vercors used the silk for their

armbands," I said. Suddenly the white silk left by Dickie's body became much more important.

"For remembrance," Kaz said. "To never forget who was responsible."

"The German assault was brutal, even by their standards," Vigot said. "They employed SS troops, along with Russian and Ukrainian volunteers, even some French fascists. The worst of a very bad bunch. The village of Vassieux, where many parachutes had landed, was destroyed. Civilians were tortured, then killed. *Un massacre.*"

Waiters swarmed the table, setting down plates with great flourishes. Mine was grilled lamb chops surrounded by greens. We stared at the dishes, each man unable to break through the images of death and horrors to begin the meal.

"Thank you, Lord, for the food before us and bless us with your tender mercies," Drake said, his head bowed. "Amen."

CHAPTER TWENTY-THREE

"WE HAVE A long drive and a full day ahead of us," Stewart said the next morning. The hotel had put out a breakfast spread of rolls and croissants in the bar for us, with plenty of coffee. Just the thing after a night of tossing and turning, trying to figure the angles on who wanted Dickie dead. Something was nagging at me, and I knew I had to stop trying to tease it out of my tired brain. All that did was drive it down deeper into my subconscious. "Colonel Harding will give you the details."

"I'll be going with you as far as Digne," Harding said. "We're recruiting additional scouts to accompany our units as they push into the Vosges near the German border. The OSS detachment with Seventh Army is desperate for more scouts and guides, so we've put out the word to Resistance groups asking for anyone who is familiar with the area. They'll take any volunteers up to Seventh Army."

"We have a large number of *maquis* who are bringing us names of collaborators, so it will take a while to conduct all of our business," Laurent said. "Once we have the volunteers in place, we will start with our investigation, which may take two days."

"There is also a humanitarian effort underway," Stewart chimed in, unable to resist the limelight for long. "The Special Operations Executive has sent representatives to make cash contributions to families who suffered because of helping their agents. There are many who lost their homes and lives."

"This mission has the blessing of General de Gaulle," Laurent offered. "While he has prohibited SOE from conducting any further operations on French soil, that decree does not apply to humanitarian efforts in liberated areas."

"We already have a number of names out to the authorities, and the search is on," Stewart said. "I understand Inspector Vigot is about to make his first arrest. It is an excellent start, but one sadly marred by the senseless death of Major Thorne. We leave in twenty minutes, gentlemen."

"So glad he spared a moment for Dickie," Kaz said, nibbling on a croissant. "Senseless, he says."

"There was sense in it, we just need to understand who it made sense to," I said, grabbing a cup of coffee and heading for Laurent.

"Colonel, I wanted to catch you before we headed out. Yesterday you said you were going to check on Danton and Jean-Paul," I said. "Find anything?"

"Yes, I did, Captain. Danton was diverted to Digne to help recruit more scouts. It was thought that a Frenchman would help in recruitment efforts," Laurent said. "Quite logical."

"I guess so. What about Jean-Paul?"

"That is somewhat different. Jean-Paul is overdue for his assignment. He should have reported to his superiors in Chaumont by now. He has not, and he is not with Cathedral any longer," Laurent said. As he spoke, he looked to the side, avoiding my eyes. And the truth.

"What is it you're not saying, Colonel? How do you know who is and isn't with Cathedral?"

"Come," Laurent said, his hand on my arm, leading me into a corner of the bar. Kaz caught my eye, and he moved in our direction, coffee cup in hand, ready to intercept anyone who barged in.

"This is unofficial," Laurent whispered. "No one else here knows. Please respect that, Captain."

"As far as I can, I will," I said.

"Danton is my informant. We at *Direction générale des études et recherches* received word of a plot against the SOE a month ago," Laurent said, watching the flow of people in the room.

"Danton called you with information the morning of Dickie's murder," I said.

"Yes, he did. All he could say was that Jean-Paul was planning something with Cathedral, but he did not know what it involved. His first guess had been the black market, but that morning he told me it involved the missing francs in Digne. He had no idea Jean-Paul was also at the hotel."

"You trust Danton?"

"Yes. It was he who reported that the plot originated with survivors of the Maquis du Vercors. There are many more scattered throughout southern France. Those who came to Algiers were willing to carry on the fight by working with the OSS and SOE. Not all are."

"Because the Allies didn't come to their aid," I said.

"Yes. But Resistance people know the SOE well, better than your OSS. It was SOE on the other end of the radio in Algiers who failed the *maquisards*, as they saw it. But it is less widely known that some senior French officers were also against sending aid. That is the real reason the Maquis du Vercors were flown out of Algiers so abruptly."

"They were close to learning those names?" I asked.

"Yes. Too close, which accounts for the sudden departure. I needed to be sure contact was broken between those men and an unknown source within our own government. Now my job is to find the ring-leaders and protect SOE personnel in France."

"But there are only a handful left, correct? No more operational groups by the order of General de Gaulle," I said.

"*Exactement.* There are still a number in administrative roles, and the humanitarian missions Colonel Harding described. Also, several SOE officers have been transferred to the regular forces and are now serving in our nation. Major Thorne was but the first victim. I had not expected them to strike so soon, and against a man who was never part of any operations in France. I had all the men who came to Algiers with Danton vetted thoroughly, including Jean-Paul. None were seen as threats," Laurent said. "But I fear we may have been wrong." I could see one way he'd been wrong. Where better to study your enemy and pick targets than at the Algiers headquarters of OSS and SOE?

"Why didn't you say anything?"

"Orders, Captain Boyle. The new French government does not wish the embarrassment of brave Resistance men turning on our allies. Allies that we need, very much more than we admit, I must say." This

time Laurent drilled me with his eyes. Now there was more he wanted
to say.

"You shot at us," I said. "With a silencer, from behind those trucks.
You timed it with the explosions on the demolitions range."

"Yes. I hoped it would alert you to the possibility of a traitor. I am
sorry to have come so close to Lieutenant Kazimierz. Please give him
my apologies. I know you keep no secrets from the baron."

"The matchbox from the Fleur de Sel, in Digne, which we found
in your room, that was a clue as well?" I asked.

"Of course. I hoped it would spur you to investigate the café. You
didn't miss the symbolism of the broken match, did you? In any case,
we have information that one of the suspects, a Resistance fighter
with the *nom de guerre* Octave, frequents the café and uses it to receive
messages. Octave may well be the leader, but we have no idea who
he is."

"Colonel, it was nice of you to try and tip us off, but I have the
feeling you're also using us as your stalking horse," I said.

"Ah, the hunter's ruse. Perhaps so, Captain. But remember, behind
the false horse is a man with a weapon. I have one more thing for you,"
Laurent said, withdrawing a photograph from his pocket. "A picture
of Jean-Paul, taken when he arrived in Algiers. It was flown in yesterday. I have already confirmed with Baptiste this was the man he
saw. The staff at the desk could not say."

"Thanks," I said. "No picture or description of Octave?"

"No. He was with the *maquis* in the Vercors, but we have not been
able to find anyone who fought with him. They are all in graves, high
in the mountains. He is a ghost, so stay alert, my friend. Commander
Stewart may be next."

"What was that all about?" Kaz asked as Laurent strolled off. I filled
him in on the news.

"Astounding," Kaz said, absently running his hand through his hair
where Laurent's bullet had almost given him a new part. "Although I
understand the French keeping this a secret. A plot against the SOE,
should it succeed, could weaken de Gaulle's government. They depend
on the Americans and the English for everything that keeps their army
in the field. It is a matter of national honor."

"Looks like Dickie was the opening salvo in their war," I said. "He was in the wrong place at the wrong time."

"Let us go, gentlemen," Stewart announced from the doorway. "Drake, bring the jeep around!"

"Why could it not have been Stewart?" Kaz muttered, as we grabbed our bags and followed.

Why indeed? He was the obvious target, a senior member of SOE Algiers Section F, responsible for activities in southern France. He had to have had a major role in the Vercors debacle. It didn't make sense.

"Boyle!" Colonel Harding called out as we assembled by the jeeps. "I've got news, for you both."

"Good news, I hope," I said.

"Excellent news," Harding said. "SOE contacted Seventh Army to ask for transportation and a driver for one of their representatives to work with Christine Granville on distributing funds to families of Resistance fighters. They'll meet us in Digne."

"You gave the job to Big Mike? We could use an extra hand," I said.

"I did. But the icing on the cake is SOE offered the job to Diana Seaton, and she accepted. For once she'll have a safe assignment, and you two can see each other. I also received a radio message from Diana's father. Sir Richard says Angelika is doing very well, and he has a live-in nurse to look after her. So, no need to worry about her, Lieutenant, while Miss Seaton is away."

"Oh, damn," I said. Diana was headed our way, in uniform, as an SOE officer.

"She will be a target," Kaz said, his eyes fixed on mine. "We must warn her."

"What are you two talking about?" Harding demanded.

CHAPTER TWENTY-FOUR

I'D LAID IT all out for Harding. Laurent's real role, his attempts to steer us in the right direction, the mysterious Octave, and the plot against SOE. He'd seen the implication right away.

"Miss Seaton and Big Mike are on the road to Digne right now," Harding said. "At least no one expects them, except for Christine Granville. She's in danger too. Let's go."

We left Nice with Stewart and Laurent in the lead, Drake at the wheel. Harding trailed them, leaving Kaz and me to eat their dust.

"We need to know more about Octave," Kaz said, his voice raised against the sound of the road. "These clandestine names are proving effective. There is no way to check his original identity."

"We have to ask around," I said. "He had to be involved in the Vercors uprising. Sooner or later, someone will recognize it."

"Billy, there were four thousand *maquis* on the Vercors plateau," Kaz said. "That does not even count those Resistance groups who fought on the low ground, blocking the German advance. There were many who worried the plateau could become a death trap and fought only on the approaches. Octave could be one of them, avenging his lost compatriots."

"Needle in a haystack territory," I said, downshifting as we took a sharp, climbing corner.

"Perhaps. The only thing we have going for us is that Octave survived. Nearly seven hundred fighters did not, as well as over two hundred civilians killed in reprisals," Kaz said.

And that Octave was angry enough to take revenge. Angry men

stood out in a crowd, at least until they decided to do more than spit words. We needed to watch for a guy who hung back, watched, and waited for his chance.

"He's looking for retribution," I said. "He must have lost loved ones. Friends, family."

"Again, that might encompass all who fought in the Vercors," Kaz said. "The Germans not only executed civilians, but they burned homes and farms. Women were raped. Captured *maquis* were brutally tortured before they were killed."

"There's plenty there to fuel the desire for retaliation," I said, watching the jeeps ahead slow down. "If Octave can't get at the Germans, he can at least strike against the SOE for abandoning the Resistance."

"I fear we are searching for a man made mad by the cruelty of war. It will make our search quite difficult," Kaz said as the two jeeps pulled to the side of the road. "What is the holdup ahead?"

Harding turned to us and shrugged. All I could see was Stewart unfolding a map. We'd just left the city behind. How could we be lost already?

"Check your map, Kaz, we don't have time for this," I said, driving around Harding and screeching to a halt next to the lead vehicle. Ahead, a truck lumbered down the road, aiming straight for us.

"Get back in line," Stewart shouted, stabbing his finger at the map.

"Commander, we can't take the mountain road," Drake said. "Look, it's all switchbacks and inclines. It'll take forever." Laurent added his assent as Kaz traced his finger on the map.

"We must stay on the main road, Commander, in the direction of Entrevaux," Kaz shouted.

"Look out, man, that truck is bearing down on you!" Stewart yelled, his eyes wide.

"Follow us," I said, but I didn't move. I shifted into first, my feet ready on the pedals, and my eyes on Stewart, who looked close to panic.

"All right! Go!" Stewart ordered, and I let out the clutch slowly, then hit the gas pedal hard. The jeep flew forward as I turned the wheel, slipping into the right-hand lane. The truck rolled by as the driver laid on the horn and shook his fist.

"Bâtard! Idiot!"

"Well, he's half right," Kaz said, once again hanging onto his hat.

"Sorry, but I can't help it. Stewart is fumbling with his map while Diana is headed for trouble, probably all decked out in her FANY uniform." Women serving with the SOE wore the uniform and insignia of the First Aid Nursing Yeomanry. There were thousands of them, working as coders, clerks, dispatchers, training personnel, and most famously, agents. Arriving in Digne wearing the FANY outfit, Diana might as well display a target on her back.

"He can't be that inept," Kaz said, glancing back to be sure they were still with us. "Taking the route through the mountains is absurd, especially if we want to get anything done this afternoon."

"Maybe he's more comfortable at sea," I said, stepping on it. I knew Laurent probably wouldn't reveal his true mission to Stewart, so he and Harding would be hard-pressed to explain my behavior. Not that I cared.

"Do you think Laurent mentioned anything to Stewart about the plot?" I said to Kaz, tossing a suspicious raised eyebrow in his direction.

"Do you think he wanted to be delayed on purpose?" Kaz said. "Because of the danger?"

"I don't know. Just an idea. This wasn't supposed to be a dangerous mission. Maybe Stewart got cold feet when Laurent let slip he might be a target," I said.

"I am not at all impressed by Commander Stewart, but I wouldn't call him a coward without any real evidence," Kaz said.

"Let's just say he's nervous in the service," I said. "I know I am, and Stewart is more used to back strain and paper cuts than bullets."

"Billy, the head of SOE Section F for southern France may not be a veteran of combat, but the post does require a steady hand and a rather ruthless approach," Kaz said. "He makes life-and-death decisions routinely. I don't see him scampering off into the hills at the first sign of physical danger."

"I guess so," I said, nearly convinced. I was probably reading too much into a squabble over a road map. So, I stepped on it.

The roadway cut along a riverbed, with green hills and granite-topped mountains in the distance. We zipped through towns and villages atop hillsides, their tiled roofs shimmering in the sun. The road narrowed as we drove through gorges alongside raging water and spanned gentle streams over arched stone bridges. Beautiful scenery. I hoped to share it with Diana once this was over. At a slower pace.

"Up ahead, at Le Vignon, we intersect with the Route Napoléon," Kaz said after an hour. "That will take us into Digne. We are making good time."

"Why'd they name the road after him?" I asked.

"It was the route he took when he returned from exile in Elba," Kaz said. "It was the beginning of his Hundred Days war."

"How'd that go for him?" I asked, pretty sure it wasn't well.

"Defeat at Waterloo," Kaz said. "Over forty thousand casualties, and it ended in Napoleon's abdication."

"Maybe Stewart was right about a different route," I said.

The miles flew by as we outpaced the other two jeeps. Mountains rose around us, forested peaks looming overhead, alternating with distant glimpses of stone outcroppings. We were still far from the Vercors, but I was beginning to see why this country would be good territory for the *maquis*. Not many main roads, and a lot of deep woods to disappear into.

"Do you think it was a smart idea for the Resistance to declare the Vercors Republic?" I asked Kaz. "No matter how high the plateau, they still had to defend it from fixed positions. Seems like this area would be perfect hit and run country."

"It is hard to judge," Kaz said. "I can understand their enthusiasm, given that Normandy had just been invaded. They thought help was coming soon. I don't think we know what de Gaulle's people told them, but they must have had some encouragement from SOE in Algiers."

"Four thousand fighters on the high ground can put up a good fight," I said, catching a glimpse of a faraway mountaintop wreathed in clouds.

"Yes, but many of them were very recent recruits with no training," Kaz said. "It is a miracle they fought as well as they did. Even though hundreds died and some simply fled, hundreds more melted away into the woods to fight another day."

"From what Vigot said, civilians had it pretty bad," I said, down-shifting on a curve.

"Yes. Part of the German plan was to ruin the Vercors as a base of operations," Kaz said. "That is why they burned out civilians and executed so many. The village of Vassieux was targeted specifically, because the *maquis* were in the process of building a small airstrip nearby."

"Vassieux," I said. "I've heard that name before."

"Yes, Inspector Vigot told us of it."

"No, before that," I said, suddenly remembering. "Jean-Paul told us he was from the Vercors and Vassieux was his home, remember? But he said he was unable to visit his family."

"Merciful god," Kaz said. "He was telling the truth. He is unable to visit them because they are all dead."

"Still, it doesn't tell us much, except that Jean-Paul had a motive," I said. "Unfortunately, it's the same motive hundreds of others could claim."

We wound around a hill, and, on the downward run, Digne came into sight. Nestled in the low ground beneath two rock face crests, terra-cotta roofed buildings clustered around a tall church steeple. The road narrowed quickly as it led us to the center. Stewart had told us we'd be holding our sessions in the town hall and bunking at the Hôtel de Provence nearby. We found both within the shadow of the church spire. The hotel faced a small plaza, and as I parked the jeep, I eyed the vehicles out front. Civilian cars, some of them still equipped with the wood-burning gasogene devices, along with a couple of jeeps and a military truck with French Forces of the Interior markings. Across the sun-splashed square, customers at a café sat at the outdoor tables. I spotted a few army uniforms, but my eye stopped at the table with a honey-haired woman in a brown FANY uniform.

Diana.

I knew she was in jeopardy just being here, but I felt joy as well as fear. The undercurrent of betrayal and danger only fed my desire to see her, to be with her, to hold her.

"Come on," I said, about to break into a run across the plaza.

"Billy, wait," Kaz said. "Do you see the sign? It is the Fleur de Sel, the restaurant Laurent told us about. The one which Octave frequents."

CHAPTER TWENTY-FIVE

"OCTAVE COULDN'T KNOW about Diana coming here," I said. We'd stayed by the jeep, watching the people in the square and those seated at the café. "Could he?"

"Not unless he has a contact within SOE," Kaz said. "And few people in France have ever seen a FANY insignia or know it is associated with women agents. But as soon as Diana makes her first visit to the family of a dead *résistant* and hands out payment, word will spread. Quickly."

"Hey, there's Big Mike," I said, spotting him coming out of the restaurant. Shoulders that wide were hard to miss.

"She will be well protected, Billy," Kaz said. "By all of us. So let us join our friends. I am eager for news of Angelika."

"Billy!" Diana shouted as soon as she caught my eye. She stood as I rushed to embrace her, earning amused smiles from people at the other tables. She smelled of lilacs and clean, fresh air after a rain. I had to force myself to untangle from her arms and not make a scene.

"*Vive l'amour*," a soldier at the next table exclaimed as he raised a glass of wine. I nodded in acknowledgement, noticing that although the uniforms were American, these guys were all French.

"It's great to see you," Big Mike said, shaking our hands like a politician at a county fair. "I was worried they'd never let me out of that damn hospital."

"How are you feeling?" Kaz asked as we took our seats. I squeezed Diana's hand, at a rare loss for words.

"Peachy," Big Mike said with a dismissive wave of the hand. "I had a hairline fracture, but it healed okay. The doc said as long as I don't jump out of any more airplanes, I'll be fine."

"Big Mike has been filling me in on your visit to our Russian friends," Diana said. "Very dramatic."

"Don't believe half of what he tells you," I said, unable to wipe the smile off my face. "But we have other news." I caught sight of Kaz shaking his head and noticed a waiter hovering behind me. He handed us menus and Kaz ordered a bottle of wine. So civilized to dine and drink at an establishment that might harbor a murderer.

"I thought a Grenache rosé would be enjoyable. A local wine, of course," Kaz explained as he watched the waiter depart.

"Now listen," I said, leaning in and lowering my voice.

"Christine!" Diana shouted, standing to wave. "Over here."

A tall, lean, dark-haired woman in the plaza turned and smiled as she heard her name. Dressed in a dark skirt, a thin leather jacket, and a silk scarf knotted at her neck, she looked like an elegant young Frenchwoman. Diana walked out to meet her, and they embraced. I didn't know they knew each other, but why should I be privy to the secrets of SOE?

"That's Christine Granville," Big Mike said. "She's all Diana talked about on the ride here. Except for you, Billy."

"From what we've heard of her, coming in second place would be an honor," I said.

"I assume they are working together on the SOE humanitarian mission?" Kaz asked.

"Yeah, and I'm the bagman," Big Mike said. "I've got French gold coins and British sovereigns in a money belt and stashed in my gear. What's the news?"

There wasn't time. We stood as Diana and Christine came to the table and the waiter rushed over with a chair. I noticed all eyes were on Christine. She had a presence, like royalty walking among commoners. Her eyes, set evenly above a thin, aristocratic nose, darted about, acknowledging a few onlookers, and perhaps searching for threats.

"These are your three musketeers," Christine said after Diana had introduced us. "I am pleased to finally meet you all. Especially a fellow Pole, Baron Kazimierz."

"The pleasure is mine," Kaz said, pulling out her chair for her. The Continental charm was at maximum. "Ours, I should say."

"You three are exactly as I pictured you," Christine said. "Except for Big Mike. I thought she was exaggerating about those shoulders! We shall be in good hands."

The wine arrived amidst laughter and teasing, while I worked at getting a word in edgewise. After it was poured, Christine raised her glass.

"To absent friends," she said.

We clinked glasses and drank. I told the story that Dickie had passed on, about the custom of sloshing liquor into each other's glasses.

"Delightful," Christine said. "This is from a friend of yours, Baron?"

"Yes. He was killed two days ago. Murdered, in Nice," Kaz said.

"By whom and why?" Diana asked.

"That's what we need to talk to you about," I said.

"There you are!" Stewart shouted from across the plaza. He leapt from the jeep as Drake pulled over, and strode to our table. "What was the meaning of that stunt with the truck, Captain Boyle?"

"Commander Stewart," Kaz said, rising and extending his hand in the direction of Christine and Diana. "May I present Krystyna, the Countess Skarbek, and Lady Diana Seaton?"

"Oh, yes, of course," Stewart said, collecting himself in the face of feminine nobility. "Heard of you both. Great things, of course. You are here on a charitable endeavor, I take it?" He looked everywhere but at the two women, probably wishing he could restage his entrance.

"We are here to remember the dead and help their survivors," Christine said. "It is a matter of honor, not charity."

"My apologies," Stewart managed to stammer. "Enjoy your luncheon." With that, he turned and stalked back to his jeep.

"There goes a man subject to sudden fits," Diana said. "Well done, Christine."

"I agree with the sentiment, but I do not think it was what caused Commander Stewart to exit so quickly," Kaz said. "From my seat, I had a clear view of what he spotted when he was avoiding your gaze. That sign."

Kaz nodded toward the pale blue sign above the restaurant window. FLEUR DE SEL.

"Do you know this place, Christine?" I asked.

"Yes, quite well," she said. "One of the waiters joined a Resistance cell and arranged for messages to be delivered here. The café became a drop."

"Coded messages?" Kaz asked. "Where were they hidden?"

"No. Messages in the clear. The owner, Madame Lemaire, has a terrific memory," Christine said. "Nothing was written down."

"Is the waiter here today?" I asked.

"No. He is dead," Christine said. "He was killed three days before Digne was liberated. Why is this café of interest?"

"Yeah, Billy, you were about to tell us something," Big Mike said. "Spill."

"Okay. Dickie Thorne was killed as part of some vendetta against the SOE," I began. "It looks like at least one person from the Maquis du Vercors is out for revenge. Someone who lost friends and family to German reprisals," I said.

"Because SOE didn't come to their aid?" Diana asked. I nodded my assent, checking the other tables to make sure no one was taking an interest in our conversation.

"I can understand it," Christine said in a low voice. "I was on the plateau when the Germans came. We'd been working on an airstrip, preparing for gliders and small aircraft. I'll never forget watching those huge gliders descend, thinking they were British, and then seeing the black crosses and swastikas. That sums up the Vercors, my friends. We expected help, begged for help, prepared for the help to arrive. And all we got were the filthy Boche."

"I have to say, I'm worried about you two getting caught in the crosshairs," I said, looking at Christine and Diana. "You represent the SOE, after all."

"We have avoided the crosshairs so far," Christine said, her voice hard.

"We're armed, Billy. Don't worry about us," Diana said, in a tone that told me to back off.

"What's the deal with this joint?" Big Mike asked, getting us back on track.

"We were warned that the guy behind this plot uses this place to pick up messages. That squares with what you just told us, Christine," I said. "Does the code name Octave mean anything to you?"

"No, but there are so many false identities, it would be impossible to know unless you were a close associate," she said. "That is how it is supposed to work, after all. When the Republic was declared, hundreds of young men flocked to join the fight. Each was told to adopt a *nom de guerre*, and perhaps it was written down, perhaps not. In any case, all records were destroyed in the fighting. It was too dangerous to leave them for the Germans or the *Milice* to find."

"You said Madame Lemaire has a good memory for messages," I said.

"Yes, she may recall the name," Christine said. "I will ask her after the midday meal. I am sure she is very busy at the moment."

"Let's eat," Big Mike said. "Unless you think Octave is inside sprinkling poison into the pot."

As always, Big Mike knew what was important. We ordered the cassoulet on Christine's recommendation, and dove into the food while catching up with each other. I watched Kaz question Diana about Angelika, eager for news about her health. Diana told him about the nurse her father had hired to care for his sister full time, and how quickly Angelika was recovering.

Before being freed from Ravensbrück under the auspices of the Swedish Red Cross, Angelika had been subjected to gruesome medical experiments. Fortunately, they hadn't permanently crippled her, and there was hope for close to a full recovery even though her legs would be forever scarred.

Once Kaz was satisfied with the news, he turned his attentions to Christine and asked about possible mutual acquaintances. The Polish nobility was a small club, one that had few survivors after years of Nazi occupation. As they found they had several friends in common—all dead as far as they knew—they lapsed into Polish and edged closer to each other. Two voices whispered mournfully, a valiant, dying breed on a battlefield so far from their homeland.

CHAPTER TWENTY-SIX

"HOW LONG WILL you be in Digne?" I asked Diana in the lobby of the hotel. "Will I see you tonight?" Kaz and I had stashed our gear in our room and were about to hoof it over to the town hall to catch up with Harding.

"You will," she said. "Sooner than that. We need to get to Madame Schenck and warn her about tonight. Then Christine and I will visit Madame Lemaire and ask about messages from Octave. We don't have much time."

"Let us hurry," Christine said. "We must find someplace safe for Madame Schenck. You can explain more about how you came to be involved in this plot against her on the way."

"Okay," I said, not understanding what the rush was. Cathedral had something planned for tonight, far as I could figure. "Kaz, how about you tell Harding I'll be back in a couple of hours. They won't start the meeting with the Resistance people until he's finished with recruiting the scouts anyway."

"Bah, what a waste of time that is," Christine said. "Not the scouts, that is excellent. But the gathering of names? Nothing but grudges and lies for the most part."

"We think we received valuable information in Nice," Kaz said. "But perhaps things are different here. We shall see. In any case, I will make our excuses to Commander Stewart if he inquires."

"What's Big Mike up to?" I asked as we drove off.

"He's guarding our riches," Diana said. "I think his leg bothers him more than he lets on, so I asked him to watch over our treasury. I can't wait until we've distributed it all. It makes me nervous carrying that much around."

"Take the next left," Christine said from the back seat. "And tell me why you are to take Madame Schenck away."

"Do you know Cathedral? Head of a Resistance group in Nice?" I asked.

"Yes. I heard he was still active, but with the black market," she said.

"He gave us a list of names for Stewart's investigation," I said. "A police inspector said there were some valuable leads. But Cathedral had a price. I have to take Madame Schenck into custody tonight. If I don't, he said he'd spread the word that we couldn't be trusted and not to cooperate with us. Apparently, the French government and SOE both want the mission to succeed, so we agreed."

"And what are you to do with her?" Christine asked. "There. Ahead, bear right."

"Get her out of the way. I wasn't planning on turning her over to anyone, but I wanted to keep my side of the bargain. Cathedral said she was an informer herself."

"Cathedral lies. Right at the fork and then we stay on this road," Christine said. "Madame Schenck had the misfortune to marry a man who worked for the Nazis, but she never did. She was raised here, and most people do not hold her accountable for the actions of her husband, especially now that he is dead."

"But I imagine a lot of people would like to get their hands on the two million francs," Diana said.

"Of course," Christine said. "Greed, it is powerful. I would guess that Cathedral has information as to where the money is hidden and wants any witnesses out of the way. Having you remove her will further shield him from scrutiny."

"So why the rush to get her away?" I asked.

"Because when Cathedral does not find the money, he will move on to more desperate measures," Christine said. "She must be shielded from that. I gave my word to her husband that nothing would happen to him if he helped me. He kept his word but was too foolish to run. His wife inherited my protection, and I will not let anything happen to her."

"Christine, if you know Cathedral won't find the money at the home of Madame Schenck, you must know where it is," Diana said. "Don't you?"

"There," Christine said, ignoring the question. "The house with the blue shutters."

We pulled up to a square two-story house with faded pink stucco and terra-cotta roof tiles. A half dozen fruit trees stood on one side and the other faced the mountains, which were partially wreathed in clouds. Four other houses were a stone's throw away, and I spotted a couple of curtains quickly drawn. Local gal or not, the neighbors were probably right to mind their own business when it came to the widow's visitors.

Christine walked to the side door and called out a greeting to let Madame Schenck know who it was. The door opened, and a stout woman of forty or so emerged, her gaze flickering up and down the road. She and Christine held a whispered conversation that seemed to be about me and Diana and probably our trustworthiness.

"Just a few minutes," Christine said, entering the house with Madame Schenck and shutting the door firmly.

"This is strange, Billy, even for you," Diana said.

"Hey, Christine's your friend," I said. "I'm just along for the ride. How long have you known her?"

"One mission," Diana said. "So, a lifetime."

There wasn't much more to say. We leaned against the jeep, admiring the view of the rugged hills and stony mountains. It was beautiful and quiet, both things in short supply as of late. Standing next to Diana, our shoulders leaning into each other, I felt the strength of her presence in the stillness of the moment. She smiled, and it felt like bright sunshine.

Then the door opened, and Christine escorted Madame Schenck out, carrying a small overnight bag. Diana helped her into the passenger's seat, and Madame Schenck clutched the bag in her lap. She turned to me with an appraising gaze and handed me a key.

"For tonight," Christine said. "She says to be sure to lock the door when you finish."

"I will," I said, starting the jeep, not exactly sure what I would be doing tonight, but confident that Christine would explain it to me.

We drove a bit farther out of town and took a road that quickly turned into a dirt track obscured by overgrown bushes. After a couple of twists and turns, it brought us to a small house with a large veranda. A woman, a few years younger than Madame Schenck, stood on the flagstone walkway, a Sten gun slung casually over her shoulder. She greeted Christine and the older woman with pecks on the cheek. It was smiles all around, especially when Christine dropped two gold pieces into the woman's palm.

"A safe house," Christine explained as we drove away. I started to ask a question but thought better of it. This lady knew what she was doing.

I DROPPED DIANA and Christine at Fleur de Sel and hurried to the town hall. As curious as I was about messages Octave may have left, I knew Stewart might be getting hot under the collar about my absence. Although he downplayed it, he had to be worried about Dickie's killer coming after him. Since it was my job to provide security, he'd have every right to be steamed.

The town hall was an ornate building in the middle of the block, with a wide staircase leading to the main doors. A US Army truck was parked outside and a group of Resistance fighters had gathered around. They were well armed, and I figured these had to be some of the scouts who'd come to offer their services.

There were more of them inside, about ten men gathered around a table with maps of the Vosges mountains and the French territory up to the German border. Kaz and Harding were busy interviewing volunteers, pointing to the maps and working out who knew the territory.

An American lieutenant was speaking with two of the volunteers, peppering them with questions in what sounded like decent French. He wore jump boots, looked to be in good shape, and carried himself with confidence. Which told me he must be the OSS officer who was taking the recruits up to Seventh Army.

I spotted Danton coming in behind me, leading two more fighters to the table.

"Captain Boyle, we have many who volunteer," he said. "Good men, you will see."

"Do they all know the Vosges?" I asked.

"*Oui*. Some better than others. Some the mountains, some the towns," Danton said. "I say to Lieutenant Jack that he should take them in pairs, do you see? To know more of the terrain."

"Makes sense," I said. "Have you seen Commander Stewart?"

"He was here for a moment, making the greeting, then he left," Danton said. "We do not see much of him." I couldn't decide if he meant that as a good thing overall or just the status today.

"How about in Algiers?" I asked. "Did you have much to do with him?"

"No, no. He is very important. We are just fighters in the Maquis du Vercors. There are many of us but only one head of the Section F in Algiers," Danton said.

"Do you know what he thought about sending supplies and reinforcements to the Vercors?" I asked. It still bothered me that Dickie Thorne had been targeted and not Stewart. Wishful thinking, maybe, but it still was a valid question.

"When we came to Algiers, he spoke to us," Danton said. "The *commandant* said he tried to send help, but it was someone else in SOE who decided. Another *département*."

"What about Dickie Thorne? Did he ever mention him?"

"Major Thorne? *Oui*, he said the major had been sent to Crete on a special mission. He spoke highly of him. Was he the one who decided against helping us?"

"No, he couldn't have been. He was in Crete at the time," I said.

"Strange. The *commandant* seemed to think he was sent there a short time ago," Danton said. "But perhaps I was confused."

"Did you ever hear anything about French paratroopers? I was told the French government in Algiers could have sent a battalion of paratroops."

"We heard of paratroopers every day. French, English, American. In the end, all we saw were the Boche in the sky," Danton said. "All we knew came from SOE. We had no contact with our government. Our radios and radio operators came from SOE. That is who they talked to."

"Thanks," I said. "And good luck. You're going north with the scouts?"

"Yes, because I speak the English *parfait. Excusez-moi*, I must show these men the maps," Danton said, perfectly enough.

Harding finished with one man and gave him a form to bring to the OSS second louie. He waved me over and asked what I'd been up to.

"Following up a couple of leads," I said. "We may have a stakeout tonight at the Schenck place. Somebody, probably Cathedral, is after her dough."

"Nice that you want to help her," Harding said with a raised eyebrow, "but why?"

"Every time we encountered Cathedral it was on his turf, with his boys around him," I said. "He'll probably be alone tonight. I'd like to catch him in the act and put the pressure on him. He knows something."

"All right. The other lead?"

"The restaurant we told you about," I said, not wanting to mention the name in case any of these guys were listening. "The owner relayed messages for the Resistance. Kept 'em all up here." I tapped my forehead.

"Keep me posted," Harding said, returning to the maps and his next candidate.

"Billy," Kaz said, a wide grin on his face as he stepped closer to the OSS officer he was talking to. "Come here."

"Captain Billy Boyle," I said, offering my hand and wondering what Kaz found so funny.

"Lieutenant Jack Hemingway," the OSS man said. "The baron tells me you've met my father."

"Yes, we did, outside of Paris," I said. "I can see the resemblance now that you mention the name. Glad to meet you, Jack."

"I hope my old man behaved himself," Jack said. "I heard he was running around with his own private army."

"He was itching to get to Paris," I said, leaving it at that.

"Papa can be a handful, believe me," Jack said. "Hey, what about this turnout? Most of these guys have a good knowledge of the area up north. Danton had a good idea about teaming them up."

"Yeah, he's *parfait*," I said. "How long do you expect this to take?"

"We should wrap up in an hour," Jack said. "I'll wait until morning to make the drive so we can do it in daylight. The roads get pretty rough, and there's rain coming. I'll be dropping most of these guys at Seventh Army HQ and taking a few with me to the 36th Division."

"You with an OSS detachment?" I asked.

"Yeah. We've been attached to the 36th Infantry. Pretty tough going up in the Vosges. Bad weather, steep slopes, lots of Krauts dug in with their backs to their own border. That's why we're getting a few of these guides. Maybe they know a goat path or two around the German lines. See you later, Captain."

"You did not tell him to call you Billy," Kaz whispered, still laughing to himself.

"Sins of the fathers," I said. "But he seems okay."

"His French is excellent," Kaz said. "Rare for an American. Ah, our leader makes an appearance."

Stewart strolled in, hand casually resting on his holster, Drake at his side. A wise precaution, given that a hit man could easily blend in with this crowd. Laurent followed, exchanging greetings with some of the men who were obviously more impressed by a French officer than any of us.

"Quite a good show," Stewart said to everyone and no one in particular as he made a beeline to Hemingway. "Here's the famous Lieutenant Jack. Good to see you again."

"Commander Stewart," Jack said, looking embarrassed, which made me like him better. "I'm not the famous one."

"Oh no, you're famous enough with us," Stewart went on. "Do you know, Boyle, that Jack is a world-class fly fisherman? He even carried his rod and reel when he made his jump before the invasion. One of my officers who oversaw the loading of the aircraft came back complaining that he hadn't been told about the new radio antenna Jack had been issued. He told me it was disguised as a fly rod! That's when I knew what Lieutenant Hemingway was up to."

"Good fishing in those limestone hills," Jack said. "I couldn't resist."

"Living off the land, eh?" Stewart said, clapping Jack on the shoulder. "Now, tell me, how many qualified men have you?"

"We should have at least twenty," Harding said, interrupting the gushing Stewart. "It'll be another hour or so until we finalize things."

"Not much time left in the day to start our proceedings, Colonel Laurent," Stewart said. "Shall we begin in the morning?"

"Agreed," Laurent said. "I will inform those who are already here."

"Very well, I shall leave you to it. Jack, perhaps you'd like to dine with me at the hotel? Drop by at seven or so. I'll be in the bar," Stewart said.

"My pleasure, Commander," Jack said. He looked like someone who had less than a nodding acquaintance with pleasurable experiences.

"I'm looking back at the motor pool with a new fondness," Drake said in a low voice as he brushed past me, following Stewart out. I could only smile and be glad I wasn't pressed into service as a dinner guest or a bodyguard.

"I'm going over to the café to see what Diana and Christine came up with," I told Harding.

"Let us make our own dining plans before we are invited to join Lieutenant Jack," Kaz said, giving Hemingway a wink.

"It's not nice to make fun of senior officers," Harding said, "especially when another senior officer is present. Get out of here."

"I'm gone, Colonel," I said, holding up my hands in surrender. Outside, I found Colonel Laurent passing around smokes and talking with the volunteers. I stopped, trying to pick up the thread of the conversation. All I understood were the words Cathedral, Jean-Paul, and Octave. The first name got a few nods, not surprising since Cathedral was a well-known leader along the coast. I joined the group and showed the picture of Jean-Paul but got nothing but unknowing shrugs. Same for Octave.

"No luck," Laurent said. "Several have heard of Cathedral and his network. Some have friends named Jean-Paul, but not as a *nom de guerre*. Octave they do not know. But perhaps the lessons of secrecy stay with those who fought underground, do you think?"

I told Laurent I agreed. There were plenty of reasons to keep quiet about things done during and just after the Occupation.

"How do we know Octave isn't one of these men?" I said.

"That is what I am looking into," Laurent said. "I know a few of these men by sight. I have asked them to vouch for those they know. It is not uncommon to take such precautions."

"Any results?"

"I can trust fourteen men so far," Laurent said. "I am waiting for confirmation from DGER in Algiers on the rest. Each man had to give information about his network as well as his real and clandestine names, so it will be easy to check."

"How are you in touch with Algiers?" I asked. None of us were equipped with radios.

"The same way France has been in touch with Algiers for several years," Laurent said. "Morse code. We had a DGER group in Digne, and our radio now has a place of honor in the office of the mayor."

"A French radio," I said. "Not SOE."

"Correct. DGER was able to maintain a few contacts for intelligence and political purposes, but nothing on the scale of SOE. We simply did not have the resources."

"But your groups are still functioning, unlike SOE," I said.

"*Certainement*," Laurent said. "When General de Gaulle ordered SOE to cease combat operations, most personnel left their radios behind. The locals who fought with them switched to the *Forces françaises de l'intérieur* or simply went home, thinking their job done. The SOE radios are probably gathering dust in attics, useless now that clandestine communications are no longer needed."

"Tell me, Colonel, how was secret radio contact maintained between the Vercors and Algiers? Who exactly was replying to messages from France?"

"It depended, Captain," he said. "The leadership of the Resistance, via DGER, would be in touch with the French government in Algiers, of course. Even London, at times."

"So that would be exclusively French, right?"

"Yes. But each individual network would have had its own radio operator and codes for communicating with SOE in Algiers," Laurent said. "After all, it was the English SOE that supplied the radio and the radio operator, as well as arms."

"And it was SOE that turned down requests for assistance," I said.

"My government was also slow in responding," Laurent said. "But we had relatively little aid to offer, as I mentioned. It was SOE that could have provided real help. Look at the supply drop with the American B-17s. When our people saw that, they wondered why it wasn't done every day, and why the bombers didn't strike the Germans attacking them. There were many questions left unanswered."

"Here's one more question. How were the SOE personnel in Algiers identified?"

"By code name, of course."

"So the SOE staff at headquarters would be anonymous to those in the field?"

"Perhaps," Laurent said, taking his time to think it through. "Although agents who were trained in Algiers would know the people there in some cases, especially the radio operators. It is hard to be exact."

Someone had been very exact, but about the wrong person.

CHAPTER TWENTY-SEVEN

I FOUND CHRISTINE and Diana as they were leaving the Fleur de Sel. The air had grown cold, and the late-afternoon sky was steel gray. The outdoor tables stood empty, chairs tipped against them. The look on Diana's face matched the weather.

"Madame Lemaire is frightened," Diana said, shoving her arms into a raincoat. "She went white at the mention of Octave."

"Then said she'd never heard of him," Christine said. "Only to say a minute later that he was dead. This is not a woman who frightens easily. She served the Boche in the café while she passed on messages to *résistants* in the kitchen."

"She was fighting in a cause worth dying for," I said. "But now, why die over a name? Does she have any family?"

"Her husband died years ago. One son joined the FFI and is fighting in the north. The other, her youngest, was wounded and is recovering at home. A threat against him would be most effective," Christine said, folding her arms against the chill and glancing skyward.

The sky looked ready to break open. We hustled to the hotel and made it to the door as the rain came down in slashing torrents, and lightning crackled in the distance.

"Big Mike should be rested enough," Diana said. "Should we set him free?"

"I think so. I'll get him and make arrangements with the manager," Christine said.

"What arrangements?" I asked Diana. "I thought he had to guard the gold."

"The hotel has a safe," she said, smiling. "Big Mike would not have stayed put if he didn't have to guard the briefcase. We'll just say we didn't know they had a safe."

"Are you really worried about him?" I asked as we headed for a secluded table in the restaurant. It was early for dinner, but a few drinkers were gathered around the bar, making enough noise to cover our conversation.

"He had a bit of a limp, which he refused to admit," Diana said. I held out a chair for her, but she preferred one that put her back to the wall. Some habits will never die. "He's probably fine, but I wanted to be sure he could rest. I don't know what Big Mike would do if they gave him a medical discharge."

"Funny," I said as I took my seat. "Most guys would give anything to get back home."

"What about you, Billy Boyle?" Diana said, leaning forward with her arms on the table and smiling, her hazel eyes drilling into mine. "Aren't you homesick for Boston?"

"Not at the moment," I said, taking her hand and kissing it. We were interrupted by a waiter. Diana ordered a bottle of wine and told him several more guests were expected. "Whenever I do think of home, it's all before the war. Before everything changed, you know? But it can never be like that again. We're different now. The people who never left home, they've changed too. Who knows what home is even like?"

"I understand," Diana said. "Being at Seaton Manor was like traveling back in time. It was comforting, but all the memories came with me, so the comfort only went so far. Memories of Daphne were everywhere, from family photographs to her clothes still folded neatly in the bedroom drawers. And of course, with Angelika there, it was a constant reminder of the war with all its horrors. And the occasional miracle."

"She's really doing as well as you told Kaz?"

"Yes. She's still in pain, and I didn't dwell on that, but there is hope. Father brought in an excellent nurse, and we took her to see some skilled physicians," Diana said. "I hope you and Kaz can come visit when this is all over. You must be due leave."

"That would be great," I said. "I know Kaz is eager to get back to

Angelika. And I wouldn't mind a few long walks in the countryside with no one shooting at us."

"Charming notion," Diana said. "Is Big Mike still seeing Estelle? The WAC in London?"

"No. She was transferred out. He was pretty beat up about it for a while, but that's the war for you. You make friends and then they're gone. Dead or sent away."

"Don't go away, Billy," Diana said, avoiding any mention of death. Bad luck.

"I won't," I said, with the surety of lovers who are running low on collateral. "I promise."

"Such a sweet lie," Diana said, pulling me closer and kissing me.

"Hey, you two, do your smooching on your own time," Big Mike said as he entered the dining room with Christine. "I'm hungry."

"It's early," Diana said, glancing at her wristwatch. "A bottle of wine is on its way, though."

"But we must eat now," Christine said, "if we are to stand watch at Madame Schenck's."

"Maybe you ought to fill me in," Big Mike said as he took his seat. "I thought this was supposed to be a cakewalk. Speaking of cake, let's see a menu."

We ordered food as soon as the wine was poured. With Big Mike, it was always better to get the important stuff done first.

"Start from the beginning, Billy," Diana said. "You told us Major Thorne was killed by someone upset about SOE not coming to the aid of the Vercors Republic. But what has that to do with Madame Schenck?"

"Okay. When we arrived at SPOC, someone took a shot at us," I said.

"Wait, what's SPOC and where is it?" Big Mike said.

"Start from the very beginning," Christine said. "Tell us every detail."

"Well, I guess it started in Crete," I said. "No, wait. It goes back farther than that. Palestine, 1941, I guess, although it can't have anything to do with all this. But here goes."

I told them the story of Dickie Thorne at the SOE demolitions course run by Stewart at the Haifa base in Palestine. About how Stewart offered Dickie's services as a security officer and how that went south when the Jewish militia got in and swiped a truckload of rifles, sending Stewart's career into a tailspin.

"I didn't know any of this until I was sent to Crete to find Captain Thorne," I said. "His radio was out, so I brought in orders for him to leave Crete to be part of this operation under Commander Stewart. He refused to go until he completed a planned raid, which was almost his last. Thorne thought it was strange that Stewart wanted him as his number two man since he'd always blamed him for the debacle at Haifa."

"It had been three years," Diana said. "Maybe Stewart thought it was time to forgive and forget?"

"He doesn't strike me as the type," I said, continuing with the details.

"Kaz was waiting for us in Algiers. Turned out he and Dickie were chums from their college days. As soon as we got to SPOC—the Special Project Operations Center—which was the new joint SOE and OSS headquarters, someone took a potshot at us.

"Turned out it was Colonel Laurent, trying to warn us of a plot against the mission," I said, going over the silenced pistol and the matchbox clues. "Remember, he's not part of SPOC. He represents the French government, and they don't want anything to interrupt the support the French army gets from both the British and the Americans. He was under orders not to reveal what he knew, since the French want to avoid any hint of a falling-out between allies."

"It is in his interest for the plot not to succeed, or at least not be made public," Christine said. "Since the French wish to end the war with a strong army, and they cannot do that without armaments from their allies. The problem of the Vercors Republic once again."

I agreed and returned to events at SPOC. Stewart gave Dickie a promotion to major, making a public spectacle of it. I went over what we knew of Stewart's postwar political plans until the food arrived, and we all went silent as Diana ordered another bottle of wine. This was thirsty work.

I picked up the story with the Maquis du Vercors being trained by

Corporal Drake at SPOC. That necessitated a diversion into Drake's story, and the fact that he was from Detroit, which piqued Big Mike's interest.

Then back to the *maquis* and their white silk flag and armbands. Danton and Jean-Paul, one of them here and one of them missing. Cathedral with his list of names in Nice, and Danton meeting him at the hotel the morning Dickie was killed. Jean-Paul's appearance there as well, witnessed by the barman, and the subsequent disappearance of Jean-Paul, who hadn't reported for his assignment.

"What else do you know about this Jean-Paul?" Big Mike asked. I told him he was experienced with explosives and that he came from the village of Vassieux in the Vercors, which meant his entire family was most likely dead.

"Oh, and I forgot," I added. "Courtesy of Colonel Laurent, we know that a *résistant* code-named Octave is supposedly behind this, but nobody knows who he is or what network he was a part of. He did use the café across the square as a message drop, but the owner is too scared to say anything."

"Okay, so two of the *Maquis du Vercor* were at the hotel," Big Mike said, spearing a piece of grilled sausage. "But how does that connect to the Schenck lady in this burg?"

"Cathedral's list of turncoats was good, but he had a price. We had to get Madame Schenck out of the way," I said. Diana mercifully took over so I could start to eat. She gave a brief recounting of Christine's Digne bluff and the delivery of two million francs to Schenck, alluding to the possibility that Christine knew where the dough was hidden.

For her own part, Christine sipped at her wine and smiled.

"So, someone tipped off Cathedral about the money," Big Mike said as he set down his cutlery. "A payoff. Nice is his territory, right? He fingers Thorne, or maybe does the job himself. Octave or whoever gets his revenge and Cathedral gets the money if he can find it without being spotted."

"We will stop him," Christine said. "I do not want Madame Schenck to be worried about treasure hunters. I want to send a message that she is to be left in peace."

"There you all are," Kaz said, shaking the rain from his jacket and pulling up a chair. I moved so he could sit next to Christine. "I thought the line of volunteer scouts would never end." The waiter appeared with the second bottle of wine and a glass for Kaz, who ordered a meal.

"I've been reviewing the case," I said. "From Haifa to Nice to Digne."

"We're gonna stake out the Schenck place tonight," Big Mike said. "Grab Cathedral and make him talk. We'll find out who Octave is."

"Admirable," Kaz said, tasting the wine. I couldn't tell if he meant the red wine or the plan. "If Cathedral even knows who it is. It occurred to me this afternoon that it could be any of the men who signed up today. I think Commander Stewart thinks the same, since our friend Drake has not been allowed to leave his side."

"We might get lucky tonight," I said, thinking through the possibilities with this new batch of unknown fighters in town.

"Perhaps," Kaz said. "What did you all think of Billy's summation? Any ideas?" His eyes were on Christine, but it was Big Mike who spoke up.

"Reminds me of a story," he began. "The Westside Mob in Detroit was run by Joe Tocco. This was during Prohibition. Anyway, they butted heads with the River Gang, run by the Licavoli brothers. Now Joe Tocco wasn't the easiest guy to get along with, and he made a lot of enemies. So everyone was surprised when he made peace with a mob gunman name of Sam Gianolla. Gianolla had taken out one of Joe Tocco's boys on orders from the Chicago mob. It wasn't personal, and Joe couldn't hit back without bringing down the wrath of Sicily on his head. But Joe took it personal, know what I mean?"

"He never forgot," Kaz said.

"Nope. Joe Tocco waited for the right time. He knew the River Gang was gonna make a move on his territory. He makes up with Sam Gianolla, makes him one of his right-hand men. He even gives him a car, a shiny blue Cadillac. He takes him around to fancy restaurants, makes sure everyone knows all is forgiven."

"And Sam is suddenly a target," I say.

"Yep. Remember, Sam was a killer. The River Gang knew they had to eliminate him to get to Joe Tocco," Big Mike said, taking a swig of wine. "Joe had it all set up, though. He had an inside man with the

River Gang. He passed on where he and Sam would be dining one night. Joe never showed up, but Sam did. He pulled up to the joint in his shiny blue Cadillac. They counted fifty-two bullet holes in the thing."

"What happened to Mr. Tocco?" Christine asked.

"He went to the Chicago bosses, told them the River Gang was outta control, and open war would be bad for business," Big Mike said. "That was the end of the Licavoli brothers. Joe Tocco came out smelling like a rose."

"He killed two birds with one stone," I said.

"In Poland, we say you roast two pieces of meat on one fire," Christine said. "But however it is said, Mr. Tocco was very smart. He eliminated an enemy by using him to avoid an attack on himself. As your Commander Stewart did, perhaps?"

CHAPTER TWENTY-EIGHT

MAYBE IT WAS telling the story from the very beginning that did it. Recognizing that the origins of this investigation did stretch back to Haifa and the bad blood between Thorne and Stewart. The recall from Crete. The promotion and the bombast that went along with it, dropping hints that Thorne had been involved in the decision not to support the Vercors Republic.

When all along it had been Commander Gordon Stewart.

I needed more than a gut feeling, though. I needed proof that Stewart put Dickie Thorne in danger on purpose. For that, I needed to find the bastard who'd killed Dickie.

The other bastard.

"You are a genius, Big Mike," Diana said. "And a good storyteller."

"I won't deny either," he said. "But we still gotta nail this Cathedral character and figure out if any of these Fifi guys are in on it." Big Mike used the shortened nickname a lot of GIs favored for the FFI forces.

"If Stewart set up Dickie deliberately, it would be one of the most cowardly things I have encountered in this war," Kaz said. "We must find out. And Stewart will pay, if it is true."

"I have an idea," Christine said, laying her hand on Kaz's arm. "One that might help determine if other *résistants* are involved. Piotr, didn't you say the scouts filled out paperwork?"

"Yes. Twenty-two were accepted out of more than thirty. They were asked to give their real name and address, as well as any *nom de guerre*," Kaz said. "I doubt Octave would use his code name, but perhaps,

Christine, you could review them? See if you know of any we should investigate?"

"You think they'd give their real names?" I asked.

"They are to be paid," Kaz said. "So, it is possible."

"Not a bad idea," Big Mike said. "Sam has all that stuff?"

"Yes, and he is still at the town hall. Perhaps you and I could review the materials, Christine? Unless you think we all need to stake out the Schenck residence," Kaz said.

"There is a chance it might be useful," Christine said, her eyes narrowing as she studied Kaz. "Remember, not every fighter was with an SOE network. Some joined companies that sprang up spontaneously when the Vercors Republic was announced. But I might be able to spot a questionable application, yes."

"Here comes Stewart," Diana said, her eye on the entrance to the dining room. The commander walked in, chatting away with Jack Hemingway as Drake trailed behind. I watched Kaz stare at Stewart, his hand moving to the knife by his plate.

"See that lieutenant with Stewart, Big Mike?" I said, giving Kaz a kick under the table. This wasn't the time, and especially not the place. "Look familiar?"

"Vaguely," Big Mike said. "He's a big guy. Can't place him though."

"Lieutenant Jack Hemingway," I said. "Papa's boy. Want to say hello?"

"Hell no. One Hemingway per war is my limit," Big Mike answered. "Is that Drake?"

"Yeah," I said as I waved Drake over. "Jack seems okay. He's OSS, attached to the 36th Division."

"Corporal Drake," Kaz said as he and Christine rose from the table. He first introduced Diana and Christine. "And this is our colleague, First Sergeant Mike Miecznikowski."

"I've heard a lot about you, Sarge," Drake said. He stood straight, not quite at attention, but wary. "Pleased to meet you."

"Same here. Take a load off, kid, these two are about to scram. What part of Detroit you call home?"

"Good luck tonight," Kaz said to me as he and Christine donned their jackets.

"Lock up when you leave," Christine said. "Madame Schenck has a flowerpot by the back door. Leave the key there. Good night."

"I grew up in Black Bottom," Drake said as he took a seat, glancing back to Stewart and Hemingway.

"I'm from Poletown," Big Mike said. "Detroit wants to make sure you know where you belong, eh?"

"And where you don't," Drake said, with an easy laugh.

"You still on duty?" I asked.

"Stewart said I should grab some dinner, then I was free. I guess the commander feels safe enough with Lieutenant Jack around. The French guys love him," Drake said. "He speaks the language like a native."

"Do you speak French, Corporal?" Diana asked.

"Some. And I'm learning. I might hang around a bit after the war's over," Drake said. "I've gotten used to walking in the front door, if you know what I mean."

"Black Bottom isn't the prettiest neighborhood around," Big Mike said. "But it's the only place they let Negroes live in Detroit."

"Used to be Jews and all sorts of other immigrants lived there," Drake said. "They passed through, but we got no place to go. I grew up in a wood-frame house with three other families, no running water or electricity. These days, in an American city. Can you believe that?"

"You leaving any family behind?" Big Mike asked.

"My momma lives with my sister now, in a real house, outside Chicago," Drake said. "Don't have much to go home to."

"Well then, good luck to you," Big Mike said, raising his glass. "Get some food into you, Corporal, we got a job to do tonight."

"What are the baron and Christine up to?" Drake said.

"I'd say roasting two birds over a single fire," Diana said, "if I have that right."

"Right enough," Big Mike said, as Drake looked on, confused.

THE HEAVY RAIN had turned to a steady mist that spattered on the jeep's canvas top. After only one wrong turn, Diana and I managed to navigate back to Madame Schenck's place. The three houses closest to it showed lights on, gleaming a dull yellow in the gloom. We turned around and made for a narrow path off the road, barely wide enough for the jeep. I pulled off the path and parked under the branches of a spreading chestnut tree. The jeep was well hidden, invisible from the road. No problem unless Cathedral decided to hide his own vehicle in the same spot.

It was fully dark, whatever moonlight there was obscured by the low, dark clouds. I turned up the collar on my field jacket, and the four of us ran toward the house, staying low in case Cathedral was running ahead of schedule and hiding under the fruit trees.

"We should check it out," Big Mike said. "See if the place has been broken into."

"And the grounds as well," Drake said. "No telling where he's going to look."

"Okay," I said. "I'll try the doors and windows. You keep a watch here while I circle around the house."

"I'm going with you," Diana said, withdrawing the Walther PPK .32 automatic she'd stashed in her raincoat. It was thin and deadly, the perfect weapon if you didn't want an unsightly bulge to ruin the drape of your clothing. "You need someone to watch your back."

I couldn't argue with that. With Diana close behind, I darted to a window on the side of the house. My face pressed against the stucco wall, I tried to see inside through the rain-soaked glass. All I could see was a murky darkness.

I whispered to Diana that I was going to try the front door, and to stay low at the corner of the house so we wouldn't give a nosy neighbor two silhouettes to spot. I ducked under a window and made for the doorway. I squatted next to the three steps that led up to it, thankful for the cover of the dark shadows.

I listened. A dog barked in the distance. Far-off thunder rolled against the mountains. I could hear my heartbeat and my rapid breaths. But nothing from the house. Silence had settled into its bones.

I reached for the latch and tried to turn it. Locked tight. I scurried back to Diana, and we went around the back, peeking into windows. All quiet. I checked the door with the flowerpot next to it. Around to the other side and back again to the small orchard.

"Nothing," I said to Big Mike and Drake. "If anyone's inside, they locked up after themselves and are keeping quiet."

"We'll scout the perimeter of the grounds," Big Mike said. "Along that wall in back and behind the shed." Madame Schenck kept a garden, and what looked like a toolshed stood about ten feet beyond it.

Big Mike and Drake pushed off, going around the small orchard to the stone wall behind the house. I lost them in the darkness, then picked them up as Big Mike crossed in front of the shed. I saw him opening the door and Drake checking out the inside. A few minutes later they were back, reporting nothing unusual.

"But that shed has shovels and a pickaxe," Drake said. "If someone's digging for buried treasure, that stuff could come in handy."

"We'll keep an eye on it," I said. "You three give me five minutes, then go to the back door."

I ran to the steps and unlocked the front door, easing myself in and locking it carefully behind me. As quiet as I was, the noise was enough to alert anybody inside the house. I did a fast check of the downstairs, then crept up the stairs, pistol at the ready. The stairway opened into a wide sitting area filled with junk. Boxes, lamps, and all the usual stuff that ends up being stored away and never used again. Two bedrooms faced each other. Both empty.

I went into each bedroom, checking the armoires and even looking under the beds. Nothing. A framed photograph sat on one dresser. A wedding picture, far as I could make out. Madame Schenck smiling in her white dress. Her husband looked handsome. Did he plan to become a collaborator? Did she know he harbored pro-Nazi beliefs? Who knows? War pushes and pulls people in every possible direction. Some are willing to bend, to go along. Others resist the pull of easy answers. Schenck tried to have it both ways, and almost made it. I didn't feel bad for him, not one bit. But I trusted Christine, and if she said the good madame deserved to walk away with the big payoff, so be it.

I replaced the photograph carefully and went downstairs to let everyone in.

We decided one person should stand watch upstairs to gain a better vantage point. Then one person in the kitchen, which offered a good perspective of the rear and a view out a side window. Then another in the front parlor, which would cover the front and both sides.

"Then one person circulating in case anyone needs to be spelled," I said.

We agreed Drake should take upstairs, since he was thin and light on his feet. If Big Mike came running down the stairs, it would probably alert Cathedral at fifty yards. Diana offered to take the front and suggested Big Mike for duty in the kitchen, which required the least moving about, although she was nice enough not to say that.

"Romantic, isn't it?" I whispered to Diana in the parlor. "Rain-streaked windows in the French countryside. Guns drawn, watching for shadows."

"You do need leave, Billy," Diana said, her eyes on the ground outside. "I must speak to Colonel Harding."

"I wouldn't mind a view of the English countryside, minus the weaponry," I said. "It's been a while since I've seen Seaton Manor."

"There will be rain, that I guarantee," Diana said. "Peace and quiet as well."

It had been a while since I'd had any kind of relationship with peace and quiet, and I was looking forward to renewing their acquaintance. I went upstairs, treading lightly on the steps. Drake reported nothing was moving, but the nearest house had already gone dark. Perfect conditions for Cathedral. I watched out the second bedroom window while he was in the other. I could see the shed out back and the stone wall before it faded into darkness. The mist had cleared, and thin lines of moonlight were beginning to break through the clouds.

Down in the kitchen, Big Mike was leaning against the wall by the side window. He shook his head, signaling nothing was moving.

"It could be soon," Big Mike said. "The lights went out in that house over there. Our man could be here already, waiting for all the neighbors to hit the hay."

"That's what Drake said."

"Kid seems pretty sharp," Big Mike said. "Had to be for a Negro to get into the OSS."

"Is his neighborhood as bad as he said?" I asked.

"Black Bottom? You know it. If you were getting off the boat from eastern Europe in 1880 or so, you might say it was the promised land. But nothing's changed, except the place is more run-down," Big Mike said. "Colored folk got nowhere else to go if they want to stay in Detroit. Worth it to some for the jobs."

"Nowhere out of town, but close to all those factories? Ford, Chrysler, General Motors?"

"I told you about the Black Legion, didn't I?" Big Mike said.

"Yeah. Guys who thought the Ku Klux Klan wasn't tough enough on Negroes," I said.

"Right. Before they was busted up, they had members in every police department and town hall in the area. Hell, the Detroit police chief was one of them. Anybody who made trouble, black or white, got a one-way ride courtesy of the Legion. Their main enforcer was an ex–Detroit cop. Peg Leg White, they called him. No one could touch him."

"Sounds like a reign of terror," I said.

"Things are better these days," Big Mike said. "But I can't blame Drake for not going back. It won't be all roses for him here, but it's gotta be better than Black Bottom."

I thought it would be hard to leave home behind, no matter how bad home was. But then I remembered my family leaving Ireland behind. Escaping hunger and oppression to start a new life. I guess that ship can sail both ways.

I barely heard Drake come down the stairs in a rush.

"Out back, by the shed," he hissed. "Two men."

I rushed to the window, trying to spot them.

That's when I heard the scream.

CHAPTER TWENTY-NINE

"YOU TWO STAY here and cover us," I said to Drake and Diana. "Could be a trap." They nodded. All we knew for sure is that someone let out a scream. But was it an attack, or a ruse?

"Be careful," Diana said at the door. I told her I sure as hell would. Drake nodded from his post at the kitchen window. I touched Diana's hand as I scooted out the door, thinking what a damn shame it would be to take a slug in front of the woman I love.

Big Mike and I began by scouting close to the house, then expanding our search in ever-widening circles, always keeping the house in view in case somebody tried to get at it. The scream sounded like it came from the back, but it could have come from anywhere. Sound is tricky that way. You can think you're heading for the source, but find it's really at your back. Which is a problem when the last sound you heard was a shriek.

At the edge of the fruit trees, I tapped Big Mike's arm and motioned for us to kneel. I cupped my ear and swiveled my head, signaling that we should stay put and listen. Even the sound of boots on thick grass and rustling clothes can drown out whatever noise your quarry is making. We went silent.

A light wind working its way through the trees.

Big Mike's steady breathing.

The faraway hoot of an owl.

My beating heart.

Rock falling on rock.

"There," Big Mike whispered. "The stone wall." We ran low toward the wall beyond the shed, drawn by the distinctive clattering sound of a rock falling from its place. I was right behind Big Mike, trying to see what was ahead in the darkness. He was running fast, and not for the first time I wondered how such a big guy could be so light on his feet.

Off to my left I saw a blur of movement, someone headed for the house from the direction of the stone wall. I slapped Big Mike on the back and turned, watching for another sign. I lowered my pistol to my side, and Big Mike, understanding, did the same. Drake or Diana could have left the house for some reason.

The blur returned, carrying with it the sound of boots hitting the ground. Then a flash of white, no, two flashes of bright white bounding away toward the road.

Two deer, their white tails taunting us as they fled. I could hear Big Mike stifling a laugh. They'd knocked a stone making the jump, probably heading for Madame Schenck's garden. But it wasn't deer screaming minutes ago, so it wasn't all that funny.

"Come on," I whispered, and we moved toward the garden, skirting it to come around to the back of the shed. I was beginning to think we'd heard the dying screech of some woodland creature, and this was all a wild goose chase. I stopped at the end of the garden, and once again, we knelt to listen. Big Mike leaned down to put his head next to mine.

"Maybe all four of us should search," he whispered. "We got nothing."

I heard footfalls, and my first thought was more deer had jumped the wall.

Something hit me. Big Mike, I think. I heard the smack of bodies and ended up under him, hearing a grunt and a yowl. The grunt was from whoever hit us, and the yowl was mine.

"Billy!" Big Mike shouted. I could feel arms and legs disentangling around me as I scrambled to find my automatic, which I'd dropped in the collision.

"Here," I said, which didn't make any sense, but I didn't know how to respond. I was seeing stars, but they were in addition to the ones in the heavens above. I laid my hand on metal and grasped my pistol, trying to stand and figure out how many of us there were.

I heard footsteps again, going fast, going away.

"The wall," Big Mike gasped, getting up and running to the stone wall. I followed, reaching him as he took a flashlight from his pocket and set it on top of the wall. "Stand aside."

He switched on the light, and we both scooted to the side and got low against the wall. Two shots rang out, missing us, but marking the shooter's position by the muzzle flashes. We fired and vaulted the wall, sprinting across the field. The ground sloped downward, and we stopped at the bottom where a trickling stream marked the lowest point. Beyond it a stretch of woods loomed even darker than the night.

"We'll never get him in there," Big Mike said. "But he'd get us."

"Right. You okay? What the hell happened, anyway?"

"The guy must've been running for the wall and didn't see us crouched down. Slammed right into me," Big Mike answered.

"You get a look at him?"

"All I saw was a knee."

"Hey down there!" Drake shouted from above, waving the flashlight at us. "What happened?"

"That's what we said," I muttered as we followed the beam of light uphill.

We explained what we'd encountered, and Big Mike had to mention the deer in addition to the collision.

"That might have been what kept him here so long," Diana said. "He might have thought those were men roaming the yard."

"Do you think that was Cathedral?" Drake asked.

"Could have been," I said. "But then who screamed?"

"Bambi?" Big Mike said.

"Okay, let's look around," I said, wishing we could just forget about the deer. "Might as well use the flashlight."

"A few lights went on across the way when the shooting started," Diana said. "But the houses are dark now. People have become immune to gunshots in the night."

"Can't blame 'em," I said. "I'd rather be home in bed. Let's look around."

Drake swung the flashlight in long arcs as we walked along the wall. When we reached the next property, we turned around and moved closer to the house, making a sweep of the area near the shed and the garden.

"What's that?" Diana said. The flashlight beam played over a dark hump in the grass behind the shed. As we drew closer, the outline was unmistakable.

A body.

Drake shined the flashlight on it and was rewarded with glistening dark red.

"Who is it?" I said, looking at the nearly ruined face. All I knew for certain was that it wasn't Cathedral.

An arm moved, as if in response to my voice. I'd been sure he was dead, but life still stirred in his battered body.

"*Mon ami*," I said, kneeling at his side.

"Who did this?" Diana joined in, asking in French.

The response was slurred, but his hand clawed at mine. I grasped it and squeezed. There was something frantic and final in his movements. He knew his injuries were grave.

Diana knelt and took his other hand, murmuring comfort in French. He seemed to smile, although his eyes seemed focused on the heavens above.

He spoke, softly, in a rambling French I couldn't pick up. Then I heard "Octave," followed by his last rasping breath.

"He's dead," Diana said, taking his hand and placing it on his chest. I took his other hand and did the same.

"What did he say?" Big Mike asked.

"He said he'd been a fool," Drake answered. "Then 'Octave,' then nothing."

"Let's take a look at what did it," I said, pulling down his eyelids. "Shine the light on him, he won't mind."

"Look at that," Big Mike said, as Drake focused the beam on the dead man's face. There was a sharp bruise and broken skin on his cheekbone. "He took a hit right there. That would have made me scream."

"And here," I said, turning his head. The back of his skull was matted with blood. That had been the killing blow, the swelling of blood in his brain killing him in what—half an hour? Might have been even less since we'd heard the scream.

"Looks like someone took a run at him from behind," Drake said. "He heard him, turned, and took the first hit in the face. Screamed, fell most likely, and then got that whack on the skull. Any blunt object woulda done it."

"Yeah," I said. "His killer thought the job done, then waited until he realized it was only a couple of deer stomping around. He took off, barreled into us, and that was it. We better check this guy's pockets, just in case."

"It's been done," Big Mike said, as the flashlight played over the turned-out pockets of his jacket and trousers. "No clues. No nothing."

Another dead man, and not a clue to be had.

Octave was clearly the one calling the tune.

CHAPTER THIRTY

"WE CAN'T LEAVE him here," Diana said. "Madame Schenck would come under suspicion." I had to agree. The fact that she hadn't been present wouldn't make any difference to those who'd be happy to pressure her for the location of the hidden cash.

"There's shovels in the shed," Drake said. "We could bury him in the field. No one would know."

"We could," I said. "But we might be heard. And even if he was in cahoots with Octave, he may well have been in the Resistance. He deserves better."

"Unless he's the guy who killed Thorne," Big Mike said, shining the light on the dead man's face. "Look at this."

There was a scar above one eye, and it cut right through the eyebrow. A match for the guy Drake had spotted on the staircase coming down from Dickie's room.

"Right," I said. "His size and hair color matches the description, and that scar is pretty unique."

"Let's leave him in town, somewhere he can be found," Diana said. No one had a better idea, so that's what we did. Right after I left the house key under Madame Schenck's flowerpot.

It was a cramped ride back. We left the corpse at the base of a fountain in the small square near the hotel. An early riser would spot it and call the *gendarmes*. He'd get his grave with military honors, if he was indeed due them, and his killer just might get spooked enough to make a mistake.

It was well past midnight when we shuffled into the hotel lobby.

Big Mike and Drake got their room keys, and the night manager gave me a note instead. It was from Kaz, asking me to find alternative lodgings for the night.

"Don't tell me you didn't see that one coming," Diana said in reaction to my surprise. "Now I wonder where you might find alternative accommodations at this hour?"

It didn't take long to figure out. The champagne in an ice bucket in Diana's room was a nice touch, along with the note from Christine saying she had news, and we should meet at eight o'clock for coffee.

We made good use of the champagne and the few hours of night left to us. Stolen hours, but at least we had them to steal, unlike so many others in this war who'd had all their hours taken, the living and the dead. People buried or turned to ash on the wind, people huddled in the shadows of ruined buildings mourning the loss of loved ones, people shattered in mind and spirit. Millions of them, souls beyond counting. Once these thoughts would have sent shivers of guilt through me, but on this night, I raised a glass to what joy we could find and kissed the tender skin of the woman I loved.

WE FOUND KAZ and Christine at a table in the corner of the dining room, hunched over a pot of coffee like it was a warm campfire on a winter's night.

"*Bonjour*," Christine said with a smile. Kaz raised his cup, keeping his own smile at a respectable level. "What happened last night?"

"Coffee," I croaked, and Kaz poured for us. I took one gulp, then another, and felt the familiar jolt kick in. A waiter appeared with a basket of bread and jams. Christine glanced at our coffee pot, a signal for more. Good move.

"Someone showed up," Diana said in a whisper, after her first sip. "Octave killed him. Or at least we think it was Octave."

"What? While you were there?" Kaz asked.

"Yeah. Looks like someone ambushed the guy and then bashed his brains in behind Madame Schenck's shed. We heard a noise, went out to search, and someone barreled into Big Mike and me. Knocked us over and kept on running. Then we found the guy, almost dead. He said he was a fool to trust Octave, then died."

"Octave knocked over Big Mike?" Kaz asked. "Astounding."

"Well, we were kneeling, trying to get a fix on the sound we heard," I explained. "But there's something else. The dead guy fit the description Drake gave us of the man he saw coming down the stairs right after Dickie was killed."

"The man with the scar and the burgundy tie," Kaz said.

"Well, he wasn't wearing the tie, and the scar was covered in blood, but yeah, that guy," I said. Kaz went silent.

I told them what we'd done with the body. Christine approved.

"I think in another day, Madame Schenck can return home," she said. "The neighbors saw nothing?"

"They worked very hard at not seeing anything," I said. "We exchanged a few shots with the guy as he took off, but no one asked questions."

"What conclusion do you draw from this?" Kaz said, tearing a piece of bread into small pieces and nibbling at them. He and Christine sat close enough for their arms to touch.

"It's fair to say Cathedral was being rewarded for his help in Nice," I said. "He was probably offered a chance to grab Madame Schenck's money, which is why he demanded we get her away."

"Then he sent one of his men, who was killed," Diana said. "He obviously knew something. If we could figure out what, it might help."

"The true identity of Octave," I said. "And who exactly was behind Dickie's murder."

"If the dead man was a confederate of Octave or Cathedral, the question remains, why did Dickie let him into his room?" Kaz said. "We have no other information on this man, no indication he was known by anyone involved in the mission."

"Remember, Jean-Paul was also seen at the hotel," I said. "He might have a connection to Octave. We need to find him. Soon."

"It seems there's little to confirm that this Octave is actually alive," Diana said. "He could be a ruse, a red herring to throw you off the track."

"What did you learn last night?" I asked Christine. "Did you know any of the applicants?"

"Yes, several of them," she said. "The men I know personally, I can vouch for. I recognized three other code names and Resistance groups. I have made telephone calls to check on them; however, all seem legitimate."

"But?" Diana asked. All conversation stopped as the waiter delivered a fresh pot of coffee.

"There is one name I am suspicious of. Lucien Rivet, who has worked near Saverne, a town on the northern edge of the Vosges," Christine said. "His code name is Savart."

"Is that from the name of his town?" Diana asked, pouring herself another cup of joe.

"No," Kaz said. "A savart is a unit of measurement for musical pitch intervals."

"Okay, but what does that have to do with us?" I asked, hoping they were keeping their big news until last.

"An octave is defined as the interval between one musical pitch and another," Christine said. "A savart measures the intervals, if I understand Piotr correctly."

"Close enough," Kaz said. "They are both musical terms, with savart the more esoteric, by far. It suggests to me that Octave may have switched code names but chosen one that still reminds him of the world of music, something that must hold importance for him."

"It's a bit of a stretch," I said. "I'm sure France has no shortage of musicians."

"True," Christine said. "But although Lucien Rivet recently lived in Saverne, he listed his place of birth as Vassieux. In the Vercors."

"Same as Jean-Paul," I said.

"Indeed," Kaz said. "Octave and Jean-Paul share the same village of origin, which was destroyed by the Nazis. Jean-Paul may be responsible for killing Dickie. And now, Octave—or Savart—is here."

"But wouldn't Octave be recognized?" I asked, pouring myself more coffee. I needed more caffeine to work this through. "He operated here, picked up his messages at the café."

"We saw how terrified Madame Lemaire was," Christine said. "That may explain it."

"It sounds as if they are working in tandem," Diana said. "One to kill Major Thorne and direct suspicion away from the other. That leaves Octave safe to come here as Savart."

"To kill Commander Stewart," I said. "With Cathedral out of the way, he's got to be next." Stewart was a real bastard, if I was right about how he set up Dickie as a target. But I didn't want him to get bumped off before we had a chance to expose him for what he did.

"Can you identify Savart?" Diana asked as she reached for the bread and jam.

"No," Kaz answered. "I did not take his information. Lieutenant Hemingway interviewed him early in the day. His signature and the time were on the form."

"We've got to find Hemingway," I said. "He was going to organize transport for the scouts up to Seventh Army this morning."

"Is Stewart part of that?" Christine asked.

"No reason for him to be," I said, slathering jam on a piece of bread. "We should check on him. If Savart is pulling out with the other scouts, this morning would be his last chance at Stewart."

"Unless he already has done the deed," Kaz said. "We should knock on Stewart's door to be sure he is alive. If he is not, I will endeavor to hide my joy."

"I hope he's alive," I said. "A bullet would be too quick. I want him to know the shame of a court-martial, for starters."

"If the commander has not taken precautions, then Savart may have an easy time of it," Christine said. "There are still weapons hidden in the hills. Silenced pistols, sniper rifles, and explosives are not hard to find."

"I've heard rumors," Diana said. "Some Resistance groups aren't sure the Germans won't come back. All that talk of miracle weapons has people worried, so I wouldn't be surprised."

"Well, good luck to you both," Christine said, standing as she brushed invisible crumbs from her dress. "We must pack and begin our work." Christine leaned down to kiss Kaz, the two of them holding hands for a few seconds before Christine broke loose, graced Kaz with a smile, and walked away.

"You didn't tell me," I said to Diana, as she stared at the table.

"I will leave you," Kaz said, taking Diana's hand and kissing it. "A pleasure. Stay safe, Diana. Billy, I will check on the commander and return shortly."

"I'm sorry, Billy," Diana said. "It was such a wonderful night; I didn't want to spoil it with talk of leaving. I wanted to be with you, not thinking about parting. Do you understand?"

"Yeah, I do. You're right. It was better not to think about things," I said. "Except each other."

"We must leave now," Diana said. "People are waiting for us and really need our help. It's important that we don't forget them. The families that hid our agents, fed the *résistants*, gave medical care, and sacrificed so much. Some lost their homes, others their loved ones."

"Like the people of Vassieux?" I asked.

"I don't think there's anyone left alive there," Diana said. "But there are many elsewhere. We're trying to help the survivors and show that we remember what they did. That Great Britain didn't just use them and leave them to the horror of German reprisals. It's important work."

"Then go do it," I said, taking her hand as we stood.

"You be careful, Billy," she said, planting a kiss on my cheek.

"No worries," I said. "All we need to do is have Jack point out Savart. We grab him, and crisis averted, thanks to Christine and Kaz."

I walked Diana to the lobby and waited for Kaz as she went upstairs. We'd stolen one night from this war, and I had no idea when we'd find another. At least her mission was humanitarian and would keep her out of the line of fire. And it looked like we were ready to wrap this investigation up.

"*Excusez-moi*, Captain Boyle?" The clerk at the desk waved a note in my direction. He apologized, saying it should have been delivered to my room last night. I opened it, reading that Commander Stewart had set our opening session for 0830 hours at the town hall.

I looked at my watch. It was close to nine.

"No answer from Stewart," Kaz said, coming down the stairs.

"He's already at town hall," I said.

I hoped we weren't too late.

CHAPTER THIRTY-ONE

THE FIRST THING I saw as we left the hotel was that the *gendarmes* were out. One was at the café, questioning people at their tables. The other was walking down our side of the street, notebook at the ready. What anyone here now would know about a body found at dawn, I had no idea. But reports had to be filed, and reports required witness statements.

Kaz and I jumped in the jeep and drove to the town hall. It wasn't far, but we didn't have time to spare. I pulled up as close as I could, looking for any sign of Hemingway or the scouts.

"The FFI truck is gone," Kaz said. "They may have already left."

"Hey! You guys," Big Mike shouted from the town hall steps. "Stewart's fuming that you ain't here."

"Where is he?" I asked. "Right now." I saw Big Mike's expression change. He could tell something was wrong.

"Inside," he said. "Same room we were set up in yesterday with the scouts. They're taking a quick break and he told me to come look for you. What is it?"

"Hemingway and the scouts have left?" Kaz said.

"Yeah, about an hour ago," Big Mike said.

"One of them may be Octave," I said.

"If he's gone, and Stewart is still alive, it means only one thing," Kaz said. "Explosives."

"You guys gotta slow down," Big Mike said. "What explosives?"

"Hidden caches, according to Christine. Insurance in case the

Krauts come back," I said. "We need to tell Laurent and Harding about Lucien Rivet, calling himself Savart. He could be Octave."

"Sam went up to his office on the top floor to get some papers," Big Mike said. "Laurent's in with Stewart and about a dozen Resistance guys. You serious about the explosives?"

"Dead serious," I said, running up the steps, hoping it was more like dead wrong.

Inside, the room was set up differently than yesterday. One head table at the far end in front of the windows. Chairs along the side of the room. A table and chairs set facing the head table. Men standing around, waiting. A couple of women. All of them still with the wary look of the clandestine life about them.

Stewart at the head table, talking to Laurent. Drake positioned in the corner, a good spot for a bodyguard.

Stewart noticed me. His expression went grim as he spit out my name and beckoned me forward with an imperious wave of his hand.

Which he rested on a lectern set on the table.

The lectern was emblazoned with the cross of Lorraine and the colors of the French flag.

The paint was fresh.

This lectern hadn't been here yesterday.

"Clear the room!" I shouted. "A bomb's been reported!"

"*Bombe!*" Kaz said. "*Allez, sors!*"

"What the devil?" Stewart said. I saw his mouth moving, but he was drowned out by the hubbub in the room as people started to leave, urged on by Kaz's windmilling arm. Chairs were knocked over as I moved into the room, a couple of beefy guys shoving me aside as they made for the exit.

"Move!" I shouted, locking eyes with Drake. He launched out of his corner, his eyes darting about the room for evidence of a bomb. I didn't have time to share my suspicions. I focused on Laurent, who was pulling Stewart behind him as they moved too damn slow, pushing aside chairs that had been left blocking the narrow aisle.

I caught Stewart's frantic eyes, saw his mouth gape open, as if he finally understood that his past had caught up with him.

The world shattered.

Searing white.

Sharp hard.

Smashing noise, a freight train passing through me, an iron sledge-hammer to the chest.

Backwards swirling dust.

The ceiling. Falling.

Kaz.

Where's Kaz?

A mouth, open wide, screaming.

Billy.

From so far away, a whisper.

Hands at my shoulders, dragging me.

"Billy!" My ears are ringing, and the word sounds like it's under-water, dull and flat.

Big Mike. It was his mouth. Screaming my name.

"Billy?" A different voice. Kaz. I grab his hand, trying to speak, but all I do is cough up dust. Chalky plaster. I feel their hands on me, unbuttoning my jacket, pulling at my shirt.

I relax. I know what they're doing. Looking for wounds. Shrapnel. Maybe I'm dead, or maybe I will be. I don't know since I don't feel anything. All I need to do is lie here and let them look for what might have killed me. I can see their faces through a gauzy haze of white confusion. They're frantic. In a moment, I'll know. It'll be a sad shake of the head; *he's had it* left unspoken. Or a smile, *he's okay.*

"Billy? Can you hear me? You're okay," Big Mike says, shouting into my vibrating ear. *Of course I am,* I want to tell him. *I saw you smile.* "Stay here."

He pats me on the shoulder. *Sure,* I want to say. *I'm not going any-where, pal.*

A minute later, or maybe an hour, someone gets me up. My legs feel like jelly. They put me in a chair and wash out my eyes with water. The ringing in my ears is still loud, but I can see just fine. Well enough to see Drake taken out on a stretcher, a bloody bandage around his head.

Well enough to see two more stretchers. No need for bandages there. Laurent and Stewart. Dead. Bodies shredded by the explosion. They were too close. Never stood a chance.

Now all I need to do is stand up. Then find the killer.

Both seem damned near impossible.

CHAPTER THIRTY-TWO

I BLINKED. IT hurt. I raised my hand to rub my eyes and noticed the bandages. Wait, where was I? I blinked harder, widening my eyes and trying to work out the dust and grit that seemed to crunch under my lids.

"Hey Billy, you're okay," Big Mike said. He was sitting next to me and placed his hand on my arm. "You're in your room."

"What happened?" I asked. I mean, I knew what happened, but the last thing I remembered was sitting in the town hall and watching a parade of the living and the dead pass me by. "How's Drake?"

"They got him to a hospital. He should be okay," Big Mike said. "You saved his life, and a lot of others."

"Good, good," I said, letting my head flop back down on the pillow. I worked my eyelids some more and managed to get them moist. It felt better, but now everything was hazy. "So, what happened to me? How'd I get here?"

"You tried to stand up," Big Mike said. "Kaz had told you to stay put, and you'd said okay. The second his back was turned, you got up. Didn't work out so well."

"Is that how I got hurt?" I said, raising both bandaged hands.

"Billy, you remember a loud bang? That was from the explosion," Big Mike said, his voice tinged with exasperation. I had the impression I might have asked that question before. A few times.

"Yeah, sure," I said. "I'm still a little groggy, that's all. How bad is it?"

"Splinters and scrapes," Big Mike said. "Nothing too bad. Same as your face. You're lucky you still got your peepers."

"My face?" I raised one hand and touched my cheek. Ouch.

"I told you, leave those cuts alone," Big Mike said, grabbing my hand and forcing it down to my side. "Like I said, you were lucky. Let them heal and don't make it worse."

"Sure, thanks for the reminder," I said. What I wanted to say is what my dad always said when someone called him lucky in a spot like this. *If I were really lucky, I wouldn't be lying here all bandaged up.* But it didn't seem like the right time to act the wiseacre.

"How's Kaz?" I asked. "He get hurt?"

"Naw. We were both out of the room, pulling people through the doorway fast as we could. A coupla the guys got minor cuts, that's it," Big Mike said. "Our ears were ringing for a while, that's for sure. How 'bout you?"

"Yeah, but they're better now," I lied. "Hey, open the curtains, willya? Why's it so dark in here?"

"Billy, it's almost ten o'clock. At night."

"What? I can't hang around here," I said, feeling the panic grow. Maybe it was about letting the killer get away, or maybe it was about half the day vanishing while I was laid out here. Either way, it didn't feel good.

I didn't feel so good either, I discovered as I tried to sit up.

"Big Mike?" I managed to croak. I must have drifted off. My throat was dry, and I had to force my eyelids open. I remembered not to touch them, and I wanted Big Mike to notice.

"He's gone, Billy." It was Kaz, sitting in the same chair Big Mike had been in. "How are you?"

"You tell me," I said. "What week is it?"

"Just past midnight," Kaz said. "Big Mike said you were awake two hours ago. That's a good sign. Do you remember things?"

"The explosion, sure. After that it kind of jumps all over the place," I said. "Drake's okay, right?"

"Yes. We had word from the hospital," Kaz said. "Concussion, a broken arm, and wounds to his back. But he will fully recover."

"And me? Help me sit up, willya?" Kaz put a pillow behind my head and grabbed me by the forearms, staying away from my hands.

"The doctor said you had a mild concussion," Kaz said. "Besides the cuts and bruises, your eyes need cleaning out again. He'll be here in the morning to rinse them with a saline solution."

"I didn't even know I was cut up," I said, holding up my hands.

"Shock, I would think," Kaz said. "You were close to the bomb. As it turns out, there was a theft from a local weapons cache. After word of the explosion got out, a farmer came forward to say he found the floorboards in his barn taken up. A quantity of *plastique* was missing, along with a dozen pencil detonators."

The detonator, better known by its official SOE designation as Number Ten Delay Switch, was a clever device in the shape of a pencil. When one end was crimped at the right point, acid would eat away a wire holding back the striker, releasing it to detonate after the desired delay. Stick the thing in a block of plastic explosive, and you have a ticking time bomb.

"A quantity, you said."

"Yes. He has more, and more detonators," Kaz said. "This was a relatively small charge, considering what could have been hidden within that lectern. It was enough to kill anyone within a ten-foot radius. I think our killer counted on Stewart keeping himself center stage."

"We've got to get after him, Kaz," I said. "Find out if there are any witnesses to that lectern being delivered. Have you asked about that? And Hemingway, track him down and get a description of Savart. There's a lot to do."

"Right now, you need to eat something. Then get back to sleep. We will make a plan in the morning, I promise," Kaz said. "Relax. Colonel Harding is already in radio communication with Seventh Army, tracking down Hemingway."

"His OSS team is attached to the 36th Division," I said. "Contact them."

"We will, Billy. I will be back in a few minutes with a stew the kitchen has been keeping warm for you," Kaz said. He must have thought I was better since he left me alone. I swung my legs off the bed and steadied myself with my bandaged hands. The room swayed a bit, and I gripped the mattress to hang on, which hurt my hand, so I took a deep breath. I willed the room to stop and got up slowly.

Now I was the one swaying a bit, but I got it under control and took a step.

So far so good.

I shuffled to the bathroom, wondering who'd changed me into these pajamas. Best not to ask. I reached out and held onto the door for support and caught a glimpse of myself in the mirror. At least I think it was me. There was a dark bruise by the side of one eye and cuts on both cheeks, along with a scrape on my forehead, made even more horrifying by the dried red rivulets from the application of tincture of iodine.

Could be worse.

All of a sudden, it felt worse, and the room did a Tilt-A-Whirl while I held onto the sink, forgetting the pain in my hands. The ride ended and I let go, only to find myself on the floor. I crawled to the bed on all fours, keeping steady as I noticed small splotches of red seeping through the gauze bandages.

Could be worse, I kept repeating, pulling myself into bed to wait for Kaz. Okay, I could use a good night's rest. I'd be fine in the morning. As long as I could stay away from loud noises and explosions, it'd be okay.

Could be worse. I could be dead, instead of feeling halfway there.

Kaz brought me a bowl of warm stew. I wolfed it down, told him I was feeling a lot better, and let my head hit the pillow with that lie lingering between us.

IN THE MORNING I was able to walk without the floorboards dancing beneath my feet. I washed up, and the face in the mirror didn't look quite as strange as it had last night. A local doctor showed up early, rinsed my eyes out with a saline solution, and changed the bandages on my hands. Through Kaz, he asked if I still had ringing in my ears. I told him it was better, which was pretty much true. His parting words to Kaz were that although my face might scare young children, I'd be fine.

Big Mike showed up with a pot of coffee, Colonel Harding on his heels.

"I hope you don't feel as bad as you look, Billy," Big Mike offered as his morning greeting.

"How are you feeling, Boyle?" Harding said, concern etched on his face. I would have preferred to have him tell me to get the hell out of the sack and back on the job.

"Fine, Colonel," I said. "Just got my bell rung pretty good yesterday, that's all."

"Glad to hear it," Harding said. "I haven't had any word back from the OSS at Seventh Army yet. Too damn secretive, that bunch. I'm leaving right now to see what I can learn in person."

"We filled Sam in about what Stewart was up to," Big Mike said as he poured a cup of joe and handed it to me.

"Hard to believe, but it does make sense," Harding said. "He must've thought he could sacrifice Thorne and satisfy whoever was out for SOE blood. But right now, we need to focus on this bomber."

"We'll go to the 36th Division and see if we can find Hemingway there," I said. "He may know more about where Savart was headed."

"There is even a chance Savart is with Hemingway," Kaz said. "The 36th Division is operating in the area near Saverne, where Lucien Rivet worked. It would be logical for him to be assigned there."

"Good point," I said. I should have thought of that myself. Maybe the explosion had crossed more wires in my noggin than I'd thought.

"You sure you're up to it?" Harding asked me.

"Yes sir," I said. "And we need to act fast. We have one advantage over Savart."

"What's that?" Harding asked.

"He doesn't know we're on to him. There's no reason for him to think we've made the connection about his code names. Once we get a description and know where he's been assigned, we grab him. He probably thinks he's too damn clever to be caught."

It was an advantage, but it wouldn't amount to much if we couldn't pick Savart out of a crowd. He'd been living the clandestine life in the shadows long enough to be on constant alert.

My brains might have been scrambled, but I still could figure the odds.

They weren't on our side.

CHAPTER THIRTY-THREE

I CAN'T SAY I had a spring in my step as we walked downstairs, but at least I stayed upright. I wore freshly laundered clothes and the hotel staff had polished my boots during the night. I'd rewound my bandages so I could flex my hands and use my fingers, like a fighter taping up before the first round. Of course, I looked more like a boxer after the fight, and I noticed a few double takes as I walked through the lobby. Outside, I buttoned my field jacket and turned up the collar. The wind was cold and damp, and the sky was heavy with dark clouds.

"Where to?" Big Mike said as we approached the jeep. He was carrying my duffle and a bedroll for me and tossed them in back next to Kaz.

"Town hall," I said. "I need to talk to witnesses."

"We've already done that," Big Mike said, pressing the starter. "Everyone who was there. Kaz worked with the local cops to take statements. Nobody knew nothin'."

"I don't want to talk to people who witnessed the explosion," I said. "I want to talk to people who were there before that. In the early hours."

"The *concierge*," Kaz said. "Of course."

"Like at the hotel?" Big Mike asked, backing into the roadway.

"In France, it means much more," Kaz said. "A caretaker and janitor who lives in an apartment building, for instance. The *concierge* would not live at the town hall, but his job would not just be to clean. He would oversee all that goes on to keep the building running."

"Like the delivery of new furniture," Big Mike said. "I get it, but why didn't the *gendarmes* question him?"

"They probably didn't know the lectern was new," I said. "Did I forget to mention the paint still looked wet?"

"Yes," Kaz said. "But you may be excused, due to your proximity to the *plastique*. You know, there was an old lectern in the room the day before, plain wood and varnish, with no decorations. The local officials may have thought the bomb was planted in that and not even considered a new one had been brought in."

We parked in front of town hall, next to a pile of construction materials and a truck full of debris from the explosion. Inside, we found the *concierge* in his *loge*, just off the main foyer. The door was open. It wasn't a live-in joint, but it was snug. Cleaning materials were stacked along one wall, and on the opposite side there was a table with a couple of chairs. A short man, beginning to bald but with a thick black mustache, greeted us. He was in the middle of sorting mail and looked startled at our arrival. Or our uniforms. Maybe it was my face, I had to remind myself.

"*Bonjour*," I said, going for a smile to soften my look. It didn't seem to help. Maybe he was the jumpy type. He gave Big Mike a glance and then his hands began to shake.

Kaz stepped forward in the small room, forcing us back. He let loose with a string of soothing French, leaning against the wooden table, and asking the *concierge* for his name.

Henri Poutou.

Kaz questioned him gently, translating for us as needed.

Yes, Henri told Kaz, he did arrive early every morning. Six o'clock. He was the only one here at that hour, distributing morning newspapers to each office and preparing rooms for meetings. Then he opened the doors at seven o'clock when the first clerks arrived. The bosses strolled in later.

No, he hadn't set up the conference room that morning. It had been done the night before. There was no brightly painted lectern when he'd left, he was positive. The morning of the terrible explosion he was busy cleaning the bathrooms, starting on the top floor. Sadly, he had seen nothing of the ground floor.

Yes, yes, he worked long hours indeed. But it was a very good job. Even when the Vichy bastards were in charge. He whispered, perhaps due to years of habit, that he passed on information he overheard when the Pétainist bosses were in charge. The Resistance people at the café, the Fleur de Sel—did we know it?—he told them when he stopped for a glass of wine on the way home. Ask Madame Lemaire, she will agree. Did he not reveal to them that the *Milice* were planning arrests one Sunday this summer at the village church in Tartonne? It was at great risk, but he, Henri Poutou, did his duty as a patriotic Frenchman. Ask them, ask Madame Lemaire, they will tell you.

It went on that way for a while.

Henri stopped, raising his hands in a gesture of exhaustion. He'd told us everything. His eyes darted between each of us, watching for the accusation he was obviously afraid of.

"Kaz, please tell Henri we are certain he did all he could during the Occupation," I said. "We know many *résistants* owe him their lives."

Henri relaxed as the news was delivered. He'd clearly been fearing the worst.

"Ask him if he ever heard the name Octave," I said.

It was like somebody slapped him. But he recovered, shaking his head no. Henri did not know the name. Most certainly not.

"Fine," I said. "One last question. Ask him how he knew about the brightly painted lectern with the cross of Lorraine."

Kaz had been kind and understanding in his questions. Friendly. But this one was different. He stepped closer and spoke in sharp, quick tones.

Henri's mouth gaped, as if he hoped the right words would present themselves to provide an answer. An answer that would absolve him. But that wasn't possible. If he hadn't been in the room, how could he have known about the bright paint and the cross of Lorraine? It had been blown into a thousand pieces, some of them into me.

Henri slumped against the table, shaking his head and moaning. Kaz spoke softly.

"*La vérité*," I heard him say. The truth.

It came easily. Henri had found a note at the main entrance that morning. It was addressed to him, and stated he must leave the front

door and the conference room door unlocked. He must then immediately leave the ground floor and busy himself elsewhere. If he failed
any of this, he would find his wife dead when he returned home.

Henri sobbed, saying he never knew what was intended. But the
note was signed Octave, and he knew of his reputation. How could he
leave his wife to be killed? How could he know there would be a bomb?
What good would it have done to tell anyone afterward? He would
be ruined.

Henri admitted he'd come downstairs even though he'd been told
not to. He always let the clerks in promptly at seven o'clock and
thought it best not to vary his routine. He'd stolen a quick glance into
the conference room, saw the new lectern, and left wondering if
someone had played a bad joke on him.

"How do we know he's telling the truth?" Big Mike asked. I'd seen
plenty of liars, and Henri was too anguished to be spinning a yarn.
Almost as if he understood, Henri shuffled through a worn ledger and
withdrew a folded sheet of paper, handing it to Kaz.

"It is as he described," Kaz said, handing me the note. *Octave* was
scrawled at the bottom.

"What should we do?" Big Mike said, nodding to Henri.

"Nothing," I said. "Just like he did."

We walked away, leaving Henri cradling his face in his hands. Who
was I to judge this man, who cleaned floors and bathrooms, passed on
dope to the Resistance, and feared for the life of his wife? It would be
a simple matter to tell the cops what he'd done, to show them the
threatening note from the sinister Octave. But why? Henri would be
ruined, publicly humiliated, his good deeds forgotten. It wouldn't bring
back Maxime Laurent and it wouldn't heal Drake any faster. Stewart
wasn't even worth thinking about.

"There are many ways for the war to wound people," Kaz said as
he clambered into the rear seat.

"No reason to add to his pain," Big Mike said. "Now let's see if we
can find this farm where the explosives are stashed."

"Let's swing by the Fleur de Sel first," I said. "We can check his
story and maybe get Madame Lemaire to talk."

We pulled up at the café. No one was seated outside, which given the weather wasn't a surprise. But the note on the door was. *FERMÉ.* The good madame was taking no chances.

We followed the directions the local cops had given Kaz to the farm up in the hills where the weapons cache had been hidden. I thought there might be a chance that the proprietor was more involved than he let on. He might've figured others knew what he'd kept hidden and would put two and two together after the bomb went off. The best way to cover his tracks would be to report the theft with great indignation and take whatever consequences there might be. Hard to believe a Resistance veteran would be punished for worrying about a return engagement with the Nazi occupiers.

A winding road soon turned to a narrow dirt track that dead-ended at a house set at the base of a hill. Sheep milled about in a pen next to several outbuildings and a stone barn with a steeply sloping terra-cotta roof.

"Good place to stash weapons," Big Mike said, unfolding his large frame from the jeep. "You'd hear anybody coming up that track easy enough."

"Yeah, it's not how I imagined it," I said, looking around at the rough terrain and paths leading uphill. "Be hard to make a stealthy approach."

A man came out of the barn. He was clad in mud-stained boots, worn corduroys, a threadbare jacket, and a beret. Kaz did the introductions, and the gent didn't blink at my bruises and cuts. He nodded, took a pipe from his pocket, and fired it up. He knew why we were here.

Alain Girac led us into the barn. It smelled like damp wool and manure, not surprisingly. Girac pointed to a stall that had been recently swept out. The floor was a series of wooden planks.

"This is usually covered in hay," Kaz said. "He keeps equipment in here, as well, to disguise the hiding place."

Without being asked, Girac pried up one floorboard, then another, revealing a chamber about six-by-six feet. Empty.

"The police took everything," Kaz told us. "He says they had a better hiding place in the hills when the Boche were here, but it was easier to have everything close by."

"He didn't hear a thing?" I said, my eyes on Girac. He was a tougher customer than Henri. His answer was a shrug followed by a few quick words.

"He says he is a heavy sleeper," Kaz informed us.

"Ask him if the sheep are heavy sleepers," I said. The sounds of *baa baa baa* mingled with a few higher-pitched bleats from the sheep in the pen not too far away.

Another shrug.

Kaz asked if he knew Octave.

Everybody in the Resistance knows of Octave, came the answer. But Girac had never met him, of course. It was safer that way. Less chance of betrayal if captured. Everyone talks, sooner or later, *n'est-ce pas?*

"Ask him if he knows this man," I said, showing the photograph of Jean-Paul. Kaz didn't even have to translate. The look of recognition was unmistakable, even though Girac covered it up quickly.

"Is accessory to murder a crime in France?" Big Mike asked. Kaz put the question to Girac, who answered with a torrent of words.

"If his choice would be to betray Octave or face a tribunal, he would do better by turning himself in," Kaz said.

"We're not going to turn him in," I said. "Tell him all we want is a description of Octave."

Girac couldn't give us one. He admitted the man in the photograph knocked on his door and told him to stay inside. He was held at gunpoint by Jean-Paul while another man went straight to the barn. It was late at night, and he saw nothing out of the darkened windows. Girac didn't know what they wanted the weapons for, or even how they knew of the cache. He was surprised to find only the *plastique* and detonators missing.

"Is he sure it was Octave in the barn?" Big Mike asked.

He was certain. The man pointing a gun at him said his companion would be very angry if Girac made trouble. Angry enough to take Girac's eyes out. It was something Octave had done before.

"Does the name Lucien Rivet mean anything to him? Or Savart?" I asked. No. He didn't know the man and showed no signs of awareness that Octave had assumed that identity.

"Was Octave always so violent?" I asked.

His Resistance cell was known for bravery and a willingness to take risks. All of them, save Octave, had been killed in the Vercors uprising. It was then that Octave began to earn his fearsome reputation. Girac said he was a man to fear.

He said he was sorry.

So was I. Octave still eluded us, and now we knew for sure Jean-Paul was working closely with him. We'd have to watch our backs and all points north.

CHAPTER THIRTY-FOUR

WE HAD ABOUT six hundred kilometers to drive, and we made good time, even as blowing rain coated the roads and beat a sloppy rhythm against our canvas roof. The route was more up than down, the cold increasing with every hour. As we passed through Grenoble, we began looking for supply units. Back in Algiers I'd been given orders signed by both Harding and Colonel Laurent instructing units to provide us with whatever assistance was needed. Right now, that meant warm jackets, gas, and hot food.

And maybe weapons. We were driving toward the front lines, and I'd feel better with a Thompson submachine gun close at hand. Especially since we might find ourselves shooting it out with the Jerries and Octave at the same time.

This section of road ran along a valley floor, so it was straight and smooth. We were behind a line of deuce-and-a-half trucks, which I hoped meant a nearby supply depot. Big Mike spotted the sign.

"Hey Kaz, what's that mean?" he said, pointing to a white sign with blue lettering.

"*Deuxième Corps d'Armee dépôt*," he said. "The French Second Corps supply depot. Which means French food in the mess. Delightful."

We pulled in and handed our orders to the guard at the gate. They were in English, but Kaz smoothed things out and in minutes we were being escorted into the depot. First stop was for gas. They topped off our tank and gave us a full jerrican, strapping it to the rear bumper.

"Next is the haberdashery," Kaz said. Our escort, a young lieutenant with a pencil-thin mustache, waved at us to follow his jeep, and soon we were inside a giant tent filled with shelves groaning under the weight of all sorts of clothing.

"Tell him we're headed into the Vosges, and we need cold-weather gear," I said.

The lieutenant spoke with the supply sergeant, who looked indignant at the thought of handing out his precious supplies to wandering strangers. He shook his head sadly as he perused the shelves, finally returning with two mackinaw coats, the perfect choice. For me and Kaz, at least. He looked at Big Mike and shrugged, then spoke with the lieutenant.

"He says he has nothing large enough," Kaz translated. "But he will do what he can."

We gave up after Big Mike nearly tore the seams on an overcoat he tried on. The supply sergeant must've felt sorry for him since he gave each of us warm gloves, scarves, and a couple of pairs of wool socks. Big Mike got an extra wool cap and a sweater he could stretch to get into. His M43 field jacket would keep him warm with all those extra layers, as long as he didn't have to spend a snowy night in a foxhole.

Grub was next. Our lieutenant said he had to discuss weapons with his superior officer, and we may as well eat while he did. No one argued, least of all Kaz.

On the way there, we passed truckloads of Negro soldiers, as well as columns of dark-skinned men marching along the road.

"*Tirailleurs sénégalais,*" our host informed us. "Part of the 9th Colonial Division. Three regiments of light infantrymen from French colonies in Africa."

"Too bad Drake isn't here to see this," Big Mike said. "I wonder how he's doing?"

"He's at the 21st General Hospital, about twenty miles south of Digne," Kaz said, as the lieutenant led us into the mess tent. "When this chase is over, we must visit him."

"Doesn't smell like French cooking," Big Mike said, wrinkling his nose. "It smells like Spam."

"I forgot," Kaz said. "French forces are completely supplied by the American army. I suddenly have lost my appetite."

"Well, I'm hungry," Big Mike said. "Breakfast was a long time ago."

"An hour since your last meal is a long time for you," Kaz said as we grabbed plates and utensils. The lieutenant left us, and we helped ourselves to fried Spam, lima beans, and potatoes. Kaz went light on everything but took a thick slice of fresh bread to fill out his plate. We each got a cup of coffee, the smell thick and heady in the chill air.

It was late for lunch, and the place was mostly cleared out, so we had one end of a table to ourselves. I ate to fill my stomach, but the coffee was definitely the best part of the meal. Kaz was smart to go with the bread.

Big Mike mopped up the last of his food and declared the meal delicious.

"But you have eaten in some of the finest restaurants in London," Kaz said, leaning back in his chair. "How can you call this food delicious?"

"Because I'm here, and the food's here. This ain't London, so I'll make the best of things," Big Mike said. "Besides, this coffee is better than the joe in England. They don't got the knack for it like the French."

"An admirable approach to life," Kaz said, raising his cup. "And I agree about the coffee. Very good. We must take the best where we can find it."

"You're right," I said, setting down my cup. "We really needed this rest stop, didn't we? For gas and chow."

"You mean Jack Hemingway and his passengers did the same?" Big Mike asked. "Only he didn't have orders signed by a coupla colonels."

"True," I said. "But Jack speaks the lingo perfectly, and he's a Hemingway. The French love his old man."

"He also has two or three Frenchmen with him," Kaz said. "Quite different from the three of us."

"You think Octave is with him?" I said.

"It makes sense," Big Mike said. "You've seen this road. It's the main route to the area the 36th is operating in. There's no other way to go. One tankful isn't going to get you there. Hell, between those Resistance guys and an OSS officer, they'd be able to steal all the gas they needed or talk their way in here no problem."

"Let's ask our friendly lieutenant if he's had other visitors," I said.

"Perhaps we can use their communications center to send a message to Colonel Harding at Seventh Army," Kaz said. "We should inform him of our suspicions."

"Good. We can't make 36th Division, unless we drive through the night, which would be crazy on these roads," I said.

"Division HQ is at Bruyères," Big Mike said, taking a map from his pocket and unfolding it. "If we get a few more hours in today and get some shut-eye, we should be able to get there by noon tomorrow."

"Ah, a hotel along the way," Kaz said. "Real French cooking. Excellent plan."

"Let's focus on finding Octave, okay?" I said, although I did favor Kaz's thinking. "When we get to Bruyères, we can't tip our hand. We don't want word getting out that we're after Octave, or Savart, or whatever he's going by. All we say is we need to speak with Jack Hemingway."

"Sure," Big Mike said. "Be nice to get lucky, though. If Jack stopped here, someone might have laid eyes on Octave. We might get a description." As Big Mike finished, I spotted an officer making his way to our table, the young lieutenant behind him.

"Gentlemen, welcome to our depot. I am Major Cuvier," he said, waving a hand to tell us to remain seated. "You come with most impressive orders, and I am glad to share our petrol and food. But I thought it wise to speak with you myself before handing over weapons. You understand?"

"Of course, Major," I said. "Please join us." I went ahead with the introductions while the lieutenant fetched his boss a cup of coffee, two sugars. He knew what the major liked.

Cuvier and Kaz chatted in French for a while. I could tell Kaz was breaking the ice for us, and I watched as Cuvier warmed to Kaz's cosmopolitan graces.

"Certainly, my friends, you may use the radio," Major Cuvier said. "Now, tell me, what are the weapons for?"

"We are investigating the murder of a French officer," I said. "Colonel Maxime Laurent. He was killed by a bomb, possibly planted by a Vichy fascist masquerading as a Resistance fighter." I thought it best to simplify things and leave Stewart and the Vercors out of it.

"We have two witnesses we need to interview," Kaz said. "Two men who volunteered as scouts for the American infantry. They are not under suspicion, but we need to talk with them. They may not even be aware of what they've seen."

"Ah. Since the men are scouts, they will be close to the Boche, eh? Very well. I will arrange for something more powerful than your pistols," Cuvier said, snapping orders to his lieutenant, who scurried off. "You will be safe for a while, but soon the road north leads to the Vosges. Very difficult terrain. For the attacker."

"That is where we are going, Major," I said. "Have you seen any other Americans passing through today?"

"Yes. We had a visit from the son of the great American writer, Hemingway," Cuvier said. "Lieutenant Jack. A brave and very civilized man. Oh, and the men with him, they were the scouts?"

"Yes sir," I said. "Jack is a good man. We had the good fortune of meeting his father, just before the liberation of Paris. Did you happen to speak with the scouts? There were two of them, I think." Cuvier beamed at the mention of our association with the Hemingway clan, but quickly got back to the subject.

"No, there were three, I am sure. Lieutenant Jack and two men came in here to eat, while the third scout stayed in the jeep, pleading exhaustion. They left quickly, wanting to make their destination before it became too dark. It was very early in the morning, so they should be in Bruyères this evening."

"Was this one of the men?" I asked, showing Cuvier the photograph of Jean-Paul. "Or perhaps he came through separately?"

"No," he said after studying the picture. "He is not familiar."

"Thank you, Major," I said. "That's very helpful."

Kaz went with him to the radio room, while Big Mike and I waited by the jeep for our weapons to be delivered. The lieutenant drove up in his vehicle, loaded for bear. One Thompson, one M1 Garand, and one M1 .30 Carbine. That man had a good eye for matching firepower to each of us. The light carbine fit Kaz perfectly. I took the Thompson, and Big Mike had the M1.

There were bandoliers of ammo and a sack of grenades.

"Kinda makes ya nervous, don't it, Billy?" Big Mike said, arranging everything in back. "The major thinking we need all this."

"He said the terrain was tough for the attacker," I said. "Which means easy for the defender. I hope our scouts survive."

"I hope we survive. Wasn't this supposed to be a milk run? Sunny southern France and all that bullshit? It's cold and damp, and we need all this to talk to a coupla guys to get a description."

"Harding owes us," I said. "Let's hope we live to collect."

CHAPTER THIRTY-FIVE

KAZ HAD GOTTEN a message off to Colonel Harding, telling him we'd be in Bruyères tomorrow morning, and that we suspected Octave was still with Hemingway and the scouts. He'd asked him to contact the 36th and smooth the way for us. A communiqué from a higher headquarters ought to do the trick. Military traffic was heavy on the route north, trucks laden with supplies and men barreling toward the front, with a slower but steady stream of vehicles returning. Some were empty, some carried wounded, the dead already in the ground close to where they fell.

Jean-Paul could be in any of the trucks ahead of us. It was easy enough to hitch a ride, especially if he waved down a Fifi vehicle. Or it would have been easy enough to befriend GIs who would be happy to do a favor for a real-life Resistance fighter. Jean-Paul could be anywhere.

But why, I had to wonder. Why would Octave and Jean-Paul make this journey? It would be easy for them to slip away and create another identity amidst all the confusion of the ongoing liberation of territory. Were they simply picking up the fight against the Germans now that they'd settled their vendetta against Stewart, oblivious to what we knew?

Or did they have another target in mind?

Nothing added up, nothing made sense. Nothing except the small hotel Kaz spotted from the road, which served up decent wine, good French country food, and soft beds. In that order.

■   ■   ■

THE NEXT MORNING, I bandaged my hands again and cleaned the scrapes on my face. My head still hurt and a bruise on my cheek was turning reddish blue, but I told myself I was doing better. After more of that good French coffee, I almost believed it.

The road was smooth for a while, but soon the jeep churned through muddy roads leading to Bruyères. And once, Big Mike had to take a detour through a field to get around a quagmire that had sucked in the wheels of a truck. We weren't the first to cross that field, so the wet soil had already turned into muddy ruts.

Big Mike jammed it into first and gunned his way out of the field, regaining the road and spotting a sign for Division HQ. Bruyères was a small town with a crowded center jammed with vehicles and the wreckage of recent fighting. Headquarters was in a schoolhouse at the edge of town, with a radio section on one side, antennas hidden beneath the camouflage netting.

Inside, the first room off a central hallway housed a group of clerks banging away at typewriters and answering field telephones. I asked one of the GIs for the G-2 office, figuring the Intelligence section would know how to find Lieutenant Jack.

"Your name, Captain?" asked the clerk, barely looking up from his two-fingered pecking.

"Captain William Boyle," I said, handing over my orders. "Colonel Harding may have sent a message from Seventh Army about us."

"Yes sir!" he said, jumping up and scurrying out of the room.

"Either you or Colonel Harding seem to be famous here," Kaz said.

"Or the mention of a higher HQ sends them into a tizzy," Big Mike said.

It didn't take long before the sound of boots from the hallway heralded the return of the clerk with a smartly dressed lieutenant in tow. He was a good-looking guy with wavy reddish-blond hair and good posture, the kind of fellow who made you feel a bit of a schlump.

"Captain Boyle, I'm Lieutenant Lewis, General Dahlquist's aide. Welcome to the 36th Division. How can we help?"

I introduced Kaz and Big Mike, which didn't make much of an impression. Lewis spared them a nod and quickly got back to having eyes only for me.

"We're looking to contact Lieutenant Jack Hemingway," I said. "He's with your OSS detachment. He arrived yesterday with three FFI scouts."

"Jack? Yes, I saw him when he came in. But it was two scouts, not three," Lewis said. "The general would like to see you, Captain Boyle, please follow me."

"Wait," I said. "Only two scouts?"

"The general doesn't like to be kept waiting. Your men can remain here." Lewis ordered the clerk to bring them coffee and told Big Mike and Kaz to have a seat. "Follow me, please, Captain."

Big Mike stifled a laugh as Lewis left the room. There were only one or two possible explanations. Either the general had heard of my many brave deeds, or he'd had me checked out when Harding's message came through from Seventh Army. Not only was Seventh Army two steps above the 36th Division in the chain of command, but Harding was also assigned to SHAEF, which meant he worked for General Eisenhower. A message like that, regardless of the content, was enough to make any general nervous. And if a dutiful staff officer got the dope that Eisenhower was Uncle Ike to me, I could count on a round of glad-handing and horseshit right around the corner.

I'd rather be drinking coffee with Kaz and Big Mike.

"Hey, Lewis, I'm honored to be meeting the general, but I really need to contact Hemingway," I said, following the aide up a flight of stairs.

"He's on a mission," Lewis said. "He left early this morning with Captain Greene, his OSS commander. That's all I know, since the OSS boys live in their own world. Here we are."

Lewis gave a quick knock and opened the door to a large room with a long table strewn with maps. Two officers wearing a lot of brass leaned over them, tracing their fingers across the paper.

"Captain Boyle, General," Lewis announced, then took a step back and went into parade rest.

"General Dahlquist," I said, coming to attention and offering a salute, figuring this situation called for every military courtesy I could think of. Salutes weren't necessary indoors except when reporting to a senior officer. I'd been dragged here, so it wasn't actually reporting, but close enough.

"Captain Boyle," Dahlquist said, returning the salute as his eyes lingered over the cuts on my face. "At ease. This is Colonel Owens, my chief of staff." Owens gave me a handshake and a smile. Friendly senior officers made me nervous.

"How's General Eisenhower these days?" Owens asked, leaning against the table and shaking a Lucky from a crumpled pack. He offered me one and I declined.

"I haven't seen the general in quite a while," I said. "This isn't really a SHAEF operation, we're sort of on loan to a joint SOE and OSS venture. I don't want to get in your way, sir." More like out of their way, and soon.

"Fact-finding for Ike?" Dahlquist asked. He was a tall, thick-faced guy with a long narrow nose and thin eyes. Maybe fifty or so. He looked tired. And irritable.

"Not at all, sir," I said, and launched into a quick description of our mission, and how it had gone off the rails. "We're hunting a Vichy agent disguised as a member of the Resistance who may be in this area." Not quite the truth, but less complicated.

"I did hear rumors about a bomb doing some damage south of here," Owens said. "Killed a Brit and a French officer. Also, that you're Ike's nephew. Any truth to either?"

"You're right about the bomb, Colonel. This guy has killed three good men so far, and we don't know who he's after next. It's connected to the uprising on the Vercors plateau. As far as General Eisenhower goes, there is a very distant family connection. But he's not my uncle. I'm no feather merchant, if that's what you're asking. Sir." I'd been accused before of using my connection with Uncle Ike to land a cushy office job, and I didn't like it much.

"Simmer down, Boyle," Owens said, glancing at Dahlquist. "No need to defend yourself. I have a friend at SHAEF who vouched for you. So much so that we had to wonder why you're here."

"It's nothing more than I said, sir. We're after a suspect, and Lieutenant Hemingway and the scouts assigned to you may have witnessed something."

"All right," Dahlquist said, apparently satisfied I wasn't a spy for the high command. "How can we help you?"

"I need to speak with Hemingway, but Lieutenant Lewis said he's off on an OSS mission, so that will have to wait," I said.

"We coordinated that with Captain Greene," Owens explained to his boss. "They're infiltrating an agent across the front lines. They should be back tomorrow. If they make it."

"Jack drove three scouts up here," I said, worrying about his chances crossing the front lines, twice. "But they didn't all show up, apparently."

"There were two, sir," Lewis said, stepping forward and withdrawing a small notebook from his pocket. "Henri Grandjean and Pierre Poirat. Both very familiar with the local terrain. They were assigned to 1st Battalion and went off with the leading elements at 0600 hours today from Belmont."

"Off where?" I asked, looking at the maps showing steep, wooded terrain. "Sir."

"There's a big push on, Captain. Our assignment is to secure the flank for VI Corps, and I'm doing it here, on this ridgeline overlooking the village of La Houssiére," General Dahlquist said, tapping his finger on the map. "That's the objective, and you can find your scouts there."

"It's an advance of seven kilometers," Owens explained. "Three battalions are attacking, 1st Battalion up front. They should seize the objective by tomorrow night. Once the Germans see we have the high ground above the village, they'll have to clear out of this whole area."

"Any chance I could get to the scouts now, sir?" I asked, knowing what the answer would be. I studied the map, noting the absence of the usual transparent overlay and grease pencil markings showing unit boundaries and the axis of attack. But what I could see was that those seven kilometers went along a ridgeline only two kilometers wide. A killing ground for a dug-in defender.

"Negative, Captain," Dahlquist said. "Don't interfere with my operation. Once the target is secured, I'll drive you there myself. For now, sit tight. Lewis, see to quarters for the captain and his group."

"Of course, sir, thank you," I said, as Dahlquist grabbed his helmet and jacket.

"Come on, Owens, let's get to 1st Battalion headquarters and get a look at the situation," Dahlquist said, thrusting his arms into his jacket. "Then we'll check on the other two battalions and make sure they're moving fast."

"I can contact them by radio, General," Owens said. "I'll have a situation report from all three battalions in thirty minutes."

"There's no substitute for leading from the front," Dahlquist growled. "You don't get things done sitting here. Right, Captain?"

I told him he was right. Generals usually are, in their own minds, especially.

Dahlquist and Owens bustled out, and I lingered at the map table. The topographic lines were so close together in places that the map looked almost black.

"Steep ridges, no roads," I said, running my finger from Belmont to La Houssiére. The village sat on the flat valley floor, a rail line running straight through it. "Can't take the open ground, the Kraut artillery spotters up on the ridge would call down holy hell on them."

"Yes, Captain," Lewis said. "That's why the general wants the high ground."

"Was the briefing held here?" I asked.

"Yes, last night."

"What'd you do with the overlays?" I asked. "Were there written orders?"

"I thought you said you weren't here to spy, Captain," Lewis said. "The general does things his way. He gave the orders, showed his battalion commanders the objective, and left them to accomplish it as they saw fit."

"Don't worry, Lewis, I'm just naturally nosy," I said. "Anyone here keep tabs on the local Resistance groups?"

"Sure. I'll take you down to G-2. They were the ones who requested scouts who knew the area," Lewis said, relaxing a bit as we left the general's office. "We couldn't find any local men. Most of the *maquis* around here are men who'd escaped the Vercors after they were attacked."

We went downstairs to the Intelligence section, but I was left wondering about the encounter with Dahlquist. Lewis said the general left his men to decide how to best achieve their objective. If that was true, why was he running off to battalion headquarters to lead from the front?

Maybe that was just his style. After all, he was a division commander. He had to know what he was doing.

Didn't he?

CHAPTER THIRTY-SIX

"MAJOR COLEMAN CAN answer all your questions about the *maquis* in this area," Lewis said, having explained to the G-2 staff what I was doing here. Thankfully, he left out any reference to SHAEF and Uncle Ike. Away from General Dahlquist, he seemed normal. Almost relaxed.

"Thanks. Just so I understand, you saw the two Fifis who came in with Hemingway yesterday, right?" He had, so I showed him and Major Coleman the photograph of Jean-Paul.

"Definitely not one of them," Lewis said, looking to Coleman, who agreed.

"I wonder what happened," I said. "Jack isn't the type to lose a passenger between here and Digne. He's a steady guy, unlike his old man. The writer, in case you didn't know."

"We're experts around here on writers' sons," Lewis said, cracking a smile for the first time. "I'll get you billeted, now, Captain. Excuse me."

"What'd he mean by that?" I asked Coleman.

"His old man is Sinclair Lewis. The guy who wrote *Babbitt*, ya know?" Coleman said. "Gotta admit, it's a helluva coincidence having two famous writers' sons in the outfit."

"Jeez, I didn't mean to give offense with that remark about Hemingway," I said. "But I have met the man. Ernest, I mean."

"Don't worry about it, Captain, Lewis is okay. Not touchy at all. He knows how to roll with the punches," Coleman said. He had full cheeks, sharp blue eyes, and a retreating hairline. I got the idea he knew what kind of punches Lewis had to roll with working for a guy like General Dahlquist. "Whaddya need?"

"Anything you can tell me about Resistance groups operating in this area," I said. "Particularly any connected with the Vercors uprising."

"Have a seat," Coleman said, motioning to a table stacked with files. "You know the story behind the Vercors Republic?"

"Too well," I said. "We're looking for someone who held a grudge against the Brits and us for not supporting it. Specifically, SOE and OSS."

"That's way above my pay grade, but I know there were plenty of frustrated Fifis around here for a while. Far as I can tell, the German attack on the Vercors scattered the survivors in every direction," Coleman said, leafing through a file. "The units on the plateau were hit really hard. A massacre. But there were companies on the low ground, too, blocking roads. They got chewed up, but not as bad. A lot of them managed to escape in the confusion."

"Some of them fled north, here to the Vosges?" I asked.

"Yeah. With the Krauts and their *Milice* buddies trailing them. Which made it hot for the *maquis* operating in this area," Coleman said. "Plus, we're not far from the German border. The Rhine River is only ninety kilometers from here, and the Swiss border isn't far to the east. Didn't give the Resistance much room to maneuver, so they never developed any major networks here."

"That's why you needed to bring in scouts?"

"Right. There are a few active *maquis* groups, but none are native to the area. We were glad to get those two men," Coleman said. "These woods and hills are treacherous."

"What do you think their chances are? The scouts and your men, of course."

"Good, if they keep moving," Coleman said. "The general promised strong forces would follow on, but I don't know who that would be. Dahlquist's got most of our strength moving up already."

"You sound worried," I said, my voice low and quiet.

"You didn't hear it from me," Coleman said. "All we have in reserve is a tank battalion and headquarters troops. And tanks ain't worth much in those hills."

"Nothing else?"

"Not unless you count the Nisei, and they're pretty damned chewed up," Coleman said.

"Nisei? I thought they were fighting in Italy," I said. The 442nd Regimental Combat Team was made up of second-generation Japanese Americans, most of whom had families living in relocation camps after they'd been forced out of their homes on the Pacific coast. I'd seen an article about them in *Stars and Stripes* a while ago. Their combat record in Italy was second to none.

"They've been here ten days or so," Coleman said. "Dahlquist put them right to work attacking this burg and a small village to the east, Biffontaine. They just were pulled off the line after nine days straight in heavy combat. They're in no shape to get thrown right back into the fight."

"A lot of casualties?" I asked. Coleman only shook his head. He'd said as much as he dared say to an outsider.

"The closest Resistance group is the Maquis de Lamarche," he said, unfolding a map. "They're here, in Grandvillers, guarding a couple of intersections for us. Just take the main road west, and it's the next village. Ask for Adama."

"That's his code name?"

"No. He's from French Sudan. That's his real name, his only name," Coleman said. "The Maquis de Lamarche has a fair number of French colonial troops who escaped capture in 1940 and have been living underground ever since. Adama speaks English well. He's a smart guy. Has to be, to stay alive this long."

"Yeah, I can't imagine the master race cares much about African lives," I said.

"The French aren't that happy about it either," Coleman said. "They brought a lot of colonial troops here to fight, now and back in 1940. But they want to turn their army white as fast as they can. That's why they're getting the FFI forces into uniform toot sweet. I don't think Adama is going to get the offer, even though he's proved himself a capable soldier."

"Major, who's doing the recruiting, exactly?" I asked, wondering if there was any connection to the Vercors.

"Couldn't tell you," Coleman said. "All I know is that the French army sets up shop in a town, calls in the Fifis, and enlists them. Not everybody responds, but enough do that they're fielding new units all the time. Word is they've started shipping some colonial troops back to Africa."

Coleman gave me a carton of Lucky Strikes to give to Adama and his men along with his greetings. I thanked him for his help and went off to find Kaz and Big Mike, wondering if any of the men recruited into the new French army had enough history with the Vercors uprising to warrant a deadly visit from Octave and Jean-Paul.

I found Lewis outside, talking with Kaz, Big Mike, and a GI with broad, blocky shoulders.

"Captain, I've got you squared away in Biffontaine," Lewis said. "It's close enough to the front lines that you'll be able to get word about the scouts as soon as possible. Sergeant Fukuchi will guide you there." Lewis watched me for a moment, not knowing that Coleman had told me about the 442nd troopers. I had the sense he was waiting for any sign of anti-Japanese sentiment. I know some guys felt that way, but the way I figured it, every added rifle meant fewer Fritzes trying to kill me.

"Right. Let us know when Hemingway gets back, Lieutenant," I said. Lewis said Jack was scheduled to send a radio message tonight from a safe house behind enemy lines, and he'd get word to us. With that, he left us with the Nisei sergeant.

"Tokko Fukuchi. They call me Tock," the sergeant said, nodding his head at each of us and dispensing with salutes as befitted any frontline soldier. At least one who didn't want an officer singled out for a Kraut sniper. "Geez, Captain, you go a few rounds with Joe Louis?"

"It was a bomb, all right, but not the Brown Bomber," I said, touching the tender swelling on my cheek. "Lewis said you'd show us where we're bunking."

"Yep. I'm with Headquarters Company, 100th Battalion. You'll be billeted with us in Biffontaine." Tock had jet-black hair, high cheek-bones, bags under his eyes, a cigarette dangling from his lips, and a twitch at the corner of his mouth.

"We were going to Grandvillers, to find a Resistance group," I said. "Is that on the way?"

"No. But it's not far," Tock said. "Better follow me so you don't get lost. Once you're off the main road it's easy to take a wrong turn in these woods." He shifted the strap of the Browning Automatic Rifle on his shoulder. For once, the army had picked the right guy to carry the heavy weapon. At twenty pounds, plus extra ammo, it was a hefty burden.

"Makes sense," Big Mike said, folding the map we'd been using. "The wrong turn could take you into the Black Forest the way I read this map."

"Wow. Where you from, Sarge?" Tock said, tipping his helmet back on his head and gazing up at Big Mike. "Sure grow 'em big wherever it is."

"Detroit," Big Mike said.

"The land of giants," Tock said, grinning. "One of you want to ride with me so I can point out the road to Grandvillers? Just not the big sergeant. Too much of a target."

"They call him Big Mike," I said. "And this is Lieutenant Kazimierz. He's with the British Army by way of Poland."

"I would be delighted to ride with you," Kaz said. "My Japanese is limited, but I would enjoy the practice. And please, call me Kaz."

"Kaz? That's funny," Tock said.

"Why?" Kaz asked him.

"We call a lot of guys Kaz," Tock said, chuckling. "Kazuki, Kazama, Kazunaga, Kazumura, they're all Kaz or Kazzy. You're the first Pole, though."

"I'll ride with you, Tock," I said. "I won't be a big target or bore you with questions about grammar and idioms."

"Good," said Sergeant Fukuchi, grinding out the cigarette with his boot. "Sorry, Lieutenant, but what I don't know about grammar, English and Japanese, would fill a book."

I climbed into Tock's jeep, and he watched as two GIs walked by, then gave me a sideways look.

"You're an odd bunch to show up here, Captain, if you don't mind my saying so," Tock offered as he started his jeep. "I hear you're from SHAEF. That true?"

"We're attached to SHAEF, yeah. We're looking for a couple of French Resistance types who've gone bad. You recognize this guy?" I showed him the photograph of Jean-Paul.

"Negative. That's it? Two officers from SHAEF and the biggest non-com in the ETO and you're not after bigger game? Too bad," Tock said, pulling out into the road as Kaz and Big Mike followed.

"What's bigger game around here?" I asked.

"General Dahlquist. He murdered my best friend."

CHAPTER THIRTY-SEVEN

"THAT'S A SERIOUS charge, soldier," I said, trying to sound stern while my gut told me this non-com just might know more about combat than General Dahlquist. "What happened?"

"This place," Tock said, waving his hand in the air, taking in the streets and buildings of Bruyères. Rubble littered the side of the road, and evidence of heavy fighting was displayed in the arcing sprays of bullet strikes across doors and windows. "Dahlquist wanted it. We took it."

"The 100th Battalion?" I asked. A regiment had three combat battalions, plus support troops, and the battalions were assigned much lower numbers.

"Yeah. The One-Puka-Puka," Tock said. "That's Hawaiian pidgin, Captain, and you'll hear a lot of that around here. You know we're from Hawaii, right? The 100th was in combat long before the rest of the outfit. That's why they let us keep our number. One-Puka-Puka."

"I thought the 442nd was from the West Coast," I said, as we drove by the remains of a brick building that had been blown up and burned, the charred debris smelling of wood and flesh.

"Nah, them Kotonks are okay, but without us Buddhaheads, they'd be in a world of trouble all on their own," Tock said, laughing to himself. I didn't ask for a translation, wanting to get back to his pal being murdered.

"Tell me about the attack," I said, as the road widened, and the structures became more spread out. "You're not blaming Dahlquist for doing his job, are you?"

"Hell, I wish he'd do his job, Captain," Tock said. "You want to arrest me for insubordination, go ahead. But if you want to hear what happened, I'll tell you."

"Tell me," I said. "Everything."

"Okay. But see that turn ahead? That's the road to Grandvillers. Look for that fallen pine tree and take that left. Got it?"

"Sure," I said, checking the landmark. A wrong turn at the front could be deadly.

"You got a few minutes to spare, Captain?" Tock asked. I said yes, and he pulled over to the side of the road. Big Mike did the same behind us. I waved them forward.

"Tock has a story to tell us," I said. "About Dahlquist."

"I'm all ears, but why we gotta stop here?" Big Mike said.

"Terrain," Tock said, getting out of the jeep and walking ten paces into a field. "You see them hills? Back there overlooking Bruyères, and up ahead on the road to Biffontaine?"

"Yes, Sergeant," Kaz said. "The towns are on the low ground, surrounded by high ground. I assume the Germans were defending in both the towns and in the hills?"

"You got that right, Lieutenant," Tock said. "When the division moved into the Vosges, Dahlquist wanted Bruyères for his headquarters. The 442nd had just gotten off the transports from sunny Italy. It was five hundred miles here from Marseilles, by boxcar and by foot. We were understrength, worn out, and tired. Of course, he picked us for the job of taking Bruyères the day we arrived." Tock looked up to the hills where thick stands of pine swayed in the cold wind. The twitch at the corner of his mouth went into overtime.

"That's his job, Sergeant. Maybe his own men were more worn out than you were," I said. It sounded logical, but I could tell from the anguish on Tock's face that there was more to the story.

"You think Dahlquist had it in for you because you're Nisei?" Big Mike asked.

"That'd be too simple. I wasn't there, but ask some of these Texas boys about the trouble Dahlquist got in when they landed on the coast during the invasion," Tock said. "Scuttlebutt is he's in trouble with General Patch up at Seventh Army."

"Texas?" Kaz asked.

"Yeah, them T-patchers are from Texas," Tock said, as if everyone knew. "They got that big *T* on their shoulder patches."

"Okay, but let's get back to what happened here," I said.

"Sure. I just wanted you to understand how things look. To see the lay of the land, you know," Tock said. "One-Puka-Puka was ordered to attack Bruyères. Everything was planned out. I'm with Headquarters Company, so I know everyone was ready. We were understrength, but we know how to fight. The Germans were dug in on the two hills overlooking Bruyères, and at key points in the town. They had machine guns in stone buildings covering the road going in. We knew it would be tough. Then General Dahlquist came to Battalion HQ. That made it tougher."

"I met him earlier. He gave me the impression he was a hands-on type of commander," I said.

"That's one way of putting it," Tock said. "The battalion commander briefed him on the plan of attack, which was set to launch in about thirty minutes. Then Dahlquist went on one of his famous frontline visits. He likes to shout and kick ass, you know? So he stumbles across our reserve company, or at least one platoon of it. They're waiting, in *reserve*, like they were ordered. Dahlquist doesn't like it, he thinks they're malingering or something. Who knows?"

Tock stopped, took a deep breath, exhaled, and looked to the hills again. It took a minute to pull himself together.

"You mentioned a friend of yours," I said, to bring him back and let Big Mike and Kaz know what this was all about.

"Yeah. Masanao Otake. We were sergeants together in Italy. Back in April, he got a battlefield commission. Most of our officers are *haole*, so it was a big deal for one of our own to get his lieutenant's bars. Masa was a great guy. Brave. He was the platoon leader, and Dahlquist gave him hell for sitting around during an offensive. He ordered the platoon to advance. Fifteen minutes before the full attack."

"A single platoon? Alone?" Big Mike said.

"That's what I said. Masa obeyed the order Dahlquist gave him. He could've radioed our CO, asked for confirmation. But that wasn't the kind of guy he was. He believed in *giri* and *sekinin* above all."

"Duty and responsibility," Kaz said.

"He lived and breathed it, Lieutenant. Masa led his platoon, twenty guys, against one of those stone farmhouses spitting slugs from a heavy machine gun. They took it. But they couldn't hold it, not with the rest of the battalion still waiting to push off. The Krauts counterattacked. Masa got cut down by a burst from a Schmeisser."

"What about his men?" Big Mike asked.

"A couple were wounded, but they all made it back," Tock said. "With Masa's body."

"What a waste," Kaz said.

"You see that hill?" Tock said, pointing back to where we'd started. "And that one, up the road, overlooking Biffontaine? Cost us twenty-one dead, a hundred and twenty-two wounded, and eighteen captured. I know, I saw the reports."

"Hey, Sergeant, I'm not defending what Dahlquist did, but casualties are unavoidable," I said, uncomfortable with sounding like a smug rear area officer.

"That's where you're wrong, Captain," Tock said. "Dahlquist avoided casualties to his T-patchers. That's all he cared about. You say you're here looking for a French killer. I can't help you with that, but I know where to find an American one. Okay, sorry for the stop, let's go."

"Nothing to be sorry about, pal," Big Mike said. We got back into the jeeps and drove into Biffontaine as silently as a funeral procession.

CHAPTER THIRTY-EIGHT

TOCK BROUGHT US to the 100th Battalion headquarters in Biffontaine and got us squared away with our quarters. HQ was set up in what was left of the town hall, and our billet was across the street, on the second floor of a building that was missing most of its third floor.

"The place took a beating," Tock said. "It ain't the Ritz, but at least we got pulled off the line for a rest. Nice to be in a rear area for once."

An artillery round shrieked through the air, passing over our heads and exploding behind the road we'd driven in on. Two more followed, and we all ducked as if a few inches might make any difference.

"This is a rear area?" Kaz asked.

"Peace and quiet compared to the past eight days," Tock said. "Jerry likes to keep us on our toes and brackets the road occasionally. Luckily, he ain't hit the mess tent. It's behind your building. I gotta get back, fellas. You all set?"

"We are," I said. "We'll stash our gear and then head for Grandvillers. Hey, before you go, what was all that about Buddhaheads and Kotonks?"

"Oh yeah, you wouldn't know about that, sir," Tock said, grinning. "Well, most guys from Hawaii are Buddhist, so Buddhaheads kinda came naturally to the mainland guys in the 2nd and 3rd Battalions. We all trained together at Camp Shelby, down in Mississippi, but we didn't get along."

"Why?" Big Mike asked. "Seems like you guys were all in the same boat."

"There was a lot we didn't know, coming from the islands," Tock said. "We like to have a few drinks, gamble, blow off steam, you know? But the West Coast guys didn't go in for that. We thought they were cheap and stuck-up. Looked down on us."

"Where did Kotonk come from?" Kaz asked. "It does not sound Japanese."

"It ain't, Lieutenant. After a few bar fights, one of the guys said that was the sound their heads made when they went down for the count. *Ko-tonk*, you know? It just stuck, and after things calmed down between us, even the mainlanders thought it was funny."

"How'd you work things out?" I said as I watched heavy, dark clouds rolling over the hills.

"Our CO selected a busload of guys from the 100th, me included, to take a trip to Arkansas, to see one of the internment camps," Tock said, releasing a heavy sigh. "We all thought they was like small towns, you know, with schools and shops. It was nothin' like that. Barbed wire fences and guard towers with guns aimed at everyone. Cramped quarters. No privacy. Lousy food. The government made it look real nice when they took photos for the newspapers, but it wasn't nice, not one bit."

"They let you inside?"

"Hell, Captain, all the guys in the other two battalions came from those camps. Letting a few Buddhaheads in was no big deal," Tock said. "I was just glad they let us out."

"How long did you stay?" Kaz asked.

"Long enough to get the official tour. But then we were able to talk to the families there on our own. I looked up the aunt and uncle of a guy from 2nd Battalion," Tock said. "He gave me a carton of cigarettes and Hershey bars for them. Hisato and Hisako Takamune. Nice folks. That's when it dawned on me."

"What?" Big Mike asked, turning his collar up against the freshening wind.

"When I saw how the Takamunes reacted to the gifts I'd brought, I realized the West Coast guys weren't cheapskates at all. It was like I'd given them a roll of C-notes. Those Kotonks had been sending all their dough to their families. Hell, I hadn't even noticed that while we were getting packages from home, the mainland Nisei were sending packages from Camp Shelby to their folks in the camps. Guess they were too proud to say anything."

"How bad was it?" Big Mike asked. "In the camp."

"Wooden barracks," Tock said, his eyes downcast. "Not much in the way of furniture or comfort. Blankets strung up for privacy. It really shook me, and that's no lie. But what really got me is the message the Takamunes asked me to deliver to their nephew. *Kamei ni kizu tsukeru bekarazu.*"

Tock looked at Kaz, but it was beyond his few words of Japanese.

"Never bring dishonor to the family name," Tock explained. "It's real formal, old-time Japanese. They made me memorize it. From behind the barbed wire, that was the message they sent. It really stayed with me. Things changed after that, lemme tell ya." Tock finished with a deep breath and a shake of his head.

"*Haji,*" Kaz said. "It means shame, correct? A similar concept?"

"Right," Tok said. "No *haji,* in simpler words."

"So, you stopped calling them Kotonks?" Big Mike asked.

"Aw, hell no, Sarge, they'll always be Kotonks. Take it from a Buddhahead," Tock said, brightening with a wide grin. "Good luck finding those scouts. You need anything, ask for me at Battalion HQ, okay?"

"Will do, Sergeant. Enjoy your rest," I said, looking around at the shattered town. "Such as it is."

"Go for broke, guys!" Tock said and drove off.

"That is their motto," Kaz told us. "From a Hawaiian pidgin phrase, meaning to gamble everything on one roll of the dice."

We carried our duffle bags and bedrolls up to the second floor. We were in a room overlooking the street. It had a nice view of rubble and rumbling trucks through the one intact window. Blankets were stretched across a shattered one. The door was off its hinges, and there was no need to redecorate since there wasn't a stick of furniture save for a small table that, surprisingly, still held a vase stuffed with dead flowers. A pockmarked wall completed the décor.

"Looks like we got the VIP suite," Big Mike said. "Nothing but the best for visitors from SHAEF."

"They've been busy," I said, moving to the broken window and looking out between the hanging blankets. "Too busy to worry about where to stash the likes of us. General Dahlquist has seen to that."

"Or perhaps Lieutenant Lewis had us put here to keep us out of the way," Kaz said. "Or uncomfortable enough to leave entirely."

"You might be right," I said, staring out at the heavy gray sky and the scorched buildings. Below me, men moved up and down the street, shoulders hunched against the chill, windy damp. They shuffled along, weighed down by heavy overcoats and weapons.

"This is miserable weather," Big Mike said, standing next to me at the window. "The higher the altitude, the worse it gets." He was right, and I was thankful for the mackinaw coats we'd picked up at the French depot. Which made me think about how these guys from the 442nd were outfitted.

"You notice anything different about their uniforms?" I asked as Kaz joined us to survey the street.

"You mean those heavy wool overcoats? Nobody really likes them," Big Mike said. "At least not for fighting in. Too damn heavy."

"And think about what Tock was wearing," I said.

"Geez, you're right. It was a Parsons jacket. They've been replaced by now, haven't they?" Big Mike said.

"Far as I know," I said. The M1943 Field Jacket was much warmer and more functional than the Parsons jacket, which really wasn't much more than a windbreaker. "None of them have the new boots either."

"Everyone we saw at General Dahlquist's headquarters was outfitted with the latest styles," Kaz said. "Officers and enlisted men."

"But not the 442nd," Big Mike said. "I'd sure hate to be out in the cold mud with those low-top shoes and canvas leggings." The new combat boots the army had brought out last year were a big improvement, with five-inch-high leather cuffs replacing the separate leggings and long laces that went with them.

"These guys just keep gettin' the short end of the stick, don't they?" Big Mike said, his fists set on his hips and his jaw clenched.

"Yeah, and it stinks. But we're just passing through, remember? We barely rate four shot-up walls around here," I said. "We need to catch those scouts as soon as they come off the line, then we go after Octave."

"Unfortunately, having a picture of Jean-Paul has done us little good," Kaz said. "Obtaining a description of Octave may not help either."

"Which is why I want to talk to those Resistance people in Grand-villers," I said. "Maybe we can get a line on what drew Octave and Jean-Paul to this neck of the woods."

"Better than standing around here," Kaz said. "Dead flowers are so depressing."

"Let's split up," I said. "Big Mike, let's see if we can scrounge a jeep for you from Tock's HQ. The scouts went off with the Texas boys, 1st Battalion. Get to their headquarters and see what you can find out. Then check with Lewis and see if there's any word on Hemingway."

"Sure thing," Big Mike said. "I'll go ahead and snoop around, just like Dahlquist said not to do. He sounds like a pleasant guy, so I'm sure he won't mind."

"I'm sure you can charm him, if it comes to that," Kaz said. "He's only a two-star general." Big Mike had a reputation for managing senior officers, but this one might be a challenge, I had to admit.

We headed back to headquarters. Tock was nowhere to be seen, but the supply clerk agreed to loan a jeep, with driver, to Big Mike, for a few hours. That made me think about Drake, and the truck his unit in Algiers was probably still waiting for. I hoped he was doing okay.

We waited out front, and in a few minutes a jeep pulled up driven by a skinny kid in a wool overcoat that looked bigger than him.

"Private Fred Hosakawa, at your service," he said. "Who needs a lift?"

"That'd be me," Big Mike said, introducing himself. "You know where the 36th Division's 1st Battalion HQ is?"

"No problem, Sarge," Hosakawa said. "But hey, if you're not in a hurry, could we stop at the mess tent? I'm starving."

"If you insist," Big Mike said, shooting a wink in my direction. "See you guys later."

We drove off, back the way we came, taking the turnoff for Grand-villers. Rain started to splat against the canvas top as the wind kicked up, the pine trees at the edge of the road swirling their branches crazily.

"I wonder if the Maquis de Lamarche will be at their posts in this weather," Kaz said. "It is one thing to strike with surprise and melt into the night. It is another to stand at a crossroads in the rain."

"We've seen the best and worst of these groups," I said.

"We have seen the best and worst of everything, Billy," Kaz answered. True enough.

After ten minutes of slow going on a road that threatened to turn to mud, the rain lessened, and we approached a crossroads. I didn't see a roadblock or guard post, but in a flash, we were surrounded by armed men spilling out of buildings on both sides of the street. I spotted one machine gun in a window, and I was sure it wasn't the only one.

"Well, that answers the question," Kaz said. "They are at their post. And staying dry."

"Who are you?" This came from a guy whose skin was the deepest black I'd ever seen. More to the point, he was aiming a Schmeisser submachine gun at my chest. He wore a US Army overcoat, a French helmet, and a grim, no-nonsense expression.

"Captain Billy Boyle. And I bet you're Adama. From French Sudan, according to Captain Lewis."

"Ah, the good Captain. Son of the famous writer. Yes, I am Adama. Did Lewis send you here?"

"We have some questions," I said. "How about we get out of the rain, and you tell your men to lower their weapons."

"*Certainement, mon capitaine*," Adama said, and barked out orders to his men, some of whom were almost as dark as he was. One guy jumped into the back seat as Adama told us to pull behind the building on our left, out of sight. He held a pistol at his side, taking no chances.

"We have to watch for German infiltrators," Adama said as we took the rear door into the house. "Your lines are very thin here."

"It seems General Dahlquist is concentrating his forces elsewhere," Kaz said.

"His attack on the ridge above La Houssiére?" Adama said. "He is a very foolish man, your general. Now, what do you want with me and my small group?"

CHAPTER THIRTY-NINE

"WHY IS DAHLQUIST foolish?" I asked Adama as we sat around a kitchen table. Two windows were open, a man at each watching the roadway. A wood stove worked to warm the room, but it was no match for the cold crosswind.

"We tried to warn Captain Lewis," Adama said, placing his hand on the shoulder of the man who sat next to him. "This is Adi Ba. He is from Guinea. He saw the Germans moving onto the ridges. Road-blocks. Strongpoints."

"You reported this?" I asked.

"*Oui.* I heard a great argument among the officers. The general does not like to hear news he does not agree with," Adama said. He and Adi Ba spoke quickly in French, and he continued. "His plan is to push three battalions across narrow ridgelines. Too many men, too many places to stop them. The Germans will hear them coming, of course."

"Perhaps the general will have adjusted his plan based on your information," I said.

"He told the *Japonais* that there would be no Germans in Bruyères and Biffontaine, and that was not true," Adama said. "He says what he wishes to believe, not what is."

"I've met him," I said. "I can't disagree."

"It will be very bad for the soldiers," Adama said. "Now, what do you want of us?"

"We're looking for two Resistance fighters, men who were part of the Vercors Plateau uprising," I said. "Was your group involved?"

"No, it was too far south for us," Adama said, speaking to Adi Ba, who nodded his agreement. "We were based in the forests outside of Chaumont. When we heard of the uprising, we attacked several German columns, but I doubt it had any effect. Then the Boche began to hunt us, and we came to this area. Better hiding places, but it is much colder. Why do you want these men?"

"They are renegades," Kaz said. "They have murdered three men. Two English officers and one French. They blame them for not coming to the aid of the Vercors Republic. They may be part of the Maquis du Vercors."

"And what makes you think they have come this far north?" Adama asked. "There are only Germans and Americans here. Except for you, Lieutenant, there is no English army."

"We think they may have another target," I said. "Perhaps another Frenchman. Do you know of anyone who might have fought at Vercors and fled to this area?"

Adama, Adi Ba, and the two men at the windows spoke among themselves. The other two were white, one with a gray handlebar mustache and the second with nothing at all to shave, since he looked barely fifteen or so.

"No," Adama said, as the kid darted out of the room. "We have seen no Vercors survivors. I sent Sébastien to ask the others."

"Has the French army recruited you yet?" Kaz asked. "They are bringing many of the FFI into the regular ranks."

"Lieutenant, I am *in* the French army," Adama said, slapping the table with his hand. "We two, Adi Ba and I, we did not surrender in 1940 with the rest of them. I had no desire to put my fate in the hands of the Nazis."

"It must have been hard, especially at first," Kaz said. "When there was little support for the Resistance."

"In the beginning, we worked for a farmer, who kept us out of sight and fed us for our work. This was Vichy, after all, so we did not have to worry about the Germans. But when the Boche took over, things changed. We began to fight back and found other *Tirailleurs sénégalais* who had been in hiding. Others joined us as well. Now we fight alongside the Americans, and they give us arms, clothing, and food. It is good."

"Don't you want to fight with the French army?" I asked.

"*Oui*. But they do not want Africans, Captain. Only white Frenchmen. An officer passed through just yesterday looking for *maquis* recruits. He declined our services. Perhaps if a unit of the old *Tirailleurs sénégalais* comes, they would take us."

"We saw them yesterday," I said. "North of Grenoble, at a French supply depot."

"The 9th Colonial Division," Kaz said. "Three regiments of *Tirailleurs*, and it looked like they were heading north."

"*Excellent!*" Adama said, translating for Adi Ba, whose face lit up. "They will take us, I know it. And bring us home when this war is over. How much longer can it be? The Boche are at their own border."

I didn't answer Adama's question. He was too happy with the news of his African comrades for me to spoil his good mood with a dose of reality.

"Did this French officer say where else he was headed?" I said instead. "Was he part of a recruitment drive?"

"Yes, he was spreading the news of a gathering at Langres. A general will be there to induct a large group of *maquis* into the army. He said he regretted he could not invite us, but we should tell any eligible fighters about it. White men, that is."

"That is not fair, Adama, especially since you never stopped fighting," Kaz said.

"You think that is unfair? Wait until I ask for the pay owed me since 1940," Adama said with a laugh. "Then you will see unfair."

"When is this gathering?"

"Three days from now, at noon in the town square," Adama said. "They will be making a newsreel, and there will be many dignitaries. Politicians. Langres is about one hundred and thirty kilometers to the southwest, if you wish to see."

"Perhaps we will," I said, hoping we'd get a description of Octave before then. "What was the name of the general?"

"I do not remember," Adama said. He consulted with Adi Ba, who seemed to recall. "Ah yes, General Michel Robine. Someone important from Algiers, I think."

Robine. That name was familiar. I was trying to place it when

Sébastien ran back into the room. No dice, no one knew of anyone from the Vercors.

"Thanks," I said, as Kaz and I stood to leave. I took the well-worn photograph of Jean-Paul from my pocket. "Just one more thing. Have you seen this man?"

Kaz explained in French that we were looking for this guy. Adama took it, frowned, and handed it to Adi Ba, who then passed it to Mister Mustache. Negative, until Sébastien laid eyes on it.

"*Oui, c'est Rémy*," Sébastien said, beaming at being the only one to remember.

"Rémy?" Kaz asked, tapping on the photo. Sébastien nodded eagerly, and Kaz peppered him with questions. I heard the word *Lamarche*, which was the name of their group, but couldn't keep up otherwise.

"*Merci*, Sébastien," Kaz said.

"Now I remember him, the fellow on the motorbike," Adama said. "Sébastien spoke with him, but I was not close enough to see his face."

"He came through twice yesterday," Kaz reported. "Once coming from Lamarche, and once returning."

"Sébastien is from Lamarche," Adama said. "It is the village from which we took our name, the Maquis de Lamarche."

"It is how they struck up a conversation," Kaz said. "They question everyone passing through, watching for German infiltrators. Rémy, as he called himself, was headed for Bruyères. He wore an FFI armband and carried a Lee-Enfield rifle with a telescopic sight."

"But how can we be sure Jean-Paul is really in Lamarche?" I asked. "He could have picked the name at random."

"Sébastien's father is the mayor," Kaz said. "Sébastien asked Jean-Paul to deliver a message that he was safe and well, and he agreed. Jean-Paul said he had met the mayor when he was seeking a place to stay for a few days. Sébastien thought he was genuine."

"Look," Adama said, taking a folded and worn map from his pocket and laying it out on the table. "Here we are in Grandvillers. There is Langres, where the recruitment will take place." As he traced the route, his finger crossed the village of Lamarche. It was about ten kilometers from Langres.

"The perfect spot to hide out and wait," I said.

"And there is more," Kaz said. "When Jean-Paul returned, he carried a passenger. Another FFI man with a rifle."

"What did he look like?"

"According to Sébastien, like any other man with his collar turned up, wearing an Adrian helmet, goggles, and a scarf covering his face." The Adrian was the French army helmet, the same as Adama wore. It had a wide brim and a distinctive crest along the top.

"Of course. I'd cover up riding around on a motorbike in this weather," I said. "But it has to be Octave. They probably had a prearranged meeting. All Octave had to do was skip out on Hemingway and wait."

"Rémy and this other man are the ones you seek?" Adama asked.

"Yes, and they are dangerous," Kaz said. "The war has driven them mad."

"If we see them, we will hold them for you," he said. "We are dangerous also. Ask the Boche."

We thanked them and got back into the jeep. The sky had darkened, with heavy clouds and a setting sun nearing the distant hilltops. A foggy mist settled over the ground, blurring the contours of the roadway and the pines lining it.

"Should we try for Lamarche now?" Kaz asked, as I kept to a slower pace.

"I don't think we need to," I said. "They'll probably stay put until the recruitment ceremony. No reason to barge in there tonight, after dark and in this pea soup. I'd rather go in the morning, with Big Mike for backup."

"I agree," Kaz said. "Perhaps we will hear from Lieutenant Hemingway, and we can go in with a description. Or the scouts will have returned."

"Robine," I said, half to myself, as we drew closer to Biffontaine. "I know I've heard the name before. How about you?"

"General Michel Robine," Kaz said. "No, I do not think I have ever heard the name. We could radio Colonel Harding and ask him to look into it."

"Wait, it's Brigadier General," I said as we pulled into Biffontaine. I racked my brain to figure out how I knew that. Who told me? I parked next to our quarters, and as soon as I turned off the engine it came to me.

"Drake," I said. "Drake mentioned him. He was the senior officer in Algiers who stopped the French paratroopers from being dropped into the Vercors. Laurent and Danton talked about him too."

"There certainly would be ill feeling toward Robine among the survivors," Kaz said. "If your suspicion is right, and Octave is planning an assassination attempt at the recruitment ceremony, we must proceed with caution. I have no interest in letting Dickie's killer slip away. So yes, it will be better to wait until morning."

"We can't let Jean-Paul escape," I said, rubbing my eyes and trying to think clearly. My head still hurt, a sharp pain throbbing behind my eyes. It hadn't been long since I'd walked into an explosion. Maybe Kaz should be driving. "He's our only link to Octave, the only person who knows who he is."

"Billy, have you noticed anything strange here?"

"What?" I said, still thinking through the possibilities of two snipers going after Robine.

"The town was full of troopers from the 442nd," Kaz said. "Where is everybody?"

He was right. The street was deserted. The headquarters of the 100th Battalion looked abandoned. No GIs, no jeeps, no traffic.

Artillery shrieked across the sky. Ours. Answering fire boomed from up ahead. Explosions reflected red and orange against the low-hanging clouds. It wasn't hard to figure where everyone was.

The rumble of artillery rolled along the ridges, echoing until it seemed to be all around us. But it only seemed to be close. A trick of the senses. Still, I hunched my shoulders every time a salvo shattered the forest on the ridgeline overlooking the village. Up there, in the mist, where Dahlquist's men were struggling to stay alive as the air bursts turned trees into splintered shrapnel and the ground shook with every explosive burst.

Yes, the morning would be better. For those left alive to see it.

CHAPTER FORTY

BATTALION HQ WAS cleared out, the door left swinging open. A deuce-and-a-half truck turned the corner and rolled by, loaded with crates of ammo.

"Hey, soldier, where is everyone?" I said, waving the driver down.

"Up on the ridge," he said, pointing to where shellfire was lighting the clouds. "Orders came through a few hours ago. Those Texas boys are in a helluva mess. I gotta go, Captain."

"There's a lot of trouble brewing up there," I said. "Let's see if the mess tent is still out back. Best place to look for Big Mike."

We took the alleyway, and I could smell the food cooking before I saw the tent. I wasn't surprised to find it still there. A field kitchen had to stay out of the line of fire, and cooks manning it would often bring hot food close to the front lines. A lot of guys complained about army food, but I never saw a dogface in a foxhole bitching about hot soup in his mess tin.

"Over here," Big Mike said, waving his arm. It really wasn't necessary. The plank tables were mostly empty, with just a few GIs wearing the T patch of the 36th Division. The Nisei were gone.

"What's going on?" I asked, although I could guess.

"Orders came down from Dahlquist," Big Mike said. "Looks like one of his battalions got themselves surrounded up there. He wants the 442nd to break through to them."

"But it was an attack by three battalions of the 36th," Kaz said. "What about the other two?"

"Good question," Big Mike said. "Fred Hosakawa said he heard it was elements of two battalions that were surrounded, and the rest were cut off and not making any progress. We'd gone up to the 1st Battalion HQ to find out about the scouts. When we got there, I could smell trouble. They were paralyzed, like they knew something was wrong but didn't have a clue. By the time we got back here, the order had come down. Freddie took off with Tock and the rest of the Headquarters Company. They're up there now."

"Jesus," I said. "That didn't take long. Those Nisei are already chewed up. There's going to be hell to pay on those ridges."

"Perhaps they can find another route and get around the Germans," Kaz said, with more hope than certainty.

"No. I saw the maps in Dahlquist's office," I said. "A seven-kilometer advance across hilly terrain only two kilometers wide, with drop-offs on each side. It didn't even look like he had a real plan of maneuver." I told them about the lack of overlays. In the absence of the usual procedure for headquarters to plan out the attack using grease pencils on a clear overlay of a topographic map, it seemed like Dahlquist had simply sent three battalions forward on a narrow front into the teeth of an enemy dug in on terrain tailor-made for defense.

"I spoke with a non-com at 1st Battalion," Big Mike said. "Said that was Dahlquist's style. Not big on detailed plans and then he goes forward and gets in the way, giving hell to anyone he thinks isn't moving fast enough. He also said the rest of the 36th has been ordered to dig in and support the 442nd in their attack."

"They can't do both," I said. "If they hunker down, they'll be no help at all."

"Right. Fits into what Tock was talking about. Remember—about Dahlquist during the invasion? I got the dope on that story."

"Yeah, but first listen to this. We have a line on where Jean-Paul and Octave are," I said.

"Where? Let's go get the bastards," Big Mike said.

"A village called Lamarche, which isn't far from Langres, where the French army is going to be swearing in a whole bunch of FFI fighters," I said. "All in front of newsreel cameras and correspondents." I gave him the lowdown on what Sébastien had recalled when I passed around the picture of Jean-Paul.

"We think they are waiting for the ceremony," Kaz said. "Billy remembers hearing about this General Robine. He is responsible for halting the French parachute regiment from reinforcing the Vercors."

"Makes sense," Big Mike said. "So, who has that information? If he's senior brass in Algiers, who would know he was the guy to put the kibosh on the paratroopers?"

"Any of the *maquis* who had been in touch with Algiers by radio from the Vercors," Kaz said. "I imagine once Robine was named as the officer who halted the paratroop drop, he would have become infamous."

"If he was named in the radio communiqués," I said. "If he wasn't, it might not have been until the survivors from the Maquis du Vercors arrived at the headquarters in Algiers that they learned his name."

"They were training with Drake, then departed and came back to France," Kaz said. "Quite suddenly. Laurent suspected they were up to something. I wonder if he knew of Robine's role."

"Which means there could be a person unknown to us who is working with Jean-Paul and using the code name Octave," I said.

"Or it could be someone we know," Big Mike said. "Cathedral, for one. Looks like he set up the guy who killed Dickie."

"If we have that right," I said.

"I don't think Cathedral is Octave," Kaz said. "Remember, Cathedral was at the hotel at the same time as the man with the scarred eyebrow. If Cathedral had sent him to kill Dickie, the fellow would have named him. But you said he mentioned Octave, saying he was a fool to trust him."

"Right," I said. "Cathedral is well-known. And his *maquis* group wasn't part of the Vercors battle. But I think he was after Madame Schenck's treasure."

"Perhaps Cathedral and Octave were in league," Kaz said. "Octave went to Madame Schenck's to both look for the treasure and eliminate the one person linking both men to Dickie's murder."

"What about Danton?" Big Mike asked. "He was at the hotel."

"Well, he certainly could've known about Robine from the Vercors," I said. "And he was in Algiers. But we know he was working for Laurent, trying to identify the conspirators."

"Then there is Lucien Rivet, whose codename, Savart, could just be a cover for Octave," Kaz said. "It could be that Cathedral is using one of his men, calling him Octave, and carrying out his plan through him."

"That would make sense if Cathedral had more of a connection to the Vercors," I said. "But maybe he does."

"Let's grab Jean-Paul tomorrow and wring the truth out of him," Big Mike said. "I'm tired of all this guesswork."

"We need a plan," I said. "We don't know where they are holed up, and those sniper rifles give them the advantage if they see us coming."

"Perhaps we could borrow Sébastien," Kaz said. "He might like to visit his parents."

"It would make it easier to talk to his father," I said. "He might not want to rat out two *maquisards* to the Americans. But after that? Jean-Paul knows us, and maybe Octave does as well."

"We would need two Handie-Talkies," Kaz said. "And an American helmet for myself. Jean-Paul may not recognize me in this excellent American mackinaw, with a scarf and helmet to obscure things." The SCR-536 Handie-Talkie was, as the name implied, a hand-held radio. It had a range of one mile, on a good day, which is about how long the battery lasted. But it was perfect for what we had in mind.

"We go in two jeeps," Big Mike said, picking up on the notion. "You get the scoop from the mayor and reconnoiter wherever they're hiding. Then call us in and we take 'em by surprise."

"Exactly," Kaz said, tossing a glance my way.

"I got nothing better," I said. "That's the plan."

"Okay. Let's get some food if they have anything left," Big Mike said. The cooks didn't have any hot food ready, but they loaded us up with corned beef and Swiss cheese sandwiches. We set our plates down, and Big Mike went back to talk with the mess sergeant. He came back a few minutes later with a bottle of wine and three glasses.

"I knew they'd have some vino stashed away," he said as he poured. "To the fraternity of sergeants."

"Cheers," I said, and we clinked glasses. I thought back to what Dickie had told me about toasts and suddenly felt his absence. I'd only known him a short time, and I couldn't imagine what Kaz was feeling.

"To Dickie," I said, and we touched glasses gently, as if to show that among the three of us, there could be no suspicions.

"A fine friend," Kaz said. "I shall have to visit his family when we get back to England. They'll be shattered."

We drank, and the silence settled over us, dark and cold, like the approaching night.

"Hey, Big Mike, you were starting to tell us something about Dahlquist during the invasion," I said. "What was that about?"

"I went back to Division HQ," he said, talking around a mouthful of corned beef. "Still no word from Hemingway. He shoulda radioed in by now, but they figure his radio is on the fritz. That's what they hope, anyway. He could still show up."

"Good luck to him," I said.

"Yeah, he's sure an improvement on his old man," Big Mike said. He set down his sandwich, took a swig of wine, and told the story he'd heard from another non-com at HQ.

During the invasion of southern France, the 36th Division had landed to the east of Cannes. Dahlquist's command was part of VI Corps, commanded by General Lucian Truscott. Each division commander was aboard a ship with the responsibility of getting their landing craft ashore in good order while maintaining communications with the navy and General Truscott.

Dahlquist had other ideas. He wanted to watch the landings up close. He took a launch out to an undefended promontory, which gave him a clear view of the landing craft heading for shore. It was probably a magnificent sight, but it put him out of radio contact. When the naval commander tried to contact Dahlquist about a last-minute change to one of his division's landing areas, he was nowhere to be found. That message got bumped up to General Truscott, who was livid about Dahlquist's absence. Word was, he threatened to sack him then and there, but held back because it might disrupt the invasion.

Then a few days later, the Germans managed to capture an officer carrying Dahlquist's operational plans for an attack set for the next morning. The Krauts launched a spoiler attack, which failed, but Dahlquist was still left with egg on his face over the loss of the plans.

"Dahlquist is in a heap of trouble with General Truscott," Big Mike concluded. "Truscott only needs one more screw-up to give Dahlquist the boot."

"And losing an entire battalion would more than qualify," Kaz said.

"Losing an entire battalion of his own division, that is," I said. "The 442nd is temporarily attached to the 36th. He'll be happy to sacrifice them if it saves his battalion, and his own skin."

"Which might be why he had the rest of the division remain in place as he sent the Nisei in," Big Mike said. "Minimize their casualties while the 442nd rides to the rescue."

"Damn. I hope they break through soon," I said.

"With the survival of the French scouts somewhat in doubt, and Hemingway's continued absence, our mission to Lamarche becomes even more important," Kaz said. "It may be the only way to apprehend Dickie's killer."

He was right. We were concerned about those three lives, and the life of General Robine. But compared to the struggle on those ridges and the losses the surrounded men and their rescuers were going to take, our mission seemed almost trivial.

Go for broke, guys.

CHAPTER FORTY-ONE

THE ONLY THING that made spending a cold night on a bare floor tolerable was knowing that I wasn't on a windy, wet ridgeline being shot at. I didn't sleep well, mostly worrying about the Nisei and what they were being put through. But I couldn't help the 442nd, and I couldn't do anything about Dahlquist's orders. What I could do is bring a measure of justice to the murderer of Dickie Thorne. Or revenge. After a lousy night's sleep, I wasn't too picky about which.

We got going early, fortifying ourselves with powdered eggs, Spam, and buckets of joe. Big Mike worked his scrounging magic and came away with two wooden crates of C rations. Meat and vegetable, meat and hash, meat and beans. We tossed our gear into the jeeps, uncertain where we'd be spending the night. Kaz decided he'd drive me, and I didn't argue, since my head still felt like a bell that had been rung too long and hard. Sébastien would be Big Mike's passenger.

We swung by Division HQ, and Big Mike scored two Handie-Talkies and a GI helmet for Kaz. His non-com pal confirmed there was still no sign of Lieutenant Hemingway.

"They're calling it the Lost Battalion," Big Mike said as he handed Kaz the helmet. "Dahlquist is at the 442nd HQ right now."

"Aren't they lucky," I said.

"The Lost Battalion is an unfortunate choice of words," Kaz said, setting the tin pot on his head. "If the Nazis overrun them, it will have great propaganda value, and they'll turn that phrase on its head.

Imagine what they'd say about capturing an entire American battalion? With their backs to the border, they will make the most of it."

I didn't doubt it. And I didn't doubt it might make our advance more cautious as well.

We drove off to Grandvillers, and this time our reception was a lot friendlier. Adama was willing to let Sébastien go home for a visit, and the boy was excited at the prospect, even after we explained what our purpose was. His father, the mayor, was Gaspard Marcoux, and Sébastien assured us he was a loyal Frenchman and would trust what his son told him. Kaz stressed that his father would be in no danger, and that we did not wish for Sébastien to get mixed up in this either. We promised to get him back after the recruitment drive in Langres, although I wasn't entirely sure where we'd be by then. Back in England, with this bizarre mission all sewn up, I hoped.

We consulted Adama's map and planned out our route. It looked to be about fifty miles, so we'd make it by midday, no problem. Big Mike handed over one crate of C rations to Adama's men and put the other in Kaz's jeep.

"For the kid to bring home," he said. Sébastien got the message and grinned. I'm sure he liked the idea of bringing food to his parents, but there was an ulterior motive. Jean-Paul and Octave were probably a burden to feed. The good mayor might send some of this grub their way. Sébastien carefully adjusted his FFI armband, set his beret at a jaunty angle, and slung his Schmeisser over his shoulder, ready for a victorious homecoming.

We drove southwest, leaving the heavily forested hills and descending into a valley that brought us to Épinal, a fair-sized town that had seen a lot of fighting. Wrecked German vehicles had been pushed to the side of the road, and outside of town, an American military cemetery held lines of temporary grave markers. Trucks were off-loading even more bodies.

I held my breath as we passed by, which was supposed to stop the spirit of the recently departed from entering my body. I never really believed it, but there sure were a lot of recently dead along this road, so why take a chance?

The rest of the route was through open countryside and small villages. It was cloudy, but we'd left the mist and chill of the Vosges behind. It was peaceful here, and it was strange to think about the carnage taking place an hour's drive away.

"I wonder if Diana and Christine are coming this far north on their goodwill tour?" I said. "Everything happened so fast, I didn't ask where they were headed."

"No idea," Big Mike said, giving me a wink. "But Kaz might know."

Maybe, but if Kaz and Christine were anything like Diana and me, they'd spent every moment in the present, soaking it in. Best thing to do when tomorrow might never come.

Soon we spotted a road sign for Lamarche and dropped back to put more distance between Kaz and us. Farmland gave way to gray stone buildings and narrow roads, and soon Kaz turned off the main road before the village.

"Sébastien's not going to the town hall?" I said.

"Course not, Billy," Big Mike said. "He's a kid. He's going to see his mom first."

We pulled over near the turn Kaz had taken. Sure enough, the Handie-Talkie squawked and Kaz reported in. Sébastien's mother had burst into tears when she'd opened the door. Fifteen minutes more passed, and Kaz radioed again. We were all invited for dinner tonight. Madame Marcoux had telephoned her husband to expect Sébastien shortly. She was out back killing a chicken for the pot, and they were about to leave.

"Great," Big Mike said. "Half the town probably knows by now."

"Shouldn't be a problem," I said. "Unless she invites Jean-Paul and his friend."

Kaz appeared a minute later, with Sébastien waving happily. Our secret mission was off to a great start.

I followed slowly. In a minute we were in the town proper, where stone buildings, set close to each other, loomed over the narrow roadway. There were a few trucks on the road, and a gasogene car, converted to use the gases generated by burning coal or wood. Petrol was still hard to come by for civilians. But no motorbike.

"We must be getting close to the center of the village," Big Mike said. "We should pull over."

I backed into a side street to stay out of sight and be ready to move.

"This place didn't get shot up much," Big Mike said. "It's nothing special, but the streets aren't full of rubble and wrecked vehicles."

"It's a perfect spot to hide out," I said. "Plenty of homes and farms, and a hop skip to Langres. They've got the perfect cover story too. FFI veterans waiting to join the army but wanting a few days of peace and quiet."

"And a motorbike to get around," Big Mike said. "We're damn lucky we got this lead on Jean-Paul."

Luck. We needed it. But this wasn't dumb luck. Tracking down the scouts and looking for nearby *maquis* while we waited had put us in touch with Sébastien. The lucky part was that he was from the village where Jean-Paul and Octave were hiding. A chance conversation at a crossroads had brought us here, but only because we were looking for that kind of luck.

"Luck is when preparation meets opportunity," I said, half to myself.

"What?"

"Something a Roman philosopher said. Sister Charlotte taught ancient history back when I was in the tenth grade. She had us memorize quotes. Seneca, I think it was."

"Like the Indians?" Big Mike asked.

"Yeah, I guess," I said. Sister Charlotte hadn't gone into that. Or I hadn't paid attention. We waited, figuring it would take time for the father-son reunion and then for Kaz to explain himself.

"Billy! He's in the bakery!" Kaz's tinny voice over the radio startled us. "Over."

"Repeat, over," Big Mike said, grabbing the radio.

"Jean-Paul. At the bakery. The *boulangerie* near town hall. Hurry, over."

"Where are you? Over," Big Mike said. "Go, Billy!"

I pulled out, heading in the direction Kaz had taken as Big Mike spoke with him. I guess I'd forgotten one thing about luck. It comes in two varieties, one of them bad.

"There," Big Mike said. "Head for that steeple. The town hall is on the right, fifty yards before it. The bakery is just past the church."

I could barely make out the steeple above the tiled roofs, but it was enough. I spotted the town hall on the corner, the French tricolor draped over a balcony, and Kaz's jeep parked beneath it. Empty.

I parked behind it, and we got out, grabbing our weapons. Big Mike called Kaz on the Handie-Talkie but there was no response.

"*Il est à la boulangerie,*" a voice said from the doorway.

"Monsieur Marcoux?" I asked. He was a thin man in a dark suit, threadbare at the seams. He nodded hurriedly and pointed down the road.

"*Sébastien est allé avec le lieutenant,*" he said, his face twisted in worry.

"Come on, the kid's with Kaz," I said. We bolted down the street, scaring two women who'd just stepped out of a shop. They gasped and retreated inside.

"Here," Big Mike said, grabbing my arm and pulling me through a gate leading to the churchyard. We ducked behind a curving stone wall that led down from the front steps. It gave us a good view of the bakery across an intersection on the opposite corner.

"There's a line, dammit," I said. Five people were visible outside the door, probably more inside the store.

"Look," Big Mike said. "On the left."

It was Kaz, at the corner of the building, watching the door, trying to stay out of sight.

"Yeah, and there's Sébastien across the street." He was lounging against a wall on the other side of the road, keeping watch on the back of the bakery. His weapon was partially hidden behind his back, but I noticed a passerby give him a strange look.

"Someone's going to get spooked real soon," Big Mike said. "Soon as they notice all the hardware. We gotta do something."

"You're right," I said. "And I can't use this Tommy gun, not with all those people around." The Thompson had a selector switch for full automatic or single shot, but I didn't want to panic people. They hadn't been liberated all that long ago, and the sight of an armed GI could easily set them off. I wasn't going to let our quarry escape during the confusion.

"New plan," I said. I set the Thompson against the wall and took off my helmet. I took my garrison cap from my pocket and put it on. "I'm going for a stroll. What kind of bread do you want?"

"The kind without bullets in it. Billy, are you nuts? We don't know if Octave is with Jean-Paul in there."

"No way," I said, standing up straight, my eyes glued to the bakery door. One person came out and two more joined the line. "The mayor must've told Kaz that. He'd know, wouldn't he? Besides, you don't need two people to pick up bread."

I unholstered my automatic and dropped the web belt. I unbuttoned my field jacket and stuffed my hands in the roomy pockets. You'd hardly know one hand gripped a .45 pistol.

"Don't take a shot unless you're sure," I said.

"I'm sure you're crazy. Good luck," Big Mike said.

Luck again. Time for some of the good stuff.

I walked across the street to Sébastien, staying out of the line of sight from inside the bakery. He came to attention as I approached, pulling his Schmeisser across his body. I motioned with my left hand for him to lower it and move back. He got the message and resumed his slumped lounging. A woman with a cloth bag showing a couple of baguettes strolled by, paying us no mind.

"Back door?" I asked, nodding to the rear of the store. "*Porte?*"

"*Oui, porte,*" he said, pointing with enthusiasm. I worried that he thought I wanted him to assault the place, so I did my best through gestures to let him know he needed to stay put and watch for Jean-Paul.

I strolled to the corner of the bakery. I couldn't see Kaz through the line of customers, but most of them saw me and sent hard looks my way. I hoped all they were worried about was that I might jump the line.

There was chatter inside, and suddenly the logjam was broken. Two, three, then four customers filed out and the line moved along. The smell of fresh baked bread was strong, as if it had just come out of the oven.

A fifth customer came out, a young woman in a green coat, followed by a tall, dark-haired man. Good-looking. It was Jean-Paul, and he was leaning in to speak with her, whispering. She laughed.

Jean-Paul wasn't wearing his FFI armband. He had on a short leather jacket, but it was long enough to nearly cover the pistol in his waistband. One hand grasped a sack of bread, and the other was resting on the woman's shoulder.

He hadn't seen us.

Or had he?

I saw his eyes shift focus.

Two people exited the bakery, moving in front of him. A shove, a shout, and then the woman in the green coat tumbled backward, Jean-Paul's sack thrust at her. Through the tangle of customers, I saw Jean-Paul turn away, his hand going to his jacket.

He hadn't seen me. He'd seen Kaz.

I burst through the crowd just as Jean-Paul's sack fell and the baguettes tumbled to the sidewalk. People dived for them, and as I worked to disentangle myself, I saw Kaz step out from the side of the building and aim his carbine at Jean-Paul.

I saw the split-second hesitation in Kaz's eyes as he took in the people directly behind our quarry. Jean-Paul saw it too and fired his pistol. Kaz jumped back as the slug zinged off the corner of the building.

People screamed. Most darted for cover inside the bakery. One lady grabbed loaves of bread from the sidewalk and scurried off. The woman in the green coat was still on the ground, dazed, her eyes wide as she took in the sight of Jean-Paul's gun.

He stopped. He couldn't go after Kaz and expose himself to a clear shot. Then he saw me. He was quick, I had to give him that. He turned and scooped up his lady friend, dragging her across the street, his pistol at the ready.

"*Arrêtez*," I heard Sébastien yell. But Jean-Paul didn't halt. He fired a shot and pulled his hostage back toward the church, unaware of how close Big Mike was.

"Jean-Paul, let her go," I said, walking closer, my gun hand down at my side. I glanced to where Sébastien was and saw him leaning against the wall, his submachine gun at the ready even as blood trickled down his leg.

"I will leave with her, and let her go," he said, his teeth clenched in fury. "But I will be glad to kill you if you come closer. Stop!"

"Where is Octave?" I said, coming to a halt. "Did he send you out to do the shopping?"

"Do not be a fool," Jean-Paul said. "Drop your pistol."

"You're the fool," I said, desperate to keep him talking and distracted. "Commander Stewart fooled you into killing the wrong person. Dickie Thorne was a good man and had nothing to do with the Vercors."

"Many people die, Captain. And Stewart has had his own reckoning. Who is the fool now, eh?"

I didn't dare look to see what Big Mike was doing. All I knew was that Jean-Paul was standing between Big Mike and Sébastien. He couldn't risk a shot, not with the woman and the boy at risk. Where was Kaz?

"We know what you're planning," I said. "The ceremony at Langres. General Robine. It's all over."

"You have not dropped your pistol," Jean-Paul said, moving the barrel of his and placing it against his hostage's temple. "Do it now and step back."

"Okay, okay," I said, worrying I'd pushed him too far. If he thought there was no hope for his plan, he might want to go down shooting. I placed the automatic on the ground and took a step back. "Am I right, about Robine? Just a hunch, you know."

"Be quiet," Jean-Paul said, shaking his pistol hand in fury. The woman's eyes widened, and she screamed, probably thinking she was about to be killed. *No lady*, I almost said out loud, *that would be me*.

A police siren sounded, echoing in the narrow streets. Jean-Paul scrambled backward, the woman writhing in his grasp. I heard boots from behind me, too light to be Big Mike. Jean-Paul spotted Kaz, and raised his pistol to aim at the onrushing threat. His aim lingered on me for a second.

Big Mike fired his M1. Once, twice, in the air. The sound was loud, amplified by the church stonework at his back. Jean-Paul was startled, his gaze searching out this new threat and quickly returning to me before going back to Big Mike. I knew he expected me to go for my gun.

So I did something else.

I launched myself, taking three long strides and diving to tackle the woman in the green coat, rolling and pulling her away from Jean-Paul.

I heard another loud report from the M1 and a couple of quick shots from Kaz's carbine.

The woman in the green coat was stunned. She looked at me, uncomprehending. Then she looked at Jean-Paul flat on his back. She started screaming.

Big Mike and Kaz were both good shots.

CHAPTER FORTY-TWO

"How's Sébastien?" I asked Kaz as I tried to console the woman in green. Her hands grasped at my arms as if she were drowning, and I could pull her to shore. I helped her up and walked her to the steps of the church, as safe a harbor as any. Two women from the bakery line comforted her, and she turned to them eagerly, glad to be done with me.

"A ricochet from the sidewalk," Kaz said, helping the limping Sébastien. A crowd began to grow, and they surrounded the body, staring at us, unsure of what had happened. Only the appearance of Sébastien with his FFI armband and bloody leg gave them assurance that we weren't a gang of Chicago cutthroats. Kaz led him to the church steps and gave him a handkerchief to hold against the slash on his calf.

"We should search the body," Big Mike said, handing me my Thompson.

"The *gendarmes* might have other ideas," I said. Two French cops got out of their automobile and advanced warily, at the same time Mayor Marcoux showed up and cried out at the sight of his son. The *flics* waited for instructions from the mayor, who calmed down quickly as Sébastien and Kaz explained things.

"They're busy," Big Mike said, stepping in front of the cooling corpse. "Check his pockets."

It wasn't pleasant. It looked like the M1 round took him in the throat, and Kaz's two carbine slugs had hit the center of his chest. Which meant a lot of blood pooling around the body. I patted down his trouser pockets.

Nothing. The leather jacket pockets produced nothing but a few francs. Not a single clue, not even an identity card.

His chest was a bloody, pulpy mess. I tried not to look directly at what the bullets had laid bare, using the old trick of focusing a little off to the side. It worked well enough for me to notice the outline of something in his shirt pocket. I reached in and pulled it out, sticky with blood.

"What is it?" Big Mike asked.

"A postcard," I said, feeling the scalloped edges. I wiped it on Jean-Paul's pants, cleaning it enough to see that nothing was written on the blank side. No stamp, no address. I stood and showed it to Big Mike, noticing that the mayor was headed our way, cops in tow and Kaz one step behind.

"I told the mayor how you distracted Jean-Paul when he fired at Sébastien," Kaz said. "He is most grateful." It wasn't a hundred percent true, but right now a grateful mayor was just what we needed.

"Tell him we are thankful for Sébastien's help in apprehending this dangerous criminal," I said. "The boy's a hero."

No politician could resist a heroic offspring, and Marcoux beamed with pleasure as Kaz translated. I apologized for the gunfire and said we'd hoped to capture Jean-Paul and his accomplice much more quietly. And where could we find the other man? And what did he look like?

"The mayor says he put them up in a farmhouse out on the route de Serrecourt," Kaz said. "It was abandoned after the Boche shot the owner in a reprisal. It is six kilometers to the south. Jean-Paul had asked for a remote location where they could practice with their firearms. They were to be snipers with the French army, he'd told the mayor."

"Okay," I said. "Did he get a good look at Octave?"

"Sadly, no," Kaz said. "He never saw him. He only knew there was a second man because Jean-Paul had told him a few days ago. He came to the town hall today to see if the mayor had heard any news about the ceremony in Langres. There was nothing new, but he did pass on the fact that the baker had received a shipment of flour this morning, and he should get to the bakery before it was all sold. We arrived not long after that."

"Wait, how did Jean-Paul get here?" I asked. "On his motorbike?"

"No, the mayor says he used a bicycle," Kaz said. "Sébastien said he saw one behind the bakery."

"Okay," I said. "How do we find this farmhouse?"

"Wait, look at this," Big Mike said, holding the postcard and rubbing off a streak of blood with his thumb. "It's a picture of a village. Read the caption. Sound familiar?"

"Vassieux," I said. "We know that's where Jean-Paul was from." I studied the picture. A mountain peak loomed over a small village with one church steeple and houses set along a curving road.

"He had that on his person?" Kaz asked.

"In his shirt pocket," I said. "He carried it over his heart."

Mayor Marcoux leaned in to study the postcard. "Ah, Vassieux," he said, nodding sadly as if that explained everything. Which, in truth, it did. Jean-Paul's hometown in the Vercors, and that of Octave as well, destroyed in a deadly, murderous reprisal.

"Will they show us where the farm is?" I asked, looking at the policemen. Kaz spoke with the mayor, who snapped out orders to the cops. Then he moved off to attend to his son.

"Ask them about the layout of the place," Big Mike said.

Kaz explained that it was off the road, about three hundred meters in. The ground rose upward, giving anyone in the farmhouse a good view of the approaches. Behind the house, woods encircled the top of a hill. There was a barn, where the previous owner had kept sheep. No other road besides the dirt lane off the route de Serrecourt.

We could drive straight up to the house, but that would be target practice for Octave, so I asked about any other way to get there.

"Yes," Kaz said. "There is another farm on the opposite side of the hill. They know the farmer and say he has cleared his land all the way to the top. He has tracks up to his fields and a jeep could get to the summit easily. Then we walk through the woods and come down to the rear of the farmhouse and barn."

"Simple," Big Mike said. "About time we caught a break."

I didn't want to think again about good luck or bad luck. I just wanted to get this over with.

"Hang on, I want to check something," I said. I walked behind the bakery, looking for the bicycle. It wasn't there. Not surprising, given how valuable bikes were in wartime France. Looked like somebody had taken advantage of the confusion and swiped it. Their lucky day.

We headed out of town, following the police to the farm. They explained to the farmer what we were doing, and he was enthusiastic about the venture. He was tired of all the shooting. He'd had enough of it in this war and wouldn't miss the loud target practice.

Kaz drove up the hill on a rutty dirt track. There were still crops in the fields, cabbages and other plantings that looked like root vegetables. At the top, the track leveled off and we stopped.

"Okay, let's see who's home," I said, and we moved off into the woods. Big Mike brought up the rear, and I noticed a wince as he crossed over a fallen log. His injured leg was acting up, not that he'd admit it. I brushed pine boughs aside as we came out of the forest and knelt to take in the view. Directly below us was the farmhouse. The barn was set back off to the side, just as the cops had described. We waited a few minutes, listening. Nothing. No sign of life.

"Big Mike, stay here and watch for any movement," I said. He nodded, already squinting along the sights of his M1.

Kaz and I ran low to the back of the barn, the blood thumping in my head with the exertion. I shook off a wave of dizziness as we edged our way along the side that faced away from the house. The barn door was open. I signaled Kaz to go inside, keeping my Thompson trained on the house. He dashed in, carbine at the ready.

I followed, seeing no movement in the house. The barn was empty, anything useful long gone. Kaz pointed to a space by the door. The tamped-down dirt floor was stained with oil. A jerrican stood nearby, empty, the gasoline fumes still wafting out of the opening. A tarpaulin lay on the ground, surrounded by a scattering of tools.

"The motorbike," Kaz said. "Gone."

"Damn. We need to check the house anyway," I said, whispering. But something told me we'd come up short. Again.

The back door was wide open. I eased my way inside, Thompson at the ready.

I moved along the hallway to a sitting room up front. Nothing but an overstuffed couch and a rocking chair. I waited, letting my breathing settle down. Kaz whispered that the room off the kitchen was empty. I eyed the stairs, wondering what sort of creaks it would make as we walked up.

But I wasn't nervous. An empty house has a stillness all its own. Octave could be hiding upstairs, and I wouldn't hear his breathing or even a subtle shifting of weight. But his presence, and the threat it carried, would be real. There was nothing here but emptiness.

I checked out the upstairs. Two bedrooms, dirty sheets, clothes on the floor.

Nothing.

"Tell Big Mike to come on," I said. "We came up empty." Kaz gave a whistle and waved his arms. Big Mike walked down the hill, working hard to hide his limp. Too much driving and clambering around in the woods, maybe.

"How'd he know?" Big Mike said as we gathered in front of the barn.

"Maybe he left a while ago," I suggested.

"But why would Jean-Paul remain? And go to the bakery?" Kaz said.

"The bicycle," I said, snapping my fingers. "They had to have somebody else helping them. A local, maybe, who witnessed what happened and pedaled out here to warn Octave. They could have made it in plenty of time."

"Short of questioning all the good people of Lamarche, how could we find this accomplice?" Kaz said, turning to stare out over the weed-filled fields.

"We need to contact Colonel Harding," Big Mike said. "He needs to know General Robine is in real danger."

"Right, let's get back to the 36th and use their radio," I said.

"Come here," Kaz said, walking out into the field. "Look."

A table was set up in the grass, with two chairs. Shell casings littered the ground.

"Yeah, we knew they were shooting out here," Big Mike said.

"Yes," Kaz said. "But we might learn something from this." He started pacing, taking deliberate strides, and counting out loud, making for a collection of chairs and benches set in a row. Shattered glass and pieces of metal were strewn about, the remnants of targets hit by the Lee-Enfield .303 bullets.

"Four hundred meters," Kaz said. "Octave will be targeting General Robine from a sniper's position four hundred meters out."

"Good thinking, Kaz," I said, slapping him on the shoulder. "That's the most useful thing we learned all day."

It was useful, but Octave in handcuffs would have been a lot more useful. We trudged back up the hill and down the other side, and I wondered what memento of his ruined home Octave kept in his shirt pocket.

CHAPTER FORTY-THREE

WE PULLED UP at town hall and checked on Sébastien. He wore a bandage on his leg and a big smile on his face, reclining on a couch in his father's office. A real hometown hero. We said our goodbyes to the mayor and offered regrets at not being able to stay for dinner, tempting as it was.

"Just enough time to get back for chow," Big Mike said as we stood by the jeeps. "After we check on the scouts, I mean."

"I've been thinking," I said. "All three of us don't need to go back. Why don't you head to Langres and get the lay of the land? See if you can spot any likely firing positions."

"Me?" Big Mike said. "It's not a bad idea, but Kaz speaks the lingo."

"Right. Which is why he has to be there when we talk with the scouts. We need a detailed description if we're going to spot Octave."

"Billy is right, Big Mike. It doesn't take three of us to wait around for the Lost Battalion to be rescued," Kaz said.

"Yeah, okay, I see your point," Big Mike said. "You guys gonna be all right?"

"Don't worry about us," I said. "Find a hotel before all the Fifis show up. Something with a good view. You have enough francs?"

"Here. Wait, I will be right back," Kaz said, handing Big Mike a wad of banknotes and dashing back inside town hall.

"Make sure you contact Sam," Big Mike said, busying himself with lowering the canvas top to his jeep. I followed his lead. The sun was out for a change.

"First thing," I said.

"The Hôtel du Cheval Blanc," Kaz said as he returned. "The mayor recommends it highly. Right in the center of town. It is in a former abbey and expensive enough that there should be rooms available, at least until the dignitaries show up."

"Here," I said, forking over some of my cash. "We'll look you up tomorrow night. With or without a description."

"If we don't find this guy, Sam's gotta get the French to call the ceremony off," Big Mike said. "They can enlist these recruits without all the fanfare."

"Fanfare is as important to the French government as a company of recruits," Kaz said. "They wish to show they are rebuilding their army and the French state. Even at the risk of exposure to gunfire. Remember the newsreels of General de Gaulle at the liberation of Paris? He stood tall as a Boche sniper fired on the crowd. I am sure he thought it worth his life not to hide from a German bullet and will expect no less from General Robine."

"We'll just have to do our best," I said. "Enjoy the hotel."

"I will. Beats a cold floor, I gotta admit. See you tomorrow."

"I take it you noticed how he favors his injured leg," Kaz said, as Big Mike drove away.

"Yes. After sleeping on the floor and driving today, he seems to have a bit of a limp. Not that he'd admit it," I said.

"No, nor would he appreciate anything we might say. A warm room, a comfortable bed, and a decent meal may do wonders for Big Mike. And it will be helpful for him to reconnoiter the town. A good plan, Billy. Except for the part that brings us back to those spartan quarters."

"Maybe we'll get lucky and the 442nd will have broken through to the Texas boys and our scouts will be waiting for us," I said. "Or Hemingway will have made it back."

Luck. I was beginning to think it was overrated.

The shadows were growing long by the time we got back to Biffontaine. This time, there were a lot of the Nisei back in town. Unfortunately, they were all in an aid station housed in the 100th Battalion's former headquarters.

I braked as two half-tracks churned through the muddy street, delivering litter cases to the medical personnel. Medics ran to assess the latest batch of wounded, and an ambulance blasted its horn from behind me. I quickly pulled off the road, parking in the alley next to our billet.

"You two! We need that jeep," shouted a doctor, his white apron stained with blood.

"We have two more wounded to collect, they can't wait. Get up there!"

"Where?" I asked, uncertain what his rank was.

"Up that goddamn road!"

He turned away, attending to the first litter case taken off the half-track.

"Let's go," I said. No reason to butt heads with the guy, whatever his rank was. They'd probably have the half-tracks unloaded in five minutes, and if that much time made a difference, we could sure as hell pitch in. "You okay with this, Kaz?"

"I had no other plans for the rest of the day," he said, hanging onto his helmet as I backed out and slammed it into first, jolting both of us back in our seats. We were out of town quickly, the dense, green forest to our left and the flat bottomland to the right. I slowed a bit, knowing that if we overshot our mark, we'd end up on the receiving end of a German 88.

"There," Kaz said, pointing to a cleared space in the pines. A single medic was bandaging the arm of one GI while another stood by, seeming to argue with him. Another Nisei lay on a stretcher, his leg and arm swathed in bloody field dressings.

"I saw you get shot, Danny," the medic said. "Right in the chest. What the hell you doin' walkin' around?"

"Don't worry about me," Danny said. He wore sergeant's stripes and carried a carbine. "I'm fine. I'll help these guys."

"We're supposed to pick up two wounded," I said. "You sure you're not one of them, Sarge?"

"Not my day," he said, pulling two silver dollars from his pocket. "Had 'em stacked in my shirt pocket. Slug hit 'em dead center." He was right. There was an indentation right above *In God We Trust.*

"You one lucky buggah, Danny," the medic said, slipping into what sounded like Hawaiian patois.

"Just had the wind knocked out of me," Danny said. "They thought I was dead. Hey, why they sending officers up here to collect the wounded? Who are you guys?"

"Billy, it's Tock!" Kaz said. He'd knelt by the GI on the stretcher and was close enough to see who it was through the grime on his face.

"Jesus," I said. "Let's get him on the jeep."

"You know Tock?" Danny said as he helped load the stretcher, setting one end on the hood and the other across the passenger seat.

"Yeah, he showed us around yesterday," I said. "He hurt bad?"

"Shot three times but they didn't kill him, and no internal injuries," Danny said. "Since I'm not a candidate for surgery, take Montana here to the aid station. He's got one good arm and can hold on to the stretcher."

"You mind staying here, Kaz?"

"Not as long as you come back," Kaz said, helping Montana into the rear seat while the medic checked the stretcher. Tock groaned, but thankfully he wasn't awake.

"Hey, you must be the two guys from SHAEF who are nosing around here," Danny said. "Looking for those French scouts." I told him we were.

"Billy Boyle," I said, offering my hand. "Let some of that luck rub off, willya?"

"Daniel Inouye," he said as we shook. "Take care of Tock and Montana, okay?"

I promised I would and started the jeep.

"Two morphine syrettes," the medic said, tapping the collar of Tock's field jacket, where the empty syrettes were stuck through the cloth. That was the method medics used to let the aid station know how much a guy'd been given.

"I'll be back quick," I said, turning the jeep around. Kaz waved. Sergeant Inouye was already moving back uphill, into the fight.

"You okay back there, Montana?"

"Yeah, not too bad. Don't worry, I won't let go of Tock. He saved our lives up there."

"What happened?"

"Krauts hit us hard. They waited until we made it to the crest of one of them goddamn ridges. Had a heavy machine gun chewing us up while they tried to flank us. Tock went after it with his BAR. I saw him take a slug to the leg, then roll behind a tree and tie off a bandage neat as you please. He kept after the MG but got hit again, same leg. Only make him madder. Took the bastard out, then fired on the advancing Krauts. We all did, and they lost interest in tangling with us. Tock got hit in the right arm and couldn't fire no more. That's the only reason he stopped fighting. He just couldn't lift that damn BAR. Saved our bacon, pardner."

"Someone ought to put him in for a medal," I said. "Hey, are you really from Montana? Didn't know there were many Japanese there."

"Japanese Americans, Captain. And I might have been the only one. 'Cept for my folks. See, we ain't all the same, just like you. Come from all over."

"Sorry, Montana, I didn't mean you weren't American. I didn't think."

"That's okay, Captain. If you're a pal of Tock's, you gotta be okay. No worries." His voice was fading, and I turned to check on him.

"Don't worry, I ain't letting go. Hurts too much to fall asleep."

"The medic didn't give you morphine?"

"Nah. I told him to save it for the guys on the ridge. We'll be at the aid station soon. I'm okay."

Damn right you are, soldier.

Back at the aid station they grabbed Tock's stretcher and hustled him inside.

"Where's the other guy?" the doctor asked as Montana was helped out of the jeep by a medic. "I was expecting a chest wound."

"False alarm," I said. "Sergeant Inouye now has two dented silver dollars and a helluva story to tell. I guess he was knocked for a loop by the impact, but he's fine."

"He's a good man, a natural leader. Glad he's okay. By the way, I should apologize for shouting at you before. Mainly because you out-rank me. Lieutenant Masato Hasegawa."

"I like your style, Lieutenant. Billy Boyle. I have to go back up there and get my pal. If there's anything else we can do, we'll lend a hand."

Lieutenant Hasegawa had an orderly pack up field dressings, sulfa, and more morphine syrettes for me to bring back to the medic.

"Tell Private Sujii to watch out for himself," he said. "And that he did a good job patching Tock up. He's going to pull through."

I promised I would. As I was driving back up the road, darkness began to settle in. Explosions rippled across the hills, volleys of steel slashing trees and men like the devil's own scythe. Ours, theirs, it was impossible to say.

It was horrible, but oddly, I felt good. I'd finally done something useful.

CHAPTER FORTY-FOUR

I DROVE UP with the supplies and found Private Sujii and Kaz helping a GI make his way down the steep slope. Blood dripped from his hand, but it was his feet that seemed to be the problem. He gasped and winced with every step, but I didn't see any injuries to his legs.

"Trench foot," Sujii announced. "Charley's got it bad."

"Not to mention a bullet through the arm," Kaz said, helping Charley to sit on a log.

"I could still shoot," Charley said, holding out his bleeding arm. "Until this."

Sujii went to work cutting back the wool fabric of Charley's overcoat and sprinkling sulfa on the wound. He applied a field dressing and tied it off.

"This'll hold," Sujii said. "Let's get you in the jeep."

It was easier said than done. We had to lift him into the seat, and Charley gritted his teeth as his feet hit the floor. Trench foot was painful, and the cold, wet conditions up here were perfect for bringing out the worst it had to offer.

I gave Sujii the supplies, and he said he had to move farther up the ridge. There'd been some progress, and he needed to set up a new spot to receive the wounded.

"Stay low," I said, and got into the jeep.

"Are you all right?" Kaz asked, patting Charley on the shoulder from the rear seat.

"Yeah. Except I feel like a fool for complaining about how hot it was back in Italy," he said. "Hot and dry, and I bitched about it." I swung the jeep around as Kaz held Charley's shoulder, keeping him steady.

"How's it going up there?" I asked.

"Slow, but we're pushing them back. Trouble is, they can dig right in again. And after dark, forget about it. Pitch-black up there. Can't tell if it's a Kraut, a tree, or your own buddy two feet in front of you."

"Well, I think I'd see a tree, but I'm going slow just in case," I said. With no lights, I could barely make out the narrow road in front of me.

"You the fellas looking for the French scouts?" Charley asked, cradling his wounded arm in his lap. "What'dya want with them anyway?" I gave him the short version.

"You're kidding, right? You need a better story than that, Captain. Nobody's going to believe the high command sent two officers up here 'cause some Frenchman killed a coupla guys."

"The closer we get to the front, the more illogical it sounds, I must admit," Kaz said. "But it is the truth."

"Scuttlebutt is you're investigating Dahlquist," Charley said.

"Should he be investigated?" I said.

"Guy deserves a court-martial," Charley said, a bitter laugh escaping his lips. "He got his own people surrounded, and now he's sending us through a meat grinder to save his ass. *Bakatare* all around."

"You are taking quite a chance saying so," Kaz said from the back seat. "We could put you on report."

"I don't think so," Charley said. "Officers who volunteer to take wounded off the line aren't the type. Besides, what are they going to do? Shoot me?" He laughed again, or maybe it was a stab of pain.

"Excellent point," Kaz said. "What does *bakatare* mean?"

"Idiot. Moron. Very stupid. Take your pick. Present company excluded, sirs."

"Almost there," I said, as we passed the first buildings on the outskirts of town.

"Hot and dry," Charley said to no one in particular. "What I wouldn't give for some hot, dusty, and dry right now."

The aid station was quiet, thankfully, and the medics got Charley out and carried him inside. We followed, and Doc Hasegawa asked if we'd stick around for a while. Word was the fighting had lessened as night fell, but the medical half-tracks were still making the rounds, and the doc wanted us to wait in case of an emergency.

We told him sure, and an orderly took us to a back room where a pile of bacon and Spam sandwiches had been brought over by the cooks. We put a sizeable dent in it.

"Spam tastes decidedly better the hungrier one is," Kaz said.

"And the closer to death," I said, sitting back and feeling how bone-tired I was.

"Half-tracks are on the way in," Doc Hasegawa said as he entered the room a few minutes later. "You fellas can take off whenever you want. Thanks for the help."

"No problem," I said. "How's Charley?"

"Through-and-through gunshot wound. I stitched him up, so his arm'll be fine. But it's a bad case of trench foot. We're going to evacuate him to a field hospital in the morning. Thing is, warm air makes trench foot even more painful. In the summer, I had two guys go AWOL from the hospital and come back on their own. They said it hurt too much to be warm."

"Sweet Jesus," I said. "What did you do?"

"Gave them extra socks and told 'em to keep their feet dry," he said. "But that's damn near impossible in this weather. Half the guys already have trench foot, just not as bad as Charley. Listen, I'm going to get some shuteye. Where are you bunking?"

Kaz told Hasegawa about our drafty lodgings across the street, and he quickly offered us a couple of spare cots and the use of this room. We didn't hesitate to accept.

"Who put you in that dump?" Hasegawa asked as orderlies brought in the cots and cleared space.

"Division CO," I said. "I think maybe it was a hint."

"Don't get me started on General Dahlquist," he said.

"He is not well thought of within the 442nd," Kaz said. "Perhaps it will take some time to get used to his ways."

"Oh, don't get me wrong," Hasegawa said. "I think the guy deserves a medal. The Iron Cross, for starters."

■ ■ ■

I DRIFTED OFF to sleep chuckling about Dahlquist receiving the German Iron Cross for his contribution to the war effort and managed a decent night's sleep. Being off the floor and having intact windows helped. Shortly after dawn, the noise of the medical half-tracks revving awakened us, and we shuffled out to find an urn of coffee and fresh doughnuts on a table, courtesy of the cooks in the mess tent.

"Captain, we have a stove set up out back," Doc Hasegawa said, appearing in a clean uniform and looking wide awake. "Wash up and shave first. You'll feel better now, and you'll thank me if you show up here with a facial wound. Godliness is next to cleanliness in my aid station."

"Very good, Doctor," Kaz said. "Billy is beginning to look scruffy."

"Have *you* looked in a mirror lately?" I said, feeling the two-day-old growth on my chin and wincing as I rubbed my cuts the wrong way.

"Lieutenant, that is nice work," Hasegawa said, leaning in close to study Kaz's scar. "Your surgeon had a steady hand. And I'll bet you didn't have any dirty stubble blown into the wound."

"No, that was not the case," Kaz said, turning away from the doctor's professional curiosity.

"Good advice, Doc," I said. "We'll get cleaned up."

"And change your socks!" Hasegawa barked, heading off to check on the walking wounded who'd spent the night at the aid station. We grabbed our kits and found the back door. An orderly was attending a huge wood-burning stove that held two large pots of simmering water. He ladled the water into our helmets, and we set up on a wooden table. Then came the lather and the shave, using the hot water warming our helmets.

"What next?" Kaz asked, running the razor across his cheek, crossing the scar that ran down from his eye. Did he think about Daphne every time he shaved?

"Division HQ," I said, swishing my razor in the water and trying to concentrate on the living. "Radio Colonel Harding at Seventh Army. See if Captain Lewis has any news about the scouts or Hemingway. Then head to wherever the 442nd Battalion headquarters is and check on their progress. We need to know if there's any chance of talking to the scouts today. Tomorrow will be too late."

"Agreed," Kaz said, finishing his shave. "Even if we have no description, we should be in Langres before dark."

We finished washing up, changed our socks, and made a beeline for the hot joe and doughnuts. As good as all that was, I had the sinking feeling it was going to be the high point of the day.

Then we drove to Bruyères and found Lieutenant Lewis at HQ, studying a map of the area.

"How are things going, Lieutenant?" I asked.

"Slow. Slower than the general would like," he answered, folding the map and stuffing it into his jacket. "We're heading to each of the 442nd battalions in a few minutes to motivate them."

"We helped bring in wounded from the 100th Battalion last night," I said. "I'd say they were highly motivated."

"The general's priority is to save the Lost Battalion," Lewis said. "I'm sure your efforts were appreciated. Is there something you need?"

"Two things. I need to send a radio message to my boss at Seventh Army, and I need to know if you've heard from Jack Hemingway yet."

"Nothing from Hemingway. The OSS boys aren't good at sharing information. If he'd made it back, we would have heard, no problem. But whatever is going on, they're keeping mum. Maybe ask Seventh Army to tell them to cooperate. They live in a top secret world all their own."

"We have encountered the OSS before, Lieutenant Lewis, and I must agree with your approach," Kaz said. "If we can use your communications facilities, we will make that request."

"Of course," Lewis said, calling for a GI to take us there.

"Good luck with the motivation," I said. Like a true loyal aide, Lewis kept a straight face.

"A little luck wouldn't go amiss," he said, rising to don his jacket and helmet.

"You laid it on a little thick with Lewis," I whispered to Kaz as we walked to the comms building.

"I thought he might be too suspicious of us to allow it," Kaz said. "What with the rumor we are investigating his superior. Couching it in terms of agreeing with his idea seemed wise."

"We don't really need to pressure the OSS, do we? If Hemingway isn't here, it really doesn't matter."

"Of course not," Kaz said. "But I am sure it does matter to Lieutenant Jack, wherever he may be."

Once inside, we wrote out the message for Harding.

Urgent. Assassination attempt planned for twelve noon tomorrow, Langres, at recruitment ceremony for French FFI. Target is General Michel Robine. One suspect still at large, Lucien Rivet, AKA Octave or Savart. Has sniper rifle. Shot may be planned for four hundred yards. Big Mike in Langres now, Hôtel du Cheval Blanc. Will arrive later today with possible positive identification of suspect.

"Anything else?" I asked Kaz.

"I wish there were more," Kaz said. "Let us see what we can find in the hours left to us."

We got sketchy directions to the 442nd command post. The situation was fluid, which was another way of saying HQ wasn't entirely in control of the situation. Lewis had already driven off in a radio-equipped jeep with Dahlquist and a non-com, so maybe he knew where he was going. We sure as hell didn't.

Back through Biffontaine, we took the turn for Belmont, an even smaller village nestled between the looming hills. MPs from the 36th Division manned a crossroads with an anti-aircraft emplacement next to the road. They didn't know where the 442nd was, but they told us one of their regimental headquarters was straight ahead, just off a logging road.

"General Dahlquist headed there ten minutes ago, Captain," the MP said. "Just so you know."

"Thanks, soldier," I said, and gunned the jeep, turning onto the dirt track and hoping not to get stuck in the mud. The headquarters was in a grove of pines just off the road. Camouflage netting was draped above tents and jeeps, and antennas poked into the branches.

"Is the 442nd headquarters ahead on this road, Sergeant?" Kaz asked a non-com who eyed us from his perch on a log. He squinted through the blue smoke that curled up from the butt he held cupped in one hand.

"Last I heard," he said. "General's looking for 'em too."

He took another drag on his cigarette and looked away. Other dogfaces went about their business, but they looked weary. Worn down. They'd been told to stand by and protect the flanks while another unit fought to break through to their buddies. Not exactly a morale booster.

I drove off, not knowing what to say. Nothing was best.

"I cannot understand how they can sit there," Kaz said. "Their comrades are dying."

"They have orders to sit there," I said. "Dahlquist is protecting his own people."

"Easy orders to follow," Kaz said. "But the memory will haunt them."

A volley of shellfire crashed into the forest ahead of us. Not close, but close enough to make us flinch. If we missed the Nisei HQ, we could barrel straight into a barrage, or a foxhole full of Fritzes.

I heard the shouting before we turned the corner, the unmistakable sound of Dahlquist's voice carrying in the chill air. I pulled in behind Lewis's jeep and watched as the scene played itself out. Dahlquist was going toe-to-toe with a colonel, both shouting at each other, holding nothing back.

"Let me do my job, General! We're working our way forward, but it's slow going. Casualties are heavy."

"You can't stop," Dahlquist shouted. "There's a battalion dying up there! Move!"

"We're not stopping, we're fighting a heavily dug-in force," the colonel said, his hands on his hips, not giving an inch.

"That's Colonel Miller," Kaz whispered. "As of yesterday, commanding officer of the 442nd. Private Sujii told me the previous CO was wounded."

I didn't envy him. His men, standing and watching from their foxholes, had stunned expressions on their faces. This wasn't the way senior officers acted, at least not in front of the lower ranks.

"The hell with this," Dahlquist snapped, and stalked back to his jeep. "Lewis, take me up to 100th Battalion. We'll light a fire under them."

"Yes sir," Lewis said, starting the jeep.

"Boyle!" Dahlquist shouted, taking notice of us. "You boys come along. You'll have a front-row seat, and you can tell Ike about it. Let's go!"

Lewis turned and gave a quick nod. There might have been a roll of the eyes as well, but it was hard to tell with his helmet pulled down. The sergeant in the back seat with the SCR-300 radio was stoic, a blank look on his face that said he'd seen it all before.

The rattle of rifle fire echoed off the hills. Machine guns ripped the air and multiple explosions shattered the trees. We halted at a collection point for the wounded, where two medics were stabilizing a half dozen men. Beyond them, a radio and several officers hunched over in a ditch marked the 100th Battalion's command post.

"Colonel Singles!" Dahlquist yelled, jumping from the jeep before it rolled to a halt. "I understand you're less than seven hundred meters from the Lost Battalion. Keep going, we've got to reach them!"

"That's right, General," Singles agreed. "We made progress this morning, but we came up against another line of defense. Machine guns and mortars are hurting us."

"I want the men to crawl and run forward because that's the only way to push the enemy back. Company commanders are to go to the front and drive their companies!"

"That's where they are, General," Colonel Singles replied, his mouth set in a grim line. "Those who are left alive."

"Damn it, get your men moving," Dahlquist said, ignoring what Singles was telling him. He moved up the steep hill, Captain Lewis following. Singles had no choice but to go along, shaking his head and muttering. He motioned for his headquarters staff to follow.

"Soldier, you can't do anything here, move!" Dahlquist said, standing upright and looking down at a GI hunkered behind a tree. It was Fred Hosakawa, who gaped at the sight of a general up front. "Soldier, keep going. Keep moving."

Whatever shortcomings Dahlquist had, he wasn't lacking in personal courage. He kept at the men, until enough were moving that the rest got going on their own. A few mortar rounds landed behind us, and Dahlquist laughed.

"See, Colonel? If you were still back there, you'd be blown to bits. Forward is the only way to go," Dahlquist said, his voice rising in intensity. He continued to the crest of the hill, standing in plain view. Below us, GIs scrambled down an embankment and were starting to climb up the other side, firing as they moved. Bullets whizzed through the trees as the Germans returned fire, but they were mainly targeting the advancing troops.

"General, you should really take cover," Singles advised, wisely edging to the lee side of a thick tree. Kaz and I knelt, keeping our heads low.

"You need to advance, not dig in, Singles," Dahlquist said. "Lewis, let's see that map. We must be within six hundred meters by now."

"Yes sir," Lewis said, taking the map from his pocket and unfolding it as the volume of fire picked up.

His head snapped back and plumed pink. Lewis fell into Dahlquist's embrace, a sniper's bullet to his head. Dahlquist grunted, staggering back under the lifeless load, until he let the corpse sink to the ground. His uniform was streaked red. He tried to wipe it off, but his hands came away thick with blood and bits of bone.

CHAPTER FORTY-FIVE

"My god," Dahlquist said over and over as he skittered down the hill, making for his jeep. "They were aiming for me and hit poor Lewis. My god."

Maybe they were. Maybe it was a stray shot. If it had been a sniper, he'd probably caught sight of that map being flashed around and took out the man holding it. But it suited Dahlquist to play a central role, even as Lewis's body cooled, so I said nothing. Besides, Dahlquist looked distraught, as if he might go off the deep end, and I didn't want to be the guy who had to catch him.

"What is he doing?" Kaz asked as we followed him. Dahlquist was picking up speed, and either he wanted to hightail it out of here, or he had some other plan. Colonel Singles had stayed on the hilltop, probably glad to be rid of the general, but I had the gnawing sense that someone needed to keep an eye on him.

"Let's stay close," I said, following the general to his jeep. A half-track had arrived for the wounded, and GIs were busy loading them up.

"Fire support mission," Dahlquist said. The communications sergeant did a double take at the sight of Dahlquist's bloody uniform, but he recovered and picked up the handset, contacting the field artillery.

"Shoot on Hill 345573," Dahlquist ordered as he calmly rinsed off his hands with water from a canteen.

"General, that's the position of the Lost Battalion," the sergeant said.

"Shoot on Hill 345573," Dahlquist shouted. "Don't you dare question me."

Standing to the side of the general, I made eye contact with the sergeant, shaking my head side to side. *No, don't do it.*

"Yes sir," the sergeant said, gripping the handset and repeating the order. "Shoot on Hill 345573. Repeat, Hill 345573."

"Good. Now get in front and drive to the 3rd Battalion," Dahlquist said, vaulting into the passenger's seat as if nothing unusual had happened.

With Dahlquist's back turned, the sergeant showed us the hand in which he held the SCR-300 handset. It had a built-in switch for sending and receiving that had to be pressed for a message to be transmitted. He hadn't depressed it.

"Thank god," Kaz murmured as we got into our jeep to follow. "I wonder how many other disasters his men have managed to avert."

"This has to qualify as the biggest," I said, stepping on it to keep pace with Dahlquist's jeep. "He has to be off his rocker to call in artillery on his own men."

"I sincerely hope so," Kaz said, holding on as we maneuvered through the rutted dirt track. Firing was going on all around us, or at least it sounded that way as the noise of battle echoed off the ridges on either side. We followed Dahlquist into a small field, one of the few flat and open spaces to be found.

GIs off-loaded crates of ammo from a half-track as stretcher-bearers carried wounded to be taken to the aid station. The image of Germans doing the same just a few hills away popped into my mind. It was ludicrous if you thought about it, which wasn't necessarily a good idea. Their bullets wounded our men, ours did the same to theirs, and we both carted off the wounded. A mirror image of carnage.

I shook the notion off with a shudder and trailed Dahlquist as he stalked away, taking the path the wounded had been brought in on. We dodged more litter cases and walking wounded. Six bodies had been laid to the side of the path, their lifeless eyes staring at the green branches and cloud-darkened sky beyond. All around us, trees were shattered from shellfire and craters dotted the muddy ground. Pine trees burned, sending swirls of smoke into the acrid air.

"Colonel Pursall!" Dahlquist bellowed, not sparing a moment to look down at the dead. Ahead, a tall, heavy-set officer was speaking into a Handie-Talkie, kneeling behind a tree. He was surrounded by dug-in GIs. When he saw the general, he handed the radio to a non-com and prepared himself for the onslaught. Pursall was a big guy, towering over the shorter Nisei around him. He wore glasses and looked more like a stout businessman than a combat officer.

"General," Pursall said, stepping forward. "Be careful, sir, we're under fire here."

"Pursall, order your men to fix bayonets and charge," Dahlquist said. "Now."

"General, we just pushed the Germans back," Pursall said. "You saw what it cost us. My lead companies have taken eighty percent casualties getting up here. I and K Companies are spent. Exhausted."

"I'll tell you when to stop, Colonel, and it isn't now. Get them moving!" Dahlquist shouted, punching his index finger into Pursall's chest.

"Those are my boys you're trying to kill. You're not going to kill my boys," Pursall spat back at him. He grabbed Dahlquist's bloody jacket and shook him like he was a hysterical kid. "I won't let you kill my boys. If there's any orders to be given for my boys to attack, I'll give the orders personally, and I'll lead them."

"Then do it," Dahlquist said, brushing aside Pursall's hands. The general stepped back, out of the colonel's reach. "That's a direct order."

This was worse than what we saw play out with Colonel Miller. Pursall was all but assaulting a superior officer in full view of his men. That was a court-martial offense. But Dahlquist didn't care. All he cared about was the attack, whatever the cost.

"If you think it's that simple," Pursall said, "I'd like you to come with me for a look."

Pursall walked up the narrow ridge and Dahlquist followed, the two of them still arguing. We went forward a few paces and knelt behind a blackened tree. GIs all around us watched the two officers continue to argue, knowing their fates hung in the balance. But the outcome wasn't in doubt. A colonel doesn't win arguments with a general, especially not this general.

Dahlquist returned, walking straight past us as if we didn't exist. From behind him, Pursall let loose a heavy sigh, then squared his shoulders.

"Item Company! King Company!" he shouted. "Advance."

Pursall was greeted by silence. No one moved. He unholstered his .45 automatic, turned, and began making his way up the hill.

"Damn," a Nisei near us said. "If he's going to get himself killed, we can't let him do it alone." He rose from his foxhole and followed, running hunched over. Slowly, other men joined him, until what was left of the two companies began to catch up with their colonel, who was halfway to the ridgeline, firing his pistol like a man possessed.

There was no bayonet charge, no shouting, no grand gestures, just a wave of men swallowed by the forest, firing from the hip, killing Germans and being killed. I gripped my Thompson and took a step toward the struggle.

"No, Billy," Kaz said, his hand on my shoulder. "This is not our fight. We must stay alive and stop Octave. If we were to be killed, even if the scouts survive, we would have failed everyone."

"You don't have to go with me," I said, my eyes on the Nisei disappearing into the smoke and dense woods.

"You know I would not let you go into that alone," Kaz said.

I dropped back a foot. He was right. About it all. If I went, Kaz would be at my side. In my heart, I knew we weren't here for a valiant last charge. Our job was to wait and salvage what we could of our mission if the scouts were left alive.

And my heart also knew I'd never forget the moment I watched those men advance into hell's open, gaping jaws.

WE WAITED. WE waited as a few walking wounded stumbled down from the ridge. We waited as half-tracks and ambulances rolled into the field, and stretcher-bearers dashed toward the firing. We strained to track the sounds of the fight as it faded and then echoed against the hills. Stretcher-bearers began to return slowly, descending the slope with their wounded charges carefully tied down.

"How much longer?" Kaz asked. "Until we know if they succeeded or failed?"

"How much longer before we have to leave without knowing?" I said, checking my watch. Time was running short.

Trucks and more half-tracks pulled in behind us, medics spilling out and running past us, their first-aid packs slapping against their sides.

"They did it!" Doc Hasegawa shouted, coming up from the trucks. His helmet with the bright red cross was nearly falling off his head. "They broke through!"

"You sure?" I asked.

"Damn straight I'm sure, Captain. Those Texas boys are making their way down now, more than two hundred of 'em."

"What about the 442nd?" I asked.

"Dahlquist ordered them to stay up there and continue pressing the enemy," Hasegawa said. "Like they've got any strength left."

"The general does not seem to care much for the reality of the situation," Kaz said. "Do you know when the men should get down?"

"Oh yeah, you're after the French scouts. Shouldn't be too long now," he said. "I'm waiting for the litter cases first. Some of them have been in bad shape for days. After them, the rest should come through here."

"Think it was worth it, Doc?" I asked.

"We saved more than two hundred men from being overrun," he said. "A lot of 'em would've been killed, the rest captured. I haven't seen all our casualty numbers, but I know we have at least one hundred dead, hundreds more wounded. You tell me, Captain. Was it worth it?"

Doc Hasegawa took off to organize a casualty clearing station while we waited for the Lost Battalion to make its way down. Was it worth it? That was a numbers game I wasn't willing to play.

The litter cases came first, Doc Hasegawa shouting orders to have them immediately loaded into half-tracks or to wait for on-the-spot treatment. Then guys with dirty, bloodstained bandages made their way slowly to medics who checked and cleaned their wounds.

The rest of the Lost Battalion didn't look much better, except for the big grins on their faces. I stopped a non-com at the head of the column, while Kaz kept his eye out for the scouts.

"Hey Sarge, you had two French scouts with you, right? They okay?" I said.

"Henri and Pierre?" he said, stopping to light up a smoke. "Yeah, they're back there somewhere. Good men. Pierre is a real woodsman. Helped us find water and mushrooms. The kind that won't kill ya."

"Great," I said, happy for the good news. "Glad you made it, Sarge."

"We owe it all to the 442nd," he said, nodding in the direction of the hill to the east where the Nisei were still fighting. "We thought it was the Krauts sneaking up on us, but instead the first thing I see is this short, dark-skinned guy with a helmet that looked two sizes too big. I knew right away it was the 442nd. I ran up to him and gave him a hug like he was my long-lost brother. Kinda was, right? Know the first thing he asks me? 'Do you guys need any cigarettes?' I'll never forget that. Sergeant Matt Sakumoto. I'll never forget that guy. Never."

He walked off, repeating *never* a few more times.

I ran up the line of GIs, their faces a blend of hollow-eyed exhaustion, relief, shock, and overwhelming joy. I spotted Kaz in the crowd. The two Frenchmen were unmistakable. Even with their American field jackets, the berets and leather boots marked them as FFI.

"Billy!" Kaz yelled, herding the scouts closer to me.

"What do they say?" I asked.

"Wait," Kaz said, listening as one finished speaking. "Yes, Savart drove with them and Lieutenant Jack. He left them a few kilometers from their destination, saying he had to meet a contact."

"Yeah, yeah, we know that much. What's he look like? Did he say anything about what he was up to?"

"Patience, Billy," Kaz said, and spoke to Pierre and Henri much more calmly than I just had. "No, Savart said nothing about his plans. He claimed he would rejoin them later in the day."

Kaz spoke to them again, and as they answered, I saw his eyes go wide.

"We have been fools," he said. "Savart is thin and tall. A young man with curly dark hair."

"Danton. Danton is Octave."

CHAPTER FORTY-SIX

"SHOULDN'T WE GET to a radio?" Kaz said as I sped down the road. "We can get a message to Colonel Harding."

"No," I said. "Bruyères is in the wrong direction, and we don't have time. Besides, a radio message could sit around for hours before it gets to Harding. We already told him we'll be in Langres today, so let's get there."

"Once we get clear of the front lines, we can stop and find a working telephone," Kaz said. "Call the hotel and warn Big Mike to look out for Danton."

"Good idea," I said, negotiating a muddy curve before coming out on a paved road. I floored it. "Lamarche. We have friends there."

"I thought Danton was a friend," Kaz said, holding onto his helmet. "How could we have been so wrong?"

"Colonel Laurent vouched for him," I said. "He was the one who was fooled, and we just took his word for Danton's loyalty."

"The perfect cover," Kaz said. "He worked as an undercover spy for Laurent, while all the while he was a double agent."

"Yeah, except he wasn't working for the other side," I said, blasting my horn at a slow-moving truck and passing it. "He was working for, what, the Maquis du Vercors?"

"I suspect it was closer to home," Kaz said. "Remember, we discovered that Lucien Rivet, who operated under both the code names Savart and Octave, was born in Vassieux. Therefore, Danton is from Vassieux, as was Jean-Paul. I would venture that Lucien Rivet is Danton's real name."

"He used the *nom de guerre* Danton to create a false identity and get to Algiers, where he and Jean-Paul could learn who scuttled the support for the uprising," I said. "He ingratiated himself with Laurent, gained his confidence, and pretended to help him."

"Yes. While all the time monitoring what Laurent knew about the plot and steering him in the wrong direction," Kaz said. "Octave was his cover name for this operation, and he probably used Savart to confuse things."

"That's why he told the scouts his name was Savart," I said. "Hemingway probably thought it was just another code name. But wait, wasn't there a form filled out in Rivet's name? How did Danton manage that? Hemingway knew who he was. He even mentioned what a big help he was organizing the scouts."

"Very helpful," Kaz said. "So helpful that Jack probably left much of the paperwork to him. Easy enough to slip a phony document into the pile. He probably carried it with him as proof of identity. One of his many, that is."

"He's slippery," I said. "But now we know who we're looking for, and where."

"Yes. Four hundred meters from General Robine at noon tomorrow."

Half an hour later, we pulled over in front of the town hall in Lamarche. Kaz dashed in and came back ten minutes later, saying our friend the mayor connected him with the hotel in Langres, and a message naming Danton was left for Big Mike, who was not in his room. Also, the mayor still wanted us to come to dinner.

"Speaking of food," Kaz said, "stop at the bakery. It will be nice to see it without hostage-taking." I did, and we got lucky. No lines, and bread baked that morning. We tore into the loaves and tried to come up with a plan.

"The first thing will be to look for vantage points, which I'd guess Big Mike has already done," I said. "Then we'll check those at four hundred meters from where Robine will be."

"That is something else Big Mike will have ascertained," Kaz said. "The location of the ceremony."

"Right. Say, you know anything about Langres? Ever been there?"

"No, I have not. I would surmise that since it has a decent hotel, according to the mayor, it will be large enough for one cathedral. Likely with a tall spire," Kaz said, ripping off a chunk of bread.

"If there's a town square, that's probably where the swearing-in will be held. Aren't most cathedrals in the town center? So too close for a long-range shot."

"Likely," Kaz agreed. "And harder to make a getaway as well. Distance is better. If Danton scores a hit on the first shot, he could be away before anyone realizes where it came from. Especially in a setting with stone buildings. The echo will be loud and confusing."

"Agreed. We need to focus on that high point four hundred meters from where Robine will be standing," I said. "With Big Mike already on the case, how hard can it be?"

ONE HOUR LATER, as we approached Langres, we realized just how hard it could be. Driving on a straight roadway through low-lying farmland, we caught sight of our destination.

"It is a fortress," Kaz said.

"And those twin spires look to be the highest point around, right in the center," I said.

"*Très redoutable*," Kaz said.

He was right, it was very formidable. From our viewpoint, we could see the entire town perched on a hill that dominated the countryside. Thick stone walls encompassed it, or at least the part we could see. We were used to the Vosges, where hilltops overlooked the towns. Here, the town was on the hilltop.

"There's no place for a sniper to set up, not four hundred meters away," I said, taking in the rooftops crowded in on each other. "There can't be a clear line of fire anywhere except from those cathedral towers."

"That would make sense if Danton was planning on shooting Robine as he was driven in," Kaz said. "But how could he know which direction he would arrive?"

"He can't. There must be some location where he'd have a straight line of sight to the town center," I said. "We have to find Big Mike and see what he's discovered."

We drove through a gate in the enormous granite wall that looked like something out of the Middle Ages. It was the same inside. Narrow streets with old stone buildings and quaint half-timbered houses ran in every direction with hardly a straight line to be seen.

"This is not sniper country," Kaz said. "Turn right here, it looks like a main road. We may as well find the town center and take a look."

"Good idea," I said, taking a right and coming out on a wider street. Shops were open and people were out walking. It looked like peacetime.

"Here, *Place Diderot*," Kaz said as we entered a small, diamond-shaped plaza. "There is a statue of the man himself. He must have lived here. Denis Diderot, the famous philosopher."

"Of course," I said, parking next to a staff car and a jeep with French army markings. Looked like the dignitaries were starting to arrive. "Famous even in Boston. Pretty tight space, isn't it?"

"Yes," Kaz said, craning his neck to look up at the cathedral spires overlooking the plaza. He stood on his seat and looked back the way we came. "Perhaps from that direction. These buildings are no more than four stories. I am not sure our sniper would have the height to see into the plaza from any distance."

"The spires," I said. "We need to check them. A sniper would have a field day up there."

"If Danton does not care about escaping, he will be up there," Kaz said. "But he has worked to cover his tracks at every juncture. I fear he has some other plan."

Kaz asked a passerby for directions to the Hôtel du Cheval Blanc, and we found it easily on the rue Diderot, which was basically the main street in this burg and the only straight line around. The hotel was built of heavy stone, part of the church at its back. We grabbed our packs and made for the lobby, which had a slate floor and vaulted ceilings, the lingering decor of its bygone days as an abbey.

"You're already checked in," Big Mike said, rising from a chair and folding his copy of *Stars and Stripes*. "Victor has your keys."

"You got our message?" I asked as a smiling guy at the desk handed us our room keys.

"Yeah. No sight of Danton, not that I'd expect him to be strolling around," Big Mike said. "He sure pulled one over on us. You guys want to get cleaned up, and we'll put our heads together in the bar?"

"Yeah, we better," I said, suddenly aware of how dirty and disheveled we were. "Half an hour."

"Okay," Big Mike said, returning to his seat. I noticed he still favored that leg.

"You have a limp," Kaz said. "Most pronounced."

"That's because I got it wrapped at the hospital. Tight. I'll fill you in once you don't smell so ripe. They have a laundry service here. They'll polish your boots too."

"Sorry you had such a rough time adjusting to the abbey life," I said, then arranged with Victor to have our dirty uniforms laundered. And our boots polished.

In forty minutes, we were sitting at a table in the bar. Washed, shaved, and dressed in a clean uniform and low quarter shoes, I felt almost human. My headache had faded and the ringing in my ears was down to a faint chiming. Kaz had already filled Big Mike in on the Lost Battalion, and as soon as our glasses of beer arrived, we toasted the 442nd.

"Okay, first tell us about your leg," I said. "What happened?"

"I've been busy," Big Mike said. "Mostly walking. The wall surrounding the town is two miles around, and you can walk the whole way on it. Hell, you could drive a jeep along it, it's that wide. I just began to get sore, so when I went to the hospital, I asked them to wrap it up tight."

"It was bad enough for you to go to the hospital?" I asked, knowing Big Mike wasn't a fan.

"No, I went to the Hôpital de la Haute-Marne, just a few streets away, because it has five stories. I went up on the roof to check the line of sight to the plaza. You could almost see it. If I'd had a ladder, I might have been able to."

"How?" Kaz asked.

"There's a decorative façade, if that's the right term, that goes about ten feet above the roofline. You could lean a ladder against it and maybe get a better view. I didn't get a chance since the janitor called a security guard. That's when I ended up talking to a doctor who looked at my leg. He told me to stay off it. He also promised to have the door to the roof locked and tell the guards to be on the alert."

"Okay. What about the steeples?"

"I climbed up both. A possibility, sure. But he'd be right on top of things. First off, he'd never get away, and second, he'd have to hide there ahead of time. Otherwise, there's too many chances he'd be spotted carrying his rifle," Big Mike said, taking a long gulp of beer.

"He might be mistaken for one of the FFI volunteers," Kaz said, sipping at his glass. "But I agree, the location is not optimal for Danton's purposes."

"What else?" I asked, relishing the cool beer against my throat. It was tempting to have another, but I needed what wits I had ready to roll.

"Coupla things," Big Mike said. "There's a road that empties into Diderot plaza. Rue Jean Rossat. You walk about a quarter mile and there's a house on a corner with a small turret on the third floor. It juts out just enough to give a clear view down to the plaza. I knocked on the door this morning, but some lady with a broom yelled and chased me away. Might be worth checking. I'm sure Kaz can sweet-talk her."

"Okay, what else?"

"Well, this wall. It has twelve towers built into it. Two of them are lined up with streets that feed into the plaza," Big Mike said. "Problem is, they were all built to defend the place. They have firing slits, but they all face outward."

"We should probably take a look," I said.

"I've always wanted to walk the walls of Langres," I heard from behind me. "I never thought it would be with you, Billy. Shall we?"

It was Diana. Kaz was on his feet in a second, giving her and Christine Granville those Continental pecks on both cheeks. Me, I settled for a single kiss, happy at the sight of Diana and the touch of her lips.

"My god, Billy!" Diana said, once she'd had a look at me. "What happened to your face? Are you all right?"

"Just a few scratches," I said, giving a cleaned-up version of events of the bomb blast back in Digne, as far as what happened to me, anyway. There was no cleaning up what happened to Stewart and Laurent.

"It's not over then, even after all that?" Diana said.

No, it wasn't. Danton had it in for the SOE as well as General Robine, and he was out for blood. I wanted to tell Diana and Christine to get out of town right now, but I knew that wasn't their style.

CHAPTER FORTY-SEVEN

"STAY HERE IN case Colonel Harding shows up, okay?" I said to Big Mike. "You ought to give your leg a rest anyway. Tomorrow's going to be a busy day."

"Sure," Big Mike said. "I'll tell Victor to call me as soon as Sam gets in. Good luck up on the wall. Maybe you'll spot something I missed."

"I never thought casing this burg would be so hard on him," I said to Kaz as Big Mike took the staircase to his room. We were waiting in the lobby while Diana and Christine stashed their bags.

"It is a demanding layout, certainly," Kaz said. "But I am more worried about Diana and Christine being here. Is there any chance Danton knows of their presence?"

"*We* didn't know they'd be here," I said. "You heard them, they only decided to come yesterday." Diana had told us they had two families to visit in Langres and had decided to change their itinerary to watch the festivities. They'd taken care of that business and asked for the best hotel in town. And here they were.

"I am sure Danton would be glad to take his revenge on SOE personnel as well," Kaz said. "But Robine will still be his top priority. I must admit to some understanding of his anger. Any help would have gone a long way in the Vercors. Conversely, no help at all would seem brutally inhumane after what the Nazis did in Vassieux."

"That's the trouble with revenge," I said. "Innocent people get hurt when it's delivered. Laurent and Dickie dead. Drake injured. It never goes smoothly."

"You left out Commander Stewart," Kaz said with a rueful grin.

"Hardly innocent. He's as guilty as Danton when it comes to Dickie Thorne," I said. "He made him the scapegoat to save his own skin. I can understand Danton, to a degree. Stewart, I can't fathom."

"I always found him smarmy," Christine said, belting her raincoat as she approached. "I was shocked at what he did, but after a moment's reflection, unsurprised."

"I didn't know him very long, but it was long enough," Diana said, linking her arm in mine. "So, what are you boys up to?"

We explained how the trail had led us here, and what General Michel Robine's role had been in denying assistance to the Vercors Republic, as we walked to the city wall. Kaz explained our working theory about a four-hundred-meter shot.

"I met the general in Algiers," Christine said. "Stiff-necked would best describe him. Not the kind of man to change his mind, especially when it comes to paratroop drops. I can see why Danton is after him."

"You two need to be careful as well," I said. "Danton is no fan of the Special Operations Executive. He made several comments about SOE betraying the *maquis*. At the time it sounded like empty bitterness, but now we have to take it more seriously."

"Don't worry about us," Diana said. "We can take care of ourselves. Our FANY uniforms might symbolize something to Danton, but Robine himself is more than a symbol. He's the living embodiment of betrayal."

"I might shoot him myself," Christine said as we climbed the steps to the top of the wall. "Paratroopers would have been welcome on the plateau." I'm sure she was half joking. Pretty sure.

"We were just saying how our sympathies might be with Danton, to some extent," Kaz said as we reached the top. "But we need to put those thoughts aside. We must see this from his perspective, but only as a sniper. Where would he set up? Where could he?"

"The view is magnificent," Diana said, looking to the west. White clouds drifted across a blue sky above lush, green rolling hills. The sun was edging downward, sending lengthening shadows our way.

"But this is the view that concerns us," Christine said, turning to face the town. We looked out over a jumble of terra-cotta rooflines, interspersed by bluish-gray slate on the fancier buildings. "We're not high enough to see anything."

"What about that?" Diana said, pointing to a turreted structure fifty yards along the wall.

"Big Mike said there were twelve towers built along the wall, all facing outward," I said. "Let's check it out."

The walkway was wide enough for the four of us to walk abreast. The crenelated outward-facing wall was chest high and three feet thick. The wind blew up from the valley floor, and I shivered as the damp chill hit me. The tower was tall, topped by a slender, conical slate roof.

"It's open," Kaz said, pushing on a stout oaken door that creaked on rusted hinges. We entered a circular room with stone walls. About ten feet up, the stonework ended, and wooden timbers rose, curving inward until they formed the tip of the steep roof. Light filtered in from several openings at eye level. A wooden staircase circled up, ending at two more firing slits. All facing outward. A table and two chairs were close to the openings. German ration tins littered the floor, and the sour smell of cabbage, lousy tobacco, and wet wool hung in the air. The odor of the enemy still lingered.

"It's a good thing the Germans didn't defend this place," Christine said, looking at the open ground below.

"They were too busy retreating," Kaz said. "Any troops who remained would have been encircled and trapped."

I took the stairs, testing each narrow step carefully. The centuries-old wood held, and I was rewarded with a spectacular view out a crescent-shaped opening. I could see along the wall, but not into the city. Not even close.

"This is an architecturally interesting dead end," Kaz said. We exited, and I craned my neck to look at the top of the roof.

"If there was an opening up there, facing into the city, he might have a shot," I said, pointing to the tip of the spire.

"We should split up," Diana said. "We can check the towers and meet on the other side. If they're all like this, it shouldn't take much time."

"Good idea," I said, and we walked south, arm in arm, like tourists, while Kaz and Christine went north.

"What was it like, in the Vosges?" Diana asked.

"Brutal. Cold. Muddy," I said, trying to put the experience into words. "The Nisei took heavy casualties, probably lost more men than they rescued. It was hard to stand by and wait for the French scouts. Hard to do nothing."

"I know," Diana said, tightening her grip on my arm. There wasn't much else she could say, but it felt good to hear that, and to hold her close.

The next tower was locked up tight. Judging by the rust around the lock and hinges, it hadn't been unlocked in ages. It had the same arrangement of openings, all facing outward. At the next, the door was wide open, revealing a jumble of broken furniture and debris. The next few were the same. Whether they were open or locked, there was no way to gain a line of sight into the city.

We waited at the sixth tower, figuring it was halfway around. The only difference was this one had the French tricolor flying from a lanyard that reached to the spire. I peeked inside as Diana waited to catch sight of Kaz and Christine. This one had the same table and chair setup as the first. Probably a German observation post, as that one had been. It was fairly clean, except for discarded ration containers and a moldy blanket. An orchard ladder—the kind with a narrow top for leaning against fruit trees—brought back memories of picking apples at my grandmother's farm. It was probably what they used to reach the lanyard on the roof. I climbed up the stairs, taking one last look. Nothing.

At the bottom of the steps, my foot got caught in a tangle of rope. I kicked it aside, noticing that it was a rope ladder. For a quick escape over the wall when things got hot? The Germans in this observation post were obviously ready to go at a moment's notice.

"They're here, Billy," Diana said from the doorway. Outside, Christine and Kaz reported on their patrol. It had been the same as ours. Some towers locked, others open, all of them facing outward.

"We found the remains of a German observation post, and one tower crammed with gardening tools," Kaz said. "Not surprising, since there are cultivated fields right outside the walls. But no way to see into the city streets."

"Let's get back to the hotel," I said, as the roar of motorcycle engines arose from below.

"Look," Christine said, as a half dozen motorcyclists came into view on a road that curved along the wall, heading for a gate fifty yards away. A staff car and two trucks followed, tailed by two more motorcyclists. "That could be General Robine and his entourage."

We leaned over the edge of the parapet, looking in both directions, waiting for the sound of a rifle shot. There was nothing, no noise except for the growling engines echoing off the stone walls as the column entered the city.

"Well, Robine is here. Danton is here. We are here," Kaz said. "I wonder how we shall all come together at noon tomorrow?"

"If we wait until noon, we'll be too late," I said. "Let's see if Harding's arrived, then check out the hospital and that apartment turret Big Mike told us about."

Kaz briefed Christine and Diana on what Big Mike had found, and our assessment of the church spires as an unlikely perch for Danton.

"I agree, he seems too clever to box himself in," Christine said. "If he didn't care about being caught, he could shoot Robine from ten yards away at the swearing in."

"There's got to be a spot we're missing," I said as we descended a long, wide ramp running along the interior wall.

"They must have used this to haul supplies to the towers," Kaz said. "Oxcarts full of food, arrows, spears, and stones to rain down on the attackers."

"Boiling oil?" Diana asked.

"Water, most often," Kaz said. "Heated to a boil on the wall and tipped over. Quite economical. They used burning tar as well."

"Thank goodness we've become civilized," Christine said, as we stepped off the ramp. A handful of *maquisards* walked by, with their weapons and FFI armbands on full display. They chattered excitedly, oblivious to even the charms of Diana and Christine. Two motorcycles roared by, and the *maquisards* gave them a hearty cheer.

"I hope they're as excited with army life after the first month," I said.

"Let us hope their introduction will not include the assassination of General Robine," Kaz said. "General de Gaulle will not appreciate his new French army being deprived of a leader by one of their own. A German would do quite nicely, but not a Frenchman."

"Piotr, how utterly cynical," Diana said, laughing as she walked beside me.

"My dear, I am Polish," Kaz said. "Living between Russia and Germany, one's natural inclination is to expect things to go badly." Christine laughed and gripped his arm tightly.

We found Colonel Harding at the hotel. He and Big Mike had secured a table in a private dining room where we could speak without worrying about being overheard. News of an expected sniper attack could easily spook the locals, and, apparently, keeping people calm was to be our priority.

"I received a directive from SHAEF to fully cooperate with the French Second Corps," Harding said, once we were all seated. "And the French will not take any special measures."

"It would not look good," Diana said. "Correct?"

"Absolutely," Harding said. "The French want to show a solid front to the world. Reacting to a renegade would be demeaning, it seems."

"I think that after General de Gaulle's performance in Paris, when he stood tall as German snipers fired on the crowd that had gathered to catch a glimpse of him, it would be a humiliation for any of his generals to do less," Kaz said.

"France has had enough of that," Christine said. "So, what are we allowed to do?"

"We?" Big Mike said. "This isn't your responsibility, Miss Granville."

"There are four of you," Christine said, fixing Big Mike with an icy glare. "I would say you need all the help you can get."

"Of course, we'd welcome your assistance," Harding said. "If your duties permit it."

"We are almost done with our rounds, Colonel," Diana said. "Another day or so won't matter. Thank you for your concern, Big Mike, but I don't think we'll be in any danger staring at rooftops."

"Okay," he said. "You're right about us being light on resources. Are we getting any help from the French, Sam?"

"Robine's security detail will take care of the cathedral. Normal procedure since he'll be speaking right in front of it," Harding said. "They'll have men on the rooftops around the plaza, but that's it."

"We checked out the towers along the wall, just as Big Mike did," I said. "No way they can be used."

"The streets aren't straight," Big Mike said. "He can't line up a shot from far away, too many curves and bends. But we should check out that turret, the one off the third floor."

"That, and the hospital," I said. "I'd like to be sure climbing up on that façade isn't an option for Danton."

"Probably best to check the hospital in the morning," Big Mike said. "It's exposed, and I doubt he'd spend the night exposed. But the apartment with the turret is different. He could be hiding in there."

"We'll pay a visit, right after we eat," I said. As if on cue, waiters brought in food and drink. I had to eat, but I had a bitter taste in my mouth. Defeat.

After eating dinner and sending Big Mike to rest, the four of us strolled to the plaza and through to the street where the turret offered a possible sniper's perch. Christine and Diana knocked on the door and were soon chatting amiably with an older woman in a black dress. She invited them in, along with Kaz, while I stayed outside. I stood on the corner, below the turret that jutted out from the third floor. I could see the plaza clear enough. From the turret, it would be an even better view. I rested my hand on my holster, glancing around and half expecting Danton to turn the corner.

"No," Kaz said as he held the door open for Christine and Diana. "The floor is rotten, and the doorway is boarded up. I looked out the window and the angle is wrong."

"Any window on this stretch would do, if you didn't mind hanging out halfway," Diana said.

"If Danton is right-handed, it would have to be this side," Christine said, pointing to the buildings on our left.

"We'll patrol here as soon as we check out the hospital in the morning," Kaz said.

"Why don't we come down for a stroll while you two are at the hospital?" Diana said. "No one will think twice about two women wandering around and having a cup of coffee at a café."

I knew better than to protest. I agreed, and we chose our rendezvous point, a café opposite the cathedral with a view of the street leading into the plaza. If all else failed, we could say our prayers.

CHAPTER FORTY-EIGHT

MORNING SUNSHINE BATHED the streets in a soft, yellow glow. I had hoped for rain and high winds, anything to cancel the big show or run it indoors. Instead, the fates played with my desires and produced the exact opposite. A crystal clear day, the crisp overnight air warmed by the sun, without even the whisper of a breeze to interfere with the trajectory of a high-speed bullet.

Sniper weather.

The plaza was already crowded, mostly with onlookers. A small brass band was assembling near the statue of Diderot. A few uniformed soldiers were busy setting up a microphone and running wires through a nearby doorway.

"It looks like Robine will be speaking from the steps around the statue," Diana said.

"He'll be head and shoulders above everyone else," Christine said. "An easy target."

"All right, we'll hustle over to the hospital and get back as soon as we can," I said, scanning the rooftops. "Maybe we'll get lucky, and we all can relax."

"Be careful," Diana said. "Luck means running into Danton."

"We should be back within the hour," Kaz said. "That will give us almost two hours to search the street."

"Don't worry about us," Diana said, patting the pocket of her trench coat. "We can take care of ourselves."

"And then some," I said, as we left at a brisk pace for the hospital.

"I do not like all this talk of luck, Billy," Kaz said. "I hate depending on it, like a gambler waiting to draw the right card. We need certainty, not wishes."

"You're right," I said. "The hospital is a logical spot to check out. That's what we're using. Logic, not luck. If we eliminate it as a possibility, then we move on to the next spot. Okay?"

"Oh yes, now I feel much better," Kaz said. "Perhaps we should tell General Robine he is now safe in our logical hands."

"This is that Polish cynicism, right?"

"I always prefer to be surprised when things turn out well rather than disappointed when they do not," Kaz said, as we turned the corner to find the Hôpital de la Haute-Marne.

The place was large, four stories of limestone with an ornate façade. Coming at it from the side, I could see what Big Mike had described. What looked like a fifth floor at first was just a front, decorated with all sorts of designs and swirling patterns.

Inside, Kaz asked to speak to the hospital administrator. He appeared in a few minutes and Kaz explained what we were after. I picked up the phrase *le grand sergent américain*.

At the mention of Big Mike, the guy smiled. He beckoned us to follow and led us up several flights of stairs. After the fourth floor, he unlocked a door that led to the roof and held it open, all the while speaking to Kaz.

"He promised the large American sergeant he would keep the door to the roof locked," Kaz told me. "He knows a few words of English and understood what Big Mike was worried about. He says he is a patriot and worked with the Resistance to provide care to their wounded."

"Has anyone suspicious been to the hospital?" I asked, surveying the back side of the façade. It was ten feet of flat stone, with none of the ornate carvings that decorated the front.

"No," Kaz said. "The janitors have been told to let no one access the roof, and all the ladders are locked away."

"Good," I said, nodding and smiling at our new friend. I cupped my hands and stood against the wall. "Come on, I'll give you a boost. You should be able to see over."

"All right," Kaz said, placing one foot in my hands. I lifted and felt his other boot dig into my shoulder.

"What can you see?" I grunted, as I tried to keep steady.

"I can see the cathedral spires," he said. "And perhaps one small corner of the plaza. Nothing else." I felt Kaz's foot come off my shoulder and he slid to the ground, dusting the chalky limestone from his hands. "Useless as a sniper perch."

Kaz thanked the hospital administrator, and I could make out enough to understand Kaz saying that it was very important to keep everything locked for the day.

"I saw no reason to tell him it was a poor position for a marksman," Kaz said. "He was so proud of his precautions."

"And you call yourself a cynic," I said.

We double-timed it to the plaza and found the place a lot busier. The brass band was ready to go, their threadbare blue uniforms looking like they'd spent the war years in mothballs. Curious civilians clustered together, watching the newsreel people who were unpacking their cameras. More French soldiers milled about, but there was no sign of any Fifis.

"Boyle!" Harding shouted from across the square, a pair of binoculars around his neck and a Handie-Talkie hanging from his shoulder.

"Nothing at the hospital, Colonel," I reported. "Anything here?"

"Just a bit of good news," he said. "The FFI men are forming up at the east gate. They're going to march in."

"We won't have dozens of Fifis wandering around the plaza," Kaz said. "That will make it harder for Danton to move about."

"That's what I think," Harding said. "I'm going up to the top of the cathedral spire. I can watch the soldiers on the rooftops and make sure Danton isn't among them."

"We'll scout the street and check with Diana and Christine," I said. "Where's Big Mike?"

"Over there," Harding said, pointing to a café behind the statue of Diderot. Big Mike waved, raising his Handie-Talkie. "If I spot anything, I call it in to him, and he alerts Robine's security detail. But they won't act unless it's a hundred percent certain."

"Hospital was a dead end?" Big Mike asked as Harding took off for the top of the cathedral. He was seated at a table with a good view of the plaza, the radio, a pair of binoculars, and a small cup of coffee before him.

"Yeah, no way to get a shot from there," I said. "Sounds like Robine's people are at least willing to listen to a warning."

"They're not happy about it," Big Mike said, nodding to a group of French officers seated at one of the café tables. "But they don't want Robine getting plugged on film, so they'll pull him back. But only if we have a confirmed sighting."

"Do you need these here?" I said, picking up the binoculars.

"Nope. Sam'll have a better view from above. Take 'em, and good luck."

Luck again. We didn't even say the word as we headed down the street. It would have been unlucky.

Diana and Christine were at the café opposite the cathedral. It was crowded with civilians and soldiers, and we narrowly beat two French lieutenants who were making a beeline for their table.

"Thank goodness," Christine said. "They've been buzzing around like flies."

"And we've had less luck than them," Diana said. "We've been up and down this street, snooping in hallways and shops, all for nothing. What about the hospital?"

"Dead end," I said, and explained Harding and Big Mike's setup in the plaza.

"We should continue looking on this street," Kaz said. "It has the most potential for a straight shot."

"We don't have a lot of time," I said, checking my wristwatch. "Let's get to it."

"I've been thinking about Danton's escape," Diana said, pushing her chair back and standing. "Two things. First, he may have altered his appearance. He could have short hair, and perhaps be dressed in a suit. Even small changes will help him escape notice."

"Very true," Christine said. "If you have a picture of the person in your mind's eye, you tend to overlook anything that does not match. What is the second thing?"

"If it were me, I'd want to exit through a rear door after the shooting," she said. "Which means it is most likely he will gain access through the same route."

"Therefore, we should reconnoiter the backs of these buildings," Christine said. "On the side of the street that would favor a right-handed shooter."

"Logical," Kaz said. "Odds are you are right. Shall we continue to monitor the fronts, Billy?"

"I don't have anything better to suggest," I said. "It makes sense, even if it is a long shot."

"This isn't time for jokes, Billy," Diana said.

I guess the joke was on me, but I figured it was better not to admit I'd been that thick. We moved out, Diana and Christine taking an alleyway to the rear of the buildings, while Kaz and I worked both sides of the street, taking stairs to the top floor and looking for any likely spots. We came up empty.

At the fourth building, we found a door to the roof and walked to the edge. Soldiers were stationed on rooftops two buildings down, and we stared at each other through binoculars before giving a friendly wave. There was no way to see into the plaza.

"Useless," I said as we went down the stairs. "We need a better method. Something more logical than this."

"Such as?" Kaz asked.

"We're looking around the edges, searching places we think Danton might be. But it's not working. We need to be at the center of things and look outward," I said. "Let's get to the statue."

By now the plaza was filling up. Two newsreel cameras were already at work, filming the growing crowd. The band was tuning up, and a line of soldiers was standing, at parade rest, in front of the statue.

"Half an hour, Billy," Kaz said.

I caught Big Mike's eye and he shrugged. Nothing from Harding.

I looked through the binoculars, down the street we'd just covered. Every rooftop that offered a good angle had a soldier at the edge, on guard. Across the plaza, the buildings were so close I didn't even need the binoculars. Every shooter's perch was covered.

What was I missing?

From inside the café, I heard a murmur of voices. A gaggle of officers surrounded one man. It had to be Robine, getting ready to make his entrance.

I stood on a chair, searching the perimeter through the binoculars, frantic that I'd missed something simple, some obvious spot that made sense to Danton and no one else. The more I looked, the more I knew he wasn't where we expected him to be. I tried to spot the towers on the wall from here, but all I saw was the very tips of two. No way to see into the plaza from there anyway. I was grasping at straws.

The sound of marching men, boots on stone, echoed from one of the roads. Motorcycles roared into life, and the band began to play a martial tune. The recruits were coming. Robine took a few steps closer to the microphone, still surrounded by his men.

The cameras swiveled to the side street, ready to capture the image of patriotic Frenchmen marching to the colors.

To the colors.

What did that remind me of?

Four motorcycles came into view, leading the Fifis into the plaza. They drew up, two on either side of the statue, and killed their engines. The recruits marched in, and the crowd lustily cheered them on as they formed ranks and came to attention.

The band struck up "La Marseillaise," their national anthem.

All eyes turned to the cathedral. At a flagpole above one of the spires, a huge French tricolor was hoisted up, unfurling in the breeze as the singing became even louder. Robine stood at attention, still under the awning of the café and surrounded by his officers.

The flag. The lanyard.

I stood on the chair again, focusing the binoculars on the tip of the tower's roof opposite the plaza. I was sure it was the one where I'd seen the tricolor, but it wasn't flying. Why?

The orchard ladder. The rope ladder. The lanyard.

Four hundred meters.

"The tower," I shouted to Kaz, and thrust the binoculars at him. I ran to the closest motorcycle, and before anyone could react, I switched on the ignition and took off, being none too quiet about it. The bike was a Harley-Davidson, just like we used to ride back in the Boston PD. I knew how to make it roar. It was the best way to signal to everyone that something was wrong without taking time to explain.

Because there was no time.

I took a corner way too fast and barely managed to keep the bike upright. I took another turn and spotted the ramp we'd walked down yesterday. I gunned the engine and fairly flew up it, hoping I wouldn't run into anyone on the wall. It was maybe a mile atop the wall to the tower, and I had to get there fast.

Things had fallen together in my mind. I saw it all at once, the pieces of the puzzle tumbling into place as I watched the French tricolor being raised above the cathedral.

How could the tower work as a sniper's perch?

Easy.

Place the wooden ladder against the tower. Climb up, hauling the rope ladder, and attach it to the lanyard. Instead of raising the flag, hoist up the rope. Tie off the lanyard and climb the rope ladder, probably securing it around the top of the tower. Feet in the rope ladder, you lean against the steep slate roof, take aim, and make a four-hundred-meter shot into the plaza.

I swerved, barely missing an old man walking his dog as I passed a tower. It wasn't far now, and I needed to stay alert. I didn't know if Robine had been rushed to safety, or if I'd simply been dismissed as a crazy American motorcycle thief.

Danton had two options for his escape. Melt into the city or use that rope ladder to go over the wall. Either option might involve his own motorbike.

I passed another tower. The next one was it. I slowed, just enough to avoid a skidding crash, bracing myself for the sound of Danton's Lee-Enfield.

There! The tower, complete with the orchard ladder in full view. At the top, his thin body barely visible against the slate tiles, was Danton. He was aiming his rifle, his eye up against the scope, his tunnel vision focused on nothing but the target.

A vulnerable moment for a sniper.

I gunned the engine, the bike rearing like a bronco and coming down hard. I braked and slid sideways into the tower, barely rolling off in time, hoping the noise and surprise was enough to distract him.

"Danton," I yelled, unholstering my .45 and firing one shot, hitting the slate beneath his feet. I wanted him alive. There had been death enough.

Danton had other ideas. He turned his rifle on me and fired once, sending me diving for cover along the wall as he worked the bolt. I tripped over the rear wheel of the bike, still spinning crazily in the air, and whacked my head against the stone wall. He'd fired wild, but it gave him what he wanted, one final chance to hit his target before the sound of gunfire sent everyone in the plaza running for cover.

I couldn't have that.

I stood, my vision blurred, and fired four shots, this time not caring if I blew his head off.

Now I was the one firing wild, and the ground seemed to wobble beneath me. Blood trickled down from my forehead, and I had to fall to one knee to stop from keeling over. Danton fired again, but I couldn't tell if the shot was aimed at me or Robine. Either way, it meant I'd failed.

I wiped blood from my eye and watched Danton slide down the roof, one gloved hand on the lanyard and the other gripping his rifle, his face twisted in rage and hatred. I realized too late that the angle of his slide had a purpose. He was landing on me.

My shoulder smacked against the hard stone from the impact of his body. I went blank for a moment, then tried to focus my eyes through the film of blood and stunned confusion. Where was Danton?

The snarling engine of his motorbike sounded from inside the tower, and Danton burst through the open door, his tires missing my head by inches. I made myself get up, shaking off the pain and righting my motorcycle, even as a wave of dizziness threatened to flatten me. I couldn't afford to go unconscious, not speeding after Danton.

It was less than a mile to the ramp. I didn't have much time. My pistol was somewhere on the ground back by the tower, and all I had was the weight and velocity of my bike. If Danton made it into the city, he'd have a chance at slipping away, disappearing into the warren of streets amidst the confusion.

I closed on him, his motorbike no match for the Harley. We raced along the battlements, wind whipping at my face. The wall curved, and I knew the ramp was coming up soon. I opened the throttle and came up on his rear tire, turning into it to send him into a spin. He swerved, avoiding my hit, and as I tried to steady the Harley, I scraped the edge of the parapet, metal screeching against stone that raked my calf. The bike wobbled underneath me as I fought for control. I had to slow down. Danton didn't.

I maneuvered to try again, then saw Kaz ahead, smack in the middle of the path, right in front of the ramp Danton was going for.

Kaz went into a shooting stance, gripping his Webley revolver in two hands. Danton bent over his handlebars, aiming straight for Kaz to make his escape down the sloping ramp. I braked, keeping to the side.

Danton was almost on him.

Kaz fired, then quickly stepped aside.

Danton kept moving. He didn't turn to take the ramp. His forward motion carried him straight into the battlements, crashing the bike and sending him flying over the edge to the hard ground below.

"Are you all right, Billy?" Kaz said as soon as I got off the bike. I could see his concern as he looked at the blood on my face.

"Yeah," I said, walking over to the edge and looking down at Danton. Even from this height, it was easy to see the bullet hole neatly placed between his eyes. "Robine all right?"

"I do not know," Kaz said. "I ran up here, on the theory he would make for the ramp. I didn't know which tower you were headed to."

"Sorry," I said, placing my hand on Kaz's shoulder. "There wasn't time to explain. And thanks." I leaned against the wall, taking deep breaths, and worked at not passing out.

I heard motorcycles coming up the ramp, and shouting voices. There were going to be a lot of questions.

"Do you want to search him?" Kaz asked. "There may be clues."

"No," I said. "I know what he has."

"A postcard, like Jean-Paul?"

"That, or a locket. A picture of his mother. A ring. A lock of hair from his girlfriend. A dried wildflower. A photograph of his home, or the key that unlocked the door. His father's pocket watch, his kid brother's jackknife. It doesn't really matter what it is, does it? Whatever it was, it reminded him of everything he'd lost, a crushing burden he no longer bears," I whispered, staring down at Danton's ruined body, not knowing what to think.

"If not for Dickie, I might feel compassion," Kaz said, as men surrounded us, peppering us with questions.

I had no answers.

CHAPTER FORTY-NINE

"GENERAL MICHEL ROBINE, in the best heroic tradition of the French military, did not flinch when a bullet from a German sniper narrowly missed him," Kaz read from *Le Figaro*, translating as he skimmed the newspaper article.

"Of course he didn't flinch, it was twenty feet over his head," Christine said. "The only danger was to the window it shattered."

"This is rich," Corporal Drake said, propped up in bed with a bandage around his head and one arm in a cast to his shoulder. We'd driven to the 21st General Hospital to pay him a visit the day after Langres, and Kaz had grabbed the newspaper at a kiosk when he'd noticed the headline about Robine. "What else did they make up?"

"Oh, the number of Fifi recruits is inflated," Kaz said, scanning the article.

"Does it mention Billy?" Diana asked.

"The stay-behind sniper was stopped by the quick action of General Robine's security detail. The motorcycle unit raced to the scene and prevented any further shots from being fired. The German, dressed in civilian clothes, was killed as he attempted to escape," Kaz read.

"Well, they got the motorcycle part right, sounds like," Drake said, laughing and wincing at the same time. "Can't wait to get these stitches out. Driving me crazy."

Drake's back had taken shrapnel from the bomb blast, and the doctors had said he was fortunate not to have had any damage to his spine. But it had taken over a hundred stitches to sew him back together.

"They treating you okay?" I asked from the foot of the bed, absently touching the small bandage on my forehead. My head was throbbing again, no surprise after the working over it had gotten. A mild concussion, the doctor had told me. Looking at Drake, I felt a bit less sorry for myself. Diana and Christine sat in chairs on either side of the bed, while Kaz lounged against the window.

"Well, I got a room to myself," Drake said with a wry grin. "The positive side of segregation, I guess. The chow is pretty good, and I can practice my French with some of the locals who work here."

"What's next?" Diana said. "Will you be here long?"

"Don't know. After the stitches come out, I still have to wear this cast for six weeks," Drake said. "Then, who knows? Back to the motor pool, maybe, if I can hold a wrench."

"Colonel Harding said he and Big Mike would be here soon," Kaz said. "Perhaps he will have some news."

"It'll be good to see another Detroit man," Drake said. "And thanks for visiting, all of you. It means a lot. *Et vraiment désolé* about your pal, Lieutenant. Dickie was all right in my book."

"I shall not forget him," Kaz said, turning his gaze to the window and watching the clouds roll by.

"You were a big help, Corporal. We're in your debt," I said, silently hoping that Sam Harding had been able to pull a few strings.

"Hey, goldbrick!" Big Mike said as he entered the room a few minutes later. "How ya doing?"

"Great, Sarge," Drake said, smiling. "Good to see you. What, no flowers?"

"We've got something else," Big Mike said, giving me a wink. "Sam's out talking with the doctors now, he'll be right in."

"All set," Harding said, walking in a few minutes later.

"Sir," Drake said, doing his best to sit at attention.

"I've got some news for you, Corporal," Sam said. "First, your record is clear back at the Quartermaster Truck Company in Algiers. I spoke to your CO, and he's fine with you being on detached duty, even if he never got his truck back."

"Swell, I'd hate to be put in the stockade for going AWOL when I get out of here," Drake said. "Thanks, Colonel."

"No problem, Sergeant," Harding said.

"Sir?"

"You heard me, soldier. You are now a buck sergeant, and a recipient of the Purple Heart," Harding said, giving Big Mike a nod. Big Mike pinned the medal with its purple ribbon and profile of George Washington on Drake's robe. Then he handed him two sets of stripes.

"Make sure you get those sewn on, once you stop lazing around here in your pajamas," Big Mike said. Drake beamed, and we gave him a round of applause.

"Congratulations, Sergeant Drake," I said.

"I can't believe it," Drake said. "I really thought I'd be in hot water over this, especially with Captain Sage in a POW camp."

"There's something else," Big Mike said, pulling a set of orders from his pocket and handing them to Drake. "Seems like Uncle Sam will have to get along without you. The doctors said your wounds qualify you for a medical discharge, soon as you're healed up."

"I'm going home?" Drake asked.

"Just read the orders, Sergeant," Harding said. Drake opened the envelope and read through the paperwork.

"I can't believe it," he said, a broad grin spreading across his face.

"You're repeating yourself," Big Mike said, taking the orders and reading the pertinent section. "Sergeant Elwood Drake, as soon as medically fit, will be transferred to the 203rd General Hospital, Paris, for recuperation and physical therapy. Once completed, he will receive his honorable discharge in place."

"In place?" Drake said. "Paris?"

"Only if you want it," Harding said.

"I'll be a civilian in Paris? Hell yeah! Sir," Drake said. "That's what I want. What I've been dreaming of."

"When you get to Paris, ask about the Servicemen's Readjustment Act," Harding said. "Congress passed it earlier this year. They'll pay for college, anywhere you want to go."

"Is this Christmas?" Drake said, his jaw dropping. "I can go to college in Paris and Uncle Sam will foot the bill? I don't know what to say."

"You don't have to say anything, Elwood," Big Mike said. "You earned it. Just like any other GI."

Drake had a million questions about Paris, then started talking in French to Kaz, Christine, and Diana about the Sorbonne, the West Bank, Montmartre, and all the places he'd read about. Part of me envied him. A million-dollar wound and a ticket to a new life in Paris. Part of me felt bad that his own country wouldn't give him the kind of freedom I took for granted. Like walking in the front door of any joint I felt like.

We said our farewells. Big Mike told Drake to look him up if he ever made it back to Detroit, saying all he had to do was ask any cop. Drake told him to do the same in Paris.

"Just ask for me at the Sorbonne," he said. "*Au revoir.*"

Outside, I hugged Diana goodbye. Her mission accomplished, Big Mike was driving her to a British airfield for her flight home. Christine was headed back to Algiers in the morning. It wasn't our usual mournful parting, since she'd be on leave, and I had asked Harding for the same. It was hard to believe we might both be together in the peaceful countryside at Seaton Manor in a day or two.

"I arranged leave for you both," Harding said to Kaz and me. "You've got a flight to London the day after tomorrow."

"Great," I said. "Thanks, Colonel. But what about Big Mike? He's still a little banged up and could use a rest."

"He's coming to London with me," Harding said. "We'll see about leave once he takes care of the mound of paperwork that's going to be waiting for us. We had to make a lot of promises and call in favors to get Drake's promotion and paperwork processed overnight. The army doesn't usually move this fast if you haven't noticed. Especially not when it comes to Negro soldiers."

"This was all Big Mike's idea?" Kaz asked, glancing at Christine, who waited by our jeep.

"He laid it all out, and I agreed," Harding said. "The man's got a good sense of right and wrong. But that leaves us with several rear area generals we need to make happy. Backs need to be scratched."

"Do we need to wait until the day after tomorrow? Sir?" I asked.

"Yes. I have one errand for you," Harding said. "I need you to head back to Bruyères."

"If General Dahlquist is still there, I'd rather not, sir," I said, knowing I had no choice.

"Too bad. But it's an easy job. I need you to talk with the OSS officer in charge and find out what happened to Jack Hemingway," Harding said. "It's more public relations than anything else. Hemingway's father is asking questions, and the OSS is not responding through official channels. Not even to SHAEF. I figure if you talk to the OSS officer on the ground, you can get the real story. Is Jack Hemingway dead, captured, lost, or what? We need to know before the old man goes public. Okay? You two take a drive, sweet-talk the OSS guy, and get back to me. Simple. Just stay out of trouble and you'll be fine." He handed us our travel orders, which included passage on an 0900 flight from Grenoble the day after tomorrow. Which also meant we needed to get going.

"Understood, Colonel," I said. "See you in London."

"Billy," Kaz said, pulling me aside as Harding drove off. "This does seem like a relatively simple matter, does it not?"

"It does?" I said. Then it dawned on me, as Christine watched us. It was her last night here. "Oh yeah, sure. No problem."

"I don't know if I shall ever see her again, Billy. She is a remarkable woman," Kaz said.

I couldn't argue with that, or that they didn't both deserve a night together.

CHAPTER FIFTY

WEARY AFTER THE long drive alone, I pulled into Bruyères. It felt different this time. There was snow on the ground and the sound of artillery fire was far, far away. It was almost peaceful. I avoided Division HQ where I might run into Dahlquist and made for the communications building. I figured they must be sending messages for the OSS detachment and would know where they hung their hat.

They did, and since OSS Captain Greene was a pain in the neck, constantly demanding top priority for his transmissions, the non-com in charge didn't hesitate when I asked. It helped that I came in with a carton of Lucky Strikes under my arm and left without it.

I drove to a stone building set back from the road. It had an attached garage where several vehicles, including a German staff car, were being worked on.

"Where's Captain Greene?" I asked one of the mechanics who had his head buried under the hood of the staff car.

"You're talking to him," he said, emerging from the garage and wiping oil off his hands. "Who's asking?"

"Colonel Samuel Harding, SHAEF," I said, getting out of the jeep. Greene had already forgotten me, so I didn't see the need to play nice. "But he didn't feel like taking the drive, so he sent me. He wants answers."

"I've seen Harding's name on a few messages," Greene said. "I don't like being pressured about top secret information."

"Meaning the whereabouts of Lieutenant Jack Hemingway, who

went out on patrol the same day he brought in a couple of FFI scouts?"
I asked. "That top secret info?"

"We don't like compromising our agents," Greene answered. "The
less said, the better, in my book."

"Listen, I understand," I said, going the sympathetic route. "But you
know that there's already one famous writer's son dead around here.
Hey, it's war, nothing unusual in that. But two sons of famous writers
in the same outfit within days of each other? That attracts attention.
Especially when Papa Hemingway starts asking questions. You want
a half dozen war correspondents knocking on your door asking what
the hell you're doing here?"

"Is that a threat, Captain?"

"Nope. Statement of fact. You ever meet Hemingway the elder?"

"Haven't had the pleasure," Greene said.

"Even if you do, pleasure will be in short supply," I said. Greene
shook his head, frowned, and shrugged.

"Okay. You can tell your Colonel Harding we've received confirmation Jack was captured while behind the lines escorting a French agent
to a safe house. A German POW bragged about how he'd met the son
of the great writer. Jack had been wounded in a skirmish after being
spotted, but they patched him up, and treated him like royalty. He's
probably in a POW camp in Germany by now."

"I'm glad he's alive, at least," I said. "He's a decent guy. Thanks,
Captain."

I tossed him a salute, and he returned it with a wave of his oily rag,
then went back to work on the staff car. I was going to ask if it was for
a secret mission or if he was going to have it shipped home, but
thought it best to beat a retreat and get in touch with Sam.

Back at the communications building, I wrote out a message to be
transmitted to Harding at SHAEF in London confirming that Jack
had been wounded and captured but was recovering in a POW camp.
By the time the colonel landed back in England, it would be waiting
on his desk. Mission accomplished, with time to spare.

"Where's the 442nd?" I asked the sergeant as he readied my message
for transmission. "Still up in those ridges?"

"Naw, the general's got them formed up in a field down the road," he said. "They just came off the line. The quartermaster was waiting with new boots and wool overcoats, and I'll tell ya, Captain, those boys looked like they needed them. They were in bad shape."

"Why are they in formation?" I asked, thinking they should be sleeping for a couple of days.

"Medals. Dahlquist loves to hand 'em out. Go take a gander, the general won't mind an officer from SHAEF watching him. Not one bit," he said with a chuckle, and gave me directions.

Snowflakes drifted down as I pulled over by the field. Dahlquist and a few other officers were getting out of their jeeps. The men of the 442nd were lined up in rows behind a color guard of four men who stood with the colors furled, their eyes downcast, and their features set in the stern grimness of exhaustion.

The ranks were uneven. Some rows held only a scattering of men. I spotted a few familiar faces. Sujii, wearing a red cross armband on his new overcoat. Fred Hosakawa, who'd survived the charge up the hill. Sergeant Dan Inouye, whose silver dollars had saved his life. But none of them looked my way. They looked straight ahead, staring right through Dahlquist, who waited while a newsreel camera was set up to record the event. An army photographer busied himself snapping pictures. I had a suspicion the public relations push was why the general had suddenly come up with cold-weather gear for the Nisei. Maybe some of Kaz's cynicism had rubbed off on me.

A murder of crows landed in the field, off to the side, their noisy cawing at odds with the strange silence of a few hundred men. Dahlquist looked at the crows, his face in a sneer as if taking offense at what they had to say. Then he noticed me, standing off to the side, and motioned me over.

"Glad you're here, Captain Boyle," he said, returning my salute. "You can tell Ike about this."

"I will, General," I said, and then stepped back a few feet, unwilling to be any part of his entourage, but wanting to witness the assembled men receiving their medals.

Colonel Miller, the commanding officer of the 442nd, stepped forward from the ranks and saluted Dahlquist.

"Colonel, I told you to have the whole regiment out here!" Dahlquist bellowed, scolding Miller in front of his men as if he were a child. "When I order everyone to pass in review, I mean everyone! You've disobeyed my orders."

Miller didn't reply, not right away. I could see his jaw clench and his fist tighten. He looked Dahlquist straight in the eye and finally spoke. "General, this is the whole regiment. This is all I have left. The rest are either dead or in the hospital."

Miller's eyes were watering. From sorrow, probably, although the cold was bitter enough. He turned away from the general and took his place in the painfully thin ranks of his regiment. Dahlquist mumbled something about a job well-done, then announced he'd be personally pinning a ribbon representing a Presidential Unit Citation on each member of the unit.

"It won't take as long as he thought," a voice said from behind me. It was Doc Hasegawa. "I think he didn't realize until this moment how bad the casualties were."

"Are they lined up by companies?" I asked.

"Yeah. See right behind the color guard? That's 3rd Battalion, Pursall's outfit. King Company began with one hundred and eighty-six men. There's only seventeen here. Item Company went in with about the same number. They have eight men who can stand, and most of them have trench foot."

"Those were the guys who made that final charge," I said. "Never saw anything like it. At least they can get some rest now."

"Are you kidding, Captain? Tomorrow it's back on the line for these boys. The general gets his picture in the paper, and they get the short end. Again."

"I should've known," I said. "What about you, Doc, you going to get your ribbon? Regardless of who's pinning it on, a Presidential Unit Citation is an honor."

"I can't do it," he said. "I was ordered here, and I obeyed. But I have to get back to my patients. Take care of yourself."

"You too, Doc," I said as we shook hands.

I walked closer to the color guard, now that Dahlquist and his officers were working their way through the ranks. Snow settled on the shoulders of the weary GIs as they waited. Waited for the ribbon, waited for the cameramen to pack up and leave, waited for what little rest the night had to offer.

The eight survivors of Item Company snapped to attention when Dahlquist approached them. As he pinned their ribbons on, I swear they stared right through him. No, not through—beyond him—over his head, past the swirling snows, eastward to the invisible hills and ridges cloaked in driving whiteness, where so much had been demanded of them, and where so much blood and life had been sacrificed for that treacherous ground.

HISTORICAL NOTES

I HAD LONG been interested in incorporating the stories of the Vercors Uprising and the struggles of the 442nd Regimental Combat Team in the Vosges into a Billy Boyle novel. Although these events occurred in the same geographic area, they were months apart. I constructed this novel to explore the aftermath of the doomed fight in the Vercors and to bring the Nisei GIs into Billy Boyle's investigative scope. The latter was tricky in terms of plot structure, but when I found that two French scouts assigned to the 36th Division were part of the Lost Battalion, I finally made the connection.

THE FREE REPUBLIC of Vercors was proclaimed on July 3, 1944, by an army of about four thousand *maquisards* on the massif du Vercors, or the Vercors Plateau, over five hundred miles of rugged mountain territory in southeastern France. Their plan was to organize a conventional force to battle the Germans, with hopes of rapid reinforcement by Allied forces.

After D-Day, there had been many contradictory signals from the Allies. General Eisenhower had urged partisan forces outside the invasion area to be patient and await further instructions. General de Gaulle's more emotional message was widely interpreted as an immediate call to arms. The Vercors *maquis* had the expectation that an invasion of southern France would quickly follow the Normandy landings, and that Allied paratroopers and weapons would reach them even before an invasion.

These misunderstandings were a recipe for disaster, and disaster fell on July 21, 1944. When airborne troops did land, they were German, not American or French. Nearly seven hundred *maquis* were killed, as well as two hundred civilians. The village of Vassieux, near the landing area of the German glider troops, was destroyed, and the inhabitants murdered.

Angry radio messages were sent by the *maquis* to both the Special Operations Executive in London and the Free French in Algiers, denouncing them for abandoning the Free Republic of Vercors to its fate. A unit of French paratroopers, as described in this book, did sit idle in Algiers while the fighting raged. While air transport would have been difficult without American or British cooperation, there were Free French air forces in the Mediterranean. It was not widely known at the time, but it was General de Gaulle himself who held the paratroopers back for possible use in another operation.

The plot against those responsible for this lack of assistance is entirely my creation, born out of reading so many accounts of how bitter the recriminations were from all parties concerned.

THE 442ND REGIMENTAL Combat Team is best known as the most decorated fighting unit in US military history. It was composed almost entirely of second-generation American soldiers of Japanese ancestry, known as Nisei. As originally formed in 1943, the 442nd was composed of over twenty-six hundred men from Hawaii, and fifteen hundred volunteers who came directly from concentration camps where they and their families were held under President Roosevelt's infamous Executive Order 9066.

The list of medals awarded to this regimental unit is astonishing. Twenty-one Medals of Honor, fifty-two Distinguished Service Crosses, one Distinguished Service Medal, five hundred and sixty Silver Stars (plus twenty-eight Oak Leaf Clusters for a second award), twenty-two Legion of Merit medals, fifteen Soldier's Medals, four thousand Bronze Stars (plus twelve hundred Oak Leaf Clusters for a second award), and more than four thousand Purple Hearts. The

442nd was awarded eight Presidential Unit Citations, five of them earned within a single month.

The record of the 442nd Regimental Combat Team is astounding. So is their use at the hands of General John E. Dahlquist, commanding general of the 36th Infantry Division. Much of the dialog attributed to Dahlquist in this novel is his, taken from eyewitness accounts. Many officers, especially those of the 442nd, were critical of the poor tactical decisions made by Dahlquist during the fighting in the Vosges. These include not only his use of the Nisei troops, but his orders that led to the Lost Battalion becoming cut off and surrounded. The formation described in the last chapter happened exactly as presented.

The timeline of the rescue of the Lost Battalion has been compressed by a few days for the purposes of moving the story along. I hope this has not lessened the impact of their fight against the enemy, the weather, and a superior officer who displayed little regard for their well-being.

I have tried to use the real names of those who fought with the 442nd whenever possible. Some readers may recall one-armed Senator Daniel Inouye, the long-serving senator from Hawaii. That is Sergeant Danny Inouye, who indeed was saved by two silver dollars in his shirt pocket. Promoted to lieutenant, Inouye lost his arm during the last days of the war while fighting in Italy.

I am indebted to Soho Press labelmate Naomi Hirahara and her family for allowing me to use the story of Tokko Fukuchi, her father-in-law, known by the nickname Tock in this story. Private First Class Fukuchi won the Silver Star for his actions against a superior enemy force in Italy, April 1945.

The courageous actions of Tokko Fukuchi, as well as the wounds he endured, were transferred to the Vosges in 1944 for the purposes of this story, but in a manner faithful to what transpired. He survived his wounds and walked with the aid of a leg brace for the rest of his life.

I recommend Naomi's book *Clark and Division*, set in Chicago during the aftermath of one Japanese American family's release from Manzanar in 1944, showing their struggle to regain some sense of normality after their life in California was destroyed.

Hisato and Hisako Takamune, mentioned in Chapter Thirty-Eight as residents of one of the concentration camps, were the grandparents of a friend, Lotus Russell. Her uncle, Fred Hosakawa, one of the GIs who made the final charge, served with the 442nd as a member of Headquarters Company, 100th Battalion.

A note on language: 112,000 men, women, and children of Japanese ancestry (over two-thirds of whom were American citizens) were relocated abruptly from the West Coast to the interior of the country and housed in camps, without due process or consideration for the constitutional rights of American citizens. Historically, these camps have been referred to as "internment camps." However, the proper term is concentration camp. In a concentration camp, populations are taken from where they live and confined, in a concentrated area, outside the rule of law. Use of the term "internment," in my opinion, softens the reality of the experience. I prefer to call it what it is.

CHRISTINE GRANVILLE WAS the *nom de guerre* of Krystyna Skarbek, a Polish citizen whose father was a count and whose mother came from a wealthy Jewish family. She began working for the British Special Operations Executive in 1940, gathering intelligence and traveling across eastern Europe and the Mideast. Making her escape just ahead of the advancing Nazi forces, she arrived in Cairo with secret letters and microfilm. Her superiors were convinced she must have been a German spy, given the ease with which she had obtained visas and traveled so far. Sidelined for months, she was finally fully reinstated by an SOE officer who later said, "The most useful thing I did in World War II was to reinstate Christine Granville."

The story of the brilliant and audacious rescue of her SOE partner and lover, Francis Cammaerts, is true and happened much as described here. The money paid to Albert Schenck, who should have heeded Christine's advice to run, was hidden by Madame Schenck. After the war, she attempted to exchange the two million francs for new banknotes (part of the postwar revaluation) and was arrested. Charges were dropped, but she was allowed to keep only a small percentage of the money.

Krystyna Skarbek was stateless at the end of the war, unable to return to Soviet-controlled Poland. Sadly, she was stabbed to death in

1952 by an acquaintance who had become obsessed with her. She was thirty-seven years old. Alistair Horne, a journalist who knew her well, called her "the bravest of the brave." Vera Atkins, one of the SOE spymasters, said of her, "Very brave, very attractive, but a loner and a law unto herself."

THIS BOOK BEGINS with a sea voyage to Crete, courtesy of the Levant Schooner Flotilla, an actual clandestine service ferrying agents and saboteurs across the eastern Mediterranean. The Cretan Resistance fought a devasting war against the German occupation, working so closely with the British SOE that agents could travel anywhere outside the most populated areas in relative safety.

I WAS INTRIGUED during the research for this book to come across the names of two French African colonial soldiers who evaded capture when France fell, and who continued to fight even as most of France settled into defeat and malaise. Their names were Adi Ba and Adama, and I thought they deserved to be recognized here as part of the Maquis de Lamarche.

France did use many colonial troops, in 1940 and 1944 as well. One reason for the rapid recruitment of FFI fighters into the regular French army was to eliminate the need for Black troops fighting in France. Colonial units were sent back to Africa as soon as white formations could be organized. Black soldiers who were released from German POW camps as France was liberated were denied the back pay owed to them. About thirty-five Black soldiers were killed by French guards at a demobilization camp in Thiaroye, just outside Dakar in Senegal, when they protested the withheld pay. Subsequent investigations have shown that the death toll may have exceeded three hundred.

LIEUTENANT JACK HEMINGWAY, son of Ernest, was an OSS officer. He was captured on a mission behind enemy lines while attached to the 36th Division. Jack did manage to escape, but was re-captured, and spent the remainder of the war at a POW camp in Bavaria. Wells Lewis, son of Sinclair Lewis, did meet his end at the side of General Dahlquist in the Vosges.

THE CHARACTER OF Corporal Elwood Drake is based on a Black GI described by Colonel Jerry Sage in his memoir *Sage*.

Jerry Sage was an OSS captain based in Algiers. In his book, he tells the story of trying to requisition a truck, exactly as described in Chapter Fourteen. The motor pool officer insisted that a driver accompany the truck, and designated "Corporal Drake," who is given no other name in Sage's book. But Sage does describe how helpful Drake became at training OSS agents, and how he was kept at the base under the subterfuge of maintaining that valuable truck.

Sage was later captured while on a mission behind enemy lines in France and spent three years in a German POW camp. He spent so much time in solitary confinement that he was christened the "Cooler King" and served as the model for Steve McQueen's character in the movie *The Great Escape*.

The Servicemen's Readjustment Act of 1944, mentioned by Colonel Harding, was the original GI Bill. It provided loans for mortgages and educational support. But the benefits were unevenly applied. In the New York and New Jersey suburbs, over sixty-seven thousand mortgages were insured by the GI Bill immediately after the war. Only one hundred of those went to non-whites. Many universities and colleges in the south refused to admit Blacks, and one year after the war ended, only 20 percent of returning Black GIs who had applied for educational benefits were enrolled in college. Elwood Drake may have been smart to take his discharge in place, even though life in France for a Black man would have had its own challenges.

Other than the mention in *Sage*, Corporal Drake has faded from the historical record. Was he the first Black soldier to integrate the Office of Strategic Services, or did he drive his truck back to the motor pool after Sage was captured?

I much prefer the ending I've given him.

Bonne chance, Drake.

ACKNOWLEDGMENTS

MANY THANKS TO first readers Liza Mandel, Michael Gordon, and Jeffrey Ross. Their excellent feedback and commentary as the manuscript was finalized helped to improve and clarify the storytelling.

My wife, Deborah Mandel, listens to chapter readings throughout the entire writing process, offers valuable critiques, and edits the manuscript to bring it into sharper focus. Her help and support are beyond measure.

I am fortunate to work with a great publishing house. Soho Press is superb on all levels. The talent and expertise of everyone there is evident in the final product you now hold in your hands. Also, kudos to Paula Munier and the entire team at Talcott Notch Literary Services for their ongoing guidance in bringing this and other stories to readers.